THE
VANISHED
BRIDE

THE VANISHED BRIDE

A BRONTË SISTERS MYSTERY

Bella Ellis

BERKLEY
New York

BERKLEY
An imprint of Penguin Random House LLC
1745 Broadway, New York, NY 10019

Copyright © 2019 by Rowan Coleman
Penguin Random House supports copyright. Copyright fuels creativity, encourages
diverse voices, promotes free speech, and creates a vibrant culture. Thank you for buying
an authorized edition of this book and for complying with copyright laws by not reproducing,
scanning, or distributing any part of it in any form without permission. You are supporting
writers and allowing Penguin Random House to continue to publish books for every reader.

BERKLEY and the BERKLEY & B colophon are registered trademarks of
Penguin Random House LLC.

Library of Congress Cataloging-in-Publication Data
Names: Ellis, Bella, author.
Title: The vanished bride / Bella Ellis.
Description: First edition. | New York: Berkley, 2019. |
Series: A Brontë sisters mystery; 1
Identifiers: LCCN 2019015852 | ISBN 9780593099056 (hardcover) |
ISBN 9780593099063 (ebook)
Subjects: LCSH: Missing persons—England—Fiction. | Brontë, Charlotte,
1816–1855—Fiction. | Brontë, Emily, 1818–1848—Fiction. | Brontë, Anne,
1820–1849—Fiction. | Women authors, English—19th century—Fiction. |
GSAFD: Mystery fiction | Biographical fiction | Historical fiction
Classification: LCC PR6103.O4426 V36 2019 | DDC 823/.92—dc23
LC record available at https://lccn.loc.gov/2019015852

First Edition: September 2019

Printed in the United States of America
1   3   5   7   9   10   8   6   4   2

Cover art: Artwork adapted from *The Ticket* by Auguste Toulmouche / © RMN-Grand
Palais / Art Resource; *top and middle face in dress* © Aleksey Tugolukov / Alamy
Stock Photo; *bottom face in dress* © Rekha Garton / Alamy Stock Photo
Cover design by Emily Osborne
Book design by Alison Cnockaert

For my mother, Dawn Coleman, giver of books,
teller of tales and lover of literature.

Acknowledgments

With thanks to my agent Lizzy Kremer, Maddalena Cavaciuti, and everyone at David Higham. Thank you to my brilliant editor Michelle Vega and the Berkley team—I'm so proud to be published by you. Thank you to everyone at Brontë Parsonage, Haworth, especially Sarah Laycock, Lauren Livesey and Ann Dinsdale. And to my dear friend Julie Akehurst, who I can talk Brontë to for hours on end. Also to expert historians who were so helpful and generous with their time, especially Steven Wood and Chris Nickson. And thank you to my family, who let me disappear to Yorkshire every few weeks in search of mystery and adventure on the moors.

THE
VANISHED
BRIDE

The human heart has hidden treasures,
In secret kept, in silence sealed;—
The thoughts, the hopes, the dreams, the pleasures,
Whose charms were broken if revealed.
        —"Evening Solace" by Charlotte Brontë

Haworth Parsonage, December 1851

Drawing her shawl a little closer around her, Charlotte adjusted her writing slope once more and dipped the nib of her pen back into the ink, her head bent low, nose just above the paper. Yet, just as so many times before, her hand hovered over the blank page, and it seemed impossible to put pen to paper in a house so empty of anything but the ghosts of those she loved.

All was very quiet now: even the fire in the grate seemed muffled and muted, and it felt near impossible to draw any warmth from the brightly dancing flames, almost as if she were already a ghost herself.

Papa was in his study, as he always seemed to be these days. Tabby and Martha were in the kitchen locking up for the night, even though, according to the clock that stood on the staircase, it was only a little after seven. Outside, the night leaned in against the little house, the weight of it creaking against the window glass. But even as the wind howled down the chimney breast, all that Charlotte heard was silence. All she felt was absence. All she knew was loss.

Not even Emily's beloved dog, Keeper, was here anymore to keep her company with his snuffles and barks, playfully dragging at the hems of her skirts with his teeth. At least now that the dog too was gone, Charlotte didn't have to witness his hopeful eyes searching for his mistress when the back door was opened, nor feel her own spirits rise every time the cold air blew in, bringing with it the promise of Emily back from a march across the moor. Oh, how she craved the companionship that had once seemed as commonplace as her own breath.

It had been such a short time, and yet a thousand years ago, that she had shared this table, this house, her entire life, with her siblings. Here, with what felt like the whole world at their backs, the three of them had talked, written, maddened, known and loved one another with such steadfast strength that it had been all sustaining.

Here they had laughed and argued as she had written *Jane Eyre*, and her sisters their own great works, not one of them guessing at the whirlwind they were inviting into their small, humble lives. Now Emily, Anne and Branwell were all gone to a better place, and for the sister left behind, this mortal existence was almost unbearably lonely.

And yet . . .

Charlotte's mouth curled into a small echo of a smile as she remembered what adventures they had forged together, the dangers they had faced, the shocking revelations they had uncovered and the secrets they had kept.

From the fashionable drawing rooms of London to the soirées of New York, the world had talked about "those Brontë women," who had wrought such passion and pride on the page. At first some doubted they were men, then others refused to believe they could be women.

And it made Charlotte smile to think how very little of the truth those people knew. How very little of what she and her sisters truly were.

Now her sisters and her brother, Branwell, were all dead. Not another living soul on this earth knew *everything*. Not one memory of the wonders and the horrors that they had discovered for themselves had ever been committed to paper, and any correspondence that might have revealed them had been meticulously burned by Charlotte herself.

When one day it would become Charlotte's turn to join her siblings in God's grace, all that had happened in those few glorious, thrilling years— the last years that they would be together—would die with her. No one would ever know of their adventures. Outside that very pane of glass that shook and trembled in its frame as she sat alone at the table, a universe of humanity gusted as hard as the wind in a ceaseless vortex of life and death. And all you needed in order to uncover its darkest secrets was to know exactly where to look.

It might even be said, Charlotte thought to herself with a smile, as her nib finally joined with paper and she began to forge worlds out of ink, that none had ever lived such adventurous, dangerous and exciting lives as those three women who grew up in a village no one had ever heard of, on the edge of the windswept and desolate moor.

Those were secrets that would never be told, but, oh, what wonderful secrets they were.

Prologue

The first thing Matilda French saw was the blood. There was such a quantity of it that for several moments she couldn't make sense of the blackish pool of liquid that was spreading slowly under the closed door, not until the iron scent hit her, and she was reminded at once of the day her mother died, and the smell of her blood mingled with freshly cut violets.

Only then did the inevitable violence of what she was looking at begin to make sense of itself, the realisation that *something* dreadful had happened creeping through her veins like an infection.

And yet, it was so unexpected, so strange to make such a discovery in the perfect quiet of a pre-dawn house, that at first she did not scream, she did not faint. Shock held her captive and, as if mesmerised into a trance-like state, body separated from mind, she did what she always did, not knowing what else to do: she knocked twice on the door.

"Madam?" The boards were sticky underfoot, the room still dark and full of shadows. Dawn had yet to lighten the sky outside. Her voice was barely more than a whisper; her next words made little sense in the face of such horror. "Mrs. Chester, are you well?"

When she pushed the door open, she found the room silent and empty of its occupant and covered in so much blood that she felt she might drown simply by inhaling.

As her eyes adjusted to the light, she could make out that her mistress's bed was empty, though from the head to the foot it was covered in what looked like one great ink stain spreading outwards from the centre like a monstrous butterfly.

Trembling, breath held, Mattie crossed to the window, where she dragged open the heavy curtains and loosened the window latch to let some of the damp, cold air in, sucking it in desperately. The first thin light of morning cast its veil over the room, and when finally she turned back to the bed, Mattie understood the terrible truth of what she was seeing.

Murder.

1

Haworth, 1845

Charlotte

"You cannot just stop, Emily," Charlotte half chided, half laughed as she stumbled into the back of her taller sister. "There is neither the room nor the time for stopping."

It had become the sisters' ritual in recent weeks, this circular walk about the dining room table, talking out their ideas, spinning them into thin air until they could see the words forming over their heads, lit by firelight and shaped by smoke.

It was not a grand dining room: if anything it was rather cramped, almost entirely filled with the pretty table and a rather worn, black sofa. Charlotte had chosen the wallpaper, in dusky shades of pink and grey, as modest and muted as the plumage of a pigeon. On the wall hung a portrait of Lord Horatio Nelson, national hero and military genius, still adored in the parsonage forty years after his glorious death in battle. Charlotte liked to think of him looking down his splendid nose at them, keeping watch on all their comings and goings; she found it comforting.

"I had a thought, Charlotte." Emily turned slightly to look at her sister over her shoulder with her enviable grey-blue eyes. "Yes, and a good one too, so good that I must write it down at once before it escapes me. Move."

Charlotte watched in horror as Emily scribbled her nib furiously on a sheet of blotting paper placed directly on the polished surface of the table.

"Really, Emily," she said. "Have you not vandalised this table enough? Poor Aunt Branwell would be turning in her grave if she could see how easily you disregard half a lifetime's worth of beeswax and elbow grease."

"Charlotte, it is many years since the 'E' incident, and I *was* only a child," Emily replied, obligingly moving the blotting paper onto her writing slope nevertheless. Charlotte watched as her sister's thumb searched out the initial, scratched crudely into the surface with a fruit knife many years ago, giving it a rub as if for good luck. "Some might say that carving my initial into the table was a form of ornamentation . . ."

"Aunt Branwell wouldn't," Anne said mildly, not looking up from the newspaper that she was engrossed in. "Do you remember, Charlotte? Emily did her best to hide the transgression by refusing to move her hand for an entire morning? How Aunt Branwell howled when she saw what she had done!"

"I seem to recall that Papa was quite impressed with me," Emily muttered, already half-lost to her writing.

"We may count ourselves most fortunate that we have a father so devoted to our enlightenment that a scratched tabletop is not nearly so important to him as his daughter learning to make her letters," Charlotte said fondly. "Another papa would have beaten you soundly, as our aunt surely would have liked to, don't you think, Anne?"

Desperate for distraction, Charlotte did her best to catch Anne's eye, but her youngest sister was not to be moved from her reading. With only Anne's little dog, Flossy, joining in the parade, Charlotte, sighing heavily, walked on alone, jealously observing as Emily scored her letters into her paper with the same furious energy and impatience with which she greeted much of life. If only Charlotte could find the same kind of inspiration to turn her mind away from the great unhappiness that preoccupied it; if only she could tempt her sisters to distract her with talk.

She should be content, happy even. For it had been many years since all of them lived under the same beloved roof. The fire burnt merrily in the grate, casting a warm dancing light on the walls, the snug and slightly smoky little room illuminated only a little further by the single oil lamp. Outside, the rain came hard, flung against the rectory windows like handfuls of pebbles. Below them, Haworth huddled against the cruel wind.

It was a typical Yorkshire summer.

"Nothing comes this evening." Charlotte sighed in frustration, stopping to look at the crowd of gravestones that tumbled headlong down the hillside towards the church and town beyond, as if the dead were in a hurry to return home. "My head is as empty as a blank page, and just as useless. There is far too much . . . *feeling* getting in the way of *thinking*. To even compose two good lines seems impossible to me."

"Then perhaps you should try thinking in feelings," Emily said unhelpfully as the words poured from the nib of her quill in the chaotic and ink-spattered scrawl that drove neat Charlotte to despair. Page after effortless page of jealously guarded verse filled Emily's notebooks.

"*You* may still find endless inspiration in childish fantasy, Emily," Charlotte snapped back before she could stop herself. "But *I* have grown out of our fantasy worlds of Gondal and Angria. Mine is a life burdened with more mature concerns."

"'Mature concerns' is a very novel way of describing 'lovesick,'" Emily muttered without looking up. "And I care not what you think of me, Charlotte, for the Gondals are in the midst of the First Wars, and I must bring them to victory or many will perish."

"You are impossible, Emily," Charlotte said, but with little venom. In truth she longed for the days when she was more like her sister, for wherever Emily walked, wherever she looked, Gondal formed all about her, its people meaning as much to her, if not more, than those made of flesh and blood with beating hearts. Her imagination was her freedom, Charlotte thought enviously, wishing that she too were able to leave behind the ceaseless hurt of this mundane, earthly existence for a world where all turned on her command. In that world, her heart would never be broken.

"Stop and rest, dear Charlotte," Anne said, as she set her paper down at last, regarding Charlotte with such sympathy that it felt almost unbearable to be pitied so. Charlotte knew that Anne would never mention that name, and Charlotte made a point never to speak it aloud. Even so, it resounded constantly within her.

"Come sit with me, and read *The Times* of London, it is only a few days old and there is much of interest. Brunel's steamship the SS *Great Britain* has begun its journey across the Atlantic to New York, expecting to complete the voyage in only two weeks! Can you imagine, the other side of the world in less than two weeks?" Anne paused for a moment, her pretty eyes shining at the thought of adventure, before turning the page. "And see here, it seems that for three years now in London there have been eight specially trained and educated policemen engaged entirely in the exclusive profession of 'detecting' to solve crimes, using their wit and intellect to search out the guilty. Their success has been so great that *The Times* is calling for a fleet of such individuals across the nation, though others say that a free country should remain free from the tyranny of policing. One has to wonder if those people have crimes they'd rather remain undiscovered. I'll find it for you, see here?"

"It looks very interesting, Anne." Charlotte nodded, taking a seat at the table opposite Emily and drawing the paper towards her, but even so the words would not come into focus.

Charlotte could think only of her last letter to her former tutor, Monsieur Héger: how she had poured every ounce of her being into it. And yet he did not reply. No matter how carefully she drew out the shape of her broken heart and pleaded for even a single crumb of mercy, he never replied. How could he? He was a married man certainly, and yet . . . Closing her eyes, Charlotte concentrated very carefully on folding and refolding the burst of agonising emotion that threatened to break through at any moment, and with some effort she made those feelings small again, as tiny as the books they used to make as children, enclosing them within a thick wall of self-imposed serenity. For if she did not, her misery would engulf her. There was no choice but to endure in perfect silence the pain of loving one who did not love her in return.

"Hold hard, sisters!" Branwell swung into the room, bringing with him a good portion of the evening rain dripping off the end of his nose, his ruby-red hair plastered against his pale skin, and the fug of beer and smoke radiating from him, his eyes alight with signs of gossip. "Cease your girlish witterings, for I have a terrible tale to tell!"

"Did they run out of gin at the Bull again?" Emily said, not looking up as he took the chair next to her, shaking himself like a wet dog.

"Steady yourself, for as young ladies you may find the news I have to relate both terrifying and despicable, perhaps even more than your gentle souls can tolerate."

"Tell us, Branwell." Charlotte seized on the promise of distraction like a thirsty woman discovering a well. "What has happened?"

"Word has come to Haworth that there has been a most bloody and awful killing." Branwell's black eyes glittered with ghoulish delight as he spoke, the fire seeming to leap at his words. "And the dreadful deed was carried out but a few miles from this very spot."

"A killing?" Anne's brow furrowed.

"A most violent murder, dear sister." Branwell leaned towards Anne, who reeled away from the reek of him. Charlotte was not so deterred.

"Tell us," she prompted him. "Tell us every detail at once."

"I heard it from the keg boy, who heard it from the wagon man, who heard it from the innkeeper in Arunton, near where the incident took place."

"Arunton," Charlotte said, thoughtfully. "I'm sure we have an acquaintance in Arunton. When did it happen, Branwell?"

"Yesterday, a most terrible and bloody murder, by all accounts, and but a stone's throw from our very own front door. Are you very afraid?"

"The only thing I am afraid of is that you will never get to the point," Emily said, finally putting down her pen. "Who has been killed, and who by?"

"And"—Branwell ignored Emily's question—"the criminal has absconded, stealing the body away with him. It is wholly possible that the murderer may be creeping about in the shadows outside our own home even as we speak."

"Hefting a body around?" Emily frowned. "That doesn't seem to me to be very conducive to creeping. Answer my question, who has been killed?"

"A lady and a mother." Branwell leant back in his chair. "At least that is the assumption."

"How dreadful." Anne clasped her hand to her chest. "We must ask Papa to include this poor woman and her family in his prayers."

"The assumption?" Charlotte pressed him irritably. "The poor lady is either murdered or not—there is no in between."

"Well, that, dear Charlotte, is where you are wrong." Branwell wagged his finger at her. "For it seems that in the early hours of this morning the second Mrs. Chester's bedchamber was found empty, except for great quantities of blood painted across every surface, with no sign of the young woman, nor her remains. She is feared dead, of course, but it cannot be determined with any certainty, as she is quite vanished."

"Just taken from her home? How terrifying. I've gone quite cold." Anne shuddered.

"How *interesting*," Emily added, her eyes alive with curiosity. Charlotte was caught somewhere between fascination and horror when another thought struck her.

"Do you mean Mrs. Elizabeth Chester? Of Chester Grange?" She reached for Emily's hand. "Chester Grange is where Matilda French took up the position as governess! That's who we know in Arunton. You remember Mattie, Emily—she endured that evil establishment Cowan Bridge with us until Papa removed us, and we have corresponded ever since, though I have heard less from her since she took up her position and I was in Brussels."

"Now that I think of it, I believe it was the governess that discovered the awful scene," Branwell added.

"Oh dear me." Charlotte was horror-struck. "It was Mattie that discovered the scene of the crime? Poor, dear Mattie, you remember how fragile she was, Emily?"

"Matilda—pretty, timid, rather useless at most things—yes, I recall her," Emily said. "Imagine knowing that as you slept in your bed a murderer was stalking the hallways outside your chamber door wielding a knife! Terrifying."

Emily could not have sounded less terrified if she had tried.

"Presumably we do not know there was a knife," Charlotte said, raising her eyes heavenwards. "Oh dear, poor Mattie. She will not do well with this, she will not do well at all. I must write to her at once."

Reaching for a pen, Charlotte hesitated, and then felt a little thrill as she galvanised an alternative plan of action.

"No, I shall do better than write. I shall visit, first thing tomorrow morning."

"I shall accompany you," Emily said. "I did always care for dear Martha French so."

"Matilda, dear," Charlotte said. "Chester Grange is but two hours' walk across Penistone moor. Anyone who may wish to accompany me is most welcome, as long as that person is not coming along simply to relish violence."

Emily looked longingly out the window, where the rain came down so heavily that it shrouded the town beyond in a veil of tears, and even though somewhere above the thick clouds the summer raged on, it was almost impossible to believe it. "I am done with being kept prisoner by the rain, and I am done with the inside of this house. Set me free to have my feet soaked through and frozen!"

Charlotte turned to Anne, who sat with her hands folded neatly in her lap, looking for all the world as meek and as mild as any maid has ever been, which is exactly how those who did not know her perceived her to be. She wore her mildness like a kind of disguise, Charlotte often thought, hiding a warrior within.

"Well, I can't very well let you both wander about alone," Anne said. "I feel I am duty bound to keep you both respectable."

"And I shall accompany you too," Branwell said with largesse. "You will need protecting from the crazed knifeman, after all."

"Well, brother dear," Anne replied, a little resentfully, "I fear I am rather uncertain as to who would be protecting whom if you were to come with us. As it is, we are quite capable of going alone."

"Are you *still* angry with me, Anne?" Branwell asked, as if it had been a thousand years since he made Anne's position as governess at Thorp Green, where they had both been employed, untenable. The utter humiliation of the Mrs. Robinson business was almost more than any of the Brontës could bear, especially Papa. The thought of Branwell involving himself with his employer's wife in proceedings that were bad beyond expression quite turned her stomach. And of course, the moment Branwell was dismissed under such a thundercloud of scandal, blameless Anne had to resign her position. The indignity was still fresh in her mind, it seemed.

Certainly, Anne was entitled to at least a *little* more angst at the loss of her income, not to mention the infamy that had been brought upon the family, and yet the moment she saw Branwell's expression of remorse and dejection, Charlotte could tell that Anne regretted her comments.

"Will you always hate me simply for falling in love?" he cried. "Please, I beg you, help me move as far away from what has crushed my heart as I may, and let me accompany you on your expeditions as I used to." He looked at each of his sisters in turn. "May I come?"

"Yes!" Emily said immediately.

"I think not," Charlotte added at once.

Emily glowered at her, and Charlotte could understand her disapproval. Recently, Branwell's weakness to the draw of the Black Bull and, frankly, all of Haworth's drinking establishments, had deepened considerably, and Emily thought anything that might keep Branwell away from hard liquor for a few hours must surely be good for him. It was a fair point, but Charlotte hesitated still.

"Why not?" Emily protested, taking Branwell's hand. "Despite Anne's assertion, we are but three defenceless women, embarking on a considerable walk without a man to protect us, after all."

"As if that has ever concerned you for one moment in your entire life, Emily." Charlotte laughed, softening her voice as she turned to Branwell. "Dear brother, not this time. This time your presence, though it would be welcome, would mark our visit out of the ordinary, and we do not wish to be noticed. It has always been the way of the world that it will pay attention to a man as fine as you. But we three countrywomen, they will not notice us . . . And on this occasion it will be to our advantage. Perhaps we three may even be able to discern the truth of what happened to Elizabeth Chester."

Charlotte avoided Anne's gaze, knowing that her little sister was appraising her at that very moment, trying to determine how much her planned visit to Matilda French was out of concern, and how much was down to a desperate need for distraction. In any event, Charlotte determined, one couldn't *not* go to visit a friend at such an unfortunate time just because it might also be rather fascinating.

"Well, then." Branwell sighed, collapsing on the sofa, hooking one of his long legs over the arm. "I will just have to find another way to amuse myself while you are gone. Perhaps the Black Bull."

"Perhaps church?" Charlotte suggested.

"Perhaps the Black Bull *is* my church." Branwell chuckled as Charlotte's eyes widened in horror.

"Is it truly terrible," Anne said gravely, in a bid to distract her sister, "that I am a little thrilled to think of us as three invisible lady detectors seeking out the truth? I believe we could be quite the only such creatures in all existence."

"Detectors?" Charlotte asked her. "What a curious phrase."

"Why yes, from the article in *The Times* I was telling you about. Detectors—that, my dear sisters, is what we shall be."

There was much more talk that night, stories and laughter that echoed on even after the grandfather clock on the stairs had struck midnight. And not one of the siblings noticed, as they talked and wrote and laughed, how the darkness crowded all around their bright little house, threatening to blot it out.

2

❧◦◦❧

Emily

Chester Grange rose up from the wild moorland that surrounded it like an ancient beast: horned, spiky and recently awoken from centuries of slumber.

Emily fell in love with it at once. Although it sat atop majestic terraced gardens that had once been the height of fashion, in recent years Nature had done her best to reclaim this manmade folly for her own.

Grasses grew long and heavy with seed, where they once would have been laid to lawn, and the only visible path left leading to the house itself was the weed-and-wildflower-strewn drive that the three sisters walked up. The once elegant terraces were covered in bindweed and ivy, tenacious little periwinkles and forget-me-nots growing out of every crack in the masonry, blurring the edges of Elizabethan carved stone and crumbling ramparts, winding their way all around the ancient house in a slowly tightening chokehold that threatened to obscure many of the windows.

There was nothing here to disappoint a woman who saw a story in every corner, for there was a potential mystery everywhere—from the towers and crenellations guarded by a series of foreboding gargoyles, poised to pounce on any poor soul that might be foolish enough to intrude, to the huge scattered stones that peered at her from the overgrown grass and looked as though they had once belonged to a far grander and more ancient palace.

It was like the setting of one of Tabby's endless stories of folklore, myths and the ancient ways, stories that Emily had been told all her life.

In this place there were a thousand voices: she could hear them whispering to her. And as they drew closer, Emily's smile grew ever wider at the prospect of adventure.

"Will you please stop grinning like a lunatic?" Charlotte asked her abruptly, stopping Emily with a gloved hand on her arm. Charlotte's expression, framed by her bonnet, looked so prim and so serious that Emily could not help smiling even more. "Emily, I am quite in earnest. It is most disconcerting, and I'm not sure that your rather obvious pleasure in this place or situation will give Mattie any comfort. Remember, Emily, we are respectable parson's daughters. Try your best to believe it."

Emily shrugged and galloped after her sister with a little more enthusiasm than was entirely seemly.

The back of the house was no less dilapidated than the front, but sure enough Mattie sat on a bench outside the kitchen, her head bowed, her fingers laced. She appeared to be either deep in prayer or thought, though Emily could not discern which.

"Mattie!" Emily shouted, just to see how Charlotte's cheeks coloured.

Matilda French's fair head came up sharply, and at once she sprang from her seat, hurrying towards her friends.

"Dear Charlotte," she gasped, a little out of breath as she took her friend's hands in hers. "Oh, how glad my heart is to set eyes on friendly faces! Dear Emily and Anne, what a relief to see you. I hardly know where to turn in such terrible times!"

"The news reached us in Haworth last night," Charlotte said. "We resolved to come and see you at once."

Emily endured an embrace, noting how Mattie's pale gold ringlets were a little ragged around the edges, and how purple shadows bruised the underneath of her blue eyes.

It seemed that Charlotte had been right when she said that Mattie would find the situation at Chester Grange intolerable. As they had walked here this morning, Charlotte had recounted the tale of the poor young woman. Mattie had lived the first portion of her life a beloved only daughter, but when her mother died in childbirth and her curate father was carried away with cholera, her uncle did his best to rid himself of his burden once and for all, sending her away to school to be trained for the life of a governess—a life she had never expected or wanted. And now this horror had happened under the same roof that sheltered her. Despite the hardships of Matilda's life, Charlotte had fretted as they'd marched on through the mud and heather, the poor governess was ill equipped for tragedy.

The Brontë children, however, had lived almost their whole lives without a mother, and in the knowledge that, should their father die, their home and means of support would go with him. He'd been training them to survive independently almost from their very first steps, and indeed, they had all worked as teachers and governesses in various positions until fate had brought them all home together this summer. Emily loved her father for his foresight with all her heart, even though she never liked to dwell on the day that she would be required to leave her beloved home, nursing a secret determination that it would never come.

"Come into the kitchen," Mattie said, leading Charlotte by the hand. "I am so very glad to see you, even if under such terrible circumstances. You are my first visitors, and in happier times I would have delighted in taking you on a tour of the house, but of course we may not. You understand why . . ."

"Why?" Emily asked, pretending she couldn't sense Charlotte staring at her.

"Mr. Chester is displaying such distress at his wife's disappearance, and as yet no understanding as to what has happened to her. You say the news reached you last night? What have you heard? My employer is very concerned about tattletales misconstruing events and interrupting enquiries, such as they are."

Her voice was bright as a naked flame, but strained, as she showed them into the country-house kitchen, which was, surprisingly for such a large house, entirely empty. Perhaps the staff had been sent home while the investigation took place, Emily supposed, wondering what sights lay behind the door that led to the main house.

"We heard that there was no sign of Mrs. Chester," Charlotte told Mattie, adding delicately, "and a very great deal of blood."

"That is . . . correct." Mattie's voice trembled as she spoke, before she straightened her shoulders. "I will make you some tea. Thank you so much for visiting—you can't know how glad I am to see you. There isn't anyone to talk to, you see—no one to turn to. My only friend here . . . well, that was Mrs. Chester, and I don't see how a person could be deprived of so much blood and yet live."

"You are not entirely alone, Miss French." A low rasp of a voice surprised them, and Emily turned towards the shadows, where she could just about discern a mass of darkness galvanising in the gloom. An older woman, of somewhere between fifty and sixty, lumbered into view, her small deep-set and beady eyes focused on the group of women with the singular intent of a crow. "I am always near, never forget it."

"Of course not, Mrs. Crawley." Mattie's voice trembled as she bowed her head to the older woman, who took a seat by the unlit fire to better observe them. "Please do forgive my manners. May I present to you my friends Charlotte, Emily and Anne Brontë from Haworth Parsonage, who, hearing of the news, have come to visit me and offer comfort in these dreadful times."

"Gossipmongers, then." Mrs. Crawley jammed herself deeper into the chair, a toad on a rock, dressed in mourning with a widow's veil pinned into her iron-grey hair and wearing a pair of white, cotton gloves. On the right side of her doughy face ran a scar that had healed into a raised and ugly cicatrix. The unfortunate-looking woman regarded the sisters with barely concealed disdain, as they curtseyed, taking them in and dismissing them at once as no one of any import, Emily was quite sure. Though it might be true, it rankled.

"I can assure you, Mrs. Crawley," Charlotte said, the colour in her cheeks high, "my sisters and I have no interest in speculation, only in comforting our friend in a time of distress."

"Keep to the kitchen and grounds," Mrs. Crawley told Mattie as, no sooner had she made herself comfortable, than she hauled her considerable mass out of the chair, her starched linen rustling like treetops in a high wind. Emily wondered at Mrs. Crawley wearing cotton mittens in the house, for it was unusual, to say the least. "And use the servants' china, girl! You are to be back attending to the children by four. This is not the time for shirking your responsibilities."

Mrs. Crawley lumbered towards a small inner room, which Emily could see through the open door was lined with bookshelves that held not books, but ornaments and objects that seemed as if they could not belong to such an intrinsically angry woman: a china shepherdess tending her flock, brightly shining silver thimbles and a posy of wildflowers in a cut-glass rose bowl. Even more curiously there was a photograph, a curious magical object Emily had seen only very rarely, of a sleeping, or possibly even dead, baby. She desperately wanted to find out which, but not enough to attempt to engage the toad woman in conversation.

"I will be in my parlour, should you require me," Mrs. Crawley told them with more threat than reassurance, and Emily bobbed a second little curtsey to her that only she knew was meant in an entirely disrespectful way.

"Well, she's a delight," Emily said under her breath, sitting down and picking up one of the slices of buttered bread that Mattie fanned out on a plain white plate for them rather apologetically.

"So tell us," Charlotte said, glancing at Emily's bulging cheeks as she took a seat at the table, "how fare you, my friend?"

Mattie glanced in the direction of Mrs. Crawley's room and smiled. "Indeed it's a very difficult and trying time for Mr. Chester and the dear children."

But her hand trembled as she poured the freshly brewed tea, a single amber drop falling onto the back of her hand.

"Charlotte, do you remember Cowan Bridge?"

"Of course," Charlotte replied very gravely. Emily was certain that her sister remembered Cowan Bridge just as clearly as she did. The school Papa had sent her and her sisters to shortly after their mother had died was indelibly branded on their memories.

Charlotte reached for Emily's hand. "Cowan Bridge was a despicable place, full of darkness and cruelty, where thinking was frowned upon, and any expression of joy snuffed out like a candle. It was there Emily and I first met you, Matilda dear, and there, in that terrible place, where our dear older sisters, Elizabeth and Maria, were pushed to the brink of death before being bundled into a carriage and taken away back home to finally slip away."

Charlotte needed not say more for the three of them to silently recall the horrors they had seen there, in that place that falsely claimed to be a place of God, a place that starved, beat and punished its innocent inmates routinely. Even now there were times when Charlotte would wake sharply in the night and cry out for Emily, sobbing as she recalled feeling the freezing body of her dying sister in bed next to her.

So of course none of them would ever forget Cowan Bridge. This was more than polite conversation, Emily realised. It was Mattie's way of telling them how very frightened and full of despair she was, just as she had been in that awful establishment. Emily had never felt so desperate, nor so alone, as she had in those dark and dreadful days, and if that was how Mattie was feeling now, then she must be truly afraid.

"We are here now, Mattie," Emily said, steadying Mattie's shoulder with a firm hand. "We shall help you feel safe once more."

This day had begun as an adventure, an excuse to roam free; Emily was happy to admit it. Now, though, as Mattie leaned into her embrace, Emily recalled all too vividly how women such as they had precious little defence against the cruelty of the world, and she saw the same thought returned a hundred times in her sisters' expressions of quiet determination. The wars of Gondal would have to cease fire for a little while, as long as Mattie needed them. She had the three Brontë sisters by her side until she was safe and protected.

Woe betide any that stood in their way.

3

Anne

"Say hello, Archie," Mattie implored the pretty little child that she cradled in her arms. "Say hello to these young misses!" But the golden-haired baby buried his face in her neck, winding his plump arms even tighter around her, grizzling as the village girl who Mattie said helped with the children from time to time—Jane, Anne thought her name was—looked on, about as charmed by the scene as if Mattie were coddling a sack of sugar.

"Francis!" Mattie called to the older boy, who was almost invisible in the long grass around a weed-choked pond, just standing perfectly still, gazing into the woods beyond, as if he could see something amongst the trees that the adults couldn't. "Francis, will you come and say good day to my friends as you have been taught?"

But Francis seemed not to hear her, his gaze fixed on empty shadows, not looking up even when Emily went and stood next to him, throwing what pebbles she could find lying about into the brackish water with loud plops. Charlotte followed a little way behind to admire the sound of a song-bird chirping in a cherry tree.

"This must be awfully hard for the children," Anne said as Mattie handed the baby back to Jane, who wandered off towards Francis. "The little boy, especially, even though he was just a babe in arms when his first mother died, for his stepmother to be . . . lost too—it hardly seems like a suitable place for young children at the moment, exposing them to such violence and uncertainty. They may seem oblivious to all, but young children take in much more of their circumstances than we might ever know."

Anne lowered her eyes, giving herself over for a moment to retracing her own fragile memories. "I was very little when we lost Mama. I seem to recall days and days of being told to stay silent, sitting on the floor in the smallest bedroom, cutting out bits of paper and drawing to pass the time, far too young to realise that I was waiting for my own mother's death."

"I was at my mama's bedside," Mattie said, her voice hardly more than a whisper. "I remember how she cried out in such pain, and all I wanted was for it stop. And then when she was silent, I wished she would cry out once more."

Anne reached for Mattie's hand, their fingers interlinking. Death was such a close companion to all of them that they should not have been surprised when he came calling time and again, and yet there was no hardening the human heart against grief.

Anne had been hardly older than Archie when Mama died, but the pain of those long hours had somehow still etched itself onto her mind in a series of blurred images. It had been almost impossible for her to understand the hush, the muted weeping, her father's exhausted face. Even now she wondered what she really did remember, or if the stories she'd been told so many times had passed into her memory and taken up residence. It was true that, should God ever bless her with children, she would want her sons and daughters to know her firsthand. To remember the flesh-and-blood woman she was, not a vague canonised sketch created out of thin air, like the image of her mother that had been given to her by those who had had the luck to love Maria Brontë while she was alive. But this was the innate danger of motherhood: as soon as you fulfilled your purpose of bringing life into the world, the chances that you'd be sacrificing your own in the process became very high.

"Baby Archie is missing his mama terribly," Mattie said. "He had only just learnt to ask for her, and now he does not stop. He can't understand where she is. And as for Francis . . . That poor boy, to lose one mother and then, just as he learns to trust Elizabeth, she is taken from him. And their father . . . he is too distraught to care for them."

"Could they not be sent to stay with grandparents? Mrs. Chester's parents, if Chester has none living?" Anne enquired, biting her lip as she looked at Emily standing in stalwart silence with the boy.

"The Honeychurches? Mr. Chester won't have it." Mattie shook her head anxiously. "He says the safest place for them is by his side, but how can he say that when"—catching herself, she lowered her voice considerably—"when his own wife has most likely been slaughtered in her chamber under his own roof? Why, how can any of us be safe until the culprit is caught?"

"Master Francis, come now!" Jane called to the older boy, who trudged towards her, his eyes on the ground the whole way.

"What *is* being done to discover the truth of the matter?" Emily asked, returning from the pond to walk with them. "I thought I would see men of law all over the house, search parties on the road, but it seems very sedate."

"The constable has already been, and completed his assessment of her room," Mattie told them. "There were signs of a struggle, sheets ripped and shredded, and so much blood . . . but how the assailant entered the house, and left undetected with Mrs. Chester dead or alive, none can fathom, including the constable. He spoke to Mrs. Crawley and me in turn, enquiring as to what we heard and saw, and then Mr. Chester. Mr. Chester told him there were a group of gypsies squatting in the woods, poaching his animals, and that he believes they may have taken Mrs. Chester, for they are gone now. So the constable has gone to chase down local gypsies, I suppose."

"Did you see the gypsies?" Anne asked.

"I saw them in the village once or twice. I bought some heather from one old crone, but I never saw them on the land. Mr. Chester told me not to take the boys into the woods while they were there, and to stay in sight of the house."

"I see," Emily said. "Where were they camping?"

"Up on the wood behind the house," Mattie told her, "towards Arunton."

"So they do not suspect Mr. Chester?" Emily asked. "Oftentimes it seems to be those nearest to the victim that are the architects of their demise."

"Oh, really? And how would you know such a thing?" Charlotte asked her archly.

"Read the papers," Emily said. "Look out of the window at the wife beaters, child murderers and poisoners of the village of Haworth that walk beside our own doorstep, Charlotte."

Charlotte pursed her lips, but Anne knew she could not disagree. Papa made no secret of the darker side of his work, and a simple walk down Main Street was enough to demonstrate that what Emily said was true: people were ever cruellest to those closest to them.

"The constable does not suspect Mr. Chester—he hasn't even considered him," Mattie said. "Of course he doesn't—it was Mr. Chester that appointed the constable, after all, but I . . ." She lowered her voice, leaning closer to the sisters. "For a whole year before he married again, I was here alone with Mrs. Crawley and Mr. Chester. During that time I came to know him as a decent and honourable man, and I admired him very greatly. He would often talk fondly of his first wife, and how he missed her companionship and . . . and then he announced his plans to marry again. But within a few months of his marriage to Elizabeth Chester, he'd become a stranger . . . It was as if another man had been hiding within him, waiting to emerge with ever-increasing ferocity the moment he brought home a new bride."

"He was a cruel husband then?"

"Very," Matilda said. "To see a man I had known to be gentle and kind turn on Elizabeth, who is hardly more than a child, it was—is—something I cannot fathom. When I got the job he told me his first wife had died from fever, but it was a lie. It's known locally that her death was very violent."

"You mean he killed her?" Anne gasped.

"No . . . not by his own hands, I suppose." Mattie wrapped her arms around herself as she shuddered. "Poor Imogen Chester leapt to her death from those very ramparts, and though most that live in the village live in fear of their landlord evicting any that speak against him, if you listen closely you'll hear them whisper to one another that it was Chester's cruelty hounded her to it."

"Poor, poor woman," Anne said. "To feel so lost and so alone that you would forfeit your place with God, just to escape this earthly pain."

"However the first Mrs. Chester died, it certainly is very unfortunate to lose your second wife in such unusual circumstances," Emily said. "Two wives gone, one dead and the other almost certainly so."

"Of all who could have carried out this crime, it's true that Mr. Chester would be better placed than any to cover up such a terrible deed," Anne mused. "A man in his position, in control of what law enforcement there is might expect to get away with murder, at least until he meets his maker."

"And yet there is no body," Emily said. "Why take the time to dispose of her remains but not to clear up all sign of the crime?"

"Perhaps he was interrupted," Anne said thoughtfully. "Mattie, what did you hear and see on the day before and night of the incident?"

"The day before was much like any other, except that Mrs. Chester was indisposed and had taken to her room for much of the day with a *lady's malady*. I made tea, soup and light meals for her. That night there was a terrible storm," Mattie said, her eyes clouding over as she remembered. "Lightning, wind almost tearing the windows from their hinges—so I was awake most of the night, though the children slept right through it all. The noise of the storm seemed to be amplified by the house, rain hard as showers of stones, wind howling in the chimneys. I thought . . . I thought I heard a scream, but I can't be sure." She glanced briefly at the house, looking away as if the mere sight of it terrified her. "Every night there are strange sounds and . . . occurrences."

"Occurrences?" Emily cocked her head, and Anne saw that familiar glint in her eye. Oh, how her sister loved a strange occurrence.

"It's a very old house," Mattie said, uncomfortably. "The wood creaks, the glass rattles—oftentimes, even if there is a fire in the grate, it will be so cold your breath mists in the air. And at night it's easy to imagine footsteps in the halls when all are asleep, or the sound of weeping coming from empty locked rooms. Jane won't stay here overnight for fear of the first Mrs. Chester haunting her. So that night, yes, I thought I heard a scream, but perhaps it was the screech of an owl or the call of a fox—I cannot say."

"And you were the first to find the bloody scene?" Anne asked.

"Indeed." Mattie's voice broke as she lowered her eyes. "There should be a nursemaid for the baby, but Mr. Chester will not have more staff at the hall than Mrs. Crawley and me—he is a very private man. Besides, Mrs. Chester insisted on spending as much time with the baby as any mother would. She would often say that motherhood was a privilege that should not be squandered. She loves that baby, though so much so that Mr. Chester can be rather jealous of him . . ." She paused a moment. "It had been our custom that I would bring the baby to her in the morning before breakfast. That day, though, he was still sleeping, so I took her some tea, and thank the Lord. For if he had seen what I saw . . . I cannot . . . I cannot . . ."

Mattie covered her face with her hands, turning away from the three sisters, her shoulders trembling. Anne let Charlotte take the lead, taking her friend's hands, meeting Mattie's eyes with her own until the moment of terrible recollection had passed and Mattie was calm again.

"But there were no signs of Mrs. Chester?" Emily asked thoughtfully, adding rather bluntly, "No corpse, I mean. I can't imagine, if the culprit were a passing tramp or scoundrel that had broken into the house to carry out his terrible deed, why on earth he would take the body with him. Therefore it must be that the body must hold the secret to the attacker—it's the only intelligent conclusion."

"Or could it be," Anne said, "that there is no body, that Mrs. Chester is not yet dead?"

"There was so much blood." Mattie shook her head. "Surely more than a human being could live without. I'm certain my mistress could not have survived."

There was a moment of silence among the women, where the breeze plucked at their skirts, and in the trees the crows called out to one another.

"Well, if Mr. Chester is not being properly investigated, then it is a scandal," Charlotte declared, "a scandal that must be rectified at once. We should tell Papa, or write to the press, demanding action."

"Yes," Emily said, "that's exactly what we should do. *Or*, perhaps, Charlotte, we might bring our own intelligence and resources to this matter to protect Mattie and discover the fate of Mrs. Chester. Mattie, could you take us to the room in question so that we might see it with our own eyes?"

"For what purpose, Emily?" Anne asked her sister, fascinated by her sister's sudden resolve. "Other than your morbid curiosity, what else is there to be divined from an empty room?"

"For the purpose of discovery," Emily told her sister. "Who knows what we, whose eyes are entirely new to this place and these people, might be able to discern that those who are familiar with the house might not? Our father has taught us to be curious, Anne. It is not a sin to seek an answer to a question that concerns a woman's life, surely?"

"And if Matilda's fears prove to be correct—if, indeed, Chester is the culprit, then something must be done to bring him to justice," Charlotte said. "Though I feel that a very good letter to some higher legal authority, perhaps in York or Leeds, might go a long way towards that. Perhaps apprising ourselves of the situation to the fullest possible extent before raising our concerns would be prudent. Do you agree, Anne?"

Anne met Charlotte's gaze, seeing how her sister sought out her permission.

"Well, in this world where men might beat their wives, might force themselves upon them, and, yes, might even kill them and go unpunished, where society and the law see women as little more than property, it seems as though someone should be trying to do something about it. For Elizabeth Chester's sake, and those innocent motherless children. And if that task falls upon us, as newly minted detectors, then I will not be the one to shirk it." She nodded determinedly. "Show us the room, Mattie."

"I cannot." Mattie shook her head. "Mrs. Crawley has already cleaned the bedroom where it all took place. She scrubbed every inch where there was blood, and now there is nothing to see except an empty room. Besides, we have been forbidden, and should we be caught, then there will be hell to pay."

"Well, there's a simple enough solution to that," Emily said, already stalking ahead towards the house. "We will not be caught."

4

Anne

There was something to be said for Chester's determination to employ only the minimum staff necessary, Anne thought, as she followed Charlotte and Emily through the secreted servant's corridors that seemed to riddle the oak-panelled walls of Chester Grange. At least it meant that Mattie had been able to spirit the sisters through the kitchen, where Mrs. Crawley nodded in her chair, and to the upstairs room unseen, each of them taking great care to make their footfalls as light as possible, no one exchanging even a whispered word.

Mattie had lit the stub of a candle in order to guide them through the windowless maze. The tiny pool of light cast only a very small circle of illumination into what felt for some minutes like an endless darkness. No sooner had the few feet ahead of them been thrown into light than the darkness followed on behind, so closely that a fanciful person might imagine feeling its breath upon the back of their neck.

And in the enforced quiet, Anne couldn't help but consider how these hidden staircases and back corridors, designed to keep domestic staff out of sight, afforded a wealth of opportunity for removing a body unseen—but only if one was familiar with the house and all its intricacies. Was it possible that they were walking in the footsteps of a murderer?

Never had she welcomed the touch of daylight more than when Mattie released them into a long landing, boasting a huge window at either end of it.

"And this was . . . *is* . . . Mrs. Chester's room," Mattie told them in hushed tones as she stopped in front of a chamber door and opened it. "Hurry—if they catch you in here, we'll all be for it."

Mattie stepped back as she allowed the sisters to enter, remaining outside, ostensibly to keep watch down the long shadowy hallway, although Anne felt a distinct reluctance from the governess to cross the threshold.

At first it seemed a very dark and forbidding room for a young woman, the diamond-paned window shrouded in heavy, red velvet curtains that let in only a thin drizzle of watery light.

Feeling suddenly caught inside another woman's head, Anne walked into the middle of the room, Charlotte hovering by the door squinting, Emily peering under the bed, her nose to the floor like her dog, Keeper, sniffing out a rabbit. Anne was certain that this had been a room full of sorrow and sadness long before the violent act had taken place: it seemed ingrained in every surface. She couldn't be sure what it was that told her that Elizabeth Chester was not a happy wife, but somehow it was written in the precisely positioned angle of each dressing-table ornament, the neat pairing of her pristine boots, one toe turned slightly inward, and even the dust that filmed the paintings on the wall. On her nightstand there was a sketchbook, similar to one that Anne owned herself. Turning the pages, she found watercolour sketches of the Grange and its grounds, but it was the portraits of the children that stopped Anne in her tracks. Elizabeth Chester had captured more than just likenesses in her drawings of the two boys. In Archie's portrait there was such tenderness, such love in every line: the devotion that flowed between a mother and her infant child. And in her depiction of Francis you saw the glimmer of hope in vulnerable eyes, the longing for love in his almost upturned mouth. These were drawings by a thoughtful woman, a compassionate and kind mother, who had been ripped cruelly from the face of the earth. Who had taken her, and why?

"Was the carpet here when you found the room empty?" Anne asked

Mattie, noting the faint ghost of a lighter wood where a large rug would once have lain.

"No," Mattie shook her head grimly, "it was gone when I discovered the room, and the counterpane from the bed too. The mattress has been removed since and destroyed—it was saturated. And you can see for yourself where the blood was spread around the room."

It was true that it was quite clear to see where the blood had been shed from the areas of the floor and walls that had been cleaned. A lighter shade of olive green showed through in swathes across the walls from floor to ceiling, presumably where gouts of blood had sprayed, and been washed away with such vigour that the plaster showed beneath the fraying paper. The floor around the bed had been scrubbed almost raw, leaving a negative image of gore clearly etched. Somehow it was just as shocking to Anne as if she had just walked into the still-bloody room.

"Stones," Emily said, climbing to her feet and stepping across the washed passages on the floor as if they were still pooled with red. Reaching out, she picked up a handful of pebbles from where they were piled on the mantel, their presence the only unmeasured gesture in the room. Weighing them in her palm, Emily showed the rocks to Anne and then Charlotte. "An unusual keepsake for a young woman."

"Perhaps Francis collected them for her," Charlotte said. "Remember how we were always coming home with pockets full of rocks and eggshells, feathers and moss, as if we'd found the greatest treasures on earth?"

"Perhaps." Emily slipped one of the pebbles into her pocket before returning the others to the mantel. Affronted, Anne almost asked her to put it back, but what was the point? There were a thousand stones just like those outside the window, a million more making up this landscape that she loved. If those particular pebbles had once meant something to Elizabeth Chester, then she was no longer here to remember it. Anne was filled with leaden dread. Mattie was right, the young woman who had come into this house so full of love and hope for the future was dead; what other explanation could there be for such a sense of utter desolation?

"Footsteps," Mattie hissed from outside, beckoning frantically. "Hurry!"

As the three bustled out into the corridor they heard the smart tap of a woman's shoe on the oak boards; though she had seemed heavy and slow when they first met, Mrs. Crawley was now purposeful.

Deftly, Mattie opened the panel in the wall, and all four of them crammed within, Mattie drawing the hidden door to a close just as the footsteps passed briskly by. They heard the sound of the door opposite, Elizabeth's door, open and close again, and then there was silence.

"Quickly," Mattie hissed. "She will search in here to be sure!"

They made the same journey in reverse then, but now in the total darkness, fumbling and feeling their way along the walls, at the greatest pace they could muster, at last emerging into the cool air of the vast kitchen before rapidly making their way out of doors and as far from the house as possible.

"Whatever happens next," Anne said, taking a deep and welcome breath of fresh air as she reached up to brush a cobweb out of Charlotte's hair, "I must know the truth of what happened to Elizabeth Chester. I will never sleep another night through if I don't know for sure what has become of that poor young woman. I cannot live in a world where one just as I can be made to vanish with barely a ripple. I simply will not allow it."

Her sisters didn't seek to dissuade her, for having stood in a room so markedly empty of its occupant, they were all of one accord.

5

Charlotte

"If it *was* Chester, then he has acres of land in which to hide a body," Charlotte said once the women were far enough from the house to feel at ease once more. In truth, she had not expected to be as affected by the sight of Elizabeth Chester's room as she had been, but indeed the vacant, skeletal bedframe and the intimate remains of her small and ordered life had deeply moved Charlotte. As she had looked around the room at the meager collection of usual artefacts that could be found in a thousand rooms up and down the country, she saw versions of items she herself treasured. Few knew better than Charlotte how fragile life was: it was nature's way. But so often a woman's life ended like this, abruptly and in violence. And more than that, the woman that was taken had no voice to shout for her and precious little recourse to justice, another expendable life snuffed out as if it were the normal order of things. This was no game that they had involved themselves in, Charlotte came gradually to realise, no mere distraction from her own desolation; this was life and death—and very much more likely death.

"A forest, a pond, a cellar—he had the time to remove the body, wrapped in the missing carpet, and conceal it anywhere on his twenty acres." Emily turned to her sisters, gesturing at the expanse of land, which, as far as the eye could see and beyond, came within the estate's boundaries. "It's the perfect location to commit a murder."

"But would he have the strength to do that?" Charlotte did her best to focus her mind on the puzzle rather than on the missing woman, and the remains of her paltry belongings. "Mattie told us that it had been a stormy night—it's no easy task to dig a grave in pouring rain and a lightning storm."

"It is true," Mattie told them, her eyes darting nervously from one sister to the other, "that when I ran screaming to my master to tell him what I had found, he was asleep in his bed, no trace that he had been caught outside in the rain. No sign of muddy boots, wet clothes or hair."

"What time does the household normally go to bed, Mattie?" Charlotte asked.

"Well, the children and I are in our quarters by seven at the latest," Mattie said. "I take almost all my meals with them. Mrs. Chester would take to her bed a little after that if she was able, but Mr. Chester might stay up the whole night drinking and . . . carrying on, and sometimes he insisted that his wife stay at his side."

"But Elizabeth Chester wasn't willing?" Anne asked.

Mattie shook her head. "When she married him she believed herself to have fallen in love, for as I told you, my master can be beguiling," she told Anne with the ghost of a smile that faded at once. "But once he had her, he tired of her. Gradually, over the months she turned to me, confided in me, until we called each other friends. She spoke of her love for the children, her regret and fear. She hoped every day—we both hoped—that the kind and decent man we'd both known would return. But all that happened was that the monster grew and grew. I know he beat her more than once, though she did her best to hide it even from me, but I saw the bruises. And yet, since she vanished, he's grief-stricken, almost broken."

"And that night? Had he demanded Elizabeth Chester's company that night?"

"No," Mattie said after a moment of thought. "No, as I mentioned she'd taken to her bed for most of that day."

"And Mrs. Crawley?" Charlotte asked.

"She will not retire until her master has," Mattie said. "I have found her sometimes sleeping, sitting in the porter's chair in the hallway, and she has been there all night because he has fallen unconscious on the library floor."

"But that night he was in bed, you say?"

Mattie nodded. "I do not know when he retired, but I know that he was in his chamber when I went to rouse him in the morning."

"So at some time between eight p.m. and . . . six, when you took Mrs. Chester her tea, Chester or an unknown assailant had the time and almost the free run of the house to commit his crime and remove Mrs. Chester, either dead or alive. Ten hours: it's more than enough time for any criminal, even if they waited until the stroke of midnight to gain access to the house. From what we know about the timeline we can't possibly determine yet that Chester is responsible for his wife's disappearance."

"No," Anne said, her brow deeply worried. "Perhaps not from what we've seen, Charlotte. But from what we feel, from the atmosphere in that room—I feel it, do you not?"

"I can't imagine that feelings can be the way of the detector, Anne," Charlotte said.

"Well, then, it is certain that a person intimate with the intricate hidden passages of Chester Grange could have disposed of a body with much greater ease than a stranger," Anne replied, a little defensively.

"Indeed, that could be anyone who once worked in the house in the past," Charlotte reminded Anne. "For now, though it will be difficult to leave her, Mattie must return to her duties, so that Mrs. Crawley doesn't suspect her any further, and we must take our leave. She paused. "But there is nothing to say that we must leave quickly, or via the main gates. Mattie said the gypsies had been camping in the woods, on the crest of the hill behind the house. It's as good a place as any to look for some trace of Elizabeth Chester. It seems an impossible task to search the whole of these grounds, but we must look for facts that cannot be misinterpreted, for irrefutable evidence. If we do not try to discover the fate of this woman, then who will?"

"Or we could just go home, practise the piano, embroider cushions and write poems." Emily shrugged.

Charlotte turned to her taller sister, lifting her chin a little to meet her steady gaze.

"Is that what you want, Emily?"

"No, but . . . No, I just want to make sure that you and Anne are prepared for what we are about to involve ourselves in. What we discover may be disturbing and even dangerous, and should we ourselves be found out, caught meddling, interfering, making trouble for men of high standing, then you can be sure that it will be *our* reputations, *our* lives, that will suffer as a consequence." She eyed her sisters in turn. "Our lives are quiet and plain, but they are safe and wholesome. Be sure you are prepared for what such an endeavour may cost us all, for the price may be very dear. Especially as you both have rather sensitive dispositions."

"Indeed I do not!" Anne retorted furiously, making Charlotte smile. "And at least I don't faint clear away at the prospect of speaking to people like *some* I could mention, Emily. Besides, there is a wrong here, and whatever the truth of it may be, it needs righting, and no good Christian woman should stand by and be silent out of fear. Why should it not be us to right it? Indeed, perhaps it may only be us who care enough to try."

Charlotte nodded. "Emily, you are right to speak of consequence. But I believe the decision has already been made by each of us, even if we have not spoken it aloud."

Exchanging a look, Anne and Emily nodded.

"We each of us want to know the truth of this matter, whatever it may be, and I do not believe that any of us are afraid of a little peril. As I said, we should begin by looking over the site of the supposed gypsy camp. Something useful may have been left behind, and—"

"No! You must leave at once!" Mattie started, her eyes widening in alarm as she stared over Charlotte's shoulder. "You must depart now, dear friends—my master has returned from town."

"Depart? I should think not," Charlotte said, eyeing the approaching figure on horseback, hounds following close behind. "Now seems like the perfect opportunity to get the measure of this particular man."

6

Charlotte

Charlotte stood her ground as the gentleman reined in his fine black mount, refusing to be moved a single inch by the imposing bulk of the muscular creature and his rider.

Four great brindled deerhounds came barking and bounding towards them, which might have shaken milder maidens, but not Charlotte or Anne, and especially not Emily, who at once crouched on the ground, stretching out her arms to embrace the creatures, letting them lick her face all over, snorting with laughter as they did.

"Emily, get up!" Charlotte hissed at her sister, but even Chester couldn't help but smile as he looked at Emily surrendering her neck to the dogs' tongues, and Charlotte noted that it was a pleasing smile—the sort of smile that made one feel as if one had done something good to have earned it as a reward.

"I always believe that my dogs are better judges of people than I," Chester told Emily affably. "Therefore you must be a very agreeable person, madam. If not, they would have bitten you by now. I train them to maul any unknown persons on sight."

"In my experience, dogs are much more agreeable than most humans," Emily said, using one hound's head as a prop as she clambered to her feet.

"You always know where you are with a dog; they never lie or dissemble—unlike men."

Emily's gaze was challenging—too challenging, Charlotte thought. Her younger sister knew so little of the art of subtlety.

"Forgive my sister." Charlotte stepped in front of Emily. "She forgets you have much more pressing matters on your mind than animal behaviour."

"On the contrary," Chester said. "Even a moment's release from the matters to which you refer is gratefully received, Miss . . . ?"

"Brontë, sir." Charlotte bobbed a curtsey. She thought the horse must stand more than eighteen hands, though she knew little of horses. It could be said that she knew hardly more of men, but that didn't prevent her making a judgement of the man that sat on the creature's back. Mr. Chester was well made; tall and strong, with a large and lion-like head complete with thick, dark mane; well dressed, though there was a button missing from his coat. His face, though craggy and pocked with the remnants of childhood disease, was indeed rather bracing to look at, with intense eyes. Yes, he could be called handsome, Charlotte decided. Though one's appearance had very little to do with what lay within—that was one thing of which she was certain—she could see how a man such as Mr. Chester might entice those less sensible and serious than she into his clutches.

"Miss French," Mr. Chester inclined his head at Mattie, as he steadied his steed, though his eyes remained on Charlotte, "why are you not with my sons?"

"Mrs. Crawley granted me permission to receive visitors due to the . . . present circumstances, sir, and the boys are with Jane, but I will return to them directly." Charlotte noted how Mattie looked at her employer with acute interest. It was a look of familiarity, and at least some degree of intimacy. Mattie's eyes never dropped from her employer's face for a second, and for all her talk of the man as a kind of monster, it wasn't trepidation that she saw in her friend's expression, but rather a kind of rapt fascination, like a moth attracted to a naked flame. Hadn't she looked at Monsieur Héger exactly like that? Keen to break the excruciatingly uncomfortable moment, she coughed politely, starting Mattie into action.

"Sir, may I present Misses Charlotte, Emily and Anne Brontë, daughters of the parson at Haworth."

"Under normal circumstances I'm sure I would be delighted to make your acquaintance," Mr. Chester said, his gaze travelling back towards the house as if he were already on his way. "However, as you are aware, we are . . ."

None of the women knew quite how to react when Chester simply trailed off into silence, Charlotte noting that his fine features were haggard and, yes, beset by grief. In this moment he looked nothing like she imagined a murderer would.

"Sir?" Mattie took a step forward and Charlotte's eyes widened as she saw Mattie cover his gloved hand with hers. "Do you need my assistance?"

"No, I do not, French," Chester said, withdrawing his hand abruptly. "In any event, please excuse me—there is much I must attend to."

"Of course, sir. I can only imagine your anguish," Charlotte said, glancing at Anne. "Please forgive me, but we three are so very distressed by events—may I ask, are the authorities any nearer to finding the whereabouts of Mrs. Chester?"

A cold bolt of ice threaded its way through her veins as Chester focused his gaze on her, and she saw something else churning beneath the surface of his grief: a deep whirlpool of rage.

"No," he said, "you may not. French, see to my children. That you should leave them with that idiot girl from the village at a time such as this is unforgivable."

Chester kicked his steed into a gallop, splattering mud and matter in his wake, but though her skirt took the worst of it, Charlotte did not move an inch as Mr. Chester charged away.

"Well," Anne said a few minutes later, when Mattie had returned to her charges and the sisters were ensconced in the thick woodland that ran around the back of the house. They followed Emily in their determination to search for the location of the gypsy camp, no matter how the damp earth might hem their skirts in muck or seep over their pattens and through the flimsy construction of their boots. "What do you make of Chester?"

"I hardly know," Charlotte said, watching Emily some several yards ahead muttering and gazing about her like she was entranced by some kind of vision, which to be quite honest wasn't all that unusual behaviour for Emily. "On the one hand, he seemed truly shocked and stricken with grief; on the other . . . he has an air of darkness about him."

"Shocked by what he has done, perhaps?" Anne considered, pausing to pluck a gold-green leaf from a birch. The air was heavy with the scent of rain, the full bloom of summer, and underneath it all, decay.

"Or shocked by the bloody disappearance of his wife." Charlotte met Anne's eye. "All we know is what Mattie has told us, and for one who is so afraid and wary of Chester, she seemed rather . . ."

"Attached," Anne said. "Yes, I saw that too. What does it mean, Charlotte? To say one thing with one's mouth and another with one's eyes?"

"I can't conceive"—Charlotte shook her head—"except that attraction and affection are complex impulses. The heart does not always land where it should."

Anne said nothing, simply taking Charlotte's hand in hers, a silent acknowledgement of her sister's heartbreak.

"Oh, I don't know, perhaps Emily was right when she said we should go home and write poetry and suffocate to death of boredom and nothingness; perhaps we are not cut out for detecting at all."

"Charlotte . . ." Anne stopped in her tracks. "Do you find our life so very bleak?"

Turning her head away, Charlotte sought to hide the sudden, unexpected tears that had sprung to her eyes. If Anne was shocked by her outburst, then so was she. It seemed to Charlotte that she hardly knew how heavily the sense of imprisonment and repression of spirit weighed on her, so used had she become to the captivity of her life.

"I'm sorry, Anne." When Charlotte spoke again her voice was softer. "I find it hard to be home again, after studying and working in Brussels with . . ." She could not quite bring herself to say Monsieur Héger's name, or even to think it, for even that simple address filled her with longing for the love that could not be hers. "To be home again, though it is welcome, it is also . . . frustrating. I thought I might see something of the world and life, and now . . ."

"I understand." Anne took her hand again. "My life as governess at Thorp Green was not nearly as thrilling as travelling abroad; it was ordered and dull. But I was content enough, my charges easy and mild. And then Branwell decided to allow our employer's wife to seduce him." Anne could not contain the bitterness that rose in her voice. "And he is paid twenty pounds to leave, and I, forced to resign, receive only three. There is anger here too, Charlotte—anger and frustration all laced up tightly under this damned bonnet!" Anne half laughed, her eyes widening as she covered her mouth with her other hand. "Forgive me, I forget myself."

Charlotte squeezed Anne's gloved hand.

"Perhaps the opposite is true, Anne," she said. "Perhaps you remember yourself. Let us make our lives bigger; that's what I wish for. I wish for my life to leave a mark on this sphere, no matter how small it may be."

"I've found it!" Emily called from a clearing in the woods. "There were travellers camping here for certain. The question is, were they the criminal kind?"

7

Anne

A rough clearing had been brutally made, saplings and undergrowth cut down wherever they could be, and though there was no path through the woodland, one had clearly been hewn by a number of carts and wagons, and there were all manner of prints. Anne could make out horse hoof, dog paw and a quantity of boots.

Hovering over the mass of indents etched into the soft mud, most still intact, Anne followed the trail of first one track and then another.

"Anne?" Emily questioned her.

"I'm searching for a smaller footprint, something that could be female," Anne told her. "One would expect women and children here, but if there are, they are wearing great ungainly boots."

"Interesting idea." Emily nodded in approval. "Though I note from my observations of the vagabonds who come to the parsonage door seeking alms, that they often have no choice of footwear, if they are lucky enough to have any at all. But it's an intelligent thought, to look for traces of a feminine presence hereabout."

Anne did her best not to look like she was pleased with her sister's approval as she continued her observation of the area, but inwardly she felt a small burst of pride.

There were the remains of a campfire, long branches balanced in a tripod above it to hang a pot from. Around it some fallen or crumbling masonry that had once stood in the grounds had been dragged through the mud to make makeshift seating. There seemed to be nothing more of interest here, and noticing how Emily and Charlotte were bickering once again, she turned away from them, heading a little deeper into the thicket.

The harder she looked, the more she found herself becoming lost in the sea of quietly rustling gentle green. Whatever might have happened here a few days ago, all was peaceful now, save for the song of thrush in branches above her head, heralding more rain no doubt. Now and then a silver beam of sunlight would cut through the overcast sky to dapple the world around her, and for a little while Anne forgot everything except for the sweet music of the breeze in the trees.

She had strayed out of sight of her sisters when something in the air shifted so subtly that it took her several moments to sense that the woodland had gone from feeling benign to watchful and wary.

Looking up sharply, Anne realised she was being observed, and her sisters were nowhere to be seen.

"Emily! Charlotte!" she made to call out, but found her words came out as nothing more than a rasp. Glancing around, her view hampered by the wings of her bonnet, she could not see anyone at first, but then slowly a figure came into view, stepping through the slender bows of young trees with uncanny silence.

"What do you want?" Anne asked as bravely as she knew how, falling back on her training as a governess: show no fear, for the moment you do you are lost.

"I should be asking that about you." The voice when it came was male and rough hewn with a strong accent, though not one that Anne could place locally.

Steadying herself as the man emerged fully from the undergrowth, she was grateful for once for her stays, keeping her back straight. The interloper was of middle years, Anne thought, though age was difficult to discern when life's hardships so often wore a person far beyond their years. He seemed clean enough, if unshaven, his clothes very much in need of repair, which was often true about her own garments. Anne could see no evidence of a weapon either, but she didn't suppose he would need much more than a strong grip or a heavy stone to do away with her out here in the woods, without a friend in sight.

Show no fear, she reminded herself.

"I am with my sisters," she said, finding her voice at last, before calling out. "Emily, Charlotte! They will appear directly. We are the guests of Mr. Chester, and I believe you are trespassing on his land."

He shook his head, his eyes never leaving her face.

"Whoever says that this bit of land is his or hers goes against the old gods," the man said most unexpectedly. "Men like that Chester, they put up fences, and call the land their own, with no thought for the old people, their paths and stopping places."

He took another step towards her, and Anne, unwilling to turn away from him to look for her sisters, resolved not to give an inch of ground. If it came to it she would run, following the slope of the hill downwards to where she knew the house to be situated. She would run and scream with all her might. But it had not come to that yet.

"Young girls such as you ought not to be out here alone," he told her, his voice low, with an edge of menace. "I was watching you, wandering about like a lamb who don't know it's for the slaughter. Don't you know a woman was snatched from your Mr. Chester's house just two nights since?"

"I do," Anne said, lifting her chin a little, forcing herself to meet his dark eyes. "And what do you know of it?"

She started at his bark of a laugh, shaken by the anger that underpinned it. Where were her sisters?

"The constable has already asked me and my people that question," he said, balling his fist as he spoke. "He did not like the answer he was given and you may not either."

"Do you . . ." Anne swallowed, doing her very best not to think of the swathes of washed floor and wall that had been so recently covered in a young woman's blood. "Do you mean to threaten me, sir?"

"Sir?" That snarling laugh again. "I am no gentleman."

"Anne!" It was Emily that called out first, Charlotte at her side a moment later. The second that Anne felt her sisters' presence, she had to resist every impulse of her body to simply let her knees melt away beneath her. She had told Emily that she was not afraid of peril; now was certainly not the time to reveal otherwise.

It was Emily who stepped in front of her, Charlotte encircling her waist with her arm, lending her subtle support.

"Come along," Charlotte said smartly. "We are expected. Soon there will be search parties out looking for us."

It was a neat ruse, but though the stranger might have accepted it as a means of escape, Emily did not.

"You are with the Romany people, aren't you? The ones that were camping here?" Emily asked the man. Anne noted that she had removed her bonnet sometime earlier. It swung from its knotted ribbons on the crook of her arm. "When did the constable come to see you?"

"Last night, alone, and again this morning with his paid thugs, moving us on, again and again, though we have done nothing but live as we always have done."

"Nothing?" Emily tilted her head. "Is poaching, stealing and threatening a young woman nothing?"

"I didn't threaten her," he replied. "And I cannot steal that which should belong to no one."

Emily drew a little closer to him, and to Anne's great amazement she realised that it was the man who was now caught off guard and unsure, stepping back as Emily moved forward. In that moment he did indeed look very young.

"So you didn't steal away Mr. Chester's wife, then?" Charlotte asked.

"We aren't like the fairy folk," he said. "We don't take those who don't want to come."

"Then why are you back here when the law has told you to move on?" Charlotte challenged him.

"The law?" He shook his head, disgusted. "Some half-drunk fool, loyal to any that pay him, that's no law. My people are used to being moved on, but

I came back to see what I could in the forest. When something's done in a place, it lingers and can be seen quite clearly if you know where to look. In the bend of the grass, or the break of a branch. If your so-called law sets on taking one of us, and making us swing for this, then it will be murder. I came to see if I could find the truth of it."

"Oh, I see," Emily said, once again taking the young man off guard with her enthusiasm. "I should very much like to see how you go about such a thing, but you should leave at once. If you are caught here, then it will be all the worse for your people."

"You don't believe us the killers?" he asked Emily, utterly bemused.

"I cannot know yet," Emily said. "But my sisters and I seek to make that discovery, and if you have nothing to hide you need not fear us."

"Fear you?" His laugh echoed through the canopy of leaves. "Happen you should fear the one who really bled that young girl to death, for the moment he knows of you, it will be you three that he will wish to see cut open like sows."

He turned on his heel, and within a minute it was as if he had never been there at all. Anne reached out for Charlotte's hand, and after a moment the thrush took up its song again.

"Anne, were you very frightened?" Charlotte asked her.

"Not at all," Anne said, feeling guilty at once over telling such a lie. "In any case, there are none of the traces he spoke of at the camp that I could discern. But . . . the way he spoke about cutting open a sow, it did sound an awful lot like he might be happy to do the same to a woman, don't you think?"

"He did seem to know about the blood," Emily said. "Though it is likely the idiot constable told him everything."

"The day grows late," Charlotte said. "My head is weary and full of thoughts. We should return home and make sense of all we have seen today."

"Wait." Emily walked a few steps down the slope from which Anne had been planning to make her escape. "Just a little longer. I think perhaps . . . yes, I see something up ahead."

8

Anne

Emily stepped aside to show Charlotte and Anne a second circle of blackened undergrowth with a somewhat theatrical sweep of her hand.

Anne took in the scene. A smaller fire had taken place there in the recent past, a circle of black ash fading to grey having burnt out any undergrowth within its radius, and indeed the overhanging branches of the trees that surrounded it were singed and blackened in places too, indicating that it must have been built very high and burnt very fiercely.

"There's the back of the house just beyond the trees." Anne pointed to where the turrets of the grange rose above the tree line, glad to have something else to focus on other than the heart-pounding fright that still pulsed through her veins. "It's very close to the open lawns with increased risk of discovery if something untoward was done here, other than a fire. It could just be the grounds man burning cuttings."

"This is no gardener's fire," Emily asserted. "For one thing, the site of the fire is enclosed by foliage, no pit has been dug, there are no signs of it being managed. If anything, it seems to have burnt almost out of control."

"There has been a fire here," Charlotte said with an impatient shrug, eager to be gone. It seemed their encounter had unsettled her too, and that at least gave Anne some comfort. "Hardly unusual on an estate of this size; what of it, Emily?"

"What of it?" Emily sighed with exasperation. "Why, only everything, Charlotte. If you and Anne had been paying attention to our friend in the woods instead of quaking in your shoes, perhaps you would have seen it too."

"May I suggest that you stop speaking in riddles and tell us what on earth it is that you *think* you have discovered?" Charlotte asked with more than a little condescension. It was often like this between her sisters; Anne had become familiar with it over the years. As much as Charlotte and Emily loved one another, as much as they so often relied on one another for friendship, stimulation and loyalty, they also, very often in fact, seemed moved to be as irksome to the other as was humanly possible.

"Very well, pay attention, look and do your best to think," Emily said. "Think of what we know of Chester Grange. Its six inhabitants are one small boy, one infant, one governess, one elderly housekeeper, one male and, until two days ago, one wife. Chester is the only grown man in residence here, and so when one discovers a trail in the undergrowth made of large, man-sized boots, one must assume that either he made them or a person unknown."

"One might, but one would be very naïve to assume that Chester does not employ external staff to keep such large grounds in check," Charlotte challenged Emily.

"Did you fail to notice how overgrown and unkempt the gardens were when we arrived, Charlotte?" Emily scoffed. "Besides, cast your eyes downward for a second, and you will note that what we see here is quite different from the traces of the gypsy camp. Here there are only one set of boot prints accompanied by multiple paw prints—see?" Emily knelt down by the tracks without a thought to her skirts, pressing her ungloved palm into the mud next to a paw print. "See how large the track is compared to my hand, and how it is imprinted deep into the mud? This isn't the paw of the sort of rabbiting mongrel a grounds man or poacher would have. It belongs to a large and noble animal, and there are several of them all around, meaning more than one such dog was here. Charlotte, it's perfectly clear—a lone man, accompanied by his large dogs, made these marks for all to see. Is it not obvious that it was Chester that set this fire?"

"Yes, actually," Charlotte said impatiently. "Yes, it is obvious if you insist on pointing out that a man and the dogs that he owns were abroad on his land at some point in the two days since Mrs. Chester vanished. Obvious, but hardly incriminating."

"Oh, Charlotte, dear sister"—Emily's eyes were bright—"I do not believe that the skill of detecting is one that you naturally possess."

"Do tell us, Emily," Anne replied hastily before Charlotte bit back. "You are being so very clever and I can't wait to hear more."

"Well, *I* have learned a great deal since we met Mr. Chester, the first item of which is that he told us, rather proudly in fact, that he had trained his dogs to raise the alarm and attack any intruder," Emily said. "But if it was an intruder who carried away Elizabeth Chester's body, Chester's guard dogs did not raise the alarm, nor did they stop the culprit. Either he is lying about his dogs' behaviour, or the dogs did not raise the alarm because there was no one abroad that night—aside from their master."

"That's true." Anne turned to Charlotte, noting the interest intermingled with annoyance in her expression. "Chester boasted of their viciousness—surely they would have brought down an attacker, or at least caused enough commotion to raise the alarm?"

"There was a storm that night, remember?" Charlotte said. "It is possible the dogs could not be heard over the thunder and the rain."

"That is also true," Anne said to Emily, with a small apologetic gesture. "Just as it's true that these marks must have been made after the storm had stopped, or they would have been washed away."

"Well then, perhaps . . . perhaps the body was hidden within that great empty house for a time and then carried here for disposal," Emily said emphatically.

"Emily, how can you possibly surmise that?" Charlotte questioned.

"Because there's more to see if you truly look." Emily reached into the ash, lifting something charred and unrecognisable up for inspection. "I'm very afraid that this is proof that a body was burned here—for it's a fragment of bone, is it not? From its length and shape, I'd say a rib bone."

"Human?" Charlotte gasped as she took a step closer to examine the blackened shard. Anne hung back, turning her face away. Though her older sisters might not flinch from the possibility that Emily could be holding a fragment of a dead woman in her hand, Anne couldn't feel quite so detached. And the possibility that this might be a part of the woman who had once painted those sweet and tender portraits sickened her. Poor Elizabeth Chester, if this was her end: to be tossed onto the flames, almost all traces of her existence obliterated, as if she were nothing more than waste to be disposed of.

"I cannot tell if the bone is human," Emily said, frowning at the object. "It would require a more expert eye than mine to make such a distinction. But why would anyone burn any other creature to ashes out here in the middle of the woods?"

"That is a pertinent question," Charlotte said, "but if we could find this evidence, then surely the constable could. Anyone could."

"If anyone else is looking, Charlotte," Emily said, her voice fraught with frustration. "But no one else aside from our woodland friend and myself—*ourselves*—are, not properly, anyway. Certainly not a constable who refuses to examine the most obvious suspect, and instead harasses the travelling folk. And the travelling folk themselves may well be seeking to hide the truth rather than uncover it."

"And there is this," Emily said, stepping away from the burnt ground and reaching up to trace a subtle path of destruction that had been wrought through the lower branches of the trees.

"See how the foliage around the track is broken and bowed down, leaving a trace of something happening here, just as the travelling man described," Emily said. "It is as if something of considerable weight and length was borne along at around the shoulder height of a reasonably tall man—a man about the height of Robert Chester, a man who could have been carrying the body of a woman."

Emily gestured at the scene, imploring her sisters to see what she saw so clearly. She was a person of sudden passions and great extremes, either one thing or the other, and when she had made up her mind about something it took a great deal to shake her of her conviction.

"My dear, I do see what you mean, and your theory is possible," Anne said carefully. "However, wouldn't you agree that the business of detecting isn't to make the evidence fit a theory, but to use evidence to build a theory? And I do not believe that we have enough to draw a conclusion as yet."

"Anne is right," Charlotte said. "We must . . ."

"Charlotte, who are you to say what we must and what we mustn't?" Emily began.

As her sisters quarrelled, Anne found herself following Emily's lead in one respect and unlacing her bonnet. Leaning into the cool, fresh air on her cheeks, she turned back to examine the path they had just walked along. Sure enough, though it was as faint as to be almost unnoticeable, a subtle disorder of the trees showed a clear path through the woodland.

Anne couldn't say precisely what it was that drew her back to the charred remains of the fire, but whatever it was, she found herself noticing a small, blackened item on the very edge of the burnt-out ground, its definite form standing out against the long summer grass. Indeed she hardly paid a thought to what it might be as she stooped to scoop it up, only knowing that somehow it was out of place there. The moment she touched it Anne recognised the object, and her heart filled with horror and sorrow.

"A tooth." Anne trembled as she spoke the word aloud, her sisters continuing to talk over her. With some effort she raised her voice.

"A tooth—I've found a tooth," she said, capturing their attention at last.

It was blackened by fire, but it was clearly distinguishable. The three sisters stood around Anne's open palm, their expressions grim and sombre.

"On this occasion I think we can agree that no expert is required to determine that this tooth is human," Emily said. "That the remains we have found here are of a human being."

"Oh goodness." Charlotte covered her mouth with her hand. "But this is . . . this is sickening. That poor, poor young woman. What are we to do?"

"We are to take stock," Anne said, sounding much calmer than she felt. "We are to think and plan and take an appropriate course of action. For there is no mystery that our three minds can't unravel. I am sure of it.

9

Emily

It was rather unusual for Papa to invite his daughters to take the evening meal with him in his study. He so often ate alone these days that, when the invitation was forthcoming, they felt the occasion was loaded with significance.

They hadn't precisely told Papa that they were investigating Robert Chester on suspicion of murder, but by the same token, neither had they precisely not. Could it be possible that somehow Papa had a notion they had been abroad in the countryside, creeping uninvited around country houses and making the acquaintance of dangerous-looking men in the woods? For if he had, Papa would not be amused.

"You have been gone much of the day." Papa spoke only once his plate was clean. "I have noticed the quiet."

"We walked over the moor," Charlotte said with as convincing an air of nonchalance as a schoolgirl caught in a lie. "Visiting."

"And whom did you see?" Papa asked her, directing his foggy gaze at her over the top of his spectacles. How long, Emily wondered, before the cataracts would rob him of his sight altogether?

Charlotte faltered, clearly unsure if she should mention Matilda or not. Emily knew that but a second longer of hesitation and whatever she said next would be revealed quite clearly as a lie.

"We went to Chester Grange, Papa," Emily said, as if it were an everyday occurrence. "You know the great old house, close to Arunton? You may have heard of the trouble there these few days past?"

"I have not." Papa's expression was one of fleeting curiosity. "I have been absorbed this whole day with my correspondence. I have scarcely raised my head long enough even to see a curate."

"You always work so hard for the parish, Papa," Emily said, her eyes meeting first Charlotte's and then Anne's. It seemed as though they might be safe from discovery after all.

"It is my duty to give my life over to God's work. This world is a cruel and unjust place for the weak and the needy, Emily," Papa told her very gravely. "This day alone I have written a great many letters pleading the case for more sanitary conditions in the village, and I'm afraid I am to oversee three funerals tomorrow. All infants. I must do all I can to care for my congregation, many of whom are not afforded the same comforts as you young women."

"Indeed, Papa," Charlotte said. "You are an example to us all."

"However," he added, observing each of them in turn, "I am not so preoccupied that I do not have the time to be acquainted with my daughters' whereabouts. You left early this morning without a word. It has been many years since my children were gathered here under this roof at once. Perhaps I need to remind you that you are children no longer, free to roam the moors like a little tribe of harridans, but young ladies. Sooner, rather than later, you must be employed again if you are to have any hope of security, and employment requires respectability."

"Really, Papa, we only took tea with an old school friend of Charlotte and Emily's," Anne said very sweetly. "Offering her a little comfort at a difficult time. It is true we dallied on the way home, for it was such a pretty day . . . earlier."

Emily glanced out of the window, hoping her father's poor eyesight would preclude him from noticing the evening rain lashing against the window.

"We are mindful of our responsibilities, Papa," Charlotte said. "Believe us. We do our best to emulate your good example in all we do."

"If only your brother were so devoted to goodness," Papa said with quiet sadness.

There was a moment of silence around the table, a moment where each sister looked one to the other, inwardly turning over the rights and wrongs of not being entirely honest with the man they loved and admired most in the world. That she was *not* lying, that was the thing to hold on to, Emily decided. As long as she could never be accused of lying to her father, then her conscience was clear.

After dinner, while Papa read and worked on his sermons or wrote to his parishioners offering what aid he could to the afflicted of Haworth—and there were many—they retired once more to the dining room, lighting extra candles alongside the oil lamp, so that they might see the objects they had collected that day all the more clearly.

Since their mutual return to Haworth, the evenings were usually spent writing, testing ideas and trying out words in various combinations, though not one of them felt fully satisfied with their efforts yet.

Anne often drew or worked on some of the verse that she had begun while employed at Thorp Green, while Charlotte would write in fits and starts, pausing often to stare miserably out of the window, no doubt pining for that fool Monsieur Héger of Brussels. What she had—and indeed still— saw in him, Emily was at a loss to understand. Their former tutor was a small, ill-made man, without one iota of dash or dare about him, and he was filled to his stunted brim with self-importance and a good deal more vanity than a man of such limited attractions should be. But that was Charlotte, dear Charlotte; she longed to be in love, and to be fallen in love with, for such matters loomed so very large in her head. Reaching out, Emily scratched behind Keeper's ear, smiling as he nuzzled his head into her hand, and was glad that she had never been in love, nor had any firm ambition ever to be. Her life, this house, this land, her animals, her mind—they were all enough. And that's where she and Charlotte were so profoundly different. All that Héger had to do to make Charlotte fall hopelessly in love with him during their time studying in Brussels was smile at her and call her clever. The moment he did that Charlotte was lost, and, Emily predicted, she was quite some distance from finding herself again yet.

Charlotte so badly needed the approval of others to see her own self; for Emily, though, her own self was sufficient.

And so as the last of the midsummer evening bled into an inky sky, though Anne sketched, not one of them wrote or gazed wistfully out of the window. Instead they sat in contemplation, trying to determine the best course of action to take next.

"If we can't trust Chester's constable, then perhaps Bradford," Charlotte said, sharpening her pencil with the ivory-handled fruit knife. "If not Bradford, then Leeds. Elizabeth Chester comes from an influential Leeds family—they surely wouldn't let their daughter's disappearance go unremarked upon?"

"Yet it has been two days since the incident," Anne said. "And they were not at the house—Chester would not allow the children to be sent to them. Local news spreads fast, but Leeds is a day's travel away, and there is a possibility that if Chester has not told them, they do not yet know what has become of their daughter."

"It would be exceedingly suspicious if he had not sent news to her parents at once," Emily said thoughtfully. "But then, Chester would know that."

"The point is," Anne said, "that even with what is contained within that box, we need more." Emily noticed how her sister would not look directly at the tea caddy she had set in the middle of the table: the pretty little wooden box that no longer contained tea, but instead a fragment of bone, a pebble and a single human tooth. Emily had thought it eminently sensible and clever to keep the evidence they had gathered together and in sight to help them with their deductions, but she knew that when Anne looked at the box she saw more than clues, she saw fragments of a human being whose life had been brutally ended. Taking pity on her little sister's sensibility, Emily tipped the lid shut.

"We believe we may have uncovered some circumstances of murder," she said, thoughtfully, "but we have not given any thought as to the reason why. What would motivate Robert Chester to kill his young wife and the mother of his child? What could possibly drive a man to such an act?"

"It cannot be greed," Charlotte said. "Chester is a wealthy man, landlord of much of the land surrounding the Grange."

"It could be jealousy," Anne said, lowering her eyes, clearly hesitant about what she was about to say.

"What is it, Anne?" Emily asked her. "Speak up."

"I have seen a man rage and rail with such jealousy that I am quite certain if he'd had the opportunity, he would have killed the one who slighted him." Anne paused, then continued. "Mr. Robinson, on discovering what had passed between his wife and our brother at Thorp Green . . . His rage was . . ." Emily watched Anne's expression tighten as she relived the memory of what Emily knew had been the scorching humiliation of having her own character tainted by the actions of her brother and *that* woman. ". . . quite apoplectic. And I believe if he had set eyes upon Branwell in that moment he would have gravely harmed him."

Emily sat frowning at the thought of her brother ruined by lust until quite suddenly it occurred to her that sitting around this table was achieving nothing, so just in case a change of scenery would help, she slid under the table, wrapping her arms around Keeper's neck.

"So you think that Elizabeth Chester may have . . . engaged in some indiscretion?" Emily heard Charlotte muse above. Indeed, Anne's theory seemed plausible, and though in polite society such transgressions were never spoken of between delicate young ladies, Emily and her sisters had not had much choice but to discuss them since their brother had arrived home leaving scandal in his wake, so fresh from Mrs. Robinson's bed that sometimes Emily thought he still smelt of her awful perfume. The very thought of it made her gag, and she instead inhaled Keeper's familiar scent to chase the awful memory away.

It wasn't that Emily was entirely disinterested in the desires of the flesh; country parson's daughter she might have been, but there lay open to her a universe of reading, from Byron to Chaucer, from which she could glean the sordid details of the most scandalous and intimate acts. No, it was more that she simply could not conjure anybody she had ever met with whom she would like to become so closely acquainted.

In truth, the idea made her feel a little squeamish, though she'd never admit to it. It was more that the attractions of people one was not obliged to love by dint of their being family were completely undetectable to her. Not to mention seemingly fraught with misery. One had only to look to the struggles of the people of Haworth to see infidelity, indiscretion, violence, addiction and even murder firsthand. Just a few yards down the hill, the people that her father served lived cheek to cheek with death. The overflowing graves that made up the view from her window were filled to the brim with infants, so many that they were numbered and not named on the stones that lay atop them.

Life was brutal, cruel and short. Many took happiness where they could, while they could, including Branwell. And many took revenge.

"Emily?" Charlotte was clearly repeating her name as she tapped her neat little foot impatiently. "Emily, what are you doing under there? Whatever it is, it is most unladylike."

"Thinking," Emily said, pushing her way out of the forest of chair legs. "Mattie told us that Chester has a violent temper when he drinks. We know that alcohol can quite change a man's demeanour. And if we can find something that shows Elizabeth was unfaithful, then that shows a reason—a motive for violence. We need to go back to Chester Grange."

"And what *did* you discover at Chester Grange?" Bowling into the room, Branwell dropped himself into their conversation and onto the sofa, his flaming hair unkempt, his shirt untucked. At least he seemed to be sober, and Emily was relieved to see his thumbs and finger stained with ink, indicating that he'd been writing or sketching. Perhaps he was emerging from his grief at last. Emily fervently hoped so, for in her experience unrequited love made people so terribly, terribly dull.

"Such awful goings-on, Branwell." She smiled at her brother. "It would turn your red hair white with shock."

"Somehow I doubt that it is possible to shock our brother," Charlotte muttered. "Nevertheless, I agree, we must return and we must find a reason to be invited into the house, and I believe I might know how."

Charlotte straightened her shoulders, her plan clearly giving her a great deal of pleasure, which meant that, as much as she loved her sister, Emily was instantly against it.

"Well, go on, then," Emily pressed her. "How do you propose we gain access to Chester Grange once again, short of going in disguise?"

Charlotte's shoulders slumped half an inch.

"I do not see why that is such a bad idea."

"You suggest we go in disguise?" Emily laughed. "As what? A travelling theatre troupe?"

"I suggest that you and Anne go down to Arunton village and see what knowledge you can glean from the locals," Charlotte said, determined to go on in the face of Emily's ridicule. "Chester may not have many staff, but I'm sure people from the village make deliveries to the house, care for the horses or are his tenants. They will see things and know things, even if they do not speak of them openly. Branwell will wash and brush his hair, conceive an assumed identity and present himself to Mr. Chester as a doctor new to the area, unfamiliar with Mrs. Chester's disappearance, offering his services to the family, and I shall accompany him posing as his widowed sister, now his dependent."

"Chester has eyes, you know, Charlotte," Emily said, erupting into a teasing grin. "Dark, dangerous eyes that saw you very clearly indeed."

"Ah yes, but this is where cunning comes in," Charlotte said proudly. "I shall wear a thick mourning veil under my bonnet, and he shall not be able to see my face! And while Branwell engages him in conversation, I shall go back to Mrs. Chester's room and look for evidence of a lover!" She sat back in her chair, her eye shining with delight at her idea. "Is it not ingenious?"

"Um . . ." Emily covered her mouth, failing to repress a bubble of laughter.

"What?" Charlotte questioned her.

"It's just that . . ." Anne bit her lip as she trailed off.

"Go on." Charlotte waited.

"My dear sister." Branwell tumbled from the sofa and onto his knees in front of Charlotte, taking her hand in his. "You are not recognisable by your face alone. You have a very particular . . . build: a tiny frame—a fairy frame, it could be said. You are the size of a moorland elf. That's what your sisters are trying to tell you. You'd need stilts and a veil that covered your insubstantial length not to be recognised again. And . . ." Branwell stilled Charlotte before she could retort. "Indeed Emily is no good for the task either, for she is particularly tall, has such a distinctive gait, and . . . a demeanour that once met, none shall forget."

"Then none should meet me, and we could all be happy," Emily replied, unoffended.

"It should be Anne and I who visit Chester again," Branwell continued. "For we two are the most able to change ourselves like chameleons, and to charm the very birds from the trees." He flourished a hand like a fop.

"Where are all these birds you've charmed?" Emily smiled as she looked around. "Where do you keep them?"

Branwell shrugged. "Only one of us has left a string of broken hearts across Yorkshire, Emily," he told her.

"I'm not sure you having your heart broken in a variety of locations counts as a string." Emily smiled.

"What is it that you hope Branwell and I should discover from Mr. Chester that we haven't already?" Anne asked.

"I *hope*," Charlotte said, "that you will see Mattie again, and be able to assess a little more of how she is faring at Chester Grange. And perhaps, while you look for evidence of unhappiness within the bride's chamber, Chester is more likely to speak of his situation to a man of the world—a man of medicine. Something that might show us where to look next . . ."

"I would say that Branwell is more a man of the pub," Emily muttered, elbowing Branwell, who elbowed her back.

"And if you insist on taking Anne with you," Charlotte told Branwell, "then it is up to Emily and me to go into the village and use our charm, good wit and easy nature to befriend the local people."

"In that case," Branwell said, "I suggest you start at the local inn. The inebriated are so much easier to fool."

10

Anne

"We are not expecting visitors," Mrs. Crawley said the moment she opened the door, eyeing the red-headed young gentleman and his female companion with her customary level of warmth and charm. Anne noticed how she always kept the scarred side of her face turned slightly away, perhaps an unconscious decision but nevertheless one that gave to the otherwise stony-faced and repressive woman's nature a touch of vulnerability.

"Indeed you are not, dear lady." Branwell bowed as he smiled, removing his hat in one practised move. "But I wonder if Mr. Chester might spare me a moment? My name is Patrick Hardwell, madam, and I am a young doctor setting up a new practice in the vicinity. I simply wished to introduce myself and my sister to the prominent families in the area."

Mrs. Crawley slid her gaze over to Anne, scrutinizing the blurred image behind the veil for long enough to make Anne feel a little uncomfortable. Last night she and her sisters had added layer after layer to the mourning veil, but she still wasn't entirely satisfied she wouldn't be recognised. Until that moment, Anne had been unable to decide if the prospect of being discovered was thrilling or terrifying, but suddenly she knew with utter certainty that it was the latter.

"We are not receiving any visitors," Mrs. Crawley reiterated. "I daresay you know why, and I daresay you are nothing but chancers hoping to get a look at where a poor young woman was taken from her own bed."

It was impossible to discern any sort of intent in Mrs. Crawley's growling tone, but for some reason Anne had assumed she would have no sympathy for the missing woman, checking herself for unconsciously deciding a person of such hunched and ugly appearance must be so on the inside too.

"My dear lady." Branwell's look of both hurt and shock was compelling. "My sister and I have heard nothing of such a disappearance—we only came to pay our respects." He threw a casual gesture in Anne's direction. "My poor sister, recently widowed, is regrettably lacking in any education or intellect, and has but a sweet and simple nature that has no use for idle gossip."

Behind the veil Anne quietly seethed, and made several rapid and fairly violent plans to do serious injury to her big brother in the space of but a few moments.

Mrs. Crawley thought for a moment before stepping aside and letting them in. "Because you are a medical man and Mr. Chester is very vexed with worry at present, I shall let you enter, but do not be surprised if he sends you away with the toe of his boot."

"A few minutes of his time is all I ask." Branwell bowed again, prompting Mrs. Crawley to snort as she walked away.

"She likes me, I can tell." Branwell smiled as he smoothed his unruly hair back from his face and adjusted his glasses.

Two of Chester's dogs trotted out from somewhere within the house and stopped a few paces from the visitors, bared their teeth and admitted low and menacing growls.

"I'm rather good at subterfuge, don't you think?" Branwell said, giving the animals a nervous wave, adding, "Good savage hounds, please don't kill me."

"Not *that* good," Anne muttered, "otherwise I'd still be in my position at Thorp Green."

"This is a very fine house," Branwell answered, Anne's comment running off his back like water ran off a duck. "I'll wager it has a very fine collection of wines."

"Branwell, remind yourself of our intentions," Anne said to him. "You are too like Emily sometimes, too often able to mistake your own fantasies for truth: it's a weakness that you must address if you are to become an independent man."

"But fantasies are so much more engaging than truth." Branwell half smiled and half sighed. "Were not your days at Thorp Green interminably dull? Would you not have, if the opportunity had presented itself, sought distraction, meaning even? Might one not even say that in releasing you from the yoke of servitude I am due your heartfelt thanks?"

Though there was a great deal that Anne could have said in answer to that comment, it would have taken several minutes that she did not have. So she only sighed behind her veil, her tapping foot ticking against the tiles like a metronome.

"Still yourself, woman," Branwell told her at last. "Remember you are mild and sweet. You are the epitome of what a woman should be, biddable and obedient."

Able to hold back no more, Anne kicked him swiftly and viciously in the shins just as Mrs. Crawley returned, Anne smiling broadly behind her veil as Branwell did his best to stifle a yelp.

"He'll see you," Mrs. Crawley said, and without further ceremony, turned on her heel and led them to Chester's study. They found him positioned behind a great leather-topped writing desk that would fill all four corners of their little dining room, a billowing cloud of smoke circulating around him and a wealth of paperwork scattered across the desk. On the wall behind hung a painting of a very beautiful woman dressed in blue velvet, bejewelled with lavish diamonds, a large ruby on her ring finger, holding the hand of a child of about two. It had to be the first Mrs. Chester, Imogen, Anne thought, looking into the sad blue eyes that seemed to be able to search her out behind her veil, so full of regret it was as if she had seen her fate approaching her. In Chester's left hand he held a wine glass filled to the brim with a ruddy, amber-coloured liquid that Anne would wager was not wine. Branwell licked his lips.

"Mr. . . . ?" Chester didn't bother addressing Anne.

"Hardwell, sir." Branwell extended his hand across the desk and shook Chester's firmly. "I would say it was a pleasure to make your acquaintance, but I believe you are suffering from an unfortunate turn of events."

"Crawley says you are a doctor—what kind of doctor?"

"Ah . . . a . . . medical one." Branwell nodded very seriously.

"Tell me, do you have any knowledge of the working of a man's brain?"

"Why, indeed, sir—it's my speciality."

It really was remarkable, Anne thought, how the stories just tripped off her brother's tongue, just as it was unremarkable that neither one of them had thought to acknowledge her presence in the room.

"I hardly know where to turn, Hardwell," Chester said, his voice thick with emotion. "I do not know what is to be done. It is now two nights and two days since my wife vanished in the most gruesome circumstances, and there is no trace of her to follow, no suspect to run down, save some gypsies, and I hardly think them criminal masterminds. I am . . ." Anne watched as he dragged his fingers through his dark hair. "I'm going mad with uncertainty, Hardwell. How may I quiet my mind, man?"

"Sir"—Branwell took a seat opposite Chester, leaving his sister to stand at his shoulder—"the greatest healer I know for a distressed mind is sleep, and if it does not come easily, perhaps you could procure some laudanum: there is an excellent pharmacist in Haworth. A drop or two should give you ease—mention my name."

"A drop or two would not give me ease," Chester spat. "The amount it would take to soothe me would as soon kill me, and even whisky does nothing—I'm too hardened against every vice. I began to quiet my mind long ago, you see—and now it refuses to be silenced." Anne started as Chester threw his glass into the fire, making the flame spurt and dart up for a moment. Folding her hands into her skirts, she kept her chin meekly down, but her eyes were honed on his every movement and expression. He was a man of opposites: large, dramatic gestures and small, sly expressions that told her he was, in some way, playing a version of himself, even if he wasn't entirely aware of his own subterfuge.

"Then perhaps I might suggest you speak aloud those thoughts that will not let you sleep? Shining a light on our demons is often a way to vanquish them," Branwell said cheerfully.

"Good Lord, man." Chester scowled at him. "I am not some skirt-wearing ninny."

"I only thought that perhaps . . ."

"Tell me . . ." Chester paused, sinking further into his chair, with an air of despondence so heavy it seemed to visibly weigh his shoulders down. "Have you ever heard of a man losing his memory under the influence of alcohol to such an extent that he has no recollection of hours of his life?"

"Every day!" Branwell said enthusiastically, for on this subject he was indeed an expert. "Why, a drunk man might speak words, engage in fights, even partake of certain 'pleasures'"—he lowered his voice—"and not re-member a thing about it. It is the curse of the drunk, I'm afraid."

"Why do you ask, sir?" Anne spoke before she could prevent herself, concerned that Branwell would let the moment pass.

"No concern of yours, madam," Chester said, standing abruptly. "As you are here I would like you to examine my children. This is a trying time for them also, and I do not wish for any illness to take hold of them while they are so upset."

"Of course, sir—it would be my honour."

"French!" Chester caught a glimpse of Mattie through the office door and summoned her in. The moment she saw Branwell her jaw dropped and almost all was given away when she looked at Anne. Somehow, seeing a ruse was afoot, she regained her composure in the nick of time, and Anne allowed herself to breathe in a mouth of netting again.

"Patrick Hardwell at your service." Branwell bowed at Mattie. "I am a doctor newly arrived in the vicinity, accompanied by my widowed sister."

It was a far greater biography than a woman of Mattie's standing was owed, but fortunately Chester didn't seem to notice.

"Matilda French, how do you do?" Mattie said uncertainly, bobbing a curtsey in return.

"Where are Francis and Archibald?" Chester asked her.

"Taking an afternoon nap, sir," Mattie replied, keeping her eyes on the floor. "As they always do at this time of day."

"Good, I wish you to take Dr. Hardwell and his sister to the children at once. He is to examine them and to ensure they are in good health."

"Sir." Matilda curtseyed, keeping her eyes down until she had led Branwell and Anne outside the front door and out of earshot and sight of anyone inside.

"What on earth are you doing here? Branwell? And Anne, is that you?"

"Yes, it is I," Anne said, hugging Mattie tightly. "We are on a secret mission, Mattie. We are looking for *clues* and *evidence*."

"I have no idea what you mean," Mattie said, shaking her head in confusion. "What on earth do you expect to find here?"

"Something that we shall only know when we see it," Anne said. "Show us as much of Chester Grange as you are able."

11

❧

Charlotte

"I'm not certain that this is our best strategic move," Charlotte said, looking at the outside of the alehouse. It was impossible to make out what lay within the small windows of the squat, wood-framed Elizabethan building, but whatever it was didn't seem appropriate for a respectable young woman at all. "Besides, surely all the local people are about their work at this time of day, not carousing in a drinking establishment?"

"Is Branwell?" Emily asked her.

"Branwell doesn't appear to be able to keep work." Charlotte sighed.

"Well, I don't want to go in," Emily said with some determination. "I could just wait outside. Or go home. I could go home and wait for news."

"News of what?" Charlotte looked at her.

"Anything?" Emily offered hopefully.

"I'm afraid not, Emily—you can't just join in with this enterprise when the mood takes you. If you are determined to be a detector, then you must be ready to face situations of great danger."

"I don't mind danger," Emily said. "It's polite conversation I can't abide."

"Think of it as a means to an end," Charlotte said. "We appear to be making small talk, but in fact we are interrogating witnesses."

"That does sound more interesting," Emily conceded.

"In any event, our main concern is to not draw undue attention,"

Charlotte said, casting around for a more suitable destination. "So I suggest we take the time to visit the clothier instead—perhaps they might have some interesting fabrics, and seamstresses do like to gossip, do they not?"

Without waiting for any further assent, Charlotte hooked her arm through Emily's and guided them down the street. Despite her wishes to remain incognito, the two women made a striking pair as they walked through the steep streets of Arunton, their pattens clacking on the cobbles. Though sisters, their disparity in height and gait should have made them utterly incongruous to the casual onlooker, but instead the two of them together had quite the opposite effect.

There was an indefinable bond between them that could not be ignored. In every negative space and shape their linked arms and mismatched hips created, there was a deep abiding closeness. For Charlotte and Emily had turned more corners into the unknown together than with any of the other members of their beloved family. They had been lost girls together at the dreaded Cowan Bridge, and both teacher and pupil at Roe Head school, and each had kept the other sane when they worked together at the Pensionnat Héger in Brussels, encountering challenges and difficulties whose burden they had shared equally. And perhaps more than anything, it had been Emily's companionship that had been her solace as Charlotte lost her heart to her master, Monsieur Héger. Though they rarely spoke of those few intense months, even as they were unfolding, Emily's stalwart and strong nature had been Charlotte's safe haven. Even after she left for home, Emily remained Charlotte's tacit confessor, the only other living person who truly knew the depth of Charlotte's thwarted love. And now that those days in Brussels were slipping ever further away, Emily was all that Charlotte had left of the life that she had lived there; Emily was the proof that said, "Yes, that happened, all of it. I know because I witnessed it. You have not lost your mind."

In return, Charlotte was Emily's unwitting beacon, leading her on, challenging her to reveal her own precious and jealously guarded secret: her immense, breathtaking talent.

There was trust between the two of them, and an accord that made the mismatched pair fit perfectly. And in this new business of detecting they would carry on just as they always had, infuriating and baiting each other, and never being anything less than entirely loyal.

A bell chimed as they entered the little shop.

"Good day, ladies." A pleasant-looking woman, her steel hair neatly pinned under a cap that reminded Charlotte of her much-missed aunt Branwell, greeted them. "I'm Mrs. Hardy—are you visiting for the day?"

It was a pretty little shop, bisected by a broad cloth-cutting table that also served as the counter, and floor-to-ceiling display shelves carrying a limited range of bolts of cloth, although some of them appeared rather fine, especially a coppery-looking satin silk that Charlotte immediately set her heart on. It looked, from what the sisters could see of the work in progress, as if most of their trade came from mending and remaking what had already been worn, a skill with which all the Brontë daughters had become be-grudgingly familiar.

"Good day, yes, we are visiting from Haworth." Charlotte smiled, careful not to volunteer more information than was polite. "My sister and I have a little idle time and thought to look at your fabrics. We are always most in-terested in the latest designs."

"Well, we have many patterns here, and any we do not have we can obtain," Mrs. Hardy told them proudly. "I keep abreast of the London and Paris fashions too, for why shouldn't our Yorkshire lasses look just as fine as those city ladies, if not a good deal finer?"

"Indeed," said Charlotte, assessing Mrs. Hardy. Hardworking and neat, she was the epitome of a professional Yorkshirewoman. This was the kind of woman Charlotte understood, the kind she had known all her life. The kind of woman, though her shop might be modest, who would have a knowledge and passion for her subject that were extensive, and who would most likely take great joy in conversing on such matters.

In Charlotte's experience, almost everyone wanted to feel interesting, and as soon as you had achieved that happy state, they would become ready friends. With this fine woman all she had to do was build a little trust.

"Tell me what *is* the latest fashion for sleeves? I would so appreciate your expertise."

As Charlotte talked, Emily turned her back on her sister and Mrs. Hardy, walking her fingers along the shelves of bolts of cloth, searching out stories and faces in every pattern, until they stopped on one and lingered. Glancing back at her sister, Charlotte knew that Emily was, for the moment at least, lost to another realm.

"Oh my," Charlotte said, her eyes lighting up at the sight of one of the latest patterns, featuring long fitted sleeves gathered a little around the wrists. "How pleasing the neckline is. Do you make many beautiful gowns? I can see how very fine your tailoring is."

"The most beautiful I ever made was for a lovely young bride," Mrs. Hardy preened happily. "Not her wedding gown, that came out of Leeds, but her trousseau. Such fine fabrics and designs, for she was a very particular young lady, and so beautiful."

"Was?" Charlotte asked as casually as she was able, keeping her eyes on the designs.

"It's been a long while since we've seen the lady in the village," Mrs. Hardy said, and Charlotte noticed her physically turning away from the temptation to gossip with an outsider. "We don't expect to see her again soon. It would be improper for me to say more."

"Where do you source your lace?" Charlotte said, picking up the end of a piece of finely wrought trim. "Mrs. Hardy, you have quite the most exquisite taste."

Mrs. Hardy beamed. "I employ a local maker exclusively. The woman makes it as fine as on the continent, with the benefit that you will never see this design elsewhere."

"How wonderful." Charlotte smiled. "Tell me, why do you not see the young lady anymore, has she moved away?"

Mrs. Hardy's smile faded a little.

"It's really not my place to say," she said, stoutly. "May I show you anything else?"

"Of course, I quite understand, we are from a small village—parson's daughters. I understand the importance of discretion; so many are disposed to idle gossip, are they not? I can see you are a woman of great character."

"Parson's daughters?" Mrs. Hardy's face softened. "It's a hard life for a young woman."

"We make do." Charlotte let her accent broaden just a little, as she frowned thoughtfully, lowering her head. "Tell me, is the bride you speak of Mrs. Chester of Chester Grange? For to speak true, we have heard about the trouble at the Grange. So distressing and shocking."

"Indeed it was." Mrs. Hardy chewed her lip, refusing to meet Charlotte's eyes.

"But there is cause for hope, wouldn't you say?" Charlotte casually fingered the corner of a fine wine damask that she would have dearly loved to purchase, but alas, new dresses were a luxury that was at present out of their reach. "Perhaps Elizabeth Chester will be found and all will come good."

"No good can come from that house," Mrs. Hardy blurted, her cheeks reddening with what Charlotte realised was repressed rage. "Forgive me, I shouldn't speak of it. It's just that she was such a fine and sweet young lady."

"Is," Charlotte said mildly. "Until we know her fate for certain we must say 'is.'"

"Perhaps she did run away," Mrs. Hardy said bleakly, folding and refolding a length of silk in a bid to hide her distress. "All I can say is that she was as devoted to her children as any mother could be—she would never leave them. You'd see her most afternoons out for a walk with them, her and young Miss French. You'd see how she'd always have her baby on her hip, how she'd hold young Master Francis's hand, and take real care to notice things that he might like: a beetle, maybe, or an interesting stone. That poor lad blossomed under her sweetness and love—she cared for him as if he were her own. I just can't see how she'd abandon those children. Not for anything. Not even for a . . . not for anything."

Charlotte noticed the slip, but let it pass by. If you wanted to extract a story from a stranger, timing was everything.

"How frightening to think there might be a madman abroad who has carried her away, perhaps keeping her captive even now!"

Mrs. Hardy shook her head bitterly, and Charlotte could sense the stream of words that she was doing her very best to keep dammed up behind her closed lips.

Charlotte reached out and briefly covered the other woman's hand, offering an implied reassurance of discretion. Fixing her with her clear eyes, she held Mrs. Hardy's gaze until the woman was finally hers. This was one particular skill that was Charlotte's alone, the ability to draw out any information from nearly anyone she encountered if she wished it, to will them to talk to her, to trust her. Only those she held in very high esteem or was directly related to seemed immune.

"Perhaps you have your own idea of what has happened?"

"Well, it's no secret his first wife died *by her own hand.*" The seamstress lowered her voice, as if it was indeed a very grave secret. "Been married less than two years too. Back then, and it were only five or so years ago, there were more staff up at the Grange, and I was one of them. I saw them carry away her body, limp as a rag doll. It were a terrible, terrible sight—one I shall never forget, that poor woman. Imogen Chester was a good woman. When she came to the village, we hoped things would settle up at the Grange. She made sure to know us all by name, asked after our families, sent medicine for the children . . . and she were so proud of little Francis— but she was as fragile as organza. Perhaps if she'd been cared for she might have thrived, but she was poorly done by, very poorly done by. Cruelty broke her, and I knew the minute I saw the second wife that . . . Well, she were such a slip of a girl. He's a cruel man, cold as you like, has been since he were a boy. And then there was the day I saw . . ."

Mrs. Hardy stopped herself.

"Saw?" Charlotte prompted her gently.

"I've already said too much. I meant not to, but you have such a kind face, miss, and I am so very sad for young Mrs. Chester, I quite forgot myself. But her husband is my landlord." Mrs. Hardy turned her face away from Charlotte. "I really should not say more."

"You have nothing to fear from us, madam, I assure you." Charlotte smiled. "No one will ever know what you say to us, and if it helps you unburden your heart a little, then what harm can it do?"

"Well, it's just that . . ."

"I shall take a length of this," Emily said, unloading an armful of fabric onto the counter. "Enough for a day dress."

"That?" Charlotte looked down at the fabric, raising her brows.

"Isn't it magnificent?" Emily beamed, searching about in her pockets for coins.

Charlotte didn't want to raise the subject of their straitened circumstances in front of Mrs. Hardy, but nevertheless she gave Emily a long, hard look, which she hoped conveyed her concern for her frivolous purchase. As ever, Emily remained one of the few people who was entirely oblivious to Charlotte's long, hard looks. She counted out the coins onto the counter and smiled with great satisfaction.

"It's covered with thunder clouds and lightning bolts," Charlotte stated as she stared at the curious design, as otherworldly and as wild as Emily herself. "I'm not sure I have ever seen a fabric made with such a design."

"Exactly, and the garment I shall make from it will be a great storm of a dress," Emily said happily, smiling at Mrs. Hardy as she acknowledged her for the first time. "Please have it delivered to the Parsonage at Haworth."

"Mrs. Hardy, you were saying?" Charlotte asked gently as the older woman wrapped up the material.

"I cannot say more." Mrs. Hardy had closed up again, like a daisy on a cloudy afternoon. "Except that the truth will out. One way or another, it always does."

Charlotte stood aside as Emily completed her transaction. If only Mrs. Hardy had completed her sentence, but now the moment was past, and she couldn't see a way to bring about such an opportunity again without looking suspicious.

"What did you see that day?" Emily asked Mrs. Hardy, who blinked rapidly at the question. "You were about to tell my sister of something you saw that may have something to do with the fate of Elizabeth Chester, were you not? What was it?"

Emily always was very direct.

"I was collecting piecework from my women in the village," Mrs. Hardy said. "May, it was. It was a pretty day, so I cut across the Chester woods to see the bluebells, and that's when I happened upon her."

"Elizabeth Chester?" Emily pressed.

"The very same." Mrs. Hardy nodded. "In the arms of a man who was certainly not her husband."

12

Anne

Although their second visit to the upper floors of Chester Grange was essentially as invited persons, Anne felt a deep unease as she and Branwell followed Mattie up the central staircase, watched closely by at least a dozen ancestral portraits. Grimed with decades of candle smoke and dust, they appeared to Anne like a counsel of ghosts observing her every move.

Thanks to the long windows, the upper halls were light, with high, ornately plastered ceilings. Even so it was impossible not to feel the silent clamour of a multitude of vacant rooms echoing all around them, nor their neglected chill, empty of everything but memories and secrets.

"That is the nursery, which as you can see adjoins my room," Mattie whispered, as she led Branwell and Anne from the room where the two dear little boys slumbered. "What I find most . . . *perplexing* . . . is that when there is a disturbance during the night, be it the banging, or the rattling, or a terrible, terrible cold, it *never* encroaches on the children's room. Every time I run to them, seeking to protect them from whatever it is that makes the great din outside my door, in there all is silent, peaceful and warm."

"Like a sanctuary," Anne said thoughtfully. "A protected place in the midst of such . . . danger." Anne wasn't sure why that word came to mind, but it was the way she felt, as if the whole of Chester Grange was one great steel trap, set to snap shut at any second.

"And this is my room."

Anne looked around Mattie's room—not uncomfortable, but shabby and cold. The curtained bed looked a hundred years old, and there was very little of Matilda French present, beyond a few well-thumbed novels and a rather sad collection of trinkets held in an upturned clamshell. All in all it could be any governess's room—it could have been Anne's at Thorp Green. Suddenly, she pictured row upon row of faceless unwanted women who were neither young nor pretty, neither well connected nor rich, and therefore seemed not to matter a jot. Though she had accepted it, the path of a governess had not been the life Anne would have chosen for herself, her sisters or anyone with a human heart. That awful purgatory of being neither servant nor family, that constant suspended state which was the opposite of belonging: Anne would rather do anything else than return to that work, for it was an entirely thankless existence. Just the sight of Mattie's sorry room made her want to scoop up her friend and take her home to a place where people would be pleased to see her. Perhaps, in his way, Branwell had saved her from this awful life, after all. Even so, she had a duty to support herself and contribute to her family somehow, and so it seemed an inescapable fate, and there were far worse.

"Well, so far I don't think we've found any clues," Branwell said, striding into the room, his masculinity quite at odds with the chaste simplicity of the chamber. "Not that I am entirely sure what a clue looks like. Does it have feathers, do you think, Matilda? Perhaps a tail?"

He smiled, and Mattie blushed, readily taking his arm as he escorted her out of her room. At least he made Mattie smile, Anne supposed. That was something that could be said for Branwell; his eager, almost desperate determination to chase away hurt with any kind of quick pleasure could be a balm, not just to himself but to those around him. That's probably why he had so many friends around Haworth, and further abroad. That and his willingness to foot the bill, whether he could afford it or not.

Just as she was leaving, Anne caught sight of something that she recognised, a tiny framed sampler exactly like one Charlotte had made as a girl, though not as precisely stitched. Picking it up, Anne read the Bible verse embroidered below rows of sample stitches, letters and numbers: "My *humility and the fear of the Lord. are. riches. honour and life.*" Another example of how, no matter how fiercely their minds might burn within, the world saw all of them, all women and girls, as one creature, a creature to be tamed and oppressed, heads bent over identical, meaningless pursuits.

Just as she was about to set the frame back down on the mantle, Anne felt something tucked into the back of it. Tugging at the object, she pulled out a folded scrap of torn paper. She glanced at it and tucked it into her sleeve, uncertain of what it meant, but certain that it meant something.

I live for the day when we will be ever together, your beloved R.

As she joined her companions, Anne considered the way Matilda had looked at her employer, so very differently to how she talked about him. It had been obvious that at some point after she had arrived at Chester Grange, Mattie had developed ideas about her employer. Such things weren't uncommon. It had never occurred to any of them that such an attachment could be reciprocated, but if the "R" that ended the note stood for Robert, then it seemed highly likely. If Matilda had been Chester's lover and he had married another woman, then . . . ? Perhaps Mattie French was far less innocent than any of them had presumed.

Mattie led them to another closed door, this time taking a moment to search left and right for any trace of Mrs. Crawley.

Though Anne was half expecting and half dreading another such adventure, Branwell couldn't help but grin with boyish delight as Mattie released a catch in the panelling that seemed to line the entire interior of Chester Grange, revealing another hidden door and a flight of stone steps. Once all three were crammed into the small and musty-smelling stairwell, she drew the door closed behind them.

"Where does this lead?" Branwell asked. There was a little greyish light coming from somewhere at the top of the spiral staircase, but Anne couldn't determine exactly where.

"Up to the attics," Mattie whispered. "But we can't get up there, the door is locked. This stairwell never seems to be used, as far as I can tell. I only found it by chance when I was playing hide-and-seek with Francis. I come here sometimes, just to be quiet. You have yet to tell me the reasoning behind your personas."

"We shall tell you once we are on the other side of that door," Branwell said with a grin, as they climbed the stairs. "Anne, hand me your hat pin."

Anne complied, and within two minutes Branwell had unlocked the door of the huge attic of Chester Grange to reveal the vast, dusty interior within.

Her brother's murky misdemeanours did have their uses after all.

13

Charlotte

"Well," Charlotte said, looking at Emily as they exited the clothier's. "What do you think about *that*?"

"It was a little overpriced," Emily said, looking up at the sky and noticing that clouds were thickening ominously over the church spire. "But it will be good to have something to wear that isn't about to disintegrate around me. Also that we should start home if we are to avoid the rain coming in from the west."

"I meant about Mr. Chester, but now that you mention it, where did the coin come from that paid for that fabric?"

"My own purse," Emily said, and Charlotte could tell that was the end of the matter. It was hardly her business to question her sister about a purchase that she could not begrudge her, for Emily's wardrobe was in a worse state of repair than her own.

"Mrs. Hardy saw Elizabeth in the arms of another man," she said, recalling the seamstress's ominous tone. "If Chester is the violent creature that Mattie says he is, then jealousy and betrayal are indeed powerful motives."

"Yes, agreed." Emily took Charlotte's arm as they walked back up the narrow street that was all but deserted, almost as if everyone who lived or worked in the village was set on avoiding the inquisitive strangers. "Such a revelation does add to the picture of a deeply unhappy marriage, but that is scarcely rare, is it? And still yet, it isn't what you called evidential, is it, Charlotte? After all, there are people that you and I have rather strong feelings about, but the way we feel about them isn't all they are, is it? Take poor Reverend William Weightman, for example, whose only crime was to be handsome and sweet, and inadvertently irresistible to much of the fairer sex for some unfathomable reason, and yet you were exceptionally rude about him all the time after you realised he wasn't going to fall in love with you."

"That was *not* the reason why," Charlotte insisted hotly, but she chose not to meet Emily's long look of disapproval.

"You called him Miss Celia Amelia, and accused him of being nothing more than a vain flirt," Emily reminded her. "But the truth is he died directly due to the care and attention he gave his parishioners, from living amongst them and not shying away from disease and disaster. One aspect of a man's personality does not make up the whole, Charlotte, as you well know."

"So do you suppose that Mr. Chester secretly does good works with the poor, or rescues the few animals whose heads he doesn't mount on his wall?" Charlotte contested. The truth, though she would never own it, was that Emily was right. When William Weightman first arrived in Haworth, he had rather turned *all* their heads, especially hers, and for a little while she had enjoyed their flirtation, letting her daydreams run too far too fast, which had always been her weakness.

But then came the incident of the Valentine cards.

Seeing that none of the young Brontë women had anything approaching a suitor, young Mr. Weightman had taken it upon himself to send them each a card, walking all the way to Bradford to post them. The ruse soon unravelled, and his identity was uncovered. While Anne was amused and Emily couldn't have cared less, the incident stung Charlotte more than she cared to admit. That Mr. Weightman should think of them—think of *her*—as an object of pity, plain and poor with no prospect of being loved for herself, felt almost too much to bear, and she retaliated by being unkind to him. It had not been her finest hour.

"I do not suppose he does anything of the sort," Emily said, "but boring, goody Anne says we need more of the irrefutable before we can damn Chester. One woman's opinion, though it may be eloquently and forcefully put—even though it is mine and I am most likely right—is not proof, Charlotte, no matter how compelling it may be. Mrs. Hardy's account only shows us a cruel husband—which is no new revelation—and a sweet young woman and mother who may also have been an unfaithful wife. It does not reveal a murderer."

"I suppose not," Charlotte said reluctantly, stopping under the wide, sheltering branches of the churchyard cedar tree. "Emily, I fear that I have recklessly launched us into something with which we are not equipped to deal. I imagined that the uncovering of the truth would be somehow plain, and clearly visible to an honest eye, but rather it is like the complicated plot of a particularly implausible novel. And this is not a gothic fairy tale, but involves real people, real lives, real blood spilt. What if we get it wrong? Who are we to meddle in such real-life horrors? Lives are at stake, perhaps even our own!"

"I do like some good, dark, twisted German fictions," Emily told her, reaching up to harvest a handful of needles, which she brought up to her nose, inhaling deeply. "Not those French confections you were once so fond of. And as for your question, Charlotte, who better than we, who have read every novel, and who are embarking on a journey to unravel the mysteries of writing ourselves? Why, we are experts before we have even begun! And if we should find ourselves cornered by a killer, well, at least it makes a nice change."

"I wish I was as certain as you, but I fear we may make matters worse." Charlotte frowned deeply.

"But think of that fat baby, and the other quiet child, whatever it was called," Emily said. "What will become of them if we lose the courage to discover the truth about their father? And what of the first Mrs. Chester, who could only find release in causing her own violent and painful death? Who speaks for her? And *if* something terrible has happened to Elizabeth, what about her, Charlotte? This is a world where women from every walk of life are used and thrown away once men are done with them; a world where we are required to be ever silent and obedient. Perhaps it is our duty to speak for those who cannot; to voice the silent with *our* words and make them heard."

Charlotte looked into Emily's eyes, reaching up to touch her cheek with a gloved hand.

"Just when I think I know you inside and out, you surprise me," she said.

"You will never know me inside and out," Emily told her, with a very small smile. "I am as mysterious as a sphinx."

"Well, even though I agree with you, Sphinx," Charlotte said, "what on earth can we do next?"

Charlotte glanced at the church clock. "We have half an hour remaining before we are due to meet Anne and Branwell," she said. "I believe the time has come for us to screw our courage to the sticking place and brave the inn if we are to discover more."

Emily sighed. "Haven't we done enough talking for today?"

Charlotte waved away her sister's hopeful expression.

"I'm afraid there is talking yet to be done."

Charlotte and Emily had sat for several minutes in the corner of the inn, sipping at cups of pale, cold tea, while the few patrons drinking in exhausted near silence simply ignored them. Charlotte tried not to notice the stench of stale beer or mind the air made gloomy with smoke, but this was not her natural habitat.

"Who shall you approach first?" Emily muttered, leaning a little closer to her sister.

Charlotte scanned the room, her brow furrowed.

"I have yet to decide."

"But when you do decide, what questions shall you ask them?" Emily countered.

"I don't know, Emily," Charlotte said, a little testily. "I thought perhaps the direction of the conversation would become apparent if we waited for the right opportunity."

Emily sat back in her chair, crossed her arms and looked determinedly out of the window.

"May I fetch owt else for you ladies?" the innkeeper asked them, wiping his palms on his apron, thereby making them considerably less clean.

"No, thank you." Charlotte smiled with her characteristic closed lips, conscious of her irregular teeth. Perhaps he would respond to flattery, as Mrs. Hardy had. "What a wonderful establishment you have here, and we are so glad of the refreshment."

"Passing through, are you?" Charlotte noted how the innkeeper cast his eye over them both, their worn clothes and plain faces, and they squirmed under the attention.

"We had come to visit a friend, but she is indisposed."

"Is she?" He nodded again, neither leaving nor speaking further.

"She is," Charlotte said, for the want of something to say. Emily pretended she wasn't there.

"In fact," Charlotte said, sensing the weight of Emily's expectation, "you may know her, Elizabeth Chester. The news is most distressing."

"I don't know where you have come from," he said, leaning over them, "but I will just say this: we look after our own round here. We don't appreciate those that come to gawk at other people's tragedies."

"Sir, I can assure you that is not our intention," Charlotte snapped back, her cheeks pinkening, cursing herself inwardly for the clumsy question.

"No need to stay a moment longer, then, is there?" He crossed his arms and looked at them for one more long moment. "Now get you back to your husbands or fathers, and mind them well."

"Well, that went splendidly," Emily said after he had walked away.

"And how would you do it differently?" Charlotte asked her. "Are you an expert of interrogation, Emily? Or detecting?"

"Then let us go and fetch the others, and see what they have discovered, Charlotte. I am very much more a thinker than a talker anyway."

"Are you?" Charlotte said flatly.

"What's that supposed to mean?" Emily asked her.

"It means, are you a thinker instead of a talker, or are you in fact neither?"

"Right." Emily made a face as she finished her tea with one grimacing swig. Standing up, she made rather an imposing figure in the low-ceilinged room, with her dark hair curled under her bonnet and her fierce, intense eyes reminding Charlotte of why she had once nicknamed her "The Major."

"Sir." She nodded at the innkeeper and addressed those few others in the room at large. "Gentlemen. My companion and I are seeking information about the whereabouts of one Mrs. Elizabeth Chester on behalf of the firm of solicitors Bell Brothers and Company. We realise that most people hereabouts are dependent on Chester for income and a home, but if you know anything that might lead us to being able to confirm that Mrs. Chester is alive and well or . . . the opposite, then we invite you to do what is right. If you wish to anonymously pass along information to our gentlemen employers then you may address a note to them and send it to Enoch Thomas, the Black Bull, Haworth. There is a reward for information that directly leads my employer to a firm conclusion. I bid you good day."

For a moment Charlotte was too stunned to move as she watched Emily stride out of the inn, bowing her head to make her way through the small door. After a few seconds she scuttled after Emily and into the street, hurrying to catch up with her sister, who was already marching off towards the designated meeting place at quite a pace.

"Bell Brothers and Company?" Charlotte asked her, when she finally caught up.

"Men talk to men, not to young ladies in bonnets and skirts sipping weak tea," Emily said, wrinkling her nose at the memory. "You heard him sending us back to our 'husbands' and 'fathers.' This way, if they do have information they will feel that they are giving it to someone in authority and with the right anatomical arrangement of parts."

"But . . ." Charlotte was still processing Emily's bold move. "A reward, Emily?"

"Indeed." Emily smiled at Charlotte. "One that will be received in heaven, granted—a reward nevertheless." Charlotte couldn't help but laugh at her sister's audacity.

"And where did the name 'Bell' come from?"

"I heard the church bell chime the hour, and thought of the new set of bells about to be installed in our own church, and it came to me as a flash of inspiration," Emily said proudly. "I think we can agree that I am quite brilliant."

"Emily"—Charlotte slowed her sister's pace by linking arms with her—"you can't just scatter words into the wind like wildflower seed. Words have weight; they have import, meaning and consequence. I fear you gave no consideration to any of those things when you spoke."

"Then let me reassure you, Charlotte," Emily said. "I am all too aware of all of those things. It's just that I only thought of them after I had spoken. Now let us hurry—we are late already, and I am eager to be done with this day, and home again before our own hearth, with our dogs at our feet and our cats on our laps. We have much to discuss."

14

Anne

The first thing Anne noticed was the taste of the air, sour and coated in dust. A series of long dormer windows set into the steeply sloping vaulted roof let in sharp slices of light but also cast long, far-reaching shadows, dense and watchful. And here at the very top of the old house you could hear the wind tearing at the ancient roofing, whipping and gusting in a constant elemental growl.

Wandering into the centre of the room, she slowly turned about, looking into every corner, but the room seemed entirely empty. There wasn't even an old trunk or piece of broken furniture languishing in the corner—not a single indication of what secrets Chester Grange might hold at all. Beyond this room was another and another, and it seemed to Anne that perhaps the attic continued on forever, almost as if a person could live their whole life up here and never visit the same room twice, like a maze, impossible to escape from. The thought unnerved her.

"What an interesting light," Branwell said, apparently untroubled by such thoughts. "This would make a wonderful studio, you know, Anne . . ."

"Please concentrate on the matter at hand," Anne told him as she walked slowly into the next room. "And answer me this: why is the door to the attic locked when it's hidden away behind a concealed entrance anyway? Everywhere I look I see precisely nothing at all. What on earth could it be that Chester is locking away up here?"

"Perhaps it's a safety measure," Branwell said. "To prevent any more unfortunate leapings."

"I don't like it," Mattie said, going to the window. "It feels sad, somehow."

"All attics feel sad," Branwell assured her. "It's the way of things. They are the least-cared-for part of any building, after all."

Mattie smiled wanly and, encouraged, Branwell went on. "Yes indeed, attics often feel utterly neglected . . ."

"Branwell," Anne said before Branwell could continue in his endeavour to get Mattie to fall in love with him. "Why don't you take the clockwise path, and Mattie and I the anti-clockwise, and I suppose we will meet again at some point."

"A mission!" Branwell clicked his heels together and saluted in the manner of a soldier. "I am dispatched, ladies. If I am never seen again, remember me fondly."

He paused only to bow, kissing Mattie's hand before strutting off into the next room, his whistle gradually fading away.

"I'm not sure we should have sent Branwell away," Mattie said, wrapping her arms around herself. "Even in broad daylight this place feels restless, like the shadows might pounce on us at any moment!"

"It's just a place, Mattie," Anne said, rather more steadily than she felt. "There is nothing here that can harm us, and my brother, though he is very dear to me, is not. . . ." Anne hesitated. "I wouldn't want him to turn your head, Mattie. At least not until he has his own head righted."

"Anne, I had no such inclination, I assure you," Mattie protested, a little too weakly to be convincing.

Anne walked away from Mattie and went through the next open door. It was just like the last, and the one after that, but in the final room of that wing she was stopped in her tracks, catching her breath just as Mattie followed on her heels.

For in that moment a beam of silver sunlight struck the dirty glass, and all at once a pair of handprints were illuminated in perfect gilded detail. Just as instantly the clouds rolled on and the light vanished, but Anne went to the window at once, peering at the glass. Recalling many rainy mornings of secretly making patterns on the misted windows before Aunt Branwell caught them, Anne blew her own warm breath onto the pane. Sure enough there were the palms again, impressions that seemed to press desperately against the glass.

"What can they mean?" Anne wondered as the image faded away.

"I don't like it," Mattie said, visibly shivering. "I don't like it at all, Anne. Shall we go down? The children will be awake soon, and there is nothing here to see. Shall I call out for Branwell? I shall call for him now."

"Wait a moment," Anne said, falling to her knees on the floor. Just under the window there was a wide crack in the crumbling Elizabethan masonry, wide enough to fit a hand into, and sure enough something seemed to be stuffed within.

Braving the sticky mass of cobwebs that barred the way, Anne reached in and drew out what she could see had once been a pair of long, white silk evening gloves, though now they were yellowed and dirty.

"Oh, Anne, put them down," Mattie said, horrified.

"Who would have put these here?" Anne asked, shaking the dust off one and running it through her fingers. "And why?"

As filthy as it was, the glove looked as though it had just been removed, the presence of the hand it had once adorned still visible in the puckered fingertips and slightly worn palm. Something caught Anne's eye on the second glove, and putting the first one down, she turned it over, examining it closely. From the tip of the forefinger to the wrist there was a long, reddish-brown smear, a stain that Anne thought could easily be dried blood. More than that, there was a tear, not along the hem, which had been very finely sewn, but in the fabric itself, as if it had been rent from whoever had been wearing it with quite some force. Feeling something hard within the fabric, Anne tipped the glove out, and into the palm of her hand fell a pretty, ruby-set wedding ring. Anne had seen the ring before, on the finger of the woman in the painting in Robert Chester's study.

"Look." She showed the gloves to Mattie, and also Branwell, who joined them as he completed his circuit. "Torn and possibly bloody gloves that still contain Imogen Chester's wedding ring. Why? Why would this room be kept completely clear except for a pair of ladies' dress gloves, Branwell?"

Branwell shook his head, frowning as he took the torn glove from her, turning it as gently as if it still contained a hand.

"A memento perhaps, a token of his lost wife to hold dear to him when he is overwhelmed with suffering?" Anne turned away from her brother, unable to bear the intense flash of longing in his eyes.

"But here?" she said, gesturing at the chasm. "Stuffed into a wall where they might never be seen or found again?"

Anne thought of the stuffed deer and fox heads that lined the walls of the great entrance hall. Though she couldn't say exactly why, she felt that the gloves and the portrait had something in common with those poor, unfortunate creatures.

"They are trophies," she whispered.

Looking up at the window again, the faintest glimmer of what seemed to be some scratching to the glass caught her eye, and she leaned forward to peer at it, her nose almost touching the window.

As she made sense of what she saw Anne gasped, tracing her finger through the layer of dirt that filmed the glass.

"What is it?" Branwell bent down to peer at whatever it was that Anne was captivated by.

"Tell me?" Mattie asked from beside the door. "I'm too afraid of what I might see if I look."

"It's writing," Anne said. "Words etched into the glass, perhaps with this very ring."

"And what do the words say?" Mattie's voice was tremulous.

"They say . . ." Anne felt her throat tighten with emotion. "They say, 'Dear God, please help me.'"

15

Emily

They dined with Papa once again, though he was lost in contemplation, as was sometimes his way, his snowy-haired head bent as he inwardly turned some thought over and over in his mind.

Emily liked to think it was because he was remembering Mama, who had loved him so very much, and to whom he had been utterly devoted. Emily wasn't the sort of woman who was given to sentiment, but with Papa she felt differently. Some thought of him as stern—cold, even—but Emily knew better. It was only that Papa carried all within. And though he rarely spoke of Maria, Emily could tell when Mama was in his thoughts from the faraway look in his eyes and the faint teary misting that gathered there.

Her own memory of her mother faded a little day by day, but she held on fiercely to those sacred, sharp moments of a life that were embedded so deeply in her heart: Mama's dark, bright eyes, her musical laugh and endless curiosity.

"Shall we find out, Emily?" she would often say, though Emily could no longer recall the sound of her voice.

Emily remembered how Mama never tired of answering questions or reading books—books she'd read aloud to her daughters whether they understood them or not. These were the things that Emily held on to.

These were the markers she identified with being a woman of worth, the qualities she hoped one day to discover within herself.

When she took him his tea a little later, the expression on his face was one of such sadness that Emily put her hand on his shoulder and leaned against him.

"What troubles you, Papa?" she asked him gently.

"A poor young girl, of a kind family," he told her, raising his watery eyes to her face, "late of this parish, who I helped to find a good position some weeks ago, has written to confess that she found herself to be with child; she is unwed."

A man of God, such as he, might be expected to rain fire and brimstone on such a poor, unfortunate, careless girl, but not Papa. Emily heard only sorrow in his voice, and a deep empathy for the girl's impossible predicament.

"What will you tell her to do, Papa?" Emily asked him. "I suppose she must marry the father to have a hope of being saved from ruin."

"Indeed, no," Papa said, taking her hand. "It should not be that one mistake gives rise to another, and another. I am writing to the young woman urging her not to rush into marriage but to trust the child to the care of her family with the parish's support and return to her post as a maid until enough money is saved for her to be married to her young man, for they do intend to marry. Then she and her child will have a good chance at a happy and productive life."

"You are a good, kind man, Papa," Emily said, bending to kiss him on the pink top of his head. "You show us each day that kindness and charity are the true stalwarts of faith. Take heart and don't feel that poor girl's misfortune as your fault. None could ever be as dedicated to their parish as you, Papa."

Patrick smiled at his middle daughter, reaching up to touch her cheek with his ink-stained fingers.

"And what did you children get up to today?" he asked her as if she were still a girl, his Irish accent still as strong as it ever was.

"We walked and talked, Papa, the four of us all together. It was quite as it used to be when we were small, waging battles and planning campaigns up and down the moor. It was a good day, and I am so glad to have Anne and Charlotte and Branwell home again. I am quite determined that I shall never roam again. Roe Head and Brussels were all very well, but they weren't home. You will have me with you always, Papa, until we are both very old and grey."

"Then I am content," Patrick said, though his smile was exhausted. "And blessed, my dear Emily Jane."

"'Dear God, please help me.'" Anne finished her recounting of the afternoon's events by reciting the words she had found scratched into the glass with a suitably dramatic delivery. "It was so macabre, so haunting, and I am sure that that brute is the kind of drunk that beats his wives, and abuses them to the point that they take their own life, or are robbed of it. But there was more than that—why does he keep the gloves and her wedding ring there, like a memorial? Did he imprison Imogen in the attic? Was her only escape to leap to her death? That poor woman must have felt so trapped and so alone. Robert Chester is like some terrible Bluebeard, collecting heads to mount on his wall next to the animals he has slain."

"Though . . ." Branwell added. He slipped on his coat, but did not make a move to leave, Emily noted. The longer they could keep his interest, the longer he would be kept from the variety of vice offered in the local inns. ". . . we did not find anything concrete that would back up your certainty, Anne. A blood-smeared glove is not a signed confession."

"We are hardly likely to get one of those, are we?" Emily said. "What are your thoughts, brother. You met with him. How did he strike you?"

Emily was pleased to see Branwell take a seat at the table as he thought over her question.

"I found him to be a troubled man," he said. "He struck me as bluff, indeed, and confident, as you would expect from a man in his position. But I also saw an inner turmoil, a damaged humanity." He rocked back in the chair, tilting his head back to look down his long nose at each of them in turn. "When I met Robert Chester I saw a man ravaged by hurt, a man seeking to blot out pain by any means necessary. And if that makes him capable of murder, then I suppose the same could be said of myself."

Emily shook her head. "You and Robert Chester are not in any way alike," she insisted. "You are gentle of heart, Branwell, *too* gentle. The only human souls you are likely to hurt with your actions are your own and those of the people who love you most."

There was a long, excruciating moment of silence, none at the table able to meet each other's eyes.

"Well," Branwell said at last, "I will leave you to your intriguing."

"No, do stay," Charlotte pleaded. "What are your thoughts of our discovery? Mrs. Chester, in the arms of a young man, in the woods?"

"Married women have been known to take lovers," Branwell said, smiling wryly. "The obvious conclusion: that Elizabeth Chester had a lover, her husband discovered this, killed her in a fit of rage and burnt the body, using his standing in the community to escape justice."

"There *is* something else." Anne's tone was quiet as she slipped out the scrunched-up note and added it to the tea caddy of evidence. "This was in Mattie's room, and it's signed from 'R.'"

Charlotte picked the scrap of paper up, examining it before handing it to Emily.

"'R' for Robert?" Emily mused. "What other 'R's are there?"

"None that we know of, but we have all seen the way she looks at Chester—her every move contradicts her every word. Is it possible that Mattie isn't telling us the whole truth, Charlotte? Might she and Chester have had a secret liaison? What if Elizabeth Chester wasn't her friend but her rival?"

Emily watched Charlotte's brows knit together and tried to recall all she knew of Mattie herself. She knew that Mattie was pretty, that once there had been talk of proposals when she was young, which never came to anything because Mattie had no money or property. She knew that Mattie was weak-willed and tender: their weeks at Cowan Bridge had been unrelentingly terrifying, but it was Mattie who wept and wailed at every turn, making herself into the teachers' timid little pet. But she had never thought of Mattie as duplicitous, nor cunning. That was not the Matilda French she knew. But then again, life changes a person, love changes a person, and usually for the worse: one only had to look at Charlotte's sadness and Branwell's misguided behaviour to see that. Love might not make Mattie a murderer but, yes, Emily thought, it could make her an accomplice.

"All I know," Charlotte said eventually, "is that when a person longs for love, the temptation to risk all to have it is very, very great. Even though she is our friend, we should consider Mattie's motives as suspect."

There was a short, intense silence, as Charlotte moved the little pieces of evidence they had collected around the table: the bone, the tooth, the note. Anne had left the ring and gloves where she had found them, for fear they might be missed, and besides, it felt right to leave them in that place, a kind of shrine. And then Emily remembered something, retrieving the pebble she had removed from Elizabeth Chester's room.

"What does a stone tell us?" Anne asked her.

"It meant something to Elizabeth," Emily said. "If we can discern what that something was, then perhaps it might tell us everything. We need to know more: more about Mattie's life at the Grange, more about Elizabeth's life before and after her marriage. More of Chester's first wife and the identity of the man in the woods. We need to use our brains, search the shadows, the nooks and crannies, seek out the truth wherever it might be buried. I suggest we draw up a battle plan at once."

"I would assist you," Branwell said, rising untidily from his seat. "Honestly, I would, but I must go, for I promised to help with a thing, in the . . . at the . . . There may be some work I heard tell from . . . Well, anyway, good eve, sisters."

"Branwell." Emily tried once more to delay her brother. "Your sculptor friend, Leyland. He must know a great deal about stones and rocks. Perhaps you could ask his advice on my pebble?"

"Joseph?" Branwell laughed. "He might be able to inform you on the intricacies of Italian marble, Emily, but I hardly think an artist of his talent and stature would have time to dwell on a young girl's obsession with a common pebble."

"I see," Emily said. Sometimes Branwell could be so insufferably self-important, and she knew her sisters thought the stone was insignificant. But she truly felt that if she could understand its meaning it would tell her something about Elizabeth Chester, and who was to say that that something might not be the key to the whole business? The trouble with her siblings was that they were seeking out signposts and main roads. Emily thought the truth was much more likely to be discovered down those secret and rarely trodden paths, buried deep in the undergrowth, and that was where she intended to look.

"There *are* men in the village, at present," Branwell said thoughtfully. "Men of science, studying the valley in some capacity. I spent a good deal of last night talking to one of them, affable chap, though I can't quite recall what we talked about . . . If I see them again tonight I will enquire if they know of an expert in pebbles who may assist you in your quest, Emily, *if* you will smile for me."

"Come home before you must be carried home," Emily said, smiling mirthlessly as commanded.

"Where is the fun in that?" Branwell replied, just as he closed the door.

"The trouble is," Anne said unhappily, snatching the tooth from under Charlotte's finger and putting it in the box, "I do not know where all we have discovered should lead us next."

"Oh!" Emily exclaimed, scooping Flossy onto her lap.

"Oh, what?" Charlotte looked at her over the top of her spectacles.

"In Arunton today, I had a thought which I tried to tell you, but before I could speak it, you had already moved on to the next moment, only intent on your usual path of 'Charlotte is right about everything' . . ."

"Bring yourself to the point," Charlotte said rather testily.

"Well, we have neglected to enquire in the most obvious place of Elizabeth's life," Emily said, enjoying stretching out a pause for as long she possibly could. "Elizabeth Chester's family, her parents! Didn't Mattie say they lived in Leeds? For surely if there are any in the world as concerned for her safety and well-being as we, it is they. We still do not even know if Chester has informed them of what has happened."

"Well . . ." Charlotte pressed her lips together and Emily could see that she was furious that she hadn't reached that conclusion first, which gave her a great deal of satisfaction. "*Perhaps* that is a good idea."

"There is no 'perhaps,' Charlotte," Emily said. "It is obvious."

"It is rather," Anne said, forlornly. "What very foolish and naïve detectors we are, not to think to speak to Elizabeth's family first."

"Not foolish, nor naïve," Charlotte countered. "Perfect strangers do not go charging into the home of a missing, probably murdered daughter, with possibly calamitous news, without at first establishing due cause, and we have done that. We have more than done that; we have built a picture of the circumstances surrounding Elizabeth's absence that contribute to the facts of the whole. Circumstantial evidence, one might call it."

"That's true," Anne said. "But if something terrible has happened to Elizabeth, it is a great responsibility we are undertaking here, meddling in the lives of those that we do not know. As Emily said, we must be certain that we are prepared for the consequences that our actions may unleash."

Emily thought of Papa, who even now was agonising over the fate of a young woman whose whole life had been thrown into disarray through choosing, just once, the shorter path to instant joy instead of the longer, harder road to heaven.

"It is our duty as good Christians not to hide from the dark," she said. "More than that, it is our vocation as writers to peer into it, to stare and stare until our eyes adjust to the murk, and discern every detail that we may and drag it into the light, so that those less courageous than us will see what must be seen. That is how the world is improved, sisters. That is how progress is brought about. I'm not afraid to look into the dark. The question is, now that we have come to a crucial part of this enterprise, Anne, Charlotte . . . are you?"

"No," Anne said at once, standing up. "I am not."

"Neither am I," Charlotte said. "But we must protect Papa, for you know how he worries about our welfare so, always anxious we'll get caught in another bog-burst, or set our frocks on fire. If he had any idea of what we were about, it would make him so anxious—we must protect him at all costs. As long as we continue under the name 'Bell' and keep our identities a secret and make sure that no one other than ourselves knows what our business is, then . . . it is settled. We will not turn back until we have uncovered the truth. We have a little of Aunt Branwell's money left—we can use that to pay our fares, and tomorrow we shall find their address in *Kelly's Directory* and travel to Leeds to seek out the Honeychurches. We shall tell Papa we are staying overnight to visit some Roe Head girls."

"I am not going to Leeds," Emily said. "It is a filthy hole of noise and people."

"You *just* said you were ready to go and peer into the worst kind of dark!" Charlotte challenged her.

"Indeed I am," Emily said. "But I can just as easily do that at home. I am of a mind to take the stone to John Brown."

"The stone?" Charlotte asked. "What would John know of a stone? What does a pebble matter anyway?"

"Well, he buries people under them every day, so perhaps more than you might think. And besides, this is not a Penistone stone—I know every inch of that moor as well as I know my own heart, so I can tell you that much."

"We shall go." Anne nodded at Charlotte. "Papa would never believe that Emily had friends anyway."

"It is a good plan," Charlotte said. "And now I shall return to my writing, for suddenly my head is full of ideas."

"And mine," Anne said, bending her head over the table. "Terrible, dark and dangerous ideas for what a strange, awful and wonderful world we live in."

Emily rose from her chair and went over to the window, where Keeper found the palm of her hand, nudging his head under it until she ruffled his ears.

The world was full of injustice and cruelty. She could see it, even from where she was standing. It filled the graveyard to the brim and ran down the open drains in Main Street. Charlotte would write of courage and romance, and Anne of faith and integrity. But she, she would write the harsh reality and truth that she saw with her own eyes in every direction that she looked; she would write of the fierce wild souls, intent on ripping the world apart for desire, and let the world make of it what they would. For that was how progress was made.

16

Charlotte

Charlotte was up before the sun, preparing all that she and Anne would need to take with them for an overnight stay in Leeds. She packed as lightly as possible, for it would be a walk to Keighley first, and then the seven-thirty coach from the Devonshire Arms unless a kindly, passing wagon driver took pity on them. Moving about silently, she let her little sister sleep on.

With her golden brown hair spread across the pillow, her cheeks slightly pink, she looked just as she had when she was a little girl. "Baby Anne," Aunt Branwell had insisted on calling her until the very end, and there was a strong part of Charlotte that wished she could always preserve that version of Anne too: pure, precious and unsullied by the cruelty of life. And yet Anne knew only too well already how the man-made grime that covered God's creation could work its way into your soul if you let it. Anne Brontë might look angelic, as she did now, but within her chest beat the heart of a fierce warrior. It was one of the things that set her apart from every other young woman that Charlotte had ever met—that set them all apart, Charlotte thought one could say without *too* much immodesty.

With her small trunk packed and the sun creeping up over the hill behind the house, she tiptoed out of the back door, intent on allowing herself a few still moments of solitude before the whole house was awake, to watch the rose-gold light set flame to the hills.

Her plans were soon revised, however, when she found Branwell sprawled on the back step, arm flung outward as if he had been dropped from the sky, the very model of a fallen angel.

"Brother," she muttered, shaking him firmly. The acrid stench of smoke, ale and vomit rose from him in a most unpleasant bouquet, and it took all of Charlotte's determination to be a good Christian to prevent her from stepping over him and walking out on to the moor.

"Branwell, rouse yourself," she said sharply, making him start, an empty bottle rolling onto the cobbles with a clatter. "What are you doing here, brother?"

Branwell shook his head, sitting up slightly.

"Where is here?" he asked her.

"Home, or almost home," she said, gingerly taking a seat next to him on the cool, stone step, pulling him into a seated position. "You did not manage to quite make it over the threshold."

"Oh." Branwell stared dumbly at his feet. "It's just that when I am sober it hurts, Charlotte."

"I imagine it does," Charlotte said. "Sleeping on granite cannot be comfortable."

"That's not what I mean and you know it," he said, casting her a long, sideways look.

"Of course I do," Charlotte replied. "Of course I know it, Branwell, but what use is there in this?" She gestured at him. "This spreading out of your misery, as though it's an infection seeping from your every pore?"

Charlotte wrinkled her nose as she looked at her brother, and for a moment there was only disgust in her expression.

"I loved her," Branwell said.

"You *desired* her, Branwell," Charlotte told him. "That is quite another thing."

"What would you know of desire?" Branwell asked her. "What would you know of that melding of heart, mind and body that ignites a soul into flame, that union which shows us earthly creatures glimpses of heaven. What would you know of that?"

Charlotte was quiet for a very long moment—a moment into which she compressed a lifetime of agony and rage.

"I know all that I may know," she told him, her voice tight and cold. "For if I had surrendered to my base desires as you did, my brother, what would have become of me? It would have been a very different fate to the one that you are suffering now, let me assure you."

"What would have become of you is infamy." Branwell looked at her with a shrug of his stiff shoulders. "And infamy passes, Charlotte. Scandal dies down. In a week or two no one will remember what passed between Mrs. Robinson and me; two hundred years from now there won't be a living soul that thinks of it once. But because I chose happiness, knowing that it would be fleeting, I have the rest of my life to live in the knowledge that I loved and was loved truly once, as deeply as with any man and his wife, more likely deeper than most."

Charlotte could not help but snort her disdain at these beatifications of his tawdry, base affair.

"You think it was like *he* says," Branwell said, unable to bring himself to allude to Mr. Robinson by name. "That I made a fantasy of it all? That I left Thorp Green with a quarter's pay in my purse because of *other reasons?*" Branwell asked her aghast, and plainly hurt that his sister might think of such a thing.

"No, Branwell, no, of course I do not believe that." Charlotte shook her head emphatically. "No, I know that you and she did what you did. I do not doubt it. God knows Anne saw enough of the goings-on to be your witness a thousand times over. But I'm afraid I *do* doubt that what befell you and that woman is a great love affair, Branwell. I *do* doubt there would have been no other to tempt Mrs. Robinson from the path of fidelity but you. In fact I feel sure that any young man that had come to her home would have become the focus of her attentions, though perhaps not all would have reciprocated quite so enthusiastically . . ."

"Charlotte." Branwell turned to her, and Charlotte could not help but recoil as she took in the icy blue pallor of his skin, cheeks and nose reddened by excess, his eyes sunken and hot with something akin to fever. "Please, I beg you, do not seek to diminish what was truly great, what might have been the greatest event of my life, Charlotte. Don't take that from me when it is all that I have."

"Branwell"—Charlotte sought out his frozen hand, clasping it in her own—"grant me leave to beg something of you?" Branwell nodded. "Do not let this sordid affair define your life. You have so much within you, Branwell—so much great art and poetry, goodness and light. What a waste it would be, what a sin, for you to live out the rest of your life obscure. Please: chase away these demons that you let consume you, search out what it is that makes you my brother, my companion, my Angrian friend. What you were once you could be again, only greater."

She paused, edging closer to him on the step, seeking to reanimate his frozen body with a little of her warmth.

"Do you remember those days, Branwell? You and I conquering universes together, Emily and Anne always at our heels? Can you not imagine yourself back to the boy you were then, with all the world at your feet?"

"Imagination is not my friend as it is yours, Charlotte," Branwell told her. "For it only serves to show me what I might have been, what I *could* have done if I were a better man. Be assured, I don't wish for this life that I live, but it is the life that I have made for myself, and though it is one full of regret, it is mine to own. I must deal with that torment in my own way, for I do not have one whit of your courage, sister dear."

Despite the stench that only strengthened as the sun inched its way across the courtyard, Charlotte leaned her head onto her brother's shoulder as she had often used to when they were children.

"I do believe that you and I are more alike than any others in this family," she told him gently. "All my life I've envied you the freedoms afforded to you as a man. Papa poured everything into you, so certain was he of your promise. But now I see that your freedom, your agency over your own existence, is nothing to be envied. It would have been better for you to have been born a girl, Branwell. Then you would have had to learn from the crib how to practise restraint, how to bear disappointment and expect much less than you are owed. It would have made you a much stronger person than you are as a man."

Branwell's fingers tightened around hers.

"You may be right, Charlotte," he said. "You may well be right."

"Oh, I am always right—haven't you noticed yet?" Charlotte replied with a teasing smile, growing sombre again at once. "Branwell, if you wish to die, then all you need to do is be patient, for death will come ambling around that corner at any moment for any one of us; we do not need to seek it out. I beg you, please, put away the drink, the opium, for a little while. Let your head clear and see what beauty and promise there is in the world that still waits for you to claim it."

"I do not believe that I will ever feel joy again," Branwell told her. "I scarcely even remember it, my heart and mind are so very weary."

Charlotte gathered Branwell into her arms and held him as he wept, his meagre frame shuddering against her.

"All that has happened need not be all that will happen, Branwell," she whispered as she rocked him. "The Lord loves you, he forgives you. See how the sun rises in the sky? Make this your new day too. For I need you, Brother. Who else will provide for me in my dotage?"

Branwell sat up, dragging his sleeve across his nose as he sniffed, taking in a deep breath of cool morning air.

"I was rather hoping you'd provide for me," he said, mustering something of a smile for his sister.

"Or perhaps we will all muddle on together for ever, just as we always have done." Charlotte smiled at the prospect. "Imagine that, white-haired old folk, staggering up the moor to chase the wind and tell stories. Now isn't that something to look forward to, Branwell dear?"

"It would be a very fine sight indeed," Branwell said with his best attempt at bravado, but somehow Charlotte knew that when he pictured them all old and grey, he painted himself out of every scene.

All the pain and secrets kept within, all the heartbreak and agony hidden behind corsets and bonnets and prayer books. As Charlotte took her brother's hand and brought it to her lips, she understood the attraction of his hopeless spiral. For there were times when her fury and pain burnt so brightly within she longed to tear the whole world down. Perhaps Elizabeth Chester felt the same agony; perhaps Elizabeth Chester decided to live a short and dangerous life, if it meant that, just for once, she felt truly alive.

17

Charlotte

Although between themselves Charlotte and Anne referred to Emily as the least socially adept Brontë, the truth was that none of the Brontë daughters was particularly keen on company, and for all of them any excursion into the wide world had to be mentally prepared for and endured, rather than enjoyed. Obviously, there had been hardly any time at all to prepare for this excursion, which made it particularly terrifying and therefore rather bracing all at the same time, which was something of a novelty, at least. For apart from visits to her old Roe Head friend Ellen Nussey, Charlotte couldn't recall any prolonged stay away from home that had brought her joy. Even her two years in Brussels, which for a short while had made her heart sing, ended in the loneliness and despair that had brought her home. And as for Anne, the only other place in the world that she ever wished to be was Scarborough, standing on the clifftops, marvelling at the boundless magnitude of the sea, and wondering at what might lie beyond it.

Their world was at once very small and also infinite: encompassing both the few square miles around their home that they knew and loved so well, and the whole of the universe that unfolded endlessly within their minds.

So, although they made the journey to and from home to Keighley, and onwards to Leeds, without any fuss, neither one of them felt particularly at ease with the experience.

It seemed to be the one part of their lives that practice and repetition did not make easier. The further the crowded coach carried them from Haworth, the more appealing the quiet, uneventful hearth of home seemed.

Charlotte had sent a letter the previous evening to secure their lodgings in a respectable establishment that her friend Ellen had used once in the outlying village of Headingley: close to where the flax industrialist Mr. Honeychurch kept his well-appointed home. Here you were far enough away from the grime and constant fug of smoke that hung over the city to be able to breathe easier, but not so far that you couldn't still hear the great roar of the relentless machine that it had become. As soon as they had deposited their belongings, they found their way to Victoria Crescent, and the home of the Honeychurches, an address that had not been hard to obtain the moment they had arrived—everyone in Leeds, including the landlady at their lodgings, knew the Honeychurches. Now that their only daughter was married, the family consisted of just Mr. and Mrs. Honeychurch themselves, as there were no surviving children other than Elizabeth, a sad fact that had not escaped either sister.

"Perhaps we should have sent a letter," Anne worried, as she and Charlotte stood side by side in front of the impressive double-fronted grey stone mansion. "To have prepared them for our enquiry, and to have asked if they will see us? After all, who are we but strange little countrywomen who have no business questioning them at all?"

"Anne"—Charlotte frowned at her younger sister—"we are very much more than that—*very* much more. We are educated women of intellect and purpose, and women who have made it our business to put the welfare of Mr. and Mrs. Honeychurch's daughter at our heart. Our intentions are honourable and good, and so they will see us and be glad of it, I'm sure." But Charlotte felt less certain than she sounded when she looked back up at the house, remembering Emily's words on how no one ever took a woman to have any authority. "Also, we shall tell them that we are visiting on behalf of our employers, Bell and Company, solicitors. That seems to work when it comes to adding a little gravitas."

"No good can come from all this deceit," Anne cautioned her sister unhappily. "Why can we not tell them the truth, Charlotte?"

"Because we must protect Mattie and our father," Charlotte replied. "And besides, this is not deceit, Anne." Charlotte took her sister's hands, addressing her with a phrase that they often exchanged with one another when faced with anything that gave them pause. "Take courage, Anne— don't think of it as a deception. Think of it as playing a part in one of our stories, as we did with our toy soldiers when we were little. We are players, acting out a part under the cover of another identity, that is all. We are 'under cover.'"

"Very well," Anne said, squaring her shoulders. "Though I am bound to say that being 'under cover' does not sound like a very respectable place for an unmarried young lady to be."

"Which is precisely why it is actually rather thrilling," Charlotte told her.

Mrs. Honeychurch was a fulsome and attractive woman of indeterminate age. Finely attired in the latest fashions, with pale gold hair and pretty blue eyes, she had the air of a woman of solid breeding, and that quiet, resolute certainty that came with being married, rich and beautiful. She was dressed well, in light summer cotton, not a hint of trauma or mourning about her. Charlotte was certain that Chester had not informed the Honeychurches of their daughter's disappearance, let alone the circumstances surrounding it.

Greeting Charlotte and Anne with polite bewilderment, Mrs. Honey-church called for tea and invited the sisters to sit in her richly appointed parlour, complete with a piano, satin drapes and a good deal of art on the walls that spoke more of quantity than quality, but which gave a pleasingly fashionable effect of warmth and gaiety.

"Well, I have never been so interested to know—to what do I owe the pleasure?" Mrs. Honeychurch smiled as she spoke, pouring tea from a gilt-edged pot of finest bone china, upon which fat pink roses bloomed.

Charlotte noted that there was a trace of a Yorkshire accent amongst her carefully modulated vowels, and she warmed to her at once. She always trusted a person who did not try to hide their beginnings much more than those who did.

"We work for the solicitors Bell and Company," Charlotte began.

"Young ladies working for a solicitor—how novel!" Mrs. Honeychurch smiled with delight. "Whatever next?"

"Indeed." Charlotte had to fight the urge to add further details to their story, knowing that a complicated subplot would only maximise the chances of their being discovered. "The Bell brothers, our employers, have dispatched us on their behalf. Owing to the delicate and confidential nature of our enquiry, they feel a feminine touch, though unconventional, may be warranted."

"Enquiry?" Mrs. Honeychurch looked bemused. "Perhaps it should be my husband you should speak to, Miss . . . ?"

"Call me Charlotte, please." Charlotte smiled. "And this is Anne."

She took care not to give up their surname or relationship, though she felt rather underdressed without either.

"Well, *Charlotte*," Mrs. Honeychurch replied, testing the solitary name with the tip of her tongue, "it's Mr. Honeychurch that deals with all the finances and business affairs—I'm afraid that I know nothing of them. So I suggest that you make an appointment to return and talk to him this evening, for he'll be at the mill all day. Although what he will think of you young unmarried ladies making enquiries of him, I cannot fathom. He is very traditionally minded, my Mr. Honeychurch, likes everything to be neatly in its place as ordained by God."

"But if everyone only ever stayed in their place, then self-made men such as your husband would still be labouring for another man, born into wealth by an accident of birth alone," Anne replied cheerfully, managing to completely confound Mrs. Honeychurch in one fell swoop.

"Please, Miss Anne," she said, "when you do meet him, don't say that to him, will you? For my part, I rather enjoy thinking, but Mr. Honeychurch does not like to have his beliefs questioned one little bit. It gives him terrible indigestion."

"Well, in any case, our enquiries are not related to your husband's business," Anne said more gently, glancing nervously at Charlotte. "Mrs. Honeychurch, we are concerned with you daughter, Elizabeth."

"Lizzie?" Mrs. Honeychurch blinked, and shook her head as she smiled in bemusement, but even so Anne thought she noticed an air of disquiet settling over the woman's shoulders like a gossamer-fine veil. "Oh no, your Messrs. Bell are quite behind the times. You see, my Lizzie is married now, and has been for more than two years! She lives outside of the village of Arunton with her husband, Robert Chester of Chester Grange. She has a little boy and is stepmother to another—dear little soul he is. Lizzie adores him."

Charlotte stirred another spoonful of sugar into her tea as she glanced at Anne, whose eyes widened just enough for Charlotte to understand that her sister had no idea how to respond either.

"What would solicitors possibly want with Lizzie anyway?" Mrs. Honeychurch wondered. "Has she been left a legacy, perhaps? She does have a number of distant relatives overseas, on my mother's side, who are quite wealthy, wine merchants out of Madeira. But even so, now that she is married, you'd need to talk to Chester about that. I'm sure he'd be very glad to have more of my daughter's funds added to his pot."

It was the tiniest sliver of a barb, but it was enough to encourage Charlotte to go on.

"Mrs. Honeychurch." Charlotte settled her teacup back in the saucer with a pleasing chime, and leant forward a little. "Have you had any correspondence with Mr. Chester in the last three days?"

"None," Mrs. Honeychurch said, frowning deeply. "Nor do I expect it. I receive a letter from my Lizzie once a week, but Chester would rather forget that we exist, it seems! Only once have I seen my grandson, and then I barely got a look at him." She hesitated for a moment, smoothing the ruffles of her skirt. "Is it he who has sent your firm?"

"No." Charlotte took a deep breath, and in that moment's hesitation felt a deep uncertainty. For who was she to be delivering this news to this poor unsuspecting woman? She had cheerfully, even eagerly taken on this responsibility without a thought to what consequences her words might wreak on this ordered and peaceful home. The urge to simply rise and walk away was very great, and yet a mother deserved to know the truth.

"Mrs. Honeychurch," she began again. "I do not believe that you know your daughter is missing from her home, for four days, since Monday last. That . . . that it looks as if the circumstances of departure might have been violent, and that Elizabeth may have come to very grave harm."

"Get out at once!" Mrs. Honeychurch stood up, her voice trembling with emotion as she directed them to the door. "Get out, get out! How dare you come to my house and speak such wicked, filthy lies?"

It was such an emphatic, visceral response that for a moment Charlotte and her sister were stunned into inaction.

"Mrs. Honeychurch . . ." Anne pleaded, when she had regained herself. "We are not lying: it's the truth. We came because . . . we . . . the Bells feared that you might not have been informed."

"No." Mrs. Honeychurch shook her head. "No, please. Do not say it. Admit that you are liars and leave. I don't know what scheme it is you are about, extortion or blackmail, is it? But I will not tolerate your disgusting deceit. Admit it." Mrs. Honeychurch's fury wavered, and Charlotte saw fear flood her soft features. When she spoke again her voice trembled. "Please. Please say that it is a cruel lie."

Charlotte spread her hands in helpless dismay.

"I'm so sorry, madam," she said. "We simply cannot, for we speak the truth."

"Then she has run away," Mrs. Honeychurch said emphatically. "Her papa will be furious. She is a headstrong girl, you see, full of notions. Or at least she used to be, when she was younger. But I really believed she was settled now, and she loves those two little boys. Why would she run away and leave those two darling children? It makes no sense."

"Mrs. Honeychurch . . ." Charlotte examined the distraught woman's face, choosing her words carefully. "The circumstances around her disappearance, the fact that she took nothing with her, these things would indicate that she was taken involuntarily."

"Oh my dear God." Mrs. Honeychurch folded onto her sofa, covering her face with her hands. "My dear little girl, I should have kept her with me, I should have kept her close. Did he find out, is that what happened? I have always been afraid that he would punish her if he found out."

"Did who find out what?" Charlotte asked gently, taking a tentative seat next to Mrs. Honeychurch and picking up her hand.

"I meant, I only meant that . . ." Mrs. Honeychurch looked up at her, her face blotched with red. "Who *are* you? What kind of young ladies would bring such vulgar and cruel lies into my home? Not respectable ones—I know that much."

"Madam." Anne knelt at her feet, taking her other hand. Mrs. Honeychurch did not resist. "I understand how shocking our words are, but I assure you we do not lie. Please forgive us for bringing you this awful news. What we can tell you is that there is yet hope. We do not know Elizabeth's fate entirely. Anne and I seek to discover the truth of her life—perhaps to find her friends, anyone who meant something to her once? It seems that perhaps we alone are concerned with uncovering the truth, not for Chester, not for ourselves, but for Elizabeth and for justice—I swear it."

Mrs. Honeychurch reached a hand out and touched Anne's cheek.

"You are just a slip of a girl. What can you do about justice?" she asked, her voice trembling. "You say that these four days my girl has been gone and I have not known it. I cannot accept that. I refuse to believe that as I have sewn, and walked the park, and tended to my husband and . . ." She hesitated, a glimmer of hope blossoming into a smile. "Wait, one moment. Wait, young misses, you *are* wrong. Though you may not mean it, you are misinformed about my Lizzie!"

"How so?" Charlotte asked, perplexed as Mrs. Honeychurch rose from the sofa and hurried over to a writing bureau in the corner. Hastily, Mrs. Honeychurch wiped at her tears as she fetched a bundle of letters tied with a ribbon, carefully taking one from the top of the parcel.

"You say she disappeared in the night, found gone on Monday morning, but you are wrong and here's the proof!" She smiled through her tears, her hands trembling as she held out a folded letter. "Take it and you will see. Elizabeth is quite well."

Anne and Charlotte exchanged a brief look as Charlotte took the letter, unfolded it and read the first line aloud:

"'Dear Mama, What a dreadful summer we are having at Chester Grange . . .'" She returned the letter to Mrs. Honeychurch. "It's a letter from your daughter."

"Yes, but read the date—read the date at the top of the letter, and the postmark. Both are dated yesterday, Tuesday. On Tuesday, Elizabeth was writing of her life at the hall, of the children, and yes, the weather *yesterday*, when you say she went missing in the early hours of Monday. So you see, ladies, you are quite wrong. My daughter is safe and well."

18

※

Anne

"This is most perplexing." It was Anne who spoke next, choosing her words with precise care as she rose from the floor and took the chair opposite Charlotte and Mrs. Honeychurch, who was seated once again. "We were at Chester Grange. We saw her room, and were able to ascertain that there had been a great event there, simply by looking. We met with Mr. Chester himself, who was gravely concerned for his wife . . . I swear to you we speak the truth—Elizabeth has not been seen since Monday."

"By whom has she not been seen?" Mrs. Honeychurch exclaimed, her voice high and strained. "Perhaps, whoever they are, they have poor eyesight, for I assure you my Elizabeth is at Chester Grange. Indeed, I receive my letters from her every week, with news of her and the children. She has always been such a good letter writer. She assures me every time she writes how very content she is, and never have I been more grateful to be proved wrong about my misgivings."

"You had misgivings about Elizabeth marrying Robert Chester?" Anne asked.

"Yes, well, not precisely that." Mrs. Honeychurch shifted in her seat, sitting up a little taller as she rediscovered her composure. "It's more that I had *misgivings* that she would ever be a happy wife," Mrs. Honeychurch said. "As I said, Lizzie can be very headstrong, and *original*. All her young life she wanted to be a seafarer—can you imagine that? She wanted to travel the world and paint everything she saw. At one time she was intent on becoming a professional musician—a pianist—had ideas she might fill concert halls! Mr. Honeychurch said that I indulged her too much, and perhaps I did, but she was so bright and curious. He said I did not spend enough time raising her to be a man's wife, and I feared he was right. I feared she would find it hard to make the adjustment to a good and obedient companion, but she proved me wrong. Her letters are the picture of contentment. She seems so happy with her little world, as if she'd forgotten the seven seas and all that lay beyond . . ."

Mrs. Honeychurch trailed off into thought, a faint smile on her rose-pink lips that gradually faded to nothing.

"If you wouldn't mind, Mrs. Honeychurch," Anne asked very quietly, deciding it was best not to contradict the poor, distressed woman again, "in order to allay the concerns of our client, would it be possible to see these other letters? It might help us learn a little more of Elizabeth."

"Well, I suppose so." Mrs. Honeychurch's affable demeanour was now rather frayed. "Though I don't really see what they can tell you of interest, unless you are fascinated by baby's croup, or how she has chosen to redecorate the nursery."

Mrs. Chester handed over the bundle she had been clutching to her bosom. It seemed that, once read, each letter had been refolded and slotted neatly back inside its envelope. Every letter was dated and signed, and a brief perusal revealed a chatty, warm tone, just as Mrs. Honeychurch had told them they would find.

"And you are quite sure this is your daughter's handwriting?" Charlotte asked, comparing the most recent letter with an earlier one, noting the two circular postmarks on the envelope she was holding, one for Arunton, and another for Keighley.

"Of course I am quite sure," Mrs. Honeychurch said. "I taught her to read and write myself, even though my husband thought it quite unnecessary! Now, if you are finished with your enquiry, perhaps you would like to be on your way and go and inform those spreading gossip to hold their tongues."

It was not a question. Mrs. Honeychurch, her cheeks growing pinker by the minute, stood abruptly, gesturing towards the door, as she rang for the maid once more.

"Mrs. Honeychurch." Anne gathered up all of her courage into that one moment. "I have travelled to Chester Grange twice, and toured the extent of the house, and even visited your daughter's bedchamber. There is no trace of her anywhere. If anything there is . . . the opposite."

"The opposite of a trace of her?" Mrs. Honeychurch's voice rose sharply. "I don't know what you are implying, young woman, but whatever it is it must be incorrect when there is a letter from Elizabeth here, must it not? My dear Elizabeth is safe and happy and well, and here is the proof of it! Perhaps it is some joke they are playing on you. When my Lizzie was a little girl she was always up to no good, always gallivanting around with her cousins . . . What a little tyke she was, full of life—you've never seen such a daisy."

Anne lowered her eyes the moment she understood exactly how hard Mrs. Honeychurch was struggling to keep her composure. There were tears in her eyes, and something else too: there was fear.

"Please believe us," Anne said gently, taking a step towards Mrs. Honeychurch, reaching out with a cautious hand. "We are acting only out of good wishes and concern, and we are truly sorry if we have upset you. Your letter is difficult to understand, I grant you, but even so, we still believe that Elizabeth is in grave danger. We are staying overnight at the London on Victoria Square. If you would like to talk to us again, if there is more you have to say, you will find us there."

"I am quite certain that my wife will not need to speak to you again," Mr. Honeychurch said as he entered the room, filling it with his great bulk and an excess of indignation at once.

"Sir," Charlotte began, "if you will just let us explain our concerns . . ."

"I heard quite enough of your concerns whilst I was standing in the hallway," Mr. Honeychurch told her. "Two strange women walk into my home with no credentials and take advantage of the innocent, simple nature of my good wife with such terrors? Where are the men who should be keeping you indoors where you belong?"

"Excuse me, but . . ."

"*Do not speak!*" Mr. Honeychurch roared at Anne, whose face paled with shock at being subjected to such an indignity. And yet, though she hated herself for it, she did his bidding. "You may tell whoever it is that is concerned that my daughter made a good match with Robert Chester, and that, like her mother, she knows her place as a wife and mother, and knows that obedience to her husband is second only to her obedience to God. If there were something amiss I would have heard of it directly. If you spent your time learning the same lesson then perhaps the best years of your lives would not be behind you, leaving you bitter and bored, with nothing better to do than meddle in the lives of others. Now, good day to you both, and I warn you—do not visit again."

"Frank, dear . . ." Mrs. Honeychurch began to speak.

"I did not ask for your opinion, woman!" he shouted at her. "I fear there has been rather too much of that already."

Mrs. Honeychurch closed her mouth, her eyes meeting Anne's for one long moment more, telling her more than any words ever could.

Ejected on to the street, the sisters hurried away from the Honeychurch house as fast as they were able.

"Charlotte, we are terrible, terrible people." Anne was the first to speak, her voice quivering with distress. "Poor Mrs. Honeychurch—we caused her such great agony, and in doing so answered none of our questions. I'm ashamed of us—we are hardly any better than Chester himself. As soon as we are home I shall go to Papa to confess all, and I shall write to Mrs. Honeychurch with our sincerest apologies, and tell her who we really are. I cannot bear that she believes we are the agents of deception. It isn't decent or moral."

"It was upsetting, indeed," Charlotte agreed. "But, Anne, although we didn't solve our mystery, at least now we know that we *have* one."

"You mean the letter, of course," Anne said, her mind still caught up in poor Mrs. Honeychurch's obvious misery.

"The letter," Charlotte said. "The letter. Though I cannot fathom the circumstances behind such a strange series of events. How and why would a letter be written and sent the day after Elizabeth Chester disappeared? One might be able to fake the date on a letter, but not the postmark on the envelope."

"You forget the greater mystery," Anne said, taking Charlotte's hands as they entered the boarding house, for she still felt ill at odds, as if their encounter with the Honeychurches had disjointed every part of her by at least one degree.

"What have I forgotten?" Charlotte asked her.

"Before she remembered the letter, she told us that she had always felt that Chester would harm her daughter if he found out the truth, and when we asked her what she meant, she turned the conversation away once more. The question is, Charlotte: *found out the truth about what?*"

Thought followed thought, star followed star,
Through boundless regions, on:
While one sweet influence, near and far,
Thrilled through, and proved us one.

—"Stars" by Emily Brontë

19

Emily

The light of the full moon flooded in through Emily's open shutters as, not for the first time that night, she sat up in bed, restless, her head full of tangled thoughts and snatches of dreams that would not let her mind cease long enough to sleep.

Papa snored steadily from his bedroom, Tabby and Martha had long since retired to their room, Branwell was yet to return home from wherever he was.

Swinging her legs out of bed, enjoying the rough cool of the floorboards against her bare feet, Emily went over to the window and drew back the curtains, catching her breath at the sight of the silvery netherworld that the moonlight had made out of Haworth after dark. The night seemed to invite her to marvel at its otherworldly wonder, beckoning her forth to play amongst the silver-edged shadows.

The gravestones glittered and shone, as if to herald the rising dead, and even her father's church, appearing as it did in silhouette, looked thrillingly sinister. Was that a shadowy figure standing between the tombs, Emily wondered with a delicious shudder? Was it a murderer, a grave robber or ghost? Perhaps it was the phantom of James Sutcliffe the highwayman, hanged for his crimes fifty years since and, rumour had it, buried in an unmarked grave that backed onto the pub that he used to love so much. What might it be like to converse with a ghost, Emily wondered? What secrets might they whisper to her of death?

"What a night for an adventure, eh, Keeper?" Emily said as her dog, sensing her movement, nosed open the door and padded into her room, leaning into her thighs. "What a night to be out, roaming the moors, seeking out answers. We'd be sure to bump into a gytrash or two, perhaps some wandering souls looking for their lost loves, don't you think, boy, hey?"

Keeper was not much one for thinking, but one of the things that Emily loved about him most of all was that he was an excellent listener and agreed with almost everything she said. Except perhaps that he should keep his muddy paws off the bed sheets, which meant that once she had been forced to beat that impulse out of him or else see Tabby put him out on the street to starve. Since that hateful, dark day, Keeper rarely strayed from her side, always poised to guard and protect her. Emily wondered how it was possible that a creature that had been so hurt could still love so fiercely the one who hurt them. But then this notion of love that people got so very het up about seemed to Emily to be the darkest, dangerous and most complicated human impulse of all. All Emily knew was that whenever she looked at Keeper, she felt more sorry for that day than she did for any other bad thing that she had ever done, and she would spend the rest of his life making it up to him.

"Why should we have to stay inside just because it is night?" Emily reasoned, resting her hand on his bony head. "Night is the time when all of the most interesting things happen, Keeper, so why should we not go out upon the breezy moor? It's when secrets are made and revealed, crimes are committed and lovers meet. Why does convention demand that you and I must stay confined to our beds, or baskets, just because of the absence of sun?"

Keeper had no answer for that conundrum.

"Action over conversation every time, don't you think, boy?"

Keeper very much agreed.

"You are quite right, boy. You are absolutely right."

And even though Papa always slept like a log, and Tabby was as deaf as a post, Emily made sure that she was very quiet as she got dressed, refraining from lacing on her boots until she was already outside. After filling the pockets of her skirts with the particular things she thought she might need for a nocturnal adventure with Keeper, habit made her reach for her bonnet. But then, with the wide smile of a woman being born into a brave new starlit world, she left it swinging on the peg. Tonight she'd feel the wind tugging at her loose locks and there'd be no one to tell her, "It's not the done thing, Emily." There'd be no one to tell her how to behave at all.

Oh, but it was glorious out there, atop the moor in the dead of night, midnight and moonlight and bright shining stars. As the moon rose, every blade of grass, every stone seemed to spring into life, taking on a new and strange quality that sang back to the midnight sky. The wind was as wild as it was warm, touching her relentlessly, moving through her hair and across her skin with the familiarity of a lover. And when Emily looked up at the shower of stars above her head, she could do no more than fling open her arms and embrace all of the glory of God.

Keeper too was thrilled with their midnight adventure, his nose full of the scents of rabbits and badgers as he raced back and forth, nose thrust into the long grass, circling his mistress constantly but never straying from her side for more than a few moments at a time.

Emily didn't need a destination in mind for her walk. How glorious it was to walk down to the falls and see how the wild forests tumbled down the mountainside, how the moonlight played on those falls that roared like thunder; and to march up to Ponden Kirk and stare down the valley with the whole world unravelling at her feet.

It was some time before Emily realised that she had in fact set a course for Chester Grange. As she came to the brow of a hill and was arrested by the sight of its vast hulk, hunched up against the dark, with but one light burning at the windows, she realised her unconscious compass had guided her here.

"Shall I go and take a peek, Keeper?" Emily asked her. "As we seem to be passing?"

It came as no surprise to her that Keeper was in total agreement.

"Keeper, you must stay here," Emily told her dog, using her shawl to secure him to a solid-looking young oak by his thick, leather collar. "There are other dogs on the grounds, and you are only more likely to excite them if you come with me, whereas they know me and like me. So you stay—there's a good boy."

Keeper whimpered, but reluctantly settled down in the long, cool grass to await his mistress's return, knowing, insomuch as he ever knew anything, that once she had set her mind to something she was rarely turned from it.

Before making her way to the house, Emily regarded Chester Grange from the cover of the woodland that surrounded it, grateful to God for providing her with a night as clear and as bright as this one.

The great, vast bulk of the building was dark, and there was little detail that she could make out, except for what might be the flickering light of a candle in one of the downstairs rooms. It was unlikely to yield any great revelations, but it was the only point of interest that she could see, and so, keeping her eyes fixed on that one illuminated window, she made her way slowly through the dark.

She wasn't quite halfway there when she heard the thunder of paws and growling barks of excited hounds that had caught her scent and were heading towards her at a great pace, halting a few feet from her, displaying mouthfuls of teeth. Another young woman, roaming around unaccompanied after dark, might have been afraid, but not Emily Brontë. Standing her ground, Emily waited for the dogs to relax just a little, keeping their heads low as they growled and sniffed the air.

"Good evening, friends," Emily said soothingly as she held out her hands, displaying the contents of her pockets, a handful of tasty incentives for Keeper. She had very little concern that they might be torn off by the vicious hounds that Chester had trained to kill on sight, for Emily had yet to meet a hound that didn't roll over for a few choice pieces of braised lamb.

"Good eve, fine fellows," she said, taking a few steps closer to the animals.

"You remember me, don't you? You remember me? I'm your friend Emily. That's right, good dogs. I'm your friend."

And sure enough the dogs' ears dropped, and their tails circled in greeting as they nuzzled the food out of her hands. Casting the rest of the cold meat into the long grass, Emily watched them for a moment as she emptied the rest of the unexpected feast from her pocket, and then she continued on her mission towards the great dark bulk of the building and all the terrors that might lie within.

Eventually Emily's outstretched hand met with the rough, cool stone of the house, and she traced her way along the length of the wall, pausing only to yank her skirt free when it caught in some thorny shrub, feeling a scratch along the back of her hand. She passed dark window after dark window until eventually a faint glow of orange light was cast on to the gravel path, telling her that she had arrived at her destination.

Flattening herself against the wall to the right of the window, Emily waited patiently, feeling as completely at ease in the situation, cloaked as she was by the dark and warmed by the summer night, as another girl might be taking a stroll in the afternoon sun. Soon enough a shadow crossed the window, blotting out the light for a moment. It had to be Chester.

Very, very slowly she edged herself towards the window and peered in through the glass with half of one eye. It was the window of the library that she had happened upon, the ceiling-high cases of books rising into the dark, and Emily felt that familiar pang of longing to be amongst books, turning pages and uncovering world after world of wonder. A man as oafish as Chester didn't deserve a library such as this, Emily thought irritably, for she was certain that he never read a single one of the books that were held captive by his ignorance. Waiting a moment, she risked looking in through the window with the whole of one of her eyes, and then, quite amazed at what she saw, forgot herself, and stood right in front of the window, gawking in like a child outside a sweet shop.

Chester had his back to her, and he was talking to someone sitting in the wing-backed chair next to the fire, though talking wasn't exactly the right way to describe it. From his movement and gestures it seemed more that he railed than talked, paced back and forth every second step, constantly obscuring the chair's occupant, no matter how Emily ducked and bobbed to try and get a look at them. His arms either flailed wildly or tore at his hair, and more than once he buried his face in his hands or looked up, as if he were pleading with God himself.

Then, quite suddenly, he turned towards the window, striding across the room to refill his glass from the decanter that stood on a table there. For one exhilarating moment Emily was sure that she had been discovered. But of course, Chester couldn't see her—he was simply staring into a reflection of the library, completely unaware of her standing on the other side of the glass. What shocked Emily more than his wild appearance and unkempt clothes was the sight of his tear-stained face. The beast had been crying. What kind of murderer sobbed so?

As Chester turned back to the chair, she caught the glimpse of an evening slipper, the hem of a silk dress. Could it be Elizabeth Chester that he had pinned into that chair? Might she be alive after all and held prisoner within the Grange? Frustratingly, there was simply no way to tell from outside.

Which meant that the only sensible thing to do was to break in.

20

Emily

Although Emily had never before broken into the manor house of a suspected murderer in the dead of night, it didn't occur to her once that this wasn't something she wouldn't be perfectly good at.

If she were in luck, Chester would follow the example of most people in Haworth, who rarely locked their doors at all. But then again, unlike the people of Haworth, Chester did have secrets to protect. That was the trouble with an interesting life, Emily mused. A life that contained love, passion and desire was a life fraught with needless complications. And while she found the idea that a person could love someone to the point of madness fascinating, she thought it was probably terribly miserable in real life. Her imaginary world of Gondal was where she truly lived—there, or caught in a moment of God's beauty high atop the moors. Those were the places where her heart really raced. But here, in the dead of night with the promise of infamy ahead, it beat as steady as a drum.

Frustratingly, every door Emily came across was tightly sealed with such uniformity that she didn't even bother trying the grand front door. Time was pressing: she must gain entry to be able to hear what Chester was saying before he became too drunk to talk at all.

Ever the optimist, Emily decided there was bound to be a window that would suit her purposes.

Most large houses contained a meat cellar, which although it might have no outside access, would always have a small window that she might be able to squeeze herself through, if she didn't mind the fate of her skirts too much. They were bound to have something like that at Chester Grange, Emily reasoned, determined that she would find her way in somehow. She simply had to, because this was too good an opportunity to miss. And, Emily thought cheerfully, if she had stayed at home in her bed like people were supposed to, she wouldn't have seen Chester at his nocturnal goings-on. Imagine if she solved the whole mystery tonight single-handedly? It would drive Charlotte to distraction with annoyance.

Utterly unafraid, and not even a little astounded by herself and her planned course of action, Emily methodically began to make her journey around the perimeter of the house, searching for any chink in its armour, conscious that there would be a limited period of time to catch Chester in the act with his poor captive.

Soon enough the hounds of Chester Grange joined her in her search, although they were not very helpful. Instead, they padded along at her side, her new boon companions, still scenting the traces of the meat that had been stored in her pockets and rather hopeful that more might be forth-coming.

Emily did not dissuade them, although Keeper would probably not speak to her for a week once he smelt the interlopers on her clothes. It was better to have the dogs within sight than run the risk of alerting Chester to the presence of an intruder.

Then, finally, as she scanned the upper floors, head tipped back, hands on her hips, she spied a miniature moon reflected in an open window. She had discovered a way in.

It was, she judged, just about large enough for her to fit through, skirts and all. Thank goodness she had left her petticoats at home. The only problem with the window was that it was situated on the first floor.

However, much of Chester Grange was covered in a good, sturdy net-work of mature ivy, with thick and ancient vines that looked as though they should be able to hold her weight. And although Emily had never scaled the walls of a building before, she had climbed up many trees and down several sheer cliff faces.

In the dead silence of the night she heard dozens of the tiny fingers of the ivy give way as it bore the full load of her weight, but still it held. Gradually ascending, the dogs staring up at her, still waggling their tails hopefully, Emily was concentrating so hard on finding each new hand- and foothold in the thick foliage, she wouldn't have noticed if Chester himself had come to the window and waved at her. And yet there was one point, as she neared the upper window, when she paused in her endeavour to take in the beauty of the warm, clear night and consider exactly what she was doing, imagining how she must look to the moon: this woman, in her dress and girl's shoes, fearlessly scaling a wall in search of dark deeds and terrible adventures. She smiled broadly to herself, for she was sure that she looked really rather magnificent.

Finally, she reached the window, and with only a little difficulty made her way through the opening, dragging her skirts after her, and cursing the mending that would need to be done when she heard them rip. There was a tinkle of glass, the sound of something heavy and metallic falling to the floor, but fortunately the room was unoccupied—by living beings, at least.

Instead it was full of sheet-covered furniture, of all shapes and sizes, that seemed to crowd and peer at her as she straightened, draggling a trail of ivy out of her wild, loose hair and tossing it on the floor. The board creaked beneath her feet; the night seemed to hold its breath.

"Good evening," she whispered to the shrouded figures. "Very pleased to make your acquaintance."

Squeezing her way through the maze of objects, Emily hurried on to the landing. All around her the house was silent, even the grandfather clock that stood at the top of the stairs no longer ticking, and for a moment she had a fancy that time had stood still here as a mark of respect to those who had lost their lives to this house.

The only light within the house was the sinking moon as it sailed below the horizon and, somewhere on the ground floor, the glow of firelight, casting long, flickering shadows that leapt into the hall.

As she walked along the hallway, a door halfway down the corridor swung slowly open. Emily froze to the spot, keeping perfectly still like a field mouse caught in the gaze of a hawk. There was a light coming from within the room, a light that was too cool to be firelight, too strong to be candlelight. It seemed to Emily that it was almost as if a moonbeam had been captured there. What she should do was stick to her mission and find her way quietly downstairs, but the call of the glow was too alluring.

It was only as she got closer to the room that she realised it was Elizabeth Chester's bedchamber. The moment she pushed open the door the light seemed to snuff out, and when she edged around the doorway and peered inside, the room was in shadows except for one die-straight beam of moonlight that sliced across the floor. Emily caught her breath as a small, disc-like object rolled out from the shadows in the corner of the room into the light, wobbling on its edge before it clattered flat to the floor and became still. Peering into the shadows, she did her best to discern if there was a shape—perhaps one of the children strayed from their nursery—but she could see no creature, living or dead, lurking in the corners. Taking a deep breath, Emily darted into the room, snatched the object up and thrust it into her pocket.

She could not tarry any longer.

Careful to keep herself in the sanctuary of the shadows, Emily edged her way down the great staircase, watched by the portraits and animal heads that lined the way as she descended. At the bottom she hesitated, halted momentarily by the sound of Chester's voice, which boomed and echoed in the quiet. Drawing slowly closer, Emily listened as he shouted and wept, pleaded and ranted like a lunatic.

Checking the length of the hall once more for Mrs. Crawley or anyone who might discover her, Emily crept gradually closer, stopping behind the library door, which stood usefully ajar. Peering in through the gap made by the hinges, now with a perfect view of Chester and his captive, she finally caught sight of the poor soul, and could not look away. For the first time that night, and indeed since she was a very small girl, fear speared its way into her rapidly beating heart, and she was shocked.

For there was no living person imprisoned in the chair. Instead, it was a gown—a bridal gown, a confection of lace and silk—arranged on the chair as if it were being worn. The empty sleeves were rested on the arms of the chair, and below the limply hanging beaded hem of the dress a pair of silk slippers were positioned neatly side by side.

But what really terrified and fascinated Emily all at once, what sat in the lap of the empty dress, with a bonnet trimmed with silk flowers that stopped just above its sightless brow, was a human skull.

Both horrified and mesmerised, Emily almost forgot that she was supposed to be hiding, so bizarre and compelling was the sight. Chester had even propped it up on a little pillow so that it was angled slightly upwards, forced to look up at him as he talked, as if rapt by his every word. The injustice of it, the ignominy, that whoever this poor soul had been was not free of Chester's control, even in death, was almost too much for Emily to bear, and she had to clench her fists to stop herself from marching into the library and rescuing the skull at once.

Fighting to keep her composure, she instead withdrew a little further into the shadow and forced herself to keep looking and listening. For Emily was certain that if she was patient she would hear a confession to murder: the man was conversing with a corpse, after all.

But Chester's words were slurred and thick with alcohol and self-pity. He sank to his knees before the skull, demanding to know why it had not loved him as he had loved it. He wept, burying his face in the silk and lace, begging for forgiveness and mercy, pleading for another chance.

Then, seemingly stricken with loss, he put his huge hands on either side of the skull, gazing into the cavities where eyes had once been. For a moment Emily thought that he might crush the skull to dust with his bare hands, for a man of his size and strength was surely capable of it. But then, to Emily's disgust, instead he lifted the head to his lips and kissed its grimacing mouth with perfect tenderness.

Silently retching, Emily covered her mouth, afraid that she might be about to see the unwelcome return of her supper. And yet she was *still* unable to tear herself away from the spectacle. Upon breaking the unholy embrace Chester seemed to deflate before Emily's eyes, collapsing back in despair, his flailing arms knocking the skull off of its podium, tilting it to one side so that it seemed to be gazing directly at Emily, pleading for release.

Only then did she avert her gaze, noting that the skull seemed to possess all of its teeth.

"Crawley!" Chester shouted. "Crawley! Where are you, woman? Where are you? I need you to attend me at once, dammit!"

And although dawn was still some time off yet, Emily heard movement from deep within the house, as if the old woman had been sitting up and awaiting his call. After a moment she saw the swing of the lantern illuminating Mrs. Crawley's face as she headed steadily down the corridor, directly towards where Emily was hiding.

Casting about for somewhere to hide, Emily saw the room across from the library, and prayed that the setting moon and Mrs. Crawley's lantern would not provide enough light to give her away. Darting within, she pushed the door almost closed behind her, leaving a tiny crack through which to observe the strange couple.

"What a state." Mrs. Crawley addressed Chester as she stopped in the doorway of the library, her hands on her broad hips. At once Emily understood why she had been wearing gloves the first time she had seen her, for between her fingers and thumb there was a prominent amount of webbing, so pronounced that three of her fingers were almost joined together, a condition she had read about but had not seen in the flesh before. "Have I not told you, *sir*, on more than one occasion, that if you will persist in carrying on like this, you will find all the secrets you work so hard to keep end up told to the whole world? Roaming the house at all hours, banging and crashing around like a child having a tantrum. And this . . . this mummery!

What do you expect to come from such acts? That her ghost will fill that dress, like the wind fills sails, and tell you it loves you?"

"I did not want her dead," Chester said, miserably. "I did not give her permission to die. She did it to spite me."

"Death was her only escape." Mrs. Crawley sighed heavily. "She could not stand another second of your torture. I told you to love her. I begged you to love her, but you don't have it in you. Whenever there is something good you must destroy it, and I have never understood why. If you had loved Imogen only, you would have been happy, you would have been whole. But you had to drive her mad too, didn't you? You couldn't resist destroying something so pure."

Emily was amazed that Mrs. Crawley dared to speak to him that way, and she didn't seem afraid to talk to him as though he were a disobedient child rather than her master.

She watched as Mrs. Crawley went over to where Chester was collapsed on the floor. Gently she picked up the skull and returned it to a velvet bag she had taken from somewhere in the room, giving it a long look of apology before she drew tight the drawstring cords. And then, with the bag swinging at her side, to Emily's utter astonishment she rested her palm on top of Chester's great head as if he were her pet dog. When she spoke it was with the same kindness and tender remorse Emily had used to whisper to Keeper as she had nursed the wounds that she herself had inflicted.

"There, there," Mrs. Crawley whispered soothingly to Chester as she hauled him to his unsteady feet with surprising strength. "There, there. To bed now. All of this will be but dreams by the morning."

"But what about her . . . ?" Chester gestured at the now crumpled dress.

"You go to bed," Mrs. Crawley said. "I'll take good care of her, I promise."

Chester lumbered out of the library, staggering against the wall and colliding with a huge, stuffed bear just outside the office, so close to where Emily was standing that she could smell his acrid breath. She listened as he crashed along the hall and stumbled up the stairs, hammering at every door as he passed.

Pushing the door closed, she meant to make her escape through the room's ground-floor window. The moon was now so low in the sky that only the very last traces of it were visible through the trees, and soon the dawn would start to warm the day with the kind of light that was a lot less easy to hide in.

But as she took in her surroundings she realised that she was in Chester's study, the portrait of a beautiful woman smiling wistfully down at her. This must be the painting of poor Imogen that Anne had told them about: the very same woman whose skull was even now contained in a velvet bag. Spread out across his desk were dozens of papers. Emily went to the desk, scouring the documents, looking for something that might be of interest, but just as she picked up a handful of papers, she heard Crawley's brisk footsteps approaching and the turn of the door handle.

Stuffing them into her bodice, Emily dived behind the heavy curtain that shrouded the casement window, drawing it across the width of her body, and held her breath. She heard the door open, footsteps entering the room and stopping.

As she stood there, Emily began to shiver, not from fear but intense cold. The temperature in the room had seemed to plummet so swiftly and deeply that she felt each cold breath she drew in return to the frozen air as mist.

Quite suddenly she heard the sound of breathing very close, laboured and ragged, but it was not her own, and neither did it belong to the person who stood on the other side of the curtain. For the sound came from right next to her, and just at the exact moment that she could not believe it was true, Emily also understood absolutely that she was not alone behind the thick, velvet curtain that shrouded the casement window. Very slowly she turned her head to face whatever it was that she was sharing her hiding space with, fully expecting to see the sightless eyes of a skull staring back at her. But before she could look any further, Mrs. Crawley's voice made her start and freeze.

"Leave him be," she told the room with such force that Emily wondered if Crawley had discovered her. But she made no move to pull back the curtain. "Leave him be. Leave him to me, you wretched spirit, I beg you!"

Emily heard Crawley's shoes squeak as she turned swiftly on her heel and closed the door after her with an abrupt slam.

It was with some considerable alarm that Emily realised that through the whole of Mrs. Crawley's speech a slender and freezing-cold hand had been holding hers.

"Good Christ," she gasped, snatching her frozen fingers from the grasp of cold, thin air. There was no apparition, no ghost—just the freezing chill, and an atmosphere of such deep sadness and despair that it brought tears to Emily's eyes.

Although no words were spoken, Emily heard the plea that rang in the air as clearly as a struck bell.

"I will," she whispered in reply. "I will help you, I swear it."

Reaching into her pocket Emily retrieved the object she had picked up from Elizabeth's room, turning it towards the window as she examined it. It was a button. And though she could not be sure, Emily suddenly felt entirely certain that it had once graced the coat of one Mr. Robert Chester.

21

❧ ❧ ❧

Charlotte

"Miss, there is a lady waiting for you in the sitting room," Mrs. Hepple, the boarding house owner, told Charlotte as soon as she reached the bottom of the stairs, weary from very little sleep. "She is very anxious to see you, and asked me to come and rouse you the moment she arrived first thing this morning, but I would not. I'll not disturb my paying guests for no one, no matter how grand they think themselves."

"Thank you, Mrs. Hepple," Charlotte said, glancing back at Anne. There could be no doubting who was waiting to see them. There were only two people who knew they were in Leeds, and one of them was Mrs. Honeychurch. The question was why, and whatever the reason, Charlotte feared it meant that she and Anne were in trouble.

"I'll bring you some tea," Mrs. Hepple offered. "For the lady too?"

"Yes, please, for the lady too, and please add the cost to our account." Charlotte smiled, although Mrs. Hepple appeared positively reluctant at the prospect of preparing tea for their unexpected guest, or indeed anything that strayed outside her self-prescribed remit.

Mrs. Hepple's sitting room, as she referred to it, was really more a sort of waiting room: a place where guests often waited for the stagecoach that would transport them on the next leg of their journey. It was crowded with a collection of mismatched and worn armchairs, at least two more than the room could comfortably hold. The chairs stood in a haphazard circle that rather reminded Charlotte of an awkward social occasion at which no one really knew what to say to each other, especially as one of the chairs looked for all the world as if it were trying to discreetly back out of the door. Still, as inelegant as it might have been, the room did rather reflect the uncomfortable nature of their second meeting with Elizabeth Honeychurch's mother.

"Mrs. Honeychurch." Charlotte and Anne bobbed neat curtsies, taking a seat on the rather worn sofa opposite Mrs. Honeychurch.

The poor woman looked utterly terrible, her face ravaged by tears. It took her some moments to be able to compose herself enough to speak.

"Mr. Honeychurch does not know that I am here, of course," Mrs. Honeychurch said very gravely, pressing her mouth into a thin line as Mrs. Hepple deposited tea, closing the sitting-room door behind her. "And so I do not have a great deal of time to spare if I am not to be discovered. To be here is . . . well, I am not in the habit of disobeying my husband. But I couldn't rest until I had spoken to you again."

"Then please, Mrs. Honeychurch, tell us what you have come to say."

"Your visit caused me a great deal of distress," Mrs. Honeychurch told them unhappily. "Very great distress indeed, and I have not been able to stop thinking of all that you said since you left, your words going around and around in my mind until I feared that I might go quite mad, but there is worse still. This morning we have discovered your claims are correct. After you left, Mr. Honeychurch took a carriage to Chester Grange at once to set my mind at rest, returning just before dawn. You were right. My Elizabeth is not at the Grange, discovered gone on Monday. My husband forced his way past that housekeeper woman and saw her empty room before he was ejected and . . . and he would not describe to me what lay within, and so I ask that you will, for what I can imagine is worse than any truth."

"We saw a room that had been very well cleaned, madam, which perhaps told us as much as if it had been left undisturbed." Charlotte told her as much as she was able without distressing the poor woman further or concealing the truth. "We have been told that when the governess discovered the empty room there was a quantity of blood, but no trace of your daughter."

Mrs. Honeychurch nodded stoutly, twisting a handkerchief gripped tight in both hands. "My husband and Mr. Chester had an altercation, Chester saying that Elizabeth was no longer his property. Mr. Honeychurch stirred up the constabulary in Keighley, and they seem to know less than you, so he will go to the magistrates in Leeds to ask for assistance in discovering what . . . what has happened to her, but as they are not part of the same county, I do not know if they will act, and if they do, it may be too late."

"Did you provide them with the letter you received?" Charlotte asked. Mrs. Honeychurch shook her head, bringing the letter out.

"Mr. Honeychurch says all it means is it was dated wrongly. Lizzie always was such a pudding-head, he said, and then it was delivered late. He says it means nothing of import, and that now that he is searching for Elizabeth there will be progress, and she will soon be home. I . . . I haven't been able to rest for thinking about that letter, worrying. A mother feels things, often before we know when something is wrong. I cannot know why I didn't sense that things were amiss with Lizzie, perhaps because I wanted so very much for all to be well. But now I can no longer sustain that pretence . . . Whenever I look at the letter, I feel a deep disquiet. What if it isn't a foolish mistake? What if it matters? My husband will not take my concern seriously—will you?"

"We will indeed," Anne said. "The letter should not be dismissed."

"You said yesterday that you were the only ones concerned with pursuing the truth of what happened."

"We do believe that we are the only ones doing so with full vigour." Charlotte nodded, adding as an afterthought, "On behalf of our employers, the Messrs. Bell."

"Can you explain to me who the Messrs. Bell are, and how they came to be involved?"

"They are good Christian gentlemen," Charlotte said, glancing at Anne uncertainly, seeing that Mrs. Honeychurch was expecting much more information than that. And then she thought of one of her father's letters to the press that she had transcribed for him a few weeks ago, and seized on the inspiration. "They have seen how very inadequate law enforcement is in our region. One constable covering thousands of people, usually relying on the patronage of an individual, often paid only on commission for issuing fines. This is no way to ensure justice. Criminals may expect no punishment."

"Indeed," Anne added. "The Bells have seen what great progress has been made in London with the organisation of the Metropolitan Police, and while they seek to lobby parliament for similar measures in the region, they are also determined to do what they can to restore the balance of justice."

"I see." Mrs. Honeychurch nodded. "Then please, will you continue to do so, on my behalf? I have a little money of my own that I keep apart from Mr. Honeychurch."

"We do not require your money," Anne said hurriedly, taking the letter from Mrs. Chester. "We only want to help. My sister and I were both up half the night worrying over the unhappiness we have caused you, but please believe us, it was never our intention."

"You're sisters?" Mrs. Honeychurch looked surprised, and Anne sent Charlotte a rueful look of apology.

"We are indeed," Charlotte admitted reluctantly. "With no husband or family to support us, we are compelled to seek respectable employment."

"You aren't past finding husbands quite yet," Mrs. Honeychurch said with a tearful smile. "Especially not you, Anne. What a very dear, sweet face you have. If I'd had a son that had lived I would have liked him to have married a girl as sweet looking as you."

"I am not so sure that I would be a sweet wife, though." Anne smiled weakly, sensing her sister's hurts from where she was sitting. Charlotte did her best to shrug off the comment, made by a distressed woman who hardly knew what she was saying, for it was certainly not the first time that such an observation had been made. And yet, still, it hurt her, deeper than she cared to admit.

"Well, all of last night I could not sleep either," Mrs. Honeychurch continued. "I sat and read and reread all of Lizzie's letters again, going over

every word and sentence. As I thought about the final weeks and days before her marriage, I resolved to see you again, and if judging you to be
honourable people, to tell you all I know, even though my husband would
be very greatly angered by my disobedience." Mrs. Honeychurch looked
down at her ring-laden fingers, which sparkled with heavy diamonds. "Dear
ladies, I have borne seven children during my marriage, and each save Lizzie was taken from us before they were a year old. Each bereavement was
harder to bear than the last, Miss . . ."

"Brontë," Charlotte said, feeling unable to maintain the lie in the face
of such tragic candour.

"Some people imagine that, when the death of children is so commonplace, a mother becomes hardened to it, as if each little life doesn't matter,
but I assure you that it does. Each time that tiny soul is placed in your arms
you fall in love, heart and soul—every part of you is bound to every part of
them, for haven't they been part of you for every week that you carried
them? One never gets used to the death of a child, and one never should."
Tears stood in her violet-blue eyes, as she looked at Charlotte. "I have seen
six of my children, my sweet, soft, smiling babies, cold in the ground before
I'd had a chance to hear them say 'Mama,' and on each occasion I hoped
to die myself. I even begged my husband to stop . . . to stop so that I would
not be with child again, but he said we must trust in the Lord, and he was
proven right. Because then the Lord gave us Lizzie, and she thrived, and
grew into womanhood, and seemed to me to be invincible. And oh, how I
doted on her, Misses Brontë, my dear, precious, sweet girl!"

"Of course," Charlotte said. "It's only natural that you should."

"We wanted the very best life for her, and she, a dutiful daughter, trusted
us to make the best choices for her. She came out into society on her eigh-
teenth birthday, and it was at her first ball that we met Chester. There were
so many fine-looking young men that wished to be her suitor, but we felt
that none of them really had what we wanted for Elizabeth."

"What was it that *you* wanted for her?" Anne asked.

Mrs. Honeychurch shifted a little in her chair, casting her eyes down. "It
was what my husband wanted. Mr. Honeychurch is a self-made man,

nouveau riche some would call us. Though we may have a thousandfold what they have in material wealth, they still look down on us. Mr. Honeychurch finds that intolerable. We hoped that our considerable wealth might attract a man with the kind of heritage that would see our Lizzie and her children rise in society—would give her respectability."

Charlotte nodded gravely and steeled herself against the great discomfort of having to ask the inevitable question of such a gentle and unhappy woman.

"Mrs. Honeychurch, when we met yesterday you spoke of . . . of Mr. Chester being angry enough to harm Elizabeth if he found out some truth about her. I realise how very hard this must be to do, but if you wish us to help your daughter, we need to know everything you are able to tell, no matter how shocking you might consider it. Know that whatever you reveal will go no further."

Mrs. Honeychurch shook her head again and again, pressing her handkerchief to her mouth.

Charlotte shifted a little in her seat, and after a moment moved it slightly nearer to the older woman.

"Mrs. Honeychurch," she said in little more than a whisper, taking one of her hands, "would it help you to know that we have heard that Elizabeth may have held affections for a man other than her husband?"

For a moment Mrs. Honeychurch looked shocked by the revelation, and then it was gone, and there was only sorrow.

"I told you my Elizabeth was a wild girl," she said. "That I indulged her. And she was so bright, gifted at the piano, and drawing. So I begged Mr. Honeychurch to employ two tutors for her: a young man to teach her the piano, and a young lady to improve her drawing and general learning. Her father was keen she should be accomplished, you see. I told him it would aid her pursuit of a good husband." Mrs. Honeychurch shook her head. "But after a few months it became apparent that the piano tutor, a Mr. Walters, took advantage of her sweet nature. A very large advantage. She was only fifteen, and full of ideas of falling in love, always one to follow her heart no matter where it led her, you see."

"And the attachment was discovered?"

"Indeed." Mrs. Honeychurch cast her swollen eyes down. "My Elizabeth was discovered in a . . . compromising situation with the fiend that seduced her by one of our maids."

"It is regrettable, Mrs. Honeychurch," Charlotte said gently. "But your daughter is not the first, nor will she be the last, to tread that path."

"Mr. Honeychurch said she was ruined, that no man of worth would have her if word got round, and that the humiliation of such a discovery would finish him. So he paid—he paid those that found them to keep their mouths closed. And he paid the one found with her too a great deal of money to go, and to never speak her name or come near her again. The rogue was obliged to change his name, and moved to Scarborough." She lowered her voice as she leaned forward, handing Charlotte a tightly folded piece of paper. "If I could never mention his name again, I'd be grateful. But I am ready to do whatever I can to help my Lizzie. Last night I searched my husband's desk and found this, his last known address. There were rumours, of course—we couldn't stop them all, try as we might. Elizabeth was sent away then, to a finishing school in Whitstable, until she was eighteen, and we'd hoped—we'd *hoped*—she'd put all that behind her, and it seemed that she had, when she met Robert Chester.

"When she first met him, Lizzie was quite swept away, and danced every single dance with him. I have never seen her look so happy and radiant. And after a few further meetings she was still just as overjoyed by his acquaintance. So when Chester came to us and asked for Lizzie's hand, we were as pleased as her. It seemed perfect: an old and respected name; a kind, older man; a widower; and what seemed to be a love match. They were joyous weeks, preparing for her wedding . . ." Mrs. Honeychurch trailed off, her smile faltering.

"And then, a few days before it was due to take place, we travelled to Chester Grange to receive our guests and settle Lizzie into what was to be her married home. We were . . . a little more relaxed about chaperoning her with Robert. He was, after all, to be her husband in just a day or two, so when he took her for a walk in the garden one evening after dinner . . . well, we thought no harm could come of it—it was a chance for them to become a little better acquainted, but . . ."

Mrs. Honeychurch was clearly struggling with the memory, and finding a way to articulate it seemed to be harder still.

"Misses Brontë, as unmarried women I do not wish to frighten you with matters that you may be unacquainted with . . ."

"Though unmarried, we are aware of matrimonial matters—you need not worry on our account," Charlotte assured her. Anne raised an eyebrow but said nothing.

"I had prepared—or thought I had prepared—Lizzie for what her husband would expect from her, and well . . . it's not as if she were ignorant of the *process*. Lizzie is a sensible and robust girl, and seemed prepared for intimacy. Indeed, I think she was rather thrilled that she would soon experience the full life of a woman *once more*."

She added the last two words in an excruciated whisper, adjusting herself in the chair again. This meeting, this conversation, was clearly so hard for her that it was evident how very much she must have loved her daughter even to consider sharing such private matters with virtual strangers. She must, Charlotte thought, have felt quite desperate, and how awful, how sickening it must have been to realise that it might have been the choices and decisions that she and her husband had made that had put her daughter in harm's way.

"You see, she came back from the walk with a face as white as chalk, as if she had seen a ghost, full of terror," Mrs. Honeychurch said unhappily. "And she wept the whole night. I know, for I was sleeping with her. The next morning she begged me to halt the wedding—cried her heart out, she did. Thinking it was nothing more than bridal nerves, I asked what had occurred between her and Chester, so that I might understand more what had caused her upset, but she would not speak of it. She couldn't bring herself to speak of what he had done to her."

Mrs. Honeychurch stood up suddenly and paced to the door and back, as if she couldn't contain her anxiety anymore.

"Well, we spoke on it, Mr. Honeychurch and I, and all the preparations were going on around us, all the guests arriving, and until that moment she had been so happy. We believed that if we could just calm Lizzie enough, all would be well. We set about persuading her to go ahead with her nuptials. But that evening she ran away, and when we found her she was terrified and hysterical. I said to John then that perhaps we had better face the prospect of calling off the wedding after all but . . . he refused. He would not countenance the idea—he said it would bring shame on him and his name, and that Lizzie would not do that to him again. He said that she had made a contract, and that now that contract must be honoured, and that he'd be glad when she were his responsibility no more. And so they were married."

Mrs. Honeychurch wept into her open palms. "Her poor, dear face on her wedding day, eyes red, raw from crying. I have never forgotten it."

"There were rumours that Elizabeth was not a happy bride," Charlotte said. "I believe she became good friends with the boy's governess, and that they shared such confidences. But marriage is so often a thing that must be settled into, little by little. It wasn't foolish to hope that your daughter would do just that."

"They honeymooned in Venice, but when she came back Lizzie was thin and pale, and not at all like herself. It soon became clear that she was with child, and we thought that must be the reason. Then dear little Archie was born safe, and all attempts to visit were blocked by Chester. I was afraid, and Mr. Honeychurch was very angry—we were on the point of going to Chester Grange and demanding to see her. But then the letters began to arrive, and they sounded so happy and content. So we settled down, our minds were eased. Let them have their space, my husband said. She is her husband's business now. And though it pained me more than I can say, I resolved to let my little girl go, as I must. And although I cannot say I was happy, I did my best to ignore my 'foolish notions,' as my husband calls them, and be content that she was. That was until you arrived at our house yesterday."

"And for that I am so sorry," Charlotte said.

"Please, don't apologise. After you left I read the letters again," Mrs. Honeychurch told her. "That's when I saw it. When I think of all the other times I have read and reread those words, pining for my little girl, and I had never seen it until you two young ladies came to visit."

"Seen what?" Anne asked her, sitting forward.

"When Lizzie was a little girl she was plagued with night terrors. Almost every night she'd scream the whole house down, and the only thing that would fix it would be for me to lie with her and massage lavender oil into her temples until she went to sleep.

"'I'm frightened, Mama,' she would say over and over. 'Bring me the lavender, bring me the lavender.'"

"And?" Charlotte was intrigued.

"In every single letter there is a paragraph about her childhood, and always the question, 'Do you remember how you used to bring me the lavender, Mama?' With the key four words underlined. 'Bring me the lavender.' Charlotte, Anne—I believe that in every single letter my Lizzie has been trying to tell me she is afraid and has been calling for her mama, and I . . . I have not heard her cries."

As poor Mrs. Honeychurch broke down, Anne fell on her knees before her, putting her arms around her in an act of comfort so unconscious that Charlotte wished she too had such a gift for effortless humanity as her little sister.

"Please, Charlotte and dear sweet Anne, please tell me how to find my Lizzie."

"We will use all the information that we have gathered, and our intellect, and piece them together to make a whole. And once we have done that, I feel sure that the answer will be revealed . . . though . . . though, Mrs. Honeychurch, it may be an answer that is very hard to hear."

"I know how to grieve," Mrs. Honeychurch said with a stoic nod. "Perhaps I know better than any. But I cannot bear not knowing—that would be the worst of it."

"A resolution will be reached, I swear it, no matter what it may be," Charlotte promised her, her expression very grave.

"And you'll have your Messrs. Bell to help you I suppose, won't you?" Mrs. Honeychurch pleaded, taking Charlotte's hand.

"Yes," Charlotte said, seeing how very much Mrs. Honeychurch needed the comfort and security of believing that there would be men in charge. "Yes, of course, the Messrs. Bell are running everything."

"Then, please, dear ladies, do what you must."

Such was the look of anguish on her face that Charlotte spoke before she had time to fully consider what she was saying.

"We will," she promised. "We will not rest until it is done."

22

Emily

Early-morning mist still puddled in the dips and crevices of the valley as Emily made the last few steps towards home, Keeper trotting at her side. Just as she was about to let herself in at the back and claim she'd been for a dawn walk, she spotted her father's sexton, John Brown, deep amongst the tabletop tombstones.

"Good morning, John," Emily greeted him as she walked down to see what he was about, Keeper taking himself inside for his breakfast.

"Good morning, Emily." John Brown looked up from the grave he was carefully reopening, where, Emily knew, there would already be several family coffins, in varying states of decay, piled one atop the other. On this early morning that held the promise of a bright, warm day, John would do his best to make room for yet another. Her father regularly petitioned the bishop to consecrate more ground for the dead of Haworth, for soon their bones would be poking up through the freshly dug earth. "You are up with the dawn again, I see."

"I saw the sun rise, John, and very fine it was too," Emily said, her head full to the brim of everything that she had seen last night—things so strange that, should she not have been so certain of her wakefulness, she would have considered the whole adventure to be a most extraordinary dream. Emily tilted her head to read the name on the flat stone. "Another Pickford child, John? Papa had hoped the little one might yet be saved. Will the burial be today?"

"Indeed," John nodded. "At midday."

"I shall attend." Emily nodded. "This last year has cost the Pickfords dear." She reached into her pocket and produced the pebble. "John, would you be so kind as to examine this stone for me and give your thoughts as to its origin?"

"A stone, you say?" John climbed out of the grave, wiping his hands on his breeches. If he had an opinion on Emily's bare head, her unruly hair and torn and muddy dress, he didn't feel the need to venture it, which was one of the many reasons that Emily liked him. Their maid Martha's father, he was a steady man, and a decent one, and for a man that lived amidst death every day, a surprisingly cheerful one too.

"If you would," Emily said, dropping the pebble into his palm.

"Well," the sexton said with a deep frown, "it's definitely a stone."

"You are amusing, John Brown," Emily said. "Can you discern where it might have originated? I fancy it is too light a grey, and too smooth, to be from anywhere nearby."

John Brown looked at the stone for some moments more.

"It's smooth," he said with a shrug, returning the pebble to her, "so I'd guess it's been in running water, a river or perhaps the sea, but more than that I cannot tell you, Emily."

"Thank you nevertheless, John," Emily said. "Now where might I find an expert to identify this stone? I will have to write letters to academics, I suppose, which will take time I do not have, not to mention that whenever a person addresses a single man in search of information they always suppose you are in want of a husband, when really there is nothing that a person could want less!" She looked at John. "When I say a person, I mean myself."

"Miss Emily," John said, wiping the building heat of the day off the back of his neck with a kerchief, "I cannot fathom what you are talking about, but I do believe there is no man alive whose interest you couldn't see off with your sharp tongue and fierce looks if the need arose."

"Why, thank you, John Brown," Emily said with a smile, the compliment quite lifting her mood.

As she took herself around the back of the house, she saw Branwell, pale as winter and draped over the dry stone wall that ran along the other side of the lane. Had it not been for a glimpse of his bright hair as his shoulders heaved, one might have thought he was another piece of the linen being hung out to dry there by Tabby, who was doing her best to pretend that she couldn't see the son of the house.

"Morning, Tabby," Emily called with practiced nonchalance.

"Your bed were made early, Miss Emily," Tabby said gravely. "And you already look like you've been dragged through a hedge backwards. Happen you'll see to that one?" Tabby couldn't quite bring herself to look at Branwell.

"I will, Tabby. I'm sorry, on both our accounts."

"Just don't let Mr. Brontë see you in such a state. And I've been up since the crack of dawn, cleaning the floors with fresh sand, so don't be walking on 'em," Tabby warned her. "I'll expect you in good time for your lunch, madam!"

"Indeed!" Emily said cheerfully. "I shall levitate over the floors right to the table."

Tabby's grumbled complaints about impertinence and ungratefulness faded as she returned into the parsonage through the back gate.

"Branwell," Emily said, gently rubbing his back as he retched into the meadow grass. "Are you only just coming home?"

"Are you?" He eyed her sideways between the strands of his hair, still managing a complicit smile even in extremis. "Help me right myself, Emily. For some reason my brain isn't yet willing to distinguish the difference between what is up and what is down."

"I fear that may be because your brain has entirely vacated the premises of your head, or died in situ, one or the other." Taking his hand, Emily pulled him off the wall and slung his arm around her, supporting his weight as the two of them slid down the rough stonework to sit in the grass.

"I shall never fall in love," Emily told him, wrinkling her nose. "The effects are too odious."

"Please no lectures, sister, dear Charlotte has already taken great pains to tell me all my faults and weaknesses."

"I don't lecture you, Branwell," Emily said. "I never engage in futile exercises when they can be avoided. How were the men of science?"

"The what?" Branwell looked at her, screwing his eyes up against the bright sky.

"Last night before you left you told me there were men of science surveying the land around Haworth staying at the Bull, and that you might help me find an expert on stones, or information to lead me to one?" Emily drew back from him sharply, causing him to grab for the wall, clinging on to it as if he might peel off the earth and fall into the sky.

"Ah yes, wait . . . It's coming back to me . . ." Branwell rolled over on to his side, until half his face was quite lost amongst the daisies. "We recited poetry; mine was the best. There was a good deal of singing, folk tunes, I seem to remember . . . Have you ever noticed how many of them are about people dying horribly, Emily?" Emily sighed as dramatically as she was able. "Then we had a wager on some chickens, mine was the worst and then . . . Yes! I have it. Amongst the surveyors there is a geologist named Purbeck who may or may not know something about your pebble. Obviously, to a man of such import, seeking to discover the very secrets of God's creation, your concerns are very trifling and unimportant to him, but he said that as a favour to me he would indulge your girlish interests. We may find him at Ponden Kirk this morning before he departs on the midday coach."

"This morning?" Emily scrambled to her feet. "But half the morning has gone already! And as for you . . ." She observed him, curled up like a kitten at the roadside. "You don't look in any fit state, Branwell."

"Give me a moment, Emily," Branwell said, "while I become reacquainted with gravity."

"As ever, my dear brother," Emily said, "I do not have time to waste on the weaknesses of men."

23

Emily

Emily found Mr. Purbeck halfway down the Kirk, having settled himself amongst the heather. At his side was an intriguing collection of tools displayed in an unfurled roll, a little similar to the tools the stonemason used. Emily observed him for a few moments, yet so lost in his thoughts was he that he had no inkling of her presence. He was youngish, Emily thought, about her own age—not that she considered herself young any longer—but somehow what was old for a woman was not so for a man. His thin, fair hair had been quite dishevelled by the wind, and already the bridge of his nose had caught the sun. Emily could have turned homeward in that moment and he would have never known that she was there, an option she seriously entertained—however, needs must.

"Good day to you, sir," she called out as she half climbed, half slid down the steep incline to where Mr. Purbeck was perched, offering, on arrival, a hand rather than curtseying, which under the precipitous circumstances she thought would be safer. "My name is Emily Brontë of Haworth. The parson there, Patrick Brontë, is my father and I believe you met my brother, Branwell Brontë, last night at the Bull inn. Perhaps he mentioned that I would be seeking your expert opinion as a matter of urgency?"

"I . . . oh . . . Good day, Miss . . . Brontë." Mr. Purbeck scrambled to his feet, scattering rock samples so that a sheet of his notes was carried off on the wind down the valley. "Jonathan Purbeck at your service, madam . . . miss? Your brother, you say? Is the gentleman with you?"

Emily was puzzled by the question because she was clearly alone. Perhaps Mr. Purbeck wasn't quite as intellectual as she had hoped.

"Hello," she said again. She sensed that there should be some more preamble, but she was at a loss as to what exactly that should be. "My brother, Branwell Brontë, told me you had an interest in geology, and that he had informed you that I wished to ask you about the origin of a particular piece of rock."

"Branwell Brontë." Mr. Purbeck thought for a moment. "Entertaining red-headed fellow? Excellent singing voice?" Mr. Purbeck smiled and blushed a deep shade of crimson at the same time as Emily regarded him. "I do recall mentioning that I was working up here today, but I am at a loss when it comes to your rock, Miss Brontë. Although, of course, if I can be of service to a lady in need, then it is my duty to always provide whatever assistance I may . . ." He seemed to run out of words for the moment, and Emily was glad of the respite.

It hadn't escaped her attention that Mr. Purbeck could not stop looking at her. Well, as Tabby had pointed out, she did look rather a sight, but a man with better manners might avert his eyes from her petticoat-less skirts and loose tangle of hair. Not Mr. Purbeck, it seemed. Mr. Purbeck was transfixed by her untidiness for reasons she could not possibly fathom.

"In any event, please would you take a moment to look at my stone?" Emily offered it to him in the palm of her hand, along with some leftover traces of lamb and dog hair.

"Ah . . . yes, of course." Mr. Purbeck straightened his jacket. "Although I must say never has an enquiry been so unexpected. I feel rather unprepared."

"Don't concern yourself with propriety. No one ever is up here," Emily said. "It's one of the reasons I love it so, as if we are one step from touching the clouds, wouldn't you say? The wind talks to you up here—it tells you secrets, if you listen hard enough."

"It is jolly windy." Mr. Purbeck nodded enthusiastically. "You make the most wonderful observations, Miss Brontë."

"Why *are* you here?" she asked, and his eyes lit up at the question as if he finally knew what to say at last.

"Across Europe geologists are saying that all the great valleys and mountains of the earth, such as this very valley, were created by the movement of huge planes of ice, tens of thousands of years ago, in a time, they say, when all the world was freezing. This mountain, the stones, the rifts in rocks, were all carved out by a slow-moving wall of ice that had such force that it shaped landscapes. I have come to see what evidence I can find in our own land to support such a theory, although"—he hesitated for a moment, perhaps belatedly remembering Emily's parson father—"obviously our Lord is the architect of all."

"A world covered in ice," Emily said thoughtfully, looking up the valley to where the hillside split in two. "I have always thought that valley looks as though it was ripped asunder by two great hands, but yes, a great wall of ice would work too. How interesting, Mr. Purbeck. I like your theory. My stone—what can you tell me about it?"

Mr. Purbeck took the stone from her hand, holding it in his palm as gently as if it were an egg.

"It's limestone," he told her at once, "and I believe it was picked up from a shore, worn smooth as it is by the constant embrace of the tide. The coast of Yorkshire is made up of many layers from the Jurassic period, one of which is limestone, but here you can see a vein of sandstone too, see? Here—it shows better if the rock is wet." He picked up a small flask and doused the pebble in water, revealing fine veins of pinks and golds amongst the purple-grey. "I can't pinpoint the exact place this pebble was found, of course, but I'd take an educated guess at somewhere from the coast around Scarborough."

"Scarborough—interesting." Emily took the stone back from him, turning it over in her hands, her mind rushing from one conclusion to another. "It could be a memento, a memory of a special place, one special treasured moment that can never be recaptured. A keepsake, a token between lovers even!"

"I say," Mr. Purbeck said, half-smiling, half-apprehensive of her, which was hardly surprising, Emily thought. She didn't suppose he met many like her. "Miss Brontë, forgive me for asking, but may I ask why you are making such enquiries? I do not believe that I have ever been asked such a question by a young lady before."

But Emily was already scrambling her way back up the hillside.

"Do forgive me, Mr. Purbeck," Emily called over her shoulder. "I would love to converse more—you seem quite interesting—but I'm afraid I am expected at a funeral."

24

Anne

"Goodness me, Emily, you look as though you have been up all night!" Charlotte exclaimed, as she and Anne returned home from the coach to find Emily in the kitchen, a novel propped up on the table as she kneaded dough to make a fresh batch of bread, a job she usually completed much earlier in the day.

"Then I look just as I should," Emily said, "for I am lacking in sleep after a night of extraordinary adventures, a morning of revelations and a funeral. And Tabby has just sanded the floors, so mind you only float anywhere for fear of disrupting her work."

"I heard that!" Tabby called from out the back kitchen, where she and Martha were feeding yet more linen through the mangle.

"The floor looks wonderful, Tabby!" Anne called out in appeasement.

"Extraordinary adventures indeed?" Charlotte sounded rather uninterested, imagining that Emily had been writing tales of Gondal again—people were always dying tragically in Gondal.

"Very much indeed," Emily said. "And as soon as this bread is in the oven and it's safe to talk, I shall tell you all I saw."

"And we shall tell you all we discovered in Leeds," Anne said, standing on her toes to rest her chin on Emily's shoulder to see what she was reading. "For we discovered a great deal."

"Then we shall see who had the more extraordinary time," Emily replied. "Although I must warn you now that it was definitely me."

Charlotte and Anne exchanged looks, quite sure that whatever had happened to Emily while she remained at home in Haworth, letting her imagination run away with the fairies, could not top their excursion to Leeds.

But of course they were both quite, quite wrong.

"Heavens," Charlotte said, feeling the hairs prickle and rise on the back of her neck as, with vivid, lurid detail, Emily told her sisters of *almost* all that she had witnessed at Chester Grange.

They had had to wait a short while to hear it, for Emily had been insistent that she would not repeat the tale at home, for fear of being overheard by Papa, Tabby or the still fresh and impossibly awkward new curate, Mr. Arthur Bell Nicholls.

As it was a pretty afternoon, she persuaded her weary sisters to venture out again almost as soon as they had set down their bags, and now that they had heard her story, they did not regret it, especially as the walk had taken them to the beautiful waterfall that they called Waters Meet amongst themselves. Here the water ran off the moor in a cold, clear and musical rush that reminded Anne of her cat walking along the piano keys. And it seemed that not so long ago a giant had stomped by, tossing huge boulders down the steep valley and hillsides as if they were his playthings. It was as picturesque as it was wild, with something that reflected a little piece of each sister back at them, and perhaps that was why they loved it so, as it was a kind of home for each of them. And it was here, far from any prying pairs of ears, that they could talk openly under the splendour of the sky, both together and in perfect isolation.

Once Anne had heard the full story, she couldn't decide what horrified her more: tales of Chester intimately fondling a skull, or her sister abroad at night, putting herself in terrible danger without a second thought.

"I grabbed a handful of papers from his desk as I left, but having glanced at them, they seem to be nothing more interesting than accounts and exceedingly dull correspondence."

"If anyone discovered what you have done, Emily," Charlotte said very gravely, "it would be you behind bars: stealing private papers, indeed!"

Emily nodded. "It would have been a very grave error to have been discovered. Oh, and there was something else . . ." Emily thought of the light that had led her to Elizabeth's room once again but kept it to herself. "I briefly visited Elizabeth's room again, and found this." She held out her palm. "I believe it is the button that was missing from Chester's coat. Perhaps pulled loose in a struggle?"

"It makes me shudder to look at it. Let us pray that Papa never hears of these escapades of ours—I'm quite sure it would end him prematurely," Anne said, not a little terrified by Emily's adventures.

"Agreed." Charlotte nodded. "We must be careful to keep Papa from further worry."

"Our brother is doing a good job of worrying poor Papa to death all on his own," Emily said baldly. "When Keeper and I returned home this morning we found Branwell sprawled out on the back step, without even the good sense to get himself inside."

"Again?" Charlotte said hopelessly. "I had thought our last conversation had reached within to the old Branwell, but I suppose I was wrong."

For a moment the sisters fell into silence, and Anne knew it was the same fear that quieted her sisters, as it did her—that it might not be possible to turn Branwell back from the path he was on before he met the precipice that lay at its end.

"Do you remember when he was always our leader in all things?" Anne said wistfully. "As a little girl I'd have followed him to the end of the earth; he seemed to me to have been born full of greatness."

"The greatness in him is still there," Charlotte said. "We must trust, and pray and hope that he returns to his true self. Surely a man with such promise can do nothing else but rise to it?"

"He does make me so afraid," Emily said at last, and that worried Anne deeply, for there was so very little that could make her sister feel frightened.

"To work then, detectors," she said as brightly as she was able, in an attempt to turn their thoughts from Branwell's plight. "Let's look at all the fragments we have collected and see if we can assemble them to make a whole. The bones you saw Mr. Chester . . . consorting with . . . could they have been the bones of Elizabeth?"

"I don't believe so," Emily said with confidence. "They were clean—so pristine they glowed white in the firelight. Besides, it takes time to get a skeleton articulated: Chester would have had to send the bones away to Bradford or Leeds—time that he has not had. And I saw the skull very clearly. It looked so fine and delicate in his great hands, as if he could easily crush it. I'm sure it was the skull of a woman, but it had all its teeth. There-fore, I believe it is the skull of the first Mrs. Chester that he keeps his pris-oner to this day, still resentful that she tried to escape him in death. What is not in doubt is that he is a dark and dangerous man. Chester is quite mad—he hides it reasonably well—but he is insane. And it strikes me that a man who still mourns his first wife to such a strange and unnatural ex-tent, though we know that he tormented her to her death, might not have any trouble dispatching his second wife."

Even on the warm afternoon, Anne shuddered. The evil that men were capable of terrified her much more when it was so carefully hidden behind a respectable veneer of lies.

"And then there is *this*." Charlotte took out Elizabeth's letter that Mrs. Honeychurch had given her, turning it over in her hands. "This letter, in Elizabeth's hand, is dated and postmarked as if sent from Chester Grange the day *after* she vanished."

"Could it be that Chester forged her hand and sent it to her parents to delay their discovery of her vanishment?" Emily wondered, taking the letter from Charlotte and reading it, her eyes screwed up against the sun.

"Mrs. Honeychurch is adamant that it is Elizabeth's writing," Anne said. "She schooled her herself, and I don't believe a man such as Chester could so accurately reproduce the copperplate hand of an educated young woman, do you? It has the mark of female learning all over it, when a young lady is schooled in repressing any individual part of herself, even in her handwriting."

"There is more," Charlotte said. "Elizabeth had escaped a great scandal at the age of only fifteen, after, it seems, becoming intimately entangled with her music tutor."

"The more I learn of such passions, the more destruction I see," Emily said. "I'm starting to believe the life of a hermit is the only safe one."

"From what we could deduce, it was an affair in which Elizabeth was a willing participant," Charlotte went on. "It seems Elizabeth's father paid off the tutor not to speak of it, and sent him on his way to the coast. Which makes it seem even more strange that Elizabeth was so afraid of marriage, when she perhaps knew more of what lay in store for her than many other young brides."

"It is interesting that she had a lost love," Emily said. "A lost love that was sent to the coast. Because Mr. Purbeck the geologist believes this pebble might be from the beaches around Scarborough, no less."

"Mr. Purbeck?" Charlotte raised her brows.

"An expert Branwell introduced me to." Emily waved her enquiry away, finding the business of explanation far too tedious. "I believe that we need to find this young gentleman with whom Elizabeth became embroiled. For if he was the young man that Mrs. Hardy saw Elizabeth with in the woods, then it could be that their love for each other continued, even after she married Chester. And it would certainly be enough motive for Chester to murder her. Or it could be that the jealous lover himself is the culprit."

"Agreed." Charlotte nodded. "Mrs. Honeychurch furnished us with his last known address."

"And the note—the note we found in Mattie's room," Anne reminded them. "We must not forget that. I believe we must talk to Mattie again, and try to discover the meaning behind the note, and if the 'R' could stand for Robert."

"Mattie is as sweet as an angel, and as meek," Charlotte said. "I cannot believe that she would be so seduced by a man such as Chester that she would help him conceal his awful deeds, especially when she has all but been telling us she believes him capable of the very worst. It makes no sense."

"Perhaps she wishes him brought low," Anne said thoughtfully, "brought closer to her station. We cannot rule it out, Charlotte. Love is an illness that drives its victims to strange and unnatural acts. If she did love Chester, then removing his wife would certainly be convenient."

"Anne, I simply can't countenance such a thought!" Charlotte's eyes widened in horror. "Are you suggesting that Mattie cut up Elizabeth Chester?"

"Anne is right," Emily said. "We can't rule out any possibility. For men and women are terrible creatures, and we can never truly know what they are capable of in secret. I believe that a journey to Scarborough is quite an undertaking, an expedition that I believe Anne should take, as she is the most familiar with the town, having travelled there with the Robinsons. You, Charlotte, should return to the Grange to talk to Mattie. She is your friend—you know her better than any of us and are most able to win her trust, to see if she is hiding anything, and discern what you may of her darker nature."

"Her darker nature?" Charlotte spluttered. "If you'd really known her as a girl, as I did, Emily, you'd see that such an idea is preposterous."

"If you kick a dog for long enough, one day it will bite you back," Emily said. "And anyway, it's the best plan, so shall we just get on with it?"

"I see, Major." Charlotte raised her brow. "And what shall you be doing while Anne and I are scurrying in all directions at your command?"

"I will travel with Anne to Scarborough tomorrow," Emily said, smiling fondly at Anne, "for she cannot make the journey alone."

"At the rate we are spending Aunt Branwell's legacy, we shall not have any left to invest," Charlotte said a little primly, but only, Anne knew, because she saw the sense in Emily's scheme. It was true that they were spending what few resources they had, putting themselves in positions that, if not positively perilous, were certainly unsuitable, and yet not one of them had questioned the value of these choices. They had banded together for Mattie, for Elizabeth and Imogen Chester and for themselves, determined champions of those who did not have a voice.

"We cannot travel tomorrow," Anne reminded her sisters. "For tomorrow is Sunday, and we have a duty to God and Papa."

Emily huffed, and Charlotte sighed, and yet they both accepted that Sunday was not a day for detecting, even with time so pressing.

"Monday then." Gathering her skirts, Charlotte began the walk back to the house, Anne following after her, but Emily stayed atop her rock, tipping her face back to catch the best of the sun while it was still shining.

"Coming?" Anne turned back to ask her.

"Will you not stay awhile with me, Anne?" Emily smiled. "It's been a very long time since we were in Gondal, and there is much to discover still."

Anne hesitated, caught between the world that she and Emily had created together and this life, this flesh-and-blood life, where all was as real as the mud under her shoes. Emily still loved their stories, still lived them all the time, and Anne had no idea how to tell her sister that she no longer felt the same, that what concerned her, what inspired her to want to write, were the stories of the real people around them. And yet Emily looked so hopeful, so like the child she had once been, that Anne couldn't refuse her.

"Come, then, sister," she said, holding out her hand. "Where shall we begin today? With a battle?"

Charlotte didn't mind as she watched her two sisters disappearing off into the distance, perhaps to walk up to Top Withens farm, or one of Emily's other favourite haunts. In fact she took a comfort in seeing them, hand in hand, heads bowed together, just as she always had done since they were very little children. It was reassuring to know that at least some things didn't change, and that whatever dark treacheries the world might conceal, at least she was certain of one thing: she would always have her sisters.

25

Anne

The journey to Scarborough was long and tiresome, and Anne worried throughout it, for she suspected that Papa had not been entirely convinced by their story of going to seek out prospective locations for a Brontë-run school.

"I see, I see," he'd said as he'd watched them pack a small trunk between them, his expression one of deeply etched concern. "Should you take your brother with you as escort, do you think? I know how well-versed you girls are in travelling abroad, but even so, you are but young ladies still."

Anne and Emily exchanged looks.

"Dear Papa," Emily said, "you need not fear for us, I swear it. We shall be guarded the whole way by the coachman and the train conductor, and we are expected in very respectable lodgings."

"Indeed, we would have happily taken Branwell, Papa," Anne had said delicately, "but I believe that he is served best by your influence at present. When he returns home, as I'm sure he will soon, it would be better that he would stay under your watchful eye."

The truth was that Branwell had vanished some time after Emily had found him and was yet to return. It had been two days and two nights since they had last heard from him, and Anne had sent Tabby and Martha out to all the places they thought he might be—drinking with the Heatons at

Ponden or gambling with fellows of low repute in any tavern five miles in all directions—but they hadn't discovered his whereabouts yet. It wasn't unheard of for Branwell to walk great distances to see friends, sleeping in ditches or hitching on the back of carts on his way. But previously, when he'd taken himself on such great adventures, he'd been a very different boy. He'd been hopeful, cheerful and—most importantly—sober, more often than not. Now there was always that cloak of doom that hung around him like a perpetual moonless night; a great storm of unhappiness that all those who loved him feared would engulf him entirely one day.

"My poor boy." Patrick had gone to the window, peering into the early morning as if searching out every dark crevice and cranny in the graveyard and beyond, hoping to glimpse a trace of his son. Anne knew that his eyesight was so poor that he could probably only make out the vaguest shapes and shadows in a world populated by nothing more than spectres.

"How I wish he would only stay at my side and let me keep him safe," Papa had said, turning to his younger daughters. "How I wish you all would, but of late you are constantly packing trunks and taking excursions hither and thither. If there was anything . . . *untoward*, you would speak to your father on the matter, would you not? For though I am old, I am still your protector, and a great deal wiser and more familiar with the ways of this world than you."

"Of course we would, Papa." Anne had brought his hand to her cheek, resting it against his palm for a moment before kissing it. "You need not concern yourself about Emily and me, or Charlotte, for that matter, Papa. We are simply doing what must be done in order to secure our futures, just as you have always taught us. All things being equal, Charlotte and I might run a very nice school in Scarborough, and Emily could stay here to take care of you and keep house. We should all benefit from such a scheme if we are successful."

"Well then, godspeed, my girls, godspeed." Patrick had kissed them each upon the forehead. "Come home to me soon."

Anne felt deeply uneasy about misinforming her father so, even though she could see the wisdom in it. And yet for the whole of the day-long journey, filled as it was with uncomfortably cramped coaches and smoke and steam, Emily clutching at her arm in excitement as the train came up to full speed, all she had thought of was his anxious face at the window as they had left, and how very dear he was to her. It was a sense of disquiet that she knew would not be gone until she was returned home, and all this dissembling, as interesting and compelling as it was, was very far behind them.

Though this was not her first time seeing it, Anne was still mesmerised by the sheer magnitude of the sea.

"The greatness of it," she said half to herself, half to Emily and a little to the wind as they stood side by side on the beach. "The vastness of it, Emily. And the noise, the ceaseless, wonderful poetry of noise, and all the colours. Every blue, grey and green there has ever been. Oh, how I should love to be greeted by this sight every day, to taste this air and see the gulls swooping overhead, and hear them calling."

"It is very fine," Emily said, smiling at her enraptured sister. "And so are you, Anne, when you stand before it. I don't believe I've ever seen your eyes so bright or your cheeks so full of roses. Scarborough suits you very well."

Emily poked the toe of her boot into the sand and looked around at the larger pebbles scattered here and there, picking a few up and dropping them, until she found one that resembled the pebble she'd insisted on bringing with her.

"See, these are similar," she said to Anne. "Perhaps Elizabeth and her tutor once stole away here for a day."

"Oh, Emily, just for a moment stop detecting and look around you! I don't believe that I have ever been so happy anywhere else in my life," Anne said, flinging her arms open as if to embrace the horizon. "Here, on the edge of the land, any journey seems entirely possible, any destination achievable."

Arm in arm, they took the steps up from the beachfront and into the town, Anne taking pleasure in taking the lead, securing her bonnet to her head with one hand in protection against the light-fingered and lively sea breeze.

"This is the address that Mrs. Honeychurch gave us as the last known address of Mr. Walters," Anne said, nodding towards a row of four modest little cottages that sat across the street from the church. "However, the information Mrs. Honeychurch came by is three years old. He might have moved on by now. Emily, do you suppose it was rather foolish for us to make this trip with so few facts?"

"We can only knock on the door and find out," Emily said. "Whatever lies behind it will lead us to our next appointment."

But before they could cross the road, an older lady, perhaps around forty years of age, processed down the street. She was dressed in deep mourning—a heavy widow's veil and black gloves—and yet there was a definite spring in her step as she walked, a certain expectation in her gait. Following the lady a few paces behind was a younger woman wearing such a plain and serviceable dress that it all but shouted out that hers was the role of female companion, a position that might, if such a thing was possible, be even more devoid of hope than that of a governess. At the companion's heels a small white terrier trotted behind, bringing up the rear like a little Napoleon, officious and self-important. As Anne observed the strange trio, she was intrigued to see the lady knock on the very painted cottages that they had been planning to call on. The lady waited for a few moments before whipping what looked like a sheaf of sheet music out of her companion's arms and letting herself into the little house, slamming the door behind her without revealing even a glimpse of who lay within.

"I wonder . . ." Anne said, tugging at Emily's elbow, nodding at the young woman who stood rather awkwardly outside the cottage, staring determinedly at her feet.

"What do you wonder, Anne?" Emily asked her.

"If perhaps we might have a discreet conversation with that poor young woman, and discover what she knows of the goings-on behind that door?"

"Excellent idea," Emily said. "You talk to her, I'll interview the dog."

———

"Good day." Anne spoke pleasantly to the young woman, who stood uncomfortably outside the little cottage that her mistress had disappeared into. "A fine afternoon, isn't it?"

"Isn't it?" the young woman replied politely with a little smile, though her expression was so wan and devoid of any pleasure that it might as well have been a frown.

"My sister and I are staying in Scarborough for a few weeks, and we understood that we might be able to engage a piano tutor hereabouts?" Anne went on, as Emily stooped to greet the little dog as it leapt up at her skirts, yapping and growling as if it were a mastiff. "Though foolishly we have forgotten both the name and address, only his approximate location . . . Willoughby? Walters? Do forgive me—we are the Misses Brontë: Anne and Emily. How do you do, Miss . . . ?"

Anne curtsied, and Emily followed suit, briefly nodding at the girl before returning to the dog.

"Miss Amelia Pritchard, pleased to meet you." The young woman bobbed a curtsey in return. "And I do believe you must mean Mr. Watson, who resides within this very cottage! My employer, Mrs. Moreton, is taking lessons from him as we speak. His attentions quite lift her mood."

"Indeed." Anne smiled, turning to Emily, who was letting the terrier lick her nose. "How fortunate, Emily—this *is* the address we were looking for."

"And you are to wait outside?" Anne asked. "While Mrs. Moreton is instructed? Is the cottage so very small?"

"Quite small." Miss Pritchard nodded. "Besides, Mrs. Moreton is quite clear that she cannot play in front of an audience, so we are to wait, are we not, Button? We wait and we follow, for this is our lot in life."

"Would you mind if we were to wait with you?" Anne asked, noting how her sister scooped Button into her arms, not minding the scrabble of his spiky little paws in the neckline of her dress nor how he seemed earnestly to be attempting to eat her ears.

"I'd be grateful for the company," Miss Pritchard replied.

Anne had supposed that the lesson might take half an hour, but the slow rotation of the clock hands on the church tower showed that a whole hour had elapsed by the time Mrs. Moreton emerged, securing her bonnet beneath her chin as she left, closing the door behind her.

"What are you about, Pritchard?" Mrs. Moreton asked, appearing to be rather affronted to find her companion standing with strangers. Behind the black gauze of her veil and bonnet, Anne noticed where stray strands of brown hair were escaping and that the buttons on her blouse were slightly out of step with their corresponding buttonholes.

"Begging your pardon, madam, these ladies wanted to enquire about piano lessons with Mr. Watson," Miss Pritchard explained.

"Did they?" Mrs. Moreton looked Anne and Emily up and down, taking in their distinct country-spinster looks, seeming to dismiss them at once, and lifted Button out of Emily's arms before proceeding swiftly up the street with a swish of her skirts. "Tell them he is fully engaged," she called over her shoulder. "And be swift—I have worked up quite an appetite."

26

Emily

"Good day?" Anne called out as they stepped in through the low doorway and directly into a rather shabby and disorganised little parlour with piles of books and sheet music piled up on every surface, on one wall of which stood an upright piano, its lid closed tight and filmed in dust that had not been troubled by any human hand in quite some time. "Is there a Mr. Watson at home?"

Emily advanced further into the room. To the left was a latched doorway that she guessed led to a staircase, and beside the piano another door that probably led into a dining room with a kitchen area beyond, though in a house as small as this it was just as probable that it would be one room combined.

"Emily!" Ann half whispered as she was just about to investigate the next room. "Footsteps!"

Emily still had her hand on the latch when through the door from the staircase entered a decidedly flustered young gentleman, who greeted their presence with quite some surprise.

"Good heavens!" he said, lowering the poker that he was brandishing. "I thought you must be robbers."

"Sir," Emily said, remembering a moment too late to remove her hand from the latch.

"Ladies?" Mr. Walters advanced a little further into the room, and all at once both of the Brontë detectors had quite forgotten what they were about, for no matter what he was named, the gentleman in question was rather distracting. Long, dark hair curled over his collar, his eyes were as blue as a periwinkle, and his shirt, untied at the neck as if thrown on in haste, revealed a good portion of his throat. "You find me at a disadvantage, I'm afraid."

"We . . . um . . ." Emily looked at Anne, who looked determinedly at the floor. "Piano. We came to ask about piano lessons."

"I see." Mr. Walters hastily made his shirt good, and tugged on a jacket that had been laid across the back of a battered chaise.

"Do you play already, or are you beginners?" he asked, the moment he was respectable. "I'm happy to instruct at any level."

He picked up Emily's gloved hand, unfolding her fingers in his palm.

"You have a pianist's fingers," he told her. "Long and elegant."

"Indeed, I do play very well," Emily replied, snatching her fingers back, as she felt an unfamiliar heat in her cheeks, which was most unsettling. This would not do, allowing this fop to take her off guard with his looks and his hand-holding. She must regain the offensive position at once. "Have you lived long in Scarborough, Mr. Walters?"

At the sound of his real name, Frederick Walters blanched as he looked warily from Emily to Anne

"Some years, yes," he replied carefully. "But you mean Watson. My name is Watson—the Walters fellow that you speak of is long since dead."

Emily noticed something like melancholy about his violet eyes, which reminded her a little of her dog. He seemed to her more like a man hiding from something than trying to keep something hidden. Still, this would not do, this sympathy for a fellow based only on his appearance—his very fine appearance. If he could move even her, it was hardly surprising that a young girl like Elizabeth Honeychurch had succumbed to his charms.

"Mr. Walters, may I be frank?" Emily asked, without waiting for an answer to the question, crossing to the window to look out, an altogether safer view. "We are the Brontë sisters out of Haworth; we are here on business for a company of solicitors named Bell Brothers and Company. We know that you had a position as music tutor to a Miss Elizabeth Honeychurch in Leeds prior to your arrival here, and we know that you were dismissed from that post when it was discovered that your involvement with Miss Honeychurch far exceeded that of tutor and pupil. We know everything about you, sir. Mrs. Honeychurch told us all."

"Then you know nothing," Mr. Walters said, his eyes flashing impressively, "for that is not what happened."

Charlotte had her way with people, her way of making herself their friend, eliciting their trust and drawing out every secret with one of those hypnotic looks of hers. Emily had no such recourse. The *only* way, as far as she was concerned, was by the most direct route possible, though there was a chance that one might crush the more fragile things underfoot as one went. Sometimes that was a necessary risk.

"Sir," she said, turning towards Walters slightly, her tone grave. "Why would the mother of a previously respectable young woman lie about such a thing? You make a grave error if you mistake us for fools. We are spinsters, yes, but we are not delicate in disposition, and I ask you to speak honestly with us, for it may very well be a matter of life and death."

"Life and death?" Mr. Walters shook his head, bewildered. "You had better be sure of what you speak of when you use such terms, madam."

"Emily, perhaps . . ." Anne began in a conciliatory tone, but Emily cut across her.

"We believe that Elizabeth is in very grave danger, if indeed she lives at all, sir. And we believe that you may know something that can reveal the truth of her fate, whatever it may be."

The expression of indignation fell away from Mr. Walters's handsome face at once, and forgetting propriety, he sank into a chair, leaving his two female visitors standing. Not one to pay much mind to ceremony, Emily perched on the edge of the chaise and directed Anne to join her. Finally her younger sister scuttled to her side.

"Please tell me of what you speak," he said, his voice very quiet. "Tell me what horror has befallen dear, sweet Elizabeth."

"You may know that she was married a little more than two years ago to a Mr. Chester of Arunton," Emily said. "Seven days ago, this Monday last, she vanished in the night, leaving no trace of her whereabouts except a great quantity of blood."

Emily watched Walters's expression very carefully as she revealed the awful truth, looking for any sign of dissemblance in his face, but either he was truly shocked to hear the news, or he was a very fine actor indeed, for he appeared quite stricken.

"Oh, dear God," he whispered. "Oh, dear, sweet Lizzie . . . but surely . . . Do the Messrs. Bell believe I might have had a hand in this terrible event?"

"We know that you and Mrs. Chester became entangled," Emily said. "And we know that Mrs. Chester was seen in the woods embracing a gentleman that was not her husband some weeks before she vanished. We are here to discern whether or not you were that young man, and if your attachment to Elizabeth was not ended by your dismissal, or even her marriage."

"You are quite, quite wrong." Mr. Walters shook his head. "I do not blame you for your errors, but I assure you that whoever it was Lizzie was with in the woods, it was not I, nor any man that I can think of. Mrs. Honeychurch told you the truth as she knows it, but the trouble is, ladies, Mrs. Honeychurch does not know the truth.

"Since my dealing with the Honeychurches, I have become a private person, cautious of the harm that others can do to me. I do not relish the notion of strangers coming into my home and demanding all my secrets as if it were their right. Even such admirable young ladies as yourselves."

"We do not relish it either, sir," Anne said, "and I so regret any discomfort my sister and I have brought to your door. But we fear that no one else will ask the questions that need to be asked."

"Lizzie was a girl of rare independence, cursed with a controlling father. Her behaviour often caused upheaval, but she was very dear to me nonetheless." Mr. Walters stood up. "Come with me to the garden. There you shall discover all that I have to hide."

Emily and Anne followed Walters through a small, sparsely equipped kitchen and an open door into a neat little postage stamp of a walled garden, lined with every kind of cottage flower one could imagine. A young lady sat on the minute square of grass, her long midnight curls cascading down her back. As they drew nearer, Emily saw she was intent on making a daisy chain.

"Look, Freddie." She turned and smiled as Mr. Walters and the sisters approached, lifting the chain of flowers for inspection. "The longest one yet, see?"

"I see, Clara." Mr. Walters knelt down in the grass, picking another daisy and handing it to her. "How clever you are: quite the best at daisy-chain construction that there has ever been, sister, dear."

"Who are these ladies?" Clara squinted up at Emily. "Will they play with me too?"

"We shall." Anne spoke, joining Clara on the grass. After a few more minutes of observation, it became clear to Emily that although Clara was a grown woman, she had the mind of a child of no greater age than eight.

"I don't know what truly happened with Lizzie," Frederick said, as they watched his sister. "It's true, I loved her. I loved her a great deal, just as I love Clara here, as a little sister. But I was not the source of her disgrace. I only know that Honeychurch came to me and offered me a great deal of money and a place to live if I agreed to be—not named, exactly—rather *a name* that he could tell his wife and others who had heard rumours of a seducer that undid his daughter; that whoever her real lover was, that personage was so scandalous and affronting to him that he felt compelled to control even the breath of a rumour to something more tolerable. He is an exceptionally controlling man, and Lizzie was so very reluctant to be controlled. It was a strange request, but if it protected Lizzie somehow, I wasn't averse to it, and I was fighting so hard to keep Clara and to provide for her. The wages of a tutor do not stretch far, and I feared I'd be forced to leave her to the mercy of a charity hospital, most of which are truly evil places. Honeychurch's proposal seemed . . . like a solution, if a desperate one. I agreed to it, I took his money and in return my true name was irrevocably tarnished. I can never work again as a concert pianist, and I am bound for ever to be at the bidding of the appetites of lonely women. None shall ever marry me, for I have nothing to offer. I shall never know love, or have children of my own. But that is the sacrifice I made to keep Clara somewhere safe and kind, and I cannot regret that."

"I'd marry you," Emily said, before she realised she had spoken her thought aloud. "If I was . . . looking for a husband, which I am not."

"Oh, well . . ." Frederick Walters coughed. "Thank you. That gives me some hope."

"You are pretty," Clara told Anne, winding the rope of flowers around the crown of her bonnet. "Will you come every day?"

"The truth is," Frederick Walters said, "I do not know what happened to Elizabeth—only that it was considered so damning that Mr. Honeychurch sought to hide it at any cost."

Emily turned to her sister.

"Why would any father fabricate a liaison between his daughter and a man to cover the truth?" she asked Anne. "For what could possibly be more scandalous than that?"

27

Charlotte

Matilda French bowed her fair head, directing her gaze at her hands, and Charlotte shifted a little in her chair, her small, fine fingers woven together on her lap. The curtains were drawn on the warm afternoon as the children were taking their afternoon nap, but the room still felt close and stifling hot. The direction of their conversation didn't aid matters either.

"Forgive me, Charlotte," Mattie spoke at last, her voice soft and low, "but I cannot imagine what you are implying."

Charlotte paused for a moment, discomfort dictating every line of her posture, from her erect back to her stiff shoulders. Not a word she had spoken thus far had come out exactly as she intended, for though Charlotte felt herself to be more well versed in the delicate intricacies of this world than many other unmarried women might be, when it came to articulating those delicacies she was at a loss.

"I do not mean to imply anything, Matilda," Charlotte said carefully, tasting the weight of each word on her tongue before she spoke it aloud. "I seek only to understand."

"Understand what?" Mattie still would not look at her directly, a fact that frustrated Charlotte greatly. If only she could make Matilda look directly into her eyes, then she would have a good chance at discerning what her friend was thinking and, more important, if she was hiding anything.

The trouble was she'd never really thought of Matilda French as anything but a dear, sweet girl before—rather a blank page, if anything—and so she'd never really taken the trouble to search out her pretty, blue eyes for any trace of complication. Never had a young woman looked so demure, so mild, and yet Emily was right—something was out of kilter here. Charlotte could sense it.

"I've told you all I know," Mattie continued. "That the constable organised a group of men, they searched the woods and outbuildings and abandoned properties about for more than twenty miles, and have found no trace of Mrs. Chester. They ousted the gypsies from the area, and saying it must have been one of those who found a way into the house looking for food and money and, discovering my poor mistress, carried her away."

"The travelling folk?" Charlotte asked. "We did meet one of their number in the woods the last time I visited, Mattie, and he was rather fearsome. I would not have thought him incapable of violence."

"It is not them who tortured and made my mistress so unhappy," Mattie said in something of a rush before falling silent a long moment, pulling at some unseen thread on her skirt. "And now you tell me that Mr. Honeychurch is seeking aid from Leeds, but what has Leeds to do with Arunton? We might as well be in another country as far as the law is concerned."

"Elizabeth's father has his own secrets to protect," Charlotte said. "Perhaps even at the cost of his daughter's safety, but Anne and Emily are engaged in learning more about those as we speak. And as for Chester, perhaps he does believe the travellers took his wife, or perhaps that they make the perfect scapegoat. The one that lets him live on as a bachelor once again, free from enquiry? Free to . . . marry again? What would you think of that, Matilda? If Chester looked around for a new wife, a new mother to his sons, and his gaze stopped at you. Would you be afraid or thrilled?"

Matilda did not react the way that Charlotte had expected at all, with cries of horror and denial. Instead she fell silent once again, her head angled so that Charlotte could see only the outline of her pale cheek, the sweep of her golden lashes on her flushed skin.

"Mr. Chester is a dangerous man," Matilda said after a moment. "A most angry and violent man—there is no doubt of that. And yet . . ."

"And yet? And yet, as you speak those words there is a quietness in your tone, Matilda," Charlotte said softly. "And a kind of longing. Do you believe yourself to be in love with Mr. Chester?"

Matilda shook her head, and when at last she looked up at Charlotte, there was a tear tracking down her face.

"How can I know what love is, Charlotte?" she asked, leaning forward and grabbing Charlotte's hand, pulling her tightly towards her so that their heads were just inches apart. "I have grown up in a world devoid of love, my mother and father dead when I was but a child, brought up by unkind and uninterested school mistresses. But within me there is a heart—a heart that longs for the devotion of a husband. And without there is . . . this body." Mattie gestured at her person as she whispered through tight lips. "This skin that longs to be touched, this neck that hopes to feel the brush of my husband's lips, this waist that wishes to be held. Charlotte, I am a living thing, trapped in this cage of a life; a woman made of desire—desire that I may never express, never speak of, never admit to—and in truth, Robert Chester might very well kill me as much as kiss me, but yes, sometimes I do wonder if it wouldn't be worth it just to know how it feels."

The two women gripped each other for a moment longer, their eyes locked intensely, and then Mattie released Charlotte, collapsing back into her chair, her eyes glittering, her brow beaded with perspiration.

"You have it wrong," Charlotte said quietly, "all wrong, dear Mattie. I have known those impulses that you speak of. I understand that longing, but you for your own self are worth so much more than an object to be loved or married. You are kind, you are courageous, you are honourable and decent. You are bringing light and stability into the life of two children who have no one else to show them how to be good." Charlotte turned her face to the sliver of daylight that crept in through a narrow gap in the curtains. "It is likely that you and I shall die—a long time from now, God willing—without ever having known what it is like to be a wife, but even so, our worth does not lie in being wanted, in being desired by a man. It doesn't even lie in the joy of motherhood. Our worth is our own, and you, Matilda—you are worth a thousand times more than a man like Chester, be he murderer or not."

Mattie closed her eyes, further tears falling as she seemed to listen to Charlotte's words long after they had been spoken.

"I know," she said. "I know you are right, Charlotte. I know what kind of man he is—I more than most. That I'd let myself think of him as anything but a monster appalls me. Am I so desperate to be loved? It's very hard not to despise myself."

"Has be made approaches to you, dear?" Charlotte asked her. "For you see, when Anne was in your room, she came, quite by chance, across a scrap of paper and, well . . ."

Charlotte held out the note in the palm of her hand, watching Mattie very closely as she realised what Charlotte was holding, her eyes widening in alarm and then horror.

"You shouldn't have taken this," Mattie said, snatching the note back. "This is my private business. It has nothing to do with what has happened to Elizabeth, nothing at all."

"Mattie . . . Mattie." Charlotte let her friend take the letter. "If you know something—something about what Chester's done—then you must see it's wrong to protect him? You must see that. No matter how you may feel, or how he's manipulated your feelings. If you keep him from the law, it would be a great sin, and you can be sure that the next wife to go missing would be you."

"How dare you!" Mattie stood up abruptly, closing the door between them and the children. "How dare you suggest such a thing? Mr. Chester and I were alone for many months before he married Elizabeth. And there was one time when I thought perhaps . . . when he dallied with my feelings and led me to believe that he had honourable intentions towards me. There!—you have forced the humiliating truth out of me. And then, of course, he married an heiress, and it came to nothing, nothing, Charlotte. I kept the note, like a fool, because it is the only such note I have ever been in receipt of. So I kept it, and looked at it sometimes, and dreamt of it coming from a good and decent man that truly loved me. So perhaps that makes me a fool, Charlotte, but *I* would never engage in a liaison with a married man—never. I am nothing like you, after all."

Charlotte recoiled from the comment as if Mattie had slapped her hard about her cheek. Who had been speculating about her time in Brussels with Matilda? Not her dear friend Ellen, surely, for, though Charlotte loved her, she never told her anything. And not Emily, but somehow a whisper had been heard, she was sure about it, otherwise how would Mattie know exactly how to hurt her? Dear God, if her feelings for Monsieur Héger became common gossip amongst the people she hoped respected her, then what? Without her reputation she'd be nothing.

"I think I'd better go," Charlotte said, crossing to the nursery door. "I would ask you not to speak ill of me, Mattie, and in return I will keep your secrets too."

"Charlotte, wait . . ." Mattie caught her arm just as she was leaving. "Please, Charlotte dear, I'm sorry. I didn't mean to . . . You and your sisters have taken such a keen interest in this business—so keen that it sometimes feels a little frightening. But, Charlotte, you must remember it isn't your duty to solve this mystery. Mr. Chester and Mr. Honeychurch have it in hand, and God will be their final judge. We must trust in that." Mattie let go of Charlotte's arm. "All I can hope for now is that I can get the children away safe. Please, forgive my anger and embarrassment—my cruelty. You are my friend, and I would never dishonour you with a misplaced word, I swear it."

Charlotte nodded.

"You said get the children safe?" she asked. "Not *keep* them safe, but *get* them safe? Where would they go? The baby might perhaps go to the Honeychurches, but the boy? He is not their blood."

"I hardly know what I said," Mattie said. "I only mean that I fear for them—I fear for all of us who live under his roof, who are subject to his rage."

"Of course." Briefly Charlotte kissed her friend, taking both her hands. "And yes, I suspect in our enthusiasm to find the truth that we might have been rather bullish. I am truly sorry. You are a good woman, Mattie. I know that you could never do anything that would harm another."

And that was true, Charlotte thought as she relived the conversation again and again on her way back over the moors—that was very true. And yet it was clear that Mattie was unsettled and hiding something.

The question was, what?

28

❦

Charlotte

"Miss Charlotte?" The boy from the Bull, Joseph Earnshaw, was hovering outside the back gate with Mr. Nicholls at his side as Charlotte returned. Charlotte's heart sank rather. Mr. Nicholls was a decent enough man, and Papa certainly liked him much better than the last curate. However, he did not have an easy manner about him, which for a woman who often struggled to have an easy manner herself, made it rather difficult to engage in conversation with him. To make matters worse, Tabby had thrown the laundry over the back wall to dry in the afternoon sun, and among the items displayed there were a number of patched petticoats and, yes, Charlotte groaned inwardly, even a pair of bloomers.

"Joseph?" Charlotte smiled at the lad, who was no more than eleven. "Mr. Nicholls."

"Miss Brontë." Mr. Nicholls blushed deeply as he bowed, which made Charlotte blush in return, a most irritating side effect. "Young Joseph here was after having a word with you."

Charlotte returned her gimlet gaze to John, hoping to pretend that Mr. Nicholls was no longer there, in fact rather wishing he would leave now that they had exchanged pleasantries, as there was no need for him to remain. But remain he did, hovering like an indecisive milkmaid.

Young Joseph, Charlotte knew, had done well at the new school her father had helped found in the last few months, picking up his numbers and
letters with as much speed and enthusiasm as his classmates, a fact that had
brought Papa much pride and joy. When Joseph was not at school he worked
as general dogsbody for Enoch Thomas at the Black Bull to help his widowed mother keep body and soul together.

If this was Black Bull business, then it had to be something to do with
Branwell, Charlotte thought: debts owing, or a feud coming to a boiling
point. Dear God, she hoped it wasn't Mr. Robinson demanding satisfaction
in the form of a duel again. Whatever it was, the acutely uncomfortable look
on Joseph's face did not bode well.

"Speak up, boy," Charlotte instructed him. "I have business to attend to,
and can't wait the whole day for you to spit it out."

"I . . . I feel it might be private, miss," Thomas said, looking at Mr. Nicholls, who blushed deeply again, at once reigniting Charlotte's own face in
the process.

"Ah, well—are you sure you can manage, Miss Brontë?" Mr. Nicholls
asked, no doubt doing his best to be gallant.

"Yes, Mr. Nicholls," Charlotte snapped. "I have managed almost all of
my life without your assistance. I feel sure I will not require it now."

"Right . . ." She did feel a little bad when she saw how Mr. Nicholls's face
fell, but only a little and only for a very short while, because the whole
business of him bowing and saying his good days went on altogether too
long for her to be sorry to see him go.

"Come along, then, Joseph," she said, relieved at last that the curate was
gone.

"It's just that a letter came to the pub, miss, hand-delivered." Joseph
squirmed under her unrelenting gaze, clutching a letter between his paws as
if it were a rag.

"Then it's for Mr. Branwell—I'll take it to him." Charlotte held out her
hand, but Joseph did not give her the letter.

"The complication is, miss . . ." Thomas kept a firm hold on the screwed-up document, positively writhing with discomfort. "It's that it isn't addressed to a Miss or Mr. Brontë, see, miss? It's addressed to Mr. B . . . e . . . ll and Co."

He carefully sounded out each letter.

"Oh!" Charlotte stared at the letter, at once burning with a desperate curiosity to know what was in it. "Oh, well, then. . . . give it to me and I shall deliver it to the correct recipient."

"But it's not addressed to you, miss," Joseph said. "You are a Miss Brontë, not a Mr. Bell."

"And the last I heard, you aren't the postmaster, Joseph Earnshaw, so hand it over," Charlotte demanded, but still the boy held fast. This was why she never wanted to teach boys, Charlotte reminded herself, in case the temptation ever arose again: they were utterly irritating in every respect. Adjusting her expression to something a little less stern, she tried another approach.

"By the way, Joseph, 'complication' is an excellent word to use. I hear that you are doing great things at the school, and I am sure you will go far if you keep up the good work. Now, tell me—if you didn't want someone at the parsonage to take delivery of the letter, then why did you bring it here?" At the very last moment, Charlotte remembered an encouraging smile.

"Because . . ." Joseph looked fraught with discomfort. "Because when it was handed to my master, he said he hadn't heard of any Mr. Bell in Haworth. And him that delivered it said that two bossy and nosy spinsters had given the delivery instructions, and my master told me to bring it up here and ask you about it."

He stared at her wide-eyed, as if he expected to be roasted alive in a flame of fury at any second. Instead Charlotte merely shrugged. After all, she and Emily did fit that description perfectly.

"I see," she said. "'Two insistent and curious women' would have been a better way of expressing it, Joseph—make a note of it. And though I can't think for whom the letter might be, I will take it unopened to Papa, and he will certainly help us find the correct recipients. Now, hand it over and be free of the burden."

Joseph Earnshaw did not need telling again. He stuffed the crumpled envelope into her hands and raced off back down the hill. Charlotte hurried inside, tearing the envelope open as she went.

Anne and Emily didn't return until just before supper the following day: a very long time to have to nurse the letter and its contents to herself—hours of a long, lonely evening and restless night during which she had been unable to settle, turning every puzzle piece over in her mind, still unable to make a complete picture.

"At last," Charlotte said, as soon as her sisters entered, laughing as they unlaced their bonnets. "We have much to discuss."

"Are we not allowed to even remove our boots?" Charlotte halted Emily's complaint by bringing her finger up to her lips and looking pointedly at Patrick's study. Silently she led her sisters into the dining room, closing the door behind them.

"Charlotte, we have travelled the whole day long," Emily said testily as Charlotte indicated that they should sit down. "We are tired and hot, and I would at the very least appreciate a cup of tea."

"Give me a moment and I shall fetch you your precious tea." Charlotte was exasperated. "But first I must show you this letter that came to the Bull yesterday, addressed to the Messrs. Bell." She flourished the letter with quite a good deal of melodrama.

"Oh, good—give it." Emily went to take the letter, but Charlotte whipped it behind her back, pressing herself against the wall to prevent Emily from seizing it.

"Let me see it!" Emily howled, and for a moment they were children again, fighting over a book or a toy.

"I hardly have the patience for this," Anne told them sharply. "Charlotte, let her see the letter—the ruse was Emily's idea, after all."

"Sit down and I'll tell you what is in it." Charlotte would not be moved.

Rolling her eyes, Emily crashed into a chair, Anne taking a seat beside her.

"This is because I made a discovery of the skull and went to Scarborough, isn't it?" Emily sulked. "You are green with envy, and now you want your own moment of discovery, even though all you have discovered is how to open an envelope."

"It was my quick thinking that averted disaster," Charlotte retorted, over-egging the way that she gained possession of the letter just a little. "If I had not persuaded the Earnshaw boy to give it to me, it would have gone to Papa, our detecting would have been discovered, and then all your fun would be over, Emily Jane."

"Well? Read on, then," Emily instructed, with a swipe of her hand.

"Yes, please do," Anne said wearily.

"It says that word of our enquiries in Arunton reached this individual a few days ago, and after some deep thought they decided to respond to our request for information. They do not sign their name, and indeed they explain that another has written this letter on their behalf, as they do not have the ability to read or write themselves. That means that two local people are risking Chester's wrath in creating this document—remember how worried the seamstress was of speaking ill of him? And that he is a man of violence is a matter of common knowledge."

"So many local people seem afraid of Chester," Anne said. "How I would love to make public his despicable secrets so none would ever need to be afraid of him again."

"Quite," Charlotte said, a little perturbed by the furious scowl that marred Anne's sweet face. "The author goes on to say this: 'Just before Mistress Chester's child were due to be born, Chester himself, wearing night clothes woke me in the dead of night and offered me more money than I have ever seen if I would set out at once to Bradford to fetch a particular physician. He told me it were urgent, but when I offered to fetch the Doctor Morely, who lived but a few houses away, Mr. Chester was adamant that it must be this man and no other. So I did as I was bid. At first the doctor didn't wish to attend, but when he heard Mr. Chester's name he came at once.'"

Charlotte looked up at her sisters to be sure of their full attention.

"It seems that once he had delivered the doctor, our man was instructed to wait, and he did, for several hours, until well after the sun was up. As he sat there he thought he could hear screaming and cries for help, 'a terrible plaintive wailing' he describes it as and thought that the baby must be coming, and that mother and child must be close to death. More than once he climbed off his cart to go inside and make enquiries, but then remembered that Chester had told him he would receive no payment at all if he didn't follow his instructions to the letter, and so remained where he was."

"Well, what a fine fellow that will listen to a woman screaming in agony and think of his pocket rather than her well-being," Emily said.

"If he thought that Elizabeth Chester was in labour, he'd hardly be about to crash his way in, would he?" Anne said. "You are just put out because Charlotte wouldn't let you have the letter to read."

"I don't see why she should benefit from the fruits of my genius," Emily grumbled. "Lording over us as if it were her idea to use a pseudonym. We wouldn't have this letter at all if it wasn't for my deft thinking."

"Here, take it," Charlotte said, offering her the letter as if it were a dirty rag. "I only sought to edit down the contents to the vital facts, rather than waste yet more time with you attempting to decipher this terrible handwriting."

"Indeed," Anne said thoughtfully. "That the teller of this tale found someone he trusted to write his story for him at all very much narrows down the field of who they might be. I don't imagine that there are many working folk in Arunton who have had the benefit of a proper education . . ."

"Well? Do you want it?" Charlotte thrust the letter at Emily. "Take it if you want it."

"Just finish it," Emily said, folding her arms under her bosom. "And let us be done with it."

"And so he goes on." Charlotte picked up the letter again. "At last the doctor emerged with Chester. He writes the doctor would not accept payment from Chester, and he told him in front of our informant that he never wished to hear from him again, that all debts had been repaid in full, and that Chester was a fiend and a monster."

"Really?" Emily brightened a little.

"Oh dear," Anne said.

"The physician never spoke once on the journey back to Bradford. The author tells us he cried silent tears like a woman might cry."

"What horrors had poor Elizabeth suffered that would distress a man of medicine, who must be familiar with death and injury, so deeply?" Anne asked, wide-eyed with worry.

"What indeed?" Emily considered. "I suppose it might have been some complication to do with the birth. After all, pregnancy is a perilous time for a woman."

"But if that was all there was to it, there would be no need for secrecy— no need for a particular doctor who was seven miles away in Bradford. And anyway, it was not the birth—as our correspondent tells us that Elizabeth Chester was still with child some days later, and Archie not born for another week."

"Do we know the name of the doctor?" Emily asked. "I believe it would be very interesting to talk with him."

"We do," Charlotte said. "His name is Dr. Charles Prescott of Bradford."

"Then we have our next destination," Emily declared. "And perhaps that might shed some light on the strange circumstances in Scarborough, though the more I discover of the players in this drama, the less I understand the plot."

"I have much to tell you about Mattie." Charlotte nodded. "And yes, I am none the wiser."

"Oh well"—Emily began to unpin her hair at the table—"at least Bradford is just a ten-mile walk away. We can go tomorrow. And this time I will lead the expedition."

"You?" Charlotte asked. "I am the oldest."

"That is plain to see, it's true," Emily returned.

"I am the most articulate," Charlotte said. "Strangers warm to me."

"Only until they get to know you," Emily spat back.

"Whereas you terrify them at first sight!"

"Oh for goodness' sake." Anne stood up, silencing both her sisters.

"There is a woman's life at stake here—we need justice and decency, and all you can do is bicker like children. Emily, you haven't even asked after our brother. Charlotte, you haven't mentioned him either."

"He is home, since sometime last night, in bed, sick from excess, of course!" Charlotte said, furious at the implication that she might not care for her brother.

"Then I shall go and see if I may bring him anything to ease his pain," Anne told her sternly. "We will talk again and exchange our news after supper, and until then I do not wish to hear a peep out of either of you. And I shall lead the expedition to Bradford, for the task should go to an adult, which clearly neither of you are."

Emily and Charlotte were silent until their little sister had left the room and thundered upstairs.

"Quite the tantrum," Emily muttered.

"Well, baby Anne was always the spoilt one," Charlotte agreed. Nevertheless, they argued no more.

29

Charlotte

Doctor Prescott was not at home when the sisters called. They had left home together early that morning to make the trip to Bradford after deciding that writing ahead to the doctor was not the best course of action. They did not wish to give their quarry time to prepare, and if meeting the Honeychurches had taught them anything, it was that a person's initial reaction to their concerns often revealed more than when they spoke aloud.

Charlotte had watched Anne take a quantity of ink and paper to Branwell before they left, asking him to tell Papa they were visiting once again, and to write her a story while they were gone.

"What shall it be about?" Branwell had asked, looking rather forlorn with his scarf wound all about him, even though the day was warm.

"Something exciting, like you used to tell us when we were girls," Anne said. "And you must stay here until it is finished, and be here on this sofa when we return to read it to me, swear it."

"Have no fear," Branwell said. "I will not stir until I have produced a work of shattering genius."

"Good, you must get strong in case we should need you," Anne had said, kissing his forehead.

"You never need me anymore," Branwell had muttered, but it had felt good to know where he was, safe and, if not well, at least cared for and occupied for the next few hours.

Anne's determination to take the lead on the visit seemed to have waned, so preoccupied with her thoughts was she, and so it was Emily who stepped up and rang vigorously at the bell, which was soon answered by a formidable-looking housekeeper, wide of girth, with forearms that looked like they might knead an awful lot of bread.

"Good day." The woman curtsied and looked at Emily expectantly.

"Good day," she smiled pleasantly. "We had hoped that we might be able to secure an appointment with Dr. Prescott today? We have travelled rather far, and the matter is somewhat pressing."

"The doctor does not practise from home," the housekeeper said, rather unhelpfully offering no more information, only staring at them each in turn as if her look might be enough to send them away—and in truth it almost was.

"Who is there, Hattie?" a lady called from within, joining Hattie at the door. Mrs. Prescott, Charlotte determined, was a neat, bright-looking woman of about her own age, smartly dressed and with lively eyes.

"We are Charlotte, Emily and Anne Brontë of Haworth. We hoped to speak to Dr. Prescott about our father?"

"Would that be the Reverend Patrick Brontë, by any chance?" Mrs. Prescott asked, rather unsettling the sisters, who had supposed their family name would mean very little to the doctor's wife.

"Please do come in and take tea with me. I am sure I will be able to arrange an appointment for you. Hattie, see to the tea, please?"

Hattie gave Mrs. Prescott a look of surprising resentment, given that she was only being asked to do her job, and stalked off in the direction of what must be the kitchen.

"The Misses Brontë out of Haworth?" Mrs. Prescott smiled as she showed them into her parlour. "I have read your father's letter in the *Leeds Mercury*, calling for the banning of cotton garments for children to cut accidental deaths by fire, and I must say I support him wholeheartedly. I'm

afraid that last year we saw more than a hundred infants die in such circumstances. It's a tragic waste of life, and so easily preventable."

"Indeed." Charlotte smiled. She warmed at once to Mrs. Prescott, who
spoke with clarity and vigour. She seemed as if she might be something of
a kindred spirit.

Hattie arrived with a rattling tea tray, which she delivered onto a small
walnut table with the same care that a mill worker might unload a bale of
wool. Mrs. Prescott just smiled at her serenely, glancing at the tray. "I'm
afraid Hattie has forgotten the milk, or indeed any lemon. Perhaps we could
just take our tea as it comes?"

"Of course," Charlotte said. "That is how we prefer it, in any case."

"With regard to my husband," Mrs. Prescott continued as she poured the
tea, "I'm afraid that Charles doesn't take appointments at our home—he
only makes house calls to his private patients. I am happy to ask him to call
on you in Haworth, but perhaps you might be able to give me some indication as to how you believe he will be able to help you in a way that your own
physician cannot?"

"It's . . ." Charlotte hesitated. They had not thought this far ahead.

"A personal matter," Emily added. "And one we wish to discuss with a
medic, and not a medic's wife."

Mrs. Prescott instantly bristled, Charlotte noted with interest, showing
the same resentment that she herself experienced every single time she was
dismissed because of her sex.

"What Emily means to say . . ." Anne began, risking her sister's wrath.

"I mean to say that we wish to discuss a medical matter with a medical
person, that is all," Emily told Mrs. Prescott, softening her tone a little. "I
meant no offence—I apologise."

"Of course not." Mrs. Prescott's smile had thinned somewhat. "However,
it may interest you to know that even though I do not possess a medical
degree, I attended all the same classes as my husband at university, and
indeed I did help him complete his studies. If women were allowed to grad-
uate from university, I would have a medical degree too."

"I do find that interesting," Emily said. "Very interesting."

"And I help him every day with his work. In fact, this may shock you, Miss Brontë, but I do believe that if I lived in a world where a woman would be accepted in such a profession, I would make a doctor equally as skilled as my husband." She stopped short of adding *if not more so*, but each woman in the room seemed to hear the words anyway.

"Indeed," Anne agreed vigorously. "And let me assure you, Mrs. Prescott, that if you are familiar with our father's letters then you are familiar with us, for he brought us up to seek something a little like the independence you speak of. We are all professional women, though none of us near as qualified as you."

"Then perhaps if you tell me what the matter is, I may be able to tell you if Robert is the right physician to aid you."

"Our father is almost blind with cataracts," Anne told her. "Our local doctors tell us that there is nothing that can be done for him, but an acquaintance, a Mr. Chester of Arunton, recommended your husband."

Mrs. Prescott's face blanched quite white in an instant, her hand rising unconsciously to her bosom.

"That man recommended Charles to you?" She spoke barely above a whisper, her shoulders trembling. "He dared to say my husband's name?"

"Indeed . . ." Emily went on carefully, glancing at her sisters. They could not have predicted such a strong reaction—it was a visceral display of fear and loathing, in equal measure. "On a visit to the church at Arunton. He told us that Dr. Prescott had treated Chester's wife just before the birth of her son, and that he was very well versed in the latest medical techniques."

"He is," Mrs. Prescott said, making a concerted effort to regain her composure. "He very much is, and we have done a great deal of research on the methods and practices of removing cataracts, carrying out several procedures with good results of success. I do believe that Charles would be happy to see your father. But he won't be home again until this evening, engaged as he is at the infirmary all day. So if you leave your address I will see that he writes to you to arrange an opportunity to examine your father. I know I should very much like him to help such a good, Christian man."

"Then we will trouble you no more," Charlotte said.

"Well, there is just one more thing," Emily countered, reaching in the pocket of her skirt and bringing out something wrapped in paper.

"Tell me, what do you make of these?"

"Emily, please . . ." Charlotte turned to her sister, but it was already too late. Mrs. Prescott was opening the packet and frowning at the contents, which was hardly surprising, for to be confronted with a blackened bone and a human tooth was not a regular occurrence for a respectable married lady.

"Are these related to your father's illness in some way?" she asked, looking up at Emily.

"No, they are artefacts that I discovered on a walk recently, and you are a woman of medicine—I thought you might like to satisfy my curiosity?"

"They are disturbing artefacts," Mrs. Prescott said, holding the tooth up and squinting at it. "This is certainly a human tooth: an incisor. It's an adult tooth, not milk, and from its size and relative lack of decay I would say it belonged to a woman aged between fifteen and perhaps twenty?"

"You can really narrow it down to such a small window?" Emily asked her, impressed.

"Well, you see"—Mrs. Prescott preened a little—"it's not pure enough to be from a younger woman, nor decayed or worn enough to belong to an older one. It's observation, really—that's all."

"You are marvellous," Emily said, grinning at Charlotte, who had to admit her sister's intuition to bring out the gruesome items had been the right one after all.

"And what about the bone?" Emily said. "I thought perhaps a rib."

"It is a rib." Mrs. Prescott smiled at her. "Well done."

"I have read many medical texts," Emily told her, nodding at the bone. "But not enough to confirm that it is human. Are you able to do so, by your observation?"

"The rib was found with the tooth, you say?" Mrs. Prescott ran her finger along the blackened curve of the bone.

"Yes." Emily nodded. "From the same victim?"

"No." Mrs. Prescott shook her head. "You see, a human rib bone is longer and more finely curved than this bone. I'm not an expert in zoology, but from the shape and density, I would guess that this came from a four-legged animal, most likely a pig. I can tell you with certainty that it does not belong to a human."

"Have you dissected many cadavers?" Emily asked Mrs. Prescott, with a naked, ghoulish curiosity that would have made Aunt Branwell turn in her grave.

"Dozens." Mrs. Prescott's eyes sparkled as she replied.

"Utterly marvellous," Emily said, before turning to Charlotte and Anne. "Not a human bone, sisters. This deepens the mystery!" Emily took the bone and thrust it at Charlotte. "A human tooth and a burnt pig bone found together—what on earth can it mean, unless there was a fight over a pig, or . . . ?"

"At which infirmary does your husband work?" Charlotte interrupted Emily before her enthusiasm for Mrs. Prescott's knowledge led her to say more.

"There is only one in Bradford." Mrs. Prescott stared into her teacup for a very long moment, before looking up sharply at Charlotte.

"One thing does rather puzzle me." She smiled. "Why couldn't you have simply written to my husband? It would have been so much more convenient than travelling into the city, with no certain chance of seeing him, and a letter would have been just as fast."

"Of course." Charlotte looked at Anne, who looked at Emily, who looked at the crystal chandelier as if it were the most fascinating thing she had ever seen. "It's just that our father raised us to judge the merit of a person by meeting them in person," Charlotte said after a few awkward moments. "And with a matter so precious as our dear Papa's eyesight, we felt the trip was worthwhile. And indeed it has been, just to make your acquaintance, Mrs. Prescott. I feel quite sure that if a woman such as you has consented to marry Dr. Prescott, then he must be a very fine man."

"Please, do call me Celia." Celia smiled, her colour returning, her eyes alive with curiosity. "And you are right, Miss Brontë, I am a woman of discernment and intellect. So why don't I ask Hattie to make us some more tea, and you may tell me why you are really here?"

30

Anne

"That poor, poor child," Celia said, as Anne relayed to her all that they had discovered so far of the fate of Elizabeth Chester. "The amount of blood you describe would certainly seem to indicate a violent death. Please, do go on."

Anne spoke with an earnest, calm and concise manner as she recalled with forensic care every detail of what had been discovered or reported to them. Wisely, she omitted mentioning Emily's midnight excursion, which, although it would no doubt fascinate this lively woman, had nevertheless been unlawful. The more she talked, and the more she read Celia Prescott's expressions, the more Anne was certain this intelligent and compelling woman would be a friend to them.

As Anne relayed their involvement in the case of Elizabeth Chester, she noticed her sisters fall back. Emily took herself off to a window seat, where she watched the life that unfolded outside as if she weren't anything to do with the indoors goings-on, except, of course, Anne knew that she was listening intently. People talked much more if they didn't think you were taking heed of them, Emily had long ago told her. Anne knew that for most of Emily's life folk had said of her that she was "away with the fairies," and very often she was, but also very often she wasn't. And this was one of those times.

"Did your husband talk to you about his visit to Chester Grange that night?" Anne asked Celia, as she poured yet more tea from a fine bone china teapot covered in hand-painted plump pink roses, this time adding slices of lemon to each cup.

"At first he would not," Celia said unhappily, "though in fairness, he didn't have to. I knew what Chester was capable of, and in many ways what happened to Elizabeth was my fault, and for a while—a good while— Charles blamed me for it."

"Blamed you?" Anne leaned forward a little, her lips parted in curiosity.

Celia thought for a moment as she stirred her tea. Placing her cup carefully in its saucer, she went to the parlour door and shut it firmly.

"I will tell you what I know for the sake of Elizabeth Chester," she said very gravely, so much so that even the noise from the street outside seemed to hush and fade away as she spoke. "I will tell you because in truth I fear that it was my husband and I who failed to save Imogen Chester when there was still a chance. But, dear ladies, I must ask you to swear on your honour that you will not repeat what I say here outside these four walls, for I fear the consequences may be very great for my husband and me."

Emily forgot at once to pretend not to be listening and, peeling herself off her window seat, joined her sisters as they swore to keep their silence.

"Well," Celia continued, "the story I am going to tell you is not one of murder. But it's not for the want of trying."

Outside, the late August afternoon whiled away, a wide, warm, blue sky and the last of the golden sunshine going to waste, while four women sat inside the elegant but shadowy parlour and talked of the very worst of humanity.

"When I first met Charles, seven years ago," Celia told them with a small, sad smile, "he was not the man he is today. Today he is a fine physician who works tirelessly to better the lot of the poor, although it costs him the fees he might otherwise earn from having the time to take on a greater number of wealthy patients. He is good and kind and sweet. He is the man I love with all of my heart."

Anne nodded, smiling slightly, as she thought what a wonder it must be to love and be loved as two equals, united in determination to live good lives. Perhaps Charlotte was right not to dismiss the possibility of such a marriage yet, for a marriage such as this one might bring great purpose and satisfaction with it.

"But"—Celia lowered her eyes—"when I first began to attend the university lectures, he was not like my husband of today at all. He was young, impetuous, with a fondness for excess. Like many men his age, he had friends with whom he would study, discuss science and medicine. And drink . . . and gamble."

"You cannot shock us," Emily assured Celia as she faltered. "Our brother has similar interests, and has yet to outgrow them."

"Well, there were . . . there were women too," Celia added, her mouth twitching in distaste.

"There have been women in our brother's life also—women that we fervently hope he will come to regret one day," Anne told her. "If only he would meet a woman such as you, who could elevate him to greater things."

"He'd have to stay sober for five minutes first," Emily said.

"Well, I noticed Charles at once." Celia's smile deepened at the recollection. "Even if he was a little unkempt and wild. Because in a room of earnest and imperious young men, he was the only one, aside from myself, who seemed to take true joy in what we were learning. And he spoke to me, the only other of my fellow students who would bid me a polite good day. The other men there preferred to pretend that I didn't exist, and I wasn't sorry that they did. But after a while I began to notice that he would often be seen in the company of an older man, not a student. This man was Robert Chester.

"Chester took part in, indeed instigated, many of the goings-on, even though he himself was recently married to his first wife, Imogen. As his association with Chester developed," Celia told them, "so did our acquaintance, under the guidance of my mother, of course. It was as if he had two lives: this one with me, where he'd take afternoon tea and stroll around the park under a parasol, and a life with Chester—a dangerous life, where drink and opium were taken, and women of easy virtue would often be present." Celia's forehead furrowed as she thought of those days, knitting together her raven dark brows with an expression of pain. "On one occasion—a concert recital—I met Imogen Chester. Her husband left her with myself and my family while he retired to the bar with Charles. She was still a new bride, and honestly, I have never seen a woman more striking: tall and elegant, dark hair and fair skin, and eyes that were the restless blue of the sea, ever changing. I remember them so very clearly because once I had met her gaze I couldn't look away from her—rather as with you, Charlotte." She smiled at Charlotte. "At the time I asked her how she was finding married life. Her response was so peculiar, I should have known she was very unhappy.

"'I find marriage a strange navigation,' she said, her voice sounding almost distant, as though it were coming from another. 'Like being lost in an unknown land without a compass.'

"It was such a strange comment, I think I made light of it, passed over it, but now . . . now I can only imagine how strange and frightening married life must have been for her.

"Her words stayed with me, though, and I often thought of them when I was weighing up my love for Charles against his wilder pursuits. It was one afternoon, in my mother's garden, when he confessed how he wished to end his other life, and devote all that he was to me. Tears ran down his face as he told me he wished to marry me, but could not do so in all good conscience until he had confessed every last sin and unburdened his soul. He swore on my pocket prayer book that if I would marry him, he would give up Chester's influence and debauchery, and be a good and faithful husband to me, and a good and faithful man to God. He begged me to save him from becoming a man as dark and as twisted as his 'friend.'"

"I would have said no," Anne said at once. Charlotte looked at her in surprise. "Well, I would have—a man should not need rescuing to be good and Christian. He should be capable of coming to the way of the Lord on his own account. And one that could not, would not be a good enough man for me to marry."

"There will never be a man good enough for you to marry," Emily told Anne with a smile. "You are altogether too good for this world."

Charlotte turned back to Celia. "If I loved a man who asked the same of me, I should be happy to guide him to the right path. Is that not the duty of a wife, to become the best part of her husband?"

"The truth is," Celia conceded, "by that time I was so in love with the man that I knew I couldn't countenance the idea of living without him. I realised there was a chance I would be forever lost and alone, as Imogen seemed to be, and yet I was prepared to risk it. Even if he had not been true to his word, even if the rest of my life had been as dark and as miserable as it easily might have been, I would still have married him, because my heart could not deny him."

"Yes, yes," Charlotte agreed fervently, "one cannot choose who one loves!"

"That one can't," Emily muttered to Anne, who repressed a smile.

"Happily, Charles was as good as his word. He came to me a man clean in body and soul, and the first few weeks of our married life together were as perfect and as blissful as any young woman can imagine.

"And then one night, soon after we returned from Italy, Chester came hammering on our door." Celia's smiled faded. She straightened her back as she remembered the awful night. "Charles told me to stay in my room, but of all my marriage vows, obedience is the one that tests me the most. And so I crept out of my bedroom and watched from the upstairs landing. As soon as I saw who was there, I was afraid that he was about to break his vow to me."

"What did Chester want?" Anne asked.

"In his arms was the broken and bloody body of a woman," Celia said, her voice barely more than a whisper now. "The poor creature was hardly alive, but I was able to make out from the colour of her hair that it wasn't Imogen. Chester more or less dropped her on to the hall tiles, and I heard him say, in words that I cannot repeat here, that he had kept her for a while, but tired of her whining, and when he told her that he was putting her out on the street, she flew into a rage and he had to defend himself against her. But there was not a mark on him, and she . . ." She shook her head, swallowing hard as she recalled the scene. "She was grievously injured.

"Chester asked Charles to see if he could save her, and told him to keep his name out of it. At first Charles refused, but at that point I could keep silent no more. I ran down the stairs and begged him to take the poor girl in. Finally Charles relented, sending Chester on his way.

"That night I acted as Charles's nurse for the first time. As he stitched and set bones, I bathed and soothed the poor woman, easing her pain as best I could. As we examined her we discovered more and more injuries, and we realised that she had endured an attack much worse than we had imagined."

"Oh, dear Lord," Anne whispered, turning to Emily, who had grown quite pale at such a thought.

"How terrible to think that such devils walk amongst us," Charlotte whispered, reaching out for Anne's hand. The more they heard, the less hope there seemed to be for poor Elizabeth Chester.

"Our patient was on the point of death for many days, but I stayed at her side, and with great care Charles and I brought Hattie back from the brink."

"Hattie?" Anne looked towards the door she had last seen the house-keeper walk through.

"Yes," Celia said. "I would not let her go back to her previous profession, or the workhouse. So I kept her with us. Our cook has also been rescued from the streets. Although we can't take any more here, it's my dream to find useful employment for all the women of Bradford who are forced into . . ."

"Prostitution," Emily finished for her with an approving nod. "I think you are the finest person I have ever met."

"Thank you." Celia's smile was a little puzzled. "Though I fear your opinion may alter when you hear the last part of my story. Charles was so sickened and horrified at what had happened that he wanted to go to the authorities and report Chester. It was I who begged him not to."

The sisters said nothing, and for a moment there was only silence in the room, save for the ticking of the clock, and Anne wondered if it marked what remained of Elizabeth Chester's life, or if that time had already passed.

"We were newly married," Celia explained. "Charles had only recently begun practising. If we were to do the good works we both dreamt of, my husband needed a spotless reputation in order to acquire a list of patients who could pay for treatment. Chester was—is—a man of influence. To come up against him, to try to bring to light the life he led and the terrible things that he did was a risk I was too cowardly to take. I knew that Chester had within his reach the power to ruin us. In my mind I thought that, as we had saved Hattie, we had righted Chester's wrongs, and that was enough. After I begged him, Charles relented. But it was a mistake, because now Chester thought of him as an accomplice. Shortly afterwards, I wrote to Imogen. I offered her plainly a place to go if she needed safe haven for her and her new baby. But she never replied. Then news came of Imogen's death. Chester said she had been ill, but Chester lied, and I kept on thinking of her, so alone, so isolated, and how I should have made Charles take me there to her, but I was too afraid of what I would discover. Then years passed, and we had no dealings with him—I hadn't even heard that he had remarried. And then. . . . then came the night he attended on Elizabeth Chester."

"So Chester had beaten her too, then?" Anne asked, her eyes filling with tears. "Even though she was heavy with his child?"

"And worse." Celia nodded. "That morning when he returned, Charles could not look at me, so furious was he that we had hidden Chester's true nature for so long. For a while I thought I had lost his love. It was a terrible time, to think of spending the rest of my life married to a man that hated me, and not to blame him for that hate. Then gradually he forgave me. And my husband taught me that it is a sacred duty never to turn your face away from evil. Instead we vowed always to shine a light upon it, declare it to the world, no matter what it might cost us personally."

"Which is exactly what *we* want to do," Charlotte said. "Now with a more pressing need than ever."

"The next day, Charles went to the constable, and a visit was paid to Elizabeth Chester. But, even though she was so badly hurt, she claimed that she had fainted and fallen down the stairs and the constable had no will to press her. And when I thought of my letters to Imogen I realised that he frightened his wives, threatened them sufficiently to prevent them from crying out for help. I told myself there was no more that could be done, not by me."

"To be too afraid to speak out," Anne said unhappily. "Such is the sway he had over her."

"If it should be needed, I will speak up, and so will Charles. We will not let Chester escape again," Celia told them. "Because if Elizabeth Chester is harmed, if she is murdered, Misses Brontë, make no mistake—just like Imogen's, her blood will be on my hands."

31

Emily

"What is the answer?" Emily asked, pausing for a moment on the crest of the steep hill that would lead them down to the foot of Haworth. "When we find it, will we recognise it? Perhaps we already have the answer, and we just haven't understood it yet."

"What are you talking about, Emily?" Anne turned back to her sister.

"That we need to look again at everything we have collected," Emily said, her pace quickening. "We have been looking for something like a signpost, something that will tell us exactly what has happened, but that isn't detecting, Sisters. Detecting is reading between the lines—it's seeing what is *not* there."

"Sometimes I think that all that weather you insist on going out in without your bonnet on has turned your mind to mush," Anne called after Emily as she broke into a trot, leaning into the turning of the earth. Emily squealed with joy, her arms outstretched, the wind twisting her sleeves into fluttering wings, as she embraced the freshness of the evening as if it were a purifying balm, cleansing her of all the terrible things Mrs. Prescott had told them. And just for a moment she was flying, soaring like a lark, diving like curlew. For a moment she was free of gravity and every earthly duty. In the next she was tumbling headlong into the soft spring of the heather, a rock catching at her stockings, the earth burning along her cheek as she came to a skidding halt. Rolling over, Emily tasted blood on her lip, but as she looked up at the dome of heaven arcing endlessly overhead, all she could do was laugh with joy for the sheer beauty of it all.

Her sister's bonnet-framed face peered down at her, and Emily laughed even louder as the first drops of rain cooled her cheeks.

"Mind to mush, I tell you," Anne said. "Mind to mush."

When at last they did reach home, Emily was bleeding at the knee, her face still smeared with traces of peat despite Charlotte's ministrations with spit and her handkerchief. In a great state of agitation, their father was waiting for them to come in through the door.

"Papa"—Charlotte went to him at once—"please tell me what the matter is. Is it your eyes? Or do you have a pain?"

"Charlotte," he said very gravely, addressing her, then each of the women. "Daughters, all—are you going to explain to me the comings and goings of late? The truth of it this time. I give you license to come and go as you please—you are all your own women—but as a father I am duty-bound to enquire after your welfare, physical and . . . moral. You gave me your word that you were conducting yourselves with the integrity I expect from you, but you are never here. You do not say where you go, or what you are about. Must I treat you like children after all, and confine you to the house without your supper?"

It did not help that Emily snorted a stifled laugh, like a caught-out schoolgirl.

"You laugh, Emily Jane," Patrick said sternly, smothering her giggle with a look, "and yet as poor as my eyesight is I see you, looking as unruly as a schoolboy. I have a reputation to think of, you know. Our position here is based solely on my good name, your futures on yours."

"Well, if Branwell can't shift you from your position after his carryings-on, I hardly see how a grazed knee and heather in my hair would do the trick," Emily mumbled.

"You went up onto the moors and met with a gentleman you do not know," Patrick scolded her. Emily's chin dropped. "Branwell has told me everything."

"Everything?" Charlotte gasped, looking at Anne.

"Yes, I found him writing in the dining room, so I brought him into my study to work with me. I asked him about your absences. And he told me all he knows."

"Papa," Emily said, unhappily, "how many times do you find us writing and you never bring us into your study to work alongside you!"

"You are young women!" Papa bellowed, his raised voice coinciding with a clap of thunder overhead. "Your writing is not work in the same way that it is for your brother. In Branwell we might yet find the path that will deliver his true talent to the world!" It took Emily all her might to keep her mouth closed; only the prospect of further upsetting her father made it possible.

"And I do not speak to you of your writings," he went on. "I speak to you of your carryings-on!"

"What did Branwell tell you, Papa?" Charlotte asked so quietly her voice could hardly be heard over the clatter of rain against the window.

"I told Papa of how much of Aunt Branwell's money you had spent searching out potential schools, and that you had gotten nowhere in your search and that I feared that we were rather overestimating your acumen, and that perhaps you should not be trusted with money and that I'd be happy to take charge of it for you," said Branwell, emerging from the dining room.

At least a day in front of Papa's fire had done her brother good, Emily thought. His colour was improved; he was washed and in clean attire, and it seemed that he was fully sober at last. Even so, at that exact moment she felt rather like murdering him with a fire poke.

"And a young gentleman called Mr. Purbeck came to the parsonage seeking you out, Emily," Branwell said. "You made rather an impression on him when you met him in the heather, it seems."

"I did not!" Emily said. "I have never heard of such nonsense. All that happened was I wished him a good day when we met on the moor, Papa. You know me better than any! I am not the sort to cavort through the heather with a young man. That's much more Charlotte's thing."

"Emily!" Charlotte hissed.

"I see what has happened here," Anne said, stepping forward to tuck her arm through her father's and guiding him into the cosy dining room, reversing Branwell onto the sofa as she did so. Emily and Charlotte followed behind, Charlotte going at once to warm herself by the fire.

"We have been much away from home," Anne went on. "But Branwell, who has been quite unwell, has misconstrued the extent of our expenses. After all, Papa, he isn't very good at sums, is he? Remember the missing funds at Luddenden Foot?" As Anne spoke, Emily raised an eyebrow at Branwell, who narrowed his eyes in return. Her little sister was the very definition of still waters running deep.

"And you, dearest dear Papa, have become worried where there is *no* need," Anne went on soothingly, gesturing at her sisters. "You may see with your own eyes that we are just as we have always been, Charlotte good and intelligent, myself obedient and mild and Emily is as always very much . . . herself."

Patrick peered from one daughter to the other, and Emily saw the lines of his concern ease a little as he seemed to observe that Anne was right, they were exactly as they had always been in his eyes.

"And today's excursion?" he asked them, turning to Charlotte, who looked guilty at once.

"Well, we . . ." Charlotte floundered.

"Branwell is right in that we were thinking of a school again," Anne said matter-of-factly. "Scarborough was not suitable, so we went to Bradford, to look at a location that Ellen Nussey had suggested to us might be both economical and suitable." She smiled at her father, leaning her head onto his shoulder for a moment. "That is all, Papa. We didn't want to trouble you until we had some notion of being successful." At Anne's beckoning, Papa took a seat at the table next to her.

"Now," Emily said, "isn't this lovely, here we are all together, safe and warm inside our little house, while the storm rages on without. Why don't I go and fetch us all some tea, and perhaps we can all eat supper together this evening? For it has been such a very long time, has it not?"

"Indeed, it seems like an eternity," Papa said, smiling as Anne took his hand in hers.

"You may pull the wool over Mr. Brontë's eyes," Tabby said as she helped Emily arrange a supper of cold meat, bread and tea on two trays. The steady beat of rain that was leaking through the roof in the outer kitchen could be heard drumming into the copper pot that Martha had placed beneath it, and the roar of the wind at their back, tearing off the moor at speed. "But I'm wise to you girls, don't you mistake it; whatever you are about, you be careful. Your pa's had more 'un his fair share of sadness, don't you be adding to it. Martha here's got more sense than the four of you put together, don't you, girl?"

"I hardly know," Martha said, smiling at Emily. "The Misses Brontë are the cleverest people I know, so I don't presume to judge them."

"See?" Tabby said, as if Martha had agreed wholeheartedly with her. "More sense than any of you. You forget, Miss Emily, I raised you. Your good, dear, late aunt might have seen to your manners and your lessons, but it were me that had you at my knee by the fireside, me who told you stories, nursed you when you were sick and fed you and taught you how to bake . . ."

Emily's smile faded as she saw the tears standing in Tabby's eyes reflecting the flickering kitchen candlelight, and heard the worry in her voice. Tabby, who was never scared of anything, not the ghosts and gytrash that stalked the moors of her bedtime stories or even the devil himself. Tabby, who had been so badly injured when she'd broken her leg years back that all thought she would die, but who refused to die, and who refused to be still even though she was lame and full of constant pain, was *scared* for her. And for a moment, Tabby's fear made Emily afraid too.

"Mind yourself while there is a fiend on the loose," she said, turning her back on Emily, and shrugging off the hand that Martha put on her shoulder. "That's all I'm saying."

"Don't be afraid for us, Tabby," Emily said gently, summoning back her courage. "I swear to you that we will always be safe. Not one of us would ever want to bring more grief to this house, to Papa, or to you."

Just as Emily picked up the first supper tray, a great hammering filled the house, merging once again with the thunder to make it seem as if the whole of their little house shook in its foundations.

Someone was beating on the door as if their very life depended on it. Setting down the tray, Emily ran into the hallway, where Charlotte and Anne were already at the door. As Charlotte flung it open, lightning whipped across the sky, revealing a startling image. Matilda French, drenched in rain and wrought with terror.

"Let me in, I beg you!" she cried. "Let me in before I am killed!"

32

Charlotte

"What is this?" Papa asked as Charlotte brought Mattie into the hallway, the rainwater running off of her in icy rivulets. "What has happened?"

"I cannot say, Papa," Charlotte said in a hushed tone as Anne wrapped a cloak around the woman, rubbing her arms briskly. "But I know this lady. She is my old school friend, Matilda French. Perhaps you had better take supper in your study after all, while we see to her?"

Papa looked at the hysterical woman with grave concern.

"Perhaps that would be best. When she is calmer and you have discovered what ails her, tell me how best I may assist. I can send for the doctor or her family; we can offer shelter and sustenance of course."

"Thank you, dear Papa," Charlotte said, resting her palm for a moment on his whiskers, as Anne bundled Matilda into the dining room, closely followed by Emily.

"Charlotte." Papa placed his hand over hers, trapping it for a second against his cheek. "I have believed your stories, always, because I do not wish to disbelieve my own children, who I have raised to know the consequences of deceit . . ."

"Papa . . ." He raised his other hand to silence her.

"I know that you and your sisters are engaged in some business that you see fit not to share with me, and I know this young woman is part of it and I suspect it has something to do with that terrible event at Arunton. In seeing her distress I can only commend your determination to assist your friend, and I choose to suppose it is a delicate matter that she wishes kept private. But please know that I will offer help without judgement whenever I am called upon, as the Lord directs me. And please, my dear child, keep you and your sisters safe from harm."

"You are the best of men, Papa." Charlotte took his hand and kissed it. "The very best of men."

Charlotte waited until her father's study door was shut, and until Anne had shut the door on the dining room too, before she addressed her friend.

"Mattie!" Charlotte guided her to the sofa, tears streaming down the bedraggled woman's red-raw face. Her sodden skirts were splattered with mud, and her hair was ratted and half-fallen down. With a sense of dread Charlotte noted how the lace of Mattie's collar was torn, rent from the wool of her dress with such force that it had ripped the garment itself. "Oh, my poor, poor friend, tell us at once what the matter is."

At the sight of three friendly faces at last, Mattie was once more set off, and for several minutes was too overwhelmed with emotion to be able to speak: she seemed truly inconsolable. Leaning into Charlotte's shoulder, she wept and wept until Charlotte felt the damp of her tears seep through her dress.

"Here, Mattie dear"—Anne knelt before the weeping woman—"take my handkerchief. Emily, go to the kitchen and find towels and the brandy we had last at Christmas for the pudding. It may help calm her."

"It may help calm *me*," Emily muttered as she went to search, and was immediately thwarted by the presence of Mr. Nicholls in the hallway, hovering outside her father's study. Charlotte watched the awkward encounter over the top of Mattie's head, wincing with every passing second.

"Miss Emily," he greeted her, with the same sort of shy inadequacy that he always did, Charlotte was quietly appalled to note.

"Mr. Nicholls." Emily inclined her head and went to walk around him, but in attempting to step out of her way, he stepped into it, a miscalculation that between them they performed three more times, until what little patience Emily had entirely evaporated.

"Dear Lord, please remove yourself from my path!" Emily told him, all but shoving him out of the way.

"I do apologise, Miss Emily!" he called after her as she stormed to the kitchen, but Emily did not bother replying, and for once Charlotte wasn't offended by her sister's rudeness, for she couldn't imagine anyone less interesting than her father's latest curate. Perhaps, if she got to know him, she might find that he had hidden depths, but the truth was, he'd probably be dead or disgraced within the month anyway, so it hardly seemed worth the effort.

When Emily returned with the brandy bottle, which, Charlotte suspected was somewhat lighter than when she had found it, she leant against the dining room door to prevent an extremely curious Tabby or her papa from entering and hearing details that would probably induce conniptions in both.

After a strong nip of bad brandy, Mattie, a little drier than she had been, composed herself enough to talk.

"I had to leave at once," she told Charlotte. "That very second. I couldn't even return to my room to collect anything. I feared . . . I feared for my life."

With the crackle in the grate of the fire that Anne had built up once more against the wind that battled its warmth by gusting down the chimney, her three friends were around her, and little Flossy on her lap. When Mattie began to speak, it was with a subdued, even oddly calm voice.

"What did he do to you?" Anne asked her gently.

"I was with the children in the garden," Mattie began. "It was such a pretty morning, I'd taken Francis out to learn his letters, and I was carrying Archie in my arms. I thought perhaps the air and sunlight might do something to help Francis's poor broken heart. He was very quiet and pensive, and at last, after much coaxing, he told me how much he missed his mamas, both of them, and that he hoped more than anything he wouldn't lose me too. I almost . . . I almost broke then, but I had to tell myself that all I did was for him and for the baby—to bring them to a place of safety—and that I could not turn away from that endeavour, not now, when they needed me the most. Then I saw him—Mr. Chester—walking down towards me from the house.

"'Your papa has come to see you,' I said to the boys, supposing we had best remain where we were until he reached us. It was quite a distance, and the closer to us he came, the more I realised how very fast he was walking, more like marching really. And then I saw how his fists were clenched, and finally, the expression on his face. It was bright red and masked in fury, his black eyes burning with such hate, staring right into me. Though I couldn't fathom why, I realised at once that he meant to harm me. I knew it as I know the sky is blue, or that my name is Matilda French. I took Francis's hand and began to hurry away from him. I had half an idea that I might be able to circle round to the back of the house and find a way in through the kitchen, but of course, with a small boy and a baby, I was no match for him. He was on us in seconds."

"Oh, my dear girl, how frightened you must have been," Charlotte said, raising her hand to rest it on Mattie's face. "How did you escape?"

"Wait a minute," Emily interrupted her. "She hasn't told us the middle part yet. What happened when he caught you?"

"She may not wish to," Charlotte said in that low, sensible tone of admonishment that Emily found particularly irritating.

"Of course she wants to," Emily said. "It's the most interesting bit . . . I mean the most important part of the . . . incident."

"I do not wish ever to think of it again," Mattie said, "but I shall, for I believe that the whole truth must be spoken. As he came level, he grabbed my arm, twisting it towards him, so that I was forced to let go of little Francis's hand.

"'Sir, what is the meaning of this?' I asked him, trying to keep composed, though my heart raced so, I thought that at any moment it might burst in my chest.

"'You,' he said to me, his eyes boring into me, his grip on my arm so tight I felt my bones creak under the pressure. 'I know it's you. I know it is you standing over my bed, staring at me every night, vanishing just a second after I open my eyes. I know it's your cold hands that grab at me and pinch and pull at me. You, you are trying to drive me mad with your trickery, but I will not let you, do you hear me? I will not let you!'"

"He accused you of grabbing him with cold hands?" Emily said, thoughtfully. "Interesting."

"He raised his fist, as if to strike me," Mattie went on, "and I cried out, 'Sir, I am holding your child!' With this furious growl he grabbed the baby from me and, taking hold of my wrist, dragged me back to the house. I truly believed I was about to be murdered, so I screamed and screamed, hoping that there might be someone in the stable or woods who would hear me, but none came. When we got back to the house, the boys were both frightened and crying, and Mrs. Crawley was there, waiting."

Mattie gazed into the fire as she recalled the events, the bright flames leaping in her eyes.

"'I beg you, help me!' I asked Mrs. Crawley, but her face was set like stone. There was no kindness, no compassion; it was as if she had resolved not to see me. She simply took the baby and the child and led them away. I knew then that there was no hope of help. He dragged me into his office, pinning me against his desk."

"Oh, dear Lord," Anne gasped, her eyes wide. Charlotte's hand tightened around Mattie's.

"He had his hands around my throat," Mattie continued, "and I could see this anger and hate in his eyes. 'Tell me it's you,' he said, squeezing my throat so hard that all began to go dark. 'Tell me!'"

"What did you do?" Charlotte asked her.

"Nothing," Mattie said. "Nothing—there was nothing I could do. And I believe if it hadn't have been for the painting, I would be dead now."

"The painting?" Anne asked, recalling her own visit to Chester's study. "The portrait of Imogen Chester? How did that help, Mattie?"

"It flew off the wall," Mattie told her. "Or at least that's how it seemed, in the heat of the moment, that it was torn off and thrown at him. But in any case, it fell, with a crash loud enough to distract him and hard enough for me to hear the canvas tear. He relaxed his grip on me just enough for me to be able to shove him off. And in that moment I ran. I ran and I kept running, out of the house, out of the grounds, and I didn't look back, not once. I have nothing: not my clothes, not wages, not my few belongings—nothing at all. The only place I could think of to come was here."

"And, of course, wherever I am will always be a refuge for you, Mattie," Charlotte told her. Anne nodded in agreement. "I am ashamed to say that I feel it is our fault that you have been left in such a dangerous situation. The more we discovered about Chester, the worse he was proven to be. And even though it was only today that we truly learned what an awful sort of man he is, we should have extracted you from danger sooner. I'm so sorry, Mattie—we failed you."

"That isn't true, Charlotte. I did not wish to leave those poor innocent children, nor him, if I am honest." Mattie's voice tightened in a sob as she thought of the last time she saw them. "I still do not wish to leave the boys for anything. I fear for those dear children and what will become of them. I cannot tell you how much I fear for them, and the thought of what he might do to them."

Charlotte tightened her arm around Mattie as Flossy struggled free at last, running at once to the door, scratching to be let out.

"This attack cannot pass—we must report it to the authorities at once," Charlotte told her sisters, her mouth set in determination.

"But we do not know what has happened to Elizabeth yet!" Emily exclaimed in frustration. "Chester has the law in his pocket. It's most likely the whole incident will be brushed away as the rantings of a jealous and hysterical woman, or if the truth is discovered, then it will not be our discovery!"

"Does that matter more than the lives of two small children?" Anne asked her.

"No," Emily said after a moment, in a tone that indicated she didn't entirely mean it, "but we are talking of a man who keeps the bones of his first wife under his bed; he is not a man we should cross lightly."

"B-bones . . . under his bed?" Mattie stuttered.

"Emily!" Charlotte spoke sharply, as Mattie's tears began anew. "I think we have had quite enough horror today. We have done all we may do; all that three clergyman's daughters might be expected to do; more, even. The chase is over—this terrible incident has ended the game. I will go to Papa and ask him how one goes about reporting such an attack."

"Well, you are wrong." Emily stood up abruptly. "You are damn wrong, Charlotte."

"*Emily!*" Anne stared up at her sister. "How can you speak to our sister that way? Or use such language in our father's house? And I am in accord with Charlotte: we must get the children out of danger as soon as is possible."

"Not about that," Emily said, utterly unapologetic. "About doing as much as we can, about being no more than three clergyman's daughters. Charlotte knows—*you* know, Anne—that we are more than that; that we three are much more than that. We have intellects that are a thousand times more powerful than any country constable, and something much more important and useful than *facts*."

Emily slammed her hands down on the table.

"We have imaginations," she said. "Great, powerful imaginations that enable us to see into the heads of anyone, even monsters like Chester. We can walk unseen amongst them, that great mass of humanity outside of this house, and *know* how they think and feel, what they want and what they will do to get it. I do believe that if we think for a moment, collect what we know of Chester, we can draw up a kind of portrait of him that could help us predict his next actions: a profile of his psyche—his mind and behaviour, you might say."

Anne and Charlotte exchanged a look, and Charlotte had to admit that her sister almost had her, for if anyone knew the power of imagination to interpret the world it was Emily. And she knew that each one of them would like to see this through to the end as much as she would. It was just that she and Anne felt so much more tightly bound to convention than Emily did. It often felt that their attempts to try to be proper did nothing but fetter them—and they failed over and over again anyway. Perhaps destiny simply didn't mean for them to be respectable. And yet . . . And yet all that Charlotte wanted in the world was approval. Acclaim. And to be the author of her own future. An unrespectable woman would never be allowed to achieve such heights.

"Emily, I do understand your passion. I myself have a burning need for more than just . . . *this*"—Charlotte gestured at their little dining room— "but we cannot continue, not while the children are in danger. If you asked me to predict what Chester might do next, then I would say he is a man who is quite mad, a man who we know has committed acts of great violence; a man who might look around him and, seeing his world begin to crumble, be capable of anything. This is separate from the mystery of the vanished bride."

"How can we possibly know that until we have solved the mystery? We don't know if Chester has killed his wife, or imprisoned her somewhere—or if another person has done the deed. Please, wait for just a few more minutes. Let us review everything we have, and see if we can't try and discern the truth of the matter before we give up entirely." Emily turned to Mattie, falling to her knees to take her hands in hers.

"Mattie, you must be worn out. Why don't we find you a change of clothes, you are quite close to Anne in build, and you may lie down on my bed in the little room at the front, and rest your eyes awhile? Charlotte and Anne and I just need a little more time to decide what best to do next. Would that be agreeable?"

Mattie turned to Charlotte, who thought for a moment.

"I believe that a lie-down would do you good, Mattie dear. I'll take you up, and Emily and Anne, perhaps you can fetch all the particulars so that we may examine them once more."

"Very well, Charlotte," Mattie said, allowing herself to be guided from the room.

"This is the right course," Emily whispered to Charlotte as she shepherded Mattie out of the room.

"Let us pray that it is so," Charlotte said, looking at her sister very grimly, "for to take the wrong course now could have very grave consequences."

33

Emily

When all of the physical evidence was laid out on the table, it looked disparate and paltry. Suddenly, Emily feared that she had made an error in overestimating their skills. What on earth could there be on this table that could tell them anything new?

The parlour seemed very small and close, the rain hammering down, the wind so fierce that from time to time it would gust the smoke that billowed up the chimney right back into the room, so that it seemed to Emily that the mist from the moors was creeping in through every crack and crevice.

"You looked through the papers that you took, didn't you?" Anne asked Emily, drawing the small pile of crumpled correspondence towards her, her fingers resting on the strange assortment as if she might divine some information through touch alone.

"Yes," Emily said, reaching for the souvenir pebble, and feeling the small, cool weight of it in her palm. If only she could discern the moment it marked by holding it, somehow summoning an image of that precious memory out of thin air, she felt certain it would be the key to understanding all. "Nothing interesting—estate business, as far as I can see."

"And there is nothing else that you can remember seeing or hearing on your excursion to Chester Grange that might give an indication as to what happened to Elizabeth?" Charlotte asked, examining her sister closely.

"Nothing," Emily lied.

She had chosen not to tell them of the more curious parts of her adventure—how the button materialised out of the shadows, or the icy hand that had gripped hers in Chester's study—for she knew that her sisters would dismiss it as another of her fancies, and she could not have blamed them if they did. It did seem incredible. But there was a reason other than simply fear or ridicule: that moment, whatever it had been, was hers, the promise she made there just for her to know about. And it would be a promise that she would keep alone too, for she took her vow to the dead of Chester Grange just as seriously as she took any she had ever made to the living.

Emily shuddered, feeling as if someone had just walked over her grave, and she had to wait for a moment for the touch of the world beyond to pass by before she could speak again.

"There's something here—I feel it," she muttered. "I just can't put my finger on what it is yet, but I will."

"Well, Emily," Anne said primly, re-sorting the papers into a pile, "I do believe that these dull papers you looked at actually contain a great deal of pertinent information. In fact I have discovered two things that may be useful."

Emily leant back in her chair. "Really? In amongst the accounts and bills there's a signed confession?"

"Really," Anne replied, enjoying the moment far too much. "Wasn't it you, Emily, who said that we should be reading between the lines?"

"Well, go on," Charlotte urged. "Now is not the time for theatre, Anne."

"Oh, I see—when it's you or Emily being dramatic, it's justified, but when it is I, it's 'theatre.'" Anne sighed. "Well, *firstly*, I discovered that Chester is in a great deal of debt—a huge amount, in fact. No wonder he wanted a rich young bride to fill his coffers again rather than make good his advances to poor, penniless Mattie. What's more, if it should be discovered that something has happened to her, then the vital income that he receives monthly from his father-in-law would stop, leaving him quite destitute. So now, at least, we understand why Chester wasn't in a hurry to tell Mr.

Honeychurch about Elizabeth's disappearance. He was afraid of being out of pocket."

"What a very fine gentleman he is," Emily said dryly. "A good discovery, Anne."

"I didn't really have to discover it." Anne's smile was subtle. "It was already there. I just had to look properly. Sometimes looking is more effective than gallivanting."

"But not half so much fun." Emily smiled.

"But what of the income from his tenants?" Charlotte pushed her eyeglasses up her nose, pinching her forehead, as she often did when her eyes were tired. "Surely that is sizeable."

"I cannot tell the full details from what I have here." Anne spread the papers out on the table for her sister's inspection. "But it seems to me that he has either secretly sold them or gambled much of his properties away. So the people of the village *think* it's Chester they are paying rent to—that they must bow down to him in order to keep their homes—but really it's just a façade to keep face. His creditors own most of Arunton now."

"In that case . . ." Emily had been rocking her chair onto its back two legs in precisely the way that drove Charlotte mad, but as the thought struck her she stood up, tipping the chair onto its back with a clatter. "He has no motive for murdering Elizabeth—no motive at all. Don't you see, if she dies he loses everything he has . . . unless his madness is so compelling it drove him to murder her when it would also harm himself?"

"There is more," Anne said, drawing out a fragment of creased brown paper. "Something that I believe is key—this empty parcel wrapper. It is addressed to Mrs. Elizabeth Chester, and it's postmarked the day that Elizabeth was discovered missing."

Emily reached across the table to take the large piece of ripped and creased brown paper from Anne and examined it, shaking her head.

"And?" She looked up at her sister, feeling not a little irritated that Anne was enjoying her discovery quite so much.

"Don't worry, Major," Anne said with a mischievous twinkle. "It's not your fault that you don't see it. Indeed I thought it was useless too until I saw the letter that Mrs. Honeychurch gave Charlotte, and compared the two. Look at the handwriting on both."

Charlotte pushed the letter over to Emily and held it against the address written out on the package. Both manuscripts were written in the same distinctive hand that Mrs. Honeychurch had been adamant belonged to her daughter.

"Elizabeth was at home and had taken to her bed for all of the day before she vanished—Mattie told us that she had," Charlotte said, frowning. "And here is a package in her hand posted to herself from . . ." She squinted at the postmark. "Hebden Bridge?"

"Or a letter that she had already written was taken to Hebden Bridge and posted back by another party?" Emily countered.

"For what purpose?" Anne asked her. "That's what I can't determine."

There Emily was stumped, for nothing to do with the two documents made any sense at all. And then it was as if a bolt of lightning struck her from above.

"Of course!" Emily gasped. "Of course, I see it all so clearly now! Though it was well hidden, I believe I have uncovered the truth, or at least part of it, thanks to our detecting, of course."

"What do you mean, Emily?" Charlotte asked. Emily paused for theatrical effect.

"The young man that Mrs. Hardy saw with Elizabeth in the woods was not the delicious Mr. Walters," Emily said, "but it still had to be *somebody*. Perhaps the true person Elizabeth was seduced by at fifteen. Elizabeth's liaison with this mystery man was shocking enough that her father wanted to cover it up with a less scandalous affair . . . This man, whoever he is, has to be the key to what has happened to Elizabeth. For it is this man who has set out to take back the girl who once loved him and place the blame at the most obvious suspect's feet. Don't you see? The staging of a bloody murder, the introduction of a variety of suspects, the path that led us to the tooth, the bonfire of bones. It's all set dressing—it's all an illusion made from smoke and mirrors to cast suspicion on the most suspicious man there is, Chester. When, in fact, if there was a terrible murder committed, it was not there, and not that night—it was only made to seem so to provide distraction and a perfect suspect! In the confusion, Elizabeth Chester was spirited away to another place. And when she was, she was still alive."

34

❦

Anne

"Let me explain," Emily said happily, clapping her hands together. No time for theatre, indeed, Anne thought. "While I cannot be sure that Elizabeth Chester still lives, I *can* be sure that she was not killed at Chester Grange . . ."

"Yes, we understand that much," Charlotte said, tapping her forefinger impatiently on the top of the table. Not one to be rushed, Emily crossed to the table, looking out down the hillside towards the little huddle of houses.

"Someone wanted the smokescreen of murder while they kidnapped Elizabeth. Of course, the perfect suspect to implicate in such a crime is the man that many know is a fiend, that man whose first wife killed herself rather than be married to him. Especially perfect if the true culprit was Elizabeth's erstwhile lover. However, knowing that Robert Chester would most likely have the law on his side, the travellers squatting in Chester's woods make a fine second set of suspects. The respectable classes so love to be afraid of gypsies that almost no proof is required to believe them guilty . . ."

"Or," Charlotte said, her eyes widening, "it could just *be* the group of angry travelling folk, kidnapping her away to be bride to their sultry king!"

"Oh dear, Charlotte," Anne said, shaking her head. "You should read more factual texts, I think. All that fiction has quite gone to your head. But"—she turned back to Emily—"it was Chester who told the constables about the gypsies on his land—and it was close by to their camp where we found the second fire, the rib and the tooth. Could it not have been Chester casting blame on the outsiders to conceal his own misdeeds?"

"It could have been, and I think perhaps in a way that is what he attempted, but not because he killed his second wife," Emily said. "Let me explain my reasoning."

"You are ever so fond of explaining, Emily," Anne said, dryly raising an eyebrow at Charlotte, who smirked in return. "Go on."

"A pig is an easy enough animal to acquire from any weekly market, and I daresay if you were to take it to a butcher, he'd give you back your pig, and the blood he collected from it if requested. It's my belief that the blood that was so liberally painted all around Elizabeth's room came from the same unfortunate animal as the rib, which was burnt in the grounds to cast suspicion on the residents of Chester Grange, both legal and squatters. Remember the member of the gypsy clan we met in the woods?"

"Hard to forget." Anne shuddered.

"Then you'll recall how he said something about slitting one of us open like a sow? That could show insight into the incident that only a culprit or an accessory would know. And in the meantime, Chester was so busy controlling what the constable was up to, afraid that he was about to be accused, that *we* found the false evidence instead of the idiot constable."

"But if Chester truly didn't harm Elizabeth," Charlotte asked, "then why would he have tried to misdirect the constable? An innocent man has nothing to hide!"

"Because," Anne said, her eyes widening as she looked at Emily, "he can't be sure if he is guilty or not! When Branwell and I went to visit him, and he thought that Branwell was a doctor, he asked him if a man could become so intoxicated he might forget everything he'd done whilst under the influence. That's why he looks so haunted, so guilty and so stricken. He was dead drunk on the night that Elizabeth vanished—Mattie told us so. And he knows his own terrible nature, and that he *may* have harmed her, he *may* be guilty, even if he doesn't remember it. And that might make him a very dangerous man, if he feels that he has nothing left to lose."

"Yes," Emily said, "that is entirely possible."

"Could it even be," Charlotte suggested hesitantly, "that whoever the perpetrator is somehow dosed Chester beyond what even he is used to, to induce exactly that confusion in his mind?"

"Yes." Emily nodded. "Yes, perhaps."

"However," Anne said slowly, as she sifted through all the puzzle pieces in her mind once again, "while the blood, the rib, the fire may all have come from or had to do with an animal, the tooth, also charred, did not. We know that that tooth is from a young human female—Mrs. Prescott confirmed it—it came out roots and all, so presume that it was either pulled or knocked out. That simply can't be trickery."

"No." Emily nodded gravely. "Nor can I think of an explanation for persons unknown sending a parcel to Elizabeth that she wrote to herself the day before she disappeared, except that it's some further form of misdirection, the point of which is perhaps even to lead us, or the authorities that should be investigating Elizabeth's disappearance, on this merry dance. The tooth . . . the tooth leads me to believe that whoever took her, they did so against her will. But also, I do not believe Chester is guilty of inflicting that cruelty on her this time. Which leaves us with the question: Who is our nefarious mastermind? Who is the man that has taken Elizabeth?"

"Oh, oh, perhaps Elizabeth had fallen in love with a gypsy as a young girl," Charlotte said breathlessly. "Imagine that—spreading the lie that your daughter had been seduced by a tutor would certainly be better than discovery she had consorted with such a wild creature! And perhaps, still madly in love with her, the gypsy searched for her until he found her at Chester Grange, and begged her to come with him, to a simple but passion-filled life on the road. However, Elizabeth—a reformed character and newly married woman—refused him. Unable to be denied the woman he loved, he carried her off into the night anyway!"

Charlotte's cheeks pinkened at the very idea of it.

"More books of facts," Anne said to Charlotte. "Read more books of facts, Charlotte. If we could find the gypsies again, we could ask them what they might know of pig's blood, but they might be anywhere by now."

"Tabby may know," Emily said thoughtfully. "Tabby knows all the old ways of the land. I'm certain that if she knew where the Romanies were a few days since she will know where they go next depending on the season. They are people of habit, even if civilisation keeps trying to step in their way. I'll ask her, though she is afraid for us and must be handled gently."

"Anne, you ask her," Charlotte said.

"I must admit that I do not wish to meet another gypsy alone," Anne said.

"Well, that's what we have Branwell for," Emily said. "Or at least that's what we can tell him. I fear a conversation with the travellers is essential; either they are guilty, or if not, perhaps we can persuade them to confide in us what they may know, specifically who the mysterious man Elizabeth was seen with could be."

"I believe that is Charlotte's forte," Anne said, lowering her eyes.

"I see!" Charlotte exclaimed. "So I am the one dispatched to converse with the travelling ruffians, me, the smallest and meekest of us all."

Charlotte was not amused by her sisters' laughter.

"Well, if Tabby is able to locate them, then try to think of them more as romantic rogues who might fall in love with you at any moment, Charlotte dear," Emily said once their mirth had subsided. "Meanwhile, I ponder still on the true meaning of this stone." Emily placed the stone in the centre of the table and stared at it for a long moment.

"I suppose it might . . . just be a stone?" Anne said rather quietly, not quite able to fathom Emily's fascination with the nondescript pebble. "Anyway, it would seem that, as far as we know, Elizabeth Chester wrote to herself from Hebden Bridge on the day she was ill in bed. So I suppose what we must do next is discover whether or not she has any personal connection there that might lead us to the next stage on our journey."

"But she does!" Mattie said, appearing around the door, her eyes red and puffy. "Please forgive me, I did try to rest, but as exhausted as I am, my mind would not be still for worrying about the boys. I do know of a connection between Mrs. Chester and Hebden Bridge."

"Come and sit, Mattie," Anne said, patting the seat of a chair. "And please tell us what you know."

Mattie settled next to Anne, her face washed clear of colour by tears and that particular kind of exhaustion that comes with great fear.

"After she came to live at the Grange, for a while I hated her," she said hesitantly. "I hated Mrs. Chester, I'm ashamed to admit. I believed that she had stolen Mr. Chester from me." Mattie looked mournfully at Charlotte. "I realise how foolish that sounds now, but at the time I was quite mad with grief at losing him. Though I was under no illusion that I could be rid of her for good, I thought I might find some way to drive a wedge between them if I could discover more about my rival."

"Oh, Matilda, dear," Charlotte whispered.

"Please," Mattie begged, "don't judge me too harshly. Besides, it's impossible for you to despise me any more than I despise myself. I . . . I decided to spy on her, to look for something that might turn Mr. Chester away from her. It was quite wrong of me, and I would have been dismissed if I had been discovered, but even then I sensed *something* was very wrong, even if I did not know exactly *how*. I picked up a book, Austen's *Emma*, that she had on the table, and out of it fell the last page of a letter that she had tucked away out of sight. I am ashamed to say I read the fragment. It was from a Miss Isabelle Lucas, written while Elizabeth was still engaged to Chester. As I read on, I realised that Miss Lucas had been her art tutor before she had been sent to school, and that a strong attachment had formed between the two. Within months, as I came to know Elizabeth, and to understand what it meant to be married to Robert Chester, I came to my senses and my schemes fell away, and I never thought of the letter again until now. I can't remember the exact address, but I am certain that it was somewhere in Hebden Bridge."

Mattie took Charlotte's hands in hers. "Is that helpful? That might be helpful, mightn't it? Oh, I wish I could remember it now, but as I heard Mrs. Crawley approaching I put it back and removed myself at once."

"It is very helpful indeed," Charlotte said gently, cupping Mattie's face in her hand. "Dear Mattie, do try to sleep, or you will make yourself ill with worry."

"So it's settled. If Tabby can help us, Charlotte and Branwell will be dispatched to talk to the gypsies tonight, and, Anne, you and I shall go to Hebden Bridge at first light," Emily said, looking at Charlotte the moment that Mattie had retired once more. "Do you agree?"

"I agree that I hope the gypsies are long gone," Charlotte said unhappily. "A daylight excursion to Hebden Bridge is far preferable to a midnight adventure with criminals and ne'er-do-wells."

"Would you prefer it was Emily?" Anne asked innocently.

"Certainly not," Charlotte said at once. "Though I think I shall come to Hebden Bridge too, to keep order."

"Good, because if we find Miss Lucas and ask her what she knows of her friend, she might give us a path to follow that would lead us to discovering Elizabeth's fate," Anne said. "And what shall we do about the children? I do so fear for them at the mercy of that madman. Could we not tell the authorities that we believe Chester is dangerous and still go to Hebden Bridge?" she asked Emily. "Why must it be one or the other?"

"Because if whoever took Elizabeth is watching Chester Grange, any disruption to the illusion created around Chester that casts suspicions wider than Chester himself, may unbalance them, cause them panic and, if Elizabeth still lives, perhaps even cause them to harm her further. And if Chester himself feels that he is close to being brought in for a crime he isn't sure he *didn't* commit, well, who knows what a man with nothing left to lose might do?" Emily turned to Anne. "It's a King Solomon's choice for sure, impossible to make and yet we *must*. Find Elizabeth and risk the children, or protect the children and risk Elizabeth? I say we allow one more day to search out Elizabeth. Chester has only ever hurt women, never children as far as we know, it's not his *modus operandi*. They are his legacy. I believe they are safer than Elizabeth may be, and if I am wrong, then . . . the mistake is mine."

Anne looked anxiously at Charlotte, who thought for a moment.

"We hurry," Charlotte said decisively. "We leave before dawn, and complete our business as rapidly as we may. For once we are in full possession of all the facts, we will know what to do, and how to go about it."

"And if something happens to the children while we are adventuring?" Anne asked Charlotte.

"Let us pray that it does not," Charlotte said very gravely. "Let us pray that it does not."

35

Charlotte

Quite how Charlotte found herself sitting wedged between Tabitha on one side and her brother on the other while he drove the "borrowed" Black Bull's cart with precious little skill, she wasn't sure. She only knew that she did not care for it.

At least the rain had stopped, the night was warm and the waning moon cast a bright enough light on the road. And it wasn't so very late as it might have been; the church bell had been sounding ten as Branwell drove them out of Haworth under Tabby's surly direction.

After Mattie was settled, the three of them had gone to fetch Branwell away from his room, where he had been writing in earnest, and in truth Charlotte had been sorry to disturb him from an occupation that she approved of; it was such a very rare occurrence.

"I require your protection, brother," she had told him. "For a venture into the treacherous night to aid us in our detecting. I am afraid that it may involve great danger and mayhem."

"Not now, Charlotte," Branwell had said, waving his sisters away without lifting his head from his desk. "After many weeks of futile searching, the muse is upon me, and one does not interrupt genius when she graces you with her caresses."

"Oh, so I am to face almost certain death alone, am I?" Charlotte said.

"Yes, that would be preferable if you don't mind," Branwell replied absently. Emily had cuffed him round the ear, and Anne had picked up the first sheet of his story and praised it voluminously until he had agreed to come just to make them quiet.

Tabby, it being after nine, was already in bed in her nightcap, the quilt drawn up under her chin, Martha slumbering next to her.

"What's this?" she'd said, sitting up in bed as Anne woke her as gently as she was able, all three sisters crowding round her bed while Branwell waited outside. "Is your father taken ill?"

As soon as Anne explained their request, Tabby had become agitated, about as furious as Charlotte had ever seen her, though she communicated in a series of angry whispers so as not to waken their papa. Eventually Anne had sent her and Emily downstairs, where they waited with Branwell, all of them struck dumb when Tabby herself came hobbling down the stairs. Somehow Anne had persuaded her to share her knowledge of the travellers' movements, but there was one condition.

The long and short of it was that Tabby would not tell them where the gypsy folk would be, as that broke some ancient unspoken traveller law that Tabby refused to contravene.

"I'll show you, and nothing else," she'd said. "And you'll have to fetch me a cart, because I can't walk great distances on my lame leg no more. Besides, I am old and bone weary of you children and your fanciful notions."

"We are children no more, Tabby," Branwell had said.

"You wouldn't know it," Tabby had replied.

She had not tired of this subject even as Branwell hefted her onto the cart. "You Brontë young'uns, always coming up with fanciful notions and gallivanting hither and thither. I've known spring lambs with more sense than you. I've a bit of Romany blood on my pa's side. I know what I'm about."

"And some Romany girth on her backside," Branwell whispered to Charlotte as he heaved the old lady up, forcing his sister to cover her mouth to stifle the laughter.

"I knows how to talk to them folk," Tabby repeated once they were on the road. "There are ways of dealing with them so as not to cause offence.

You mark my words, if anyone is doing any asking it's me, and me alone. You—" She pointed at Branwell, bundled up in his muffler, his battered hat pulled low over his brows. "You try to look fierce, and you, Miss Charlotte, you don't say anything at all, if such a thing is possible. You got the kind of face that would turn them agin' ye soon as they look at ye."

How rude, Charlotte thought, but given the circumstances, and the great inconvenience Tabby was suffering in order to help them, she kept the thought to herself.

Their journey, as it turned out, was not a long one. Tabby directed Branwell to drive them just two miles outside of Haworth to the hamlet of Stanbury, and a little further on until they arrived at the foot of the valley below the home of Branwell's friends the Heatons, Ponden Hall, where a stream ran off the top of the moor and through a lush meadow surrounded by thick woodland.

"The Heatons don't mind the gypsy folk here for a week or so," Tabby told Charlotte as Branwell helped her down, grimacing as he took the brunt of her weight on his wasted frame. "After all, most of them are worse blaggards than the Romany themselves."

"You are speaking of my friends," Branwell had said.

"I know it," Tabby told him, grabbing onto his arm. Her breath was laboured, her bad leg making the going twice as rough for her. She was certainly a formidable old woman, Charlotte thought with great fondness; she was finding it hard enough with her two good legs, as she half slid, half fell down the steep incline to the campsite, the long wet grass as slippery as ice. For Tabby the difficulty must have been tenfold and yet she didn't complain at all. Well, not very much at least.

Approaching the peaceful camp, Charlotte saw four wagons stationed around a fire, the glimmer of a lantern coming from within one. Two dogs barked as they approached, and a group of sturdy-looking horses, swathed in blankets for the night, whinnied restlessly.

There was only one figure seated at the fire, the hunched shape only becoming something more human looking as they drew closer. Charlotte was relieved to see that it was a woman, though the relief was short-lived.

The crone looked very old and very fearsome in the firelight, smoking a small pipe, her wide-brimmed hat tied under her chin with a striped scarf. Even in the gloom there was a glint of steel that could be detected in her gaze.

"Now then, Kezia," Tabby said, shuffling ahead. "I've come calling, seeking your wisdom."

"Come warm your sen by the fire, then," the old woman spoke without looking up from the blaze. Charlotte was alarmed to notice three, then four shadowy figures emerging from the wagon, advancing towards their vulnerable little group, close enough to be menacing but not close enough to be clearly seen.

"We don't mean you harm, Kezia," Tabby said.

"We'll see," Kezia said in a tone that Charlotte took to mean that if there were any harm to be done it would be directed at them. In the dark she reached out for Branwell's hand, feeling his fingers grip tightly around hers. "What you want with me, Tabby, coming out here in the dead of night, ghosts gathering all round. Can't be just that these fancy people want their fortunes told. Did you bring silver?"

"Aye, we did," Tabby said, drawing nearer to the fire but not troubling herself to stoop down to the low logs that had been arranged as seating. "We do not seek fortunes, only knowledge."

Ever so slowly Kezia turned her back to the fire to better look at Charlotte and her brother. Although her face was now completely obscured by shadow, Charlotte could feel the woman's eyes crawling over her. Even with the heat from the fire, she shuddered. Despite all of her rational inclinations it felt as if the gypsy woman could see right into her soul.

"Good," the old woman said. "For I'll not tell their fortunes. I'm too old now to say anything that ain't true, and sometimes what is, is too hard to hear."

"What do you mean by that?" Charlotte asked, propelled by fear before she could prevent herself. "Why do you say that? Do you hope it will make us press you further for a fortune, and spend more silver, is that it? For you might as well know we have none to spare!"

Charlotte took a step back behind her brother as the shadowy figures drew a little closer.

"Miss Charlotte, be still," Tabby told her firmly. "Don't question Kezia on what she will and will not do, she is the chief of this camp, and you owe her your respect."

"I apologise," Charlotte said meekly, from behind Branwell's shoulder.

"Hmmph." Kezia fixed her gaze on Tabby. "Give me your silver and I'll see if I know what you want."

Tabby held out her hand, into which Branwell obediently dropped two shillings. She handed them to the old woman, who tucked them inside what looked like an old stocking foot that she produced from the folds of her skirt.

"Do you know who the gentleman Mrs. Elizabeth Chester were seen with in the woods this spring, for we know it weren't her husband. Has any paid you for pig's blood and bones?" Tabby said, clearly feeling no need to dissemble. Adding in something of a rush, "Or if yourself used such materials as a ruse to take the Chester girl or helped someone else to do so."

Kezia was silent for a long time, sucking on her pipe as she observed Tabby, engaged in what Charlotte could only assume was the making up of her mind on what to do next.

"I would have stuck another with my long knife for asking me such a question Tabitha Aykroyd," she said at last, so coldly that Charlotte believed her.

"I know it." Tabby nodded grimly, and suddenly Charlotte could see why the dear old lady had been so insistent on coming with them. Oh, how she loved dear Tabby, and how she would fuss over her and take care of her as soon as this whole business was done with.

"I don't have no girl hidden here," Kezia said with such certainty that Charlotte believed her at once. "The law and a rabble of hired thugs been out here already and searched us more 'an once. They didn't find nothing, because there ain't nothing to find. We gypsies don't murder, not for pleasure or gain anyways." She looked Branwell up and down. "Revenge, maybe."

"That's what I thought," Tabby said, nodding. "But miss here was insistent we ask."

"That don't surprise me," Kezia muttered.

"Why?" Once again Charlotte simply could not prevent her mouth from speaking. "Why doesn't that surprise you? What can you possibly discern about my character after meeting me for but a few minutes?"

"Plenty," Tabby said dryly, setting Kezia to a kind of wheezing laugh. "What about the fellow in the forest, or the blood I spoke of, Kezia, and the bone. Know anything of that?"

"I'll tell you this one thing," Kezia said at length. "And this one thing only and you will ask me no more." Tabby shot Charlotte a stern warning look. "We filled a barrel with blood from a pig we found and a bag with its bones, for a gentleman who paid us most handsomely. If he is the man you speak of, I cannot say. The transaction was done at night; he said not two words. I know nothing of what he did with it, or who he was, for he was not known to I. I don't know where he came from or where he went. And if I did, I'd never tell you."

"Then our business is concluded," Tabby said. "We'll trouble you no more, Kezia. I wish you safe travels."

"Wait." Kezia barked out the command. "The fairy-sized girl, I want her to come and sit with me for a moment."

"Well, I do not wish to." Charlotte drew further behind Branwell. "I am a Christian woman. I do not believe in your magic!"

"You don't need to believe in it for it to be real," Tabby told her with a hiss. "Go and sit down, girl!"

Under great obligation, and remembering how just a few moments earlier she had been filled with great love for Tabby, Charlotte reluctantly obeyed, sitting awkwardly on the log and lifting her face to meet Kezia's. At close quarters she saw a regal woman, one whose hard life was etched deeply into her face, but who regarded her with a poise and a certain sense of self that Charlotte found enviable.

"It doesn't matter what you say to me," she said, offering Kezia her palm. "I shall not take any notice of it."

"You can keep your little hand," Kezia told her. "It's not there I see your fate, but in your face, in the lines around your eyes, the sorrow in the bend of your mouth. Be still while I look at you." Charlotte made herself hold the old woman's gaze until it was finally broken, as Kezia redirected her face towards the firelight, which made the shadows of her features leap and dance.

"There's a flame in you," Kezia said eventually. "Brightest I've ever seen, with a light that could shine on forever, if only you have the courage to let it burn."

"I have no idea what you mean by those remarks," Charlotte said.

"Oh, you do," Kezia said. "I don't, but you, you know the meaning very well."

Getting up, Charlotte drew back from the fire as quickly as she was able, rushing to the safe haven of Tabby's side.

"Will you look at my face too, old crone?" Branwell asked, bending at the waist in the hope that she might look at him. "I wish to know my fortune. I wish to know if my love will ever be my wife, and if I will find the path for my talents that will lead me to greatness."

But Kezia did not turn her face back from the fire.

"Go now," she told Tabby. "My boys are getting restless."

"I thank ye, friend," Tabby said, gesturing for Branwell's support.

"Tread carefully, fairy child," Kezia called, her voice echoing in the darkness as they left as quickly as they were able. "Danger is very close by, and it will find you."

36

Anne

Hebden Bridge was a lively little town with a sense of purpose that positively hummed in the air, Anne thought, as they alighted from the coach.

To an outsider—even to an insider—Haworth looked rather dilapidated, a collection of homes jumbled together, as if by accident, that seemed to tumble down the hillside on which it was built.

By contrast, Hebden Bridge, though equally hilly, looked like it was scrambling its way triumphantly to the very top. The textile industry had transformed and enriched the area, and the railway station had elevated its fortunes even further, opening up this once quiet corner of Yorkshire to the whole world.

To Anne it seemed as if the landscape itself had somehow got wind of its burgeoning situation, and was preening and ruffling its feathers in pride. She rather liked the energy and the modernism of it all. It seemed like a town full of possibility and opportunity.

It was also very full of people, which made it rather difficult to know where to start looking for one Miss Isabelle Lucas.

"Our first appointment should be at the church, of course," Charlotte said, holding on to her bonnet as the summer breeze picked up, bowling down the cobbled street.

Branwell had still lain abed as Charlotte joined their sisters this morning and told them of the previous night's extraordinary discovery, feeling all the while that last night's excursion had been a waking dream. However, the information that Charlotte, Tabby and Branwell had gathered from the gypsy queen was vital. An unknown man had staged the bloody scene of Elizabeth's disappearance. Not Chester, because the woman Kezia certainly knew him; he had made it his business to persecute her tribe. Whoever this man was, he had to be the one that had taken Elizabeth, knocked a tooth from her head and, they hoped, still held her captive and alive. Time was running by very fast now, and it had to be hoped that some indication of whom this man might be could be discovered here and now.

"The reverend there will be sure to have a good knowledge of his congregation," Charlotte went on, stifling a little yawn, "and even if unwilling to give us a precise address, might send someone there to bring Miss Lucas to us."

"Unless, of course, she is a Methodist, or even a Catholic," Emily said mischievously, just to see Charlotte shudder. Charlotte thought that no one else in the world except Emily knew that once, near the end of her time in Brussels, when Charlotte was very low and lonely, she had walked into a Catholic church and made her confession. Afterwards she had swiftly detailed the whole surprising matter to Emily in a letter that tried to make light of it, and Emily had told Anne, on pain of death should she ever let slip that she knew. Anne frowned at Emily: she must know how uncomfortable Charlotte felt about flirting with a faith other than the one her own papa presided over.

"Besides," Anne added, trying to gloss over the moment, "the Reverend Sutcliffe Sowden is a very good acquaintance of your Mr. Nicholls, Charlotte."

"He is not my Mr. Nicholls!" Charlotte was pleasingly appalled at the very idea.

"Nevertheless, unless we want to find another tale to tell our dear father, it's best to avoid all religious establishments," Anne reminded her. "Oh dear, I do worry about all the deceit that comes with detecting. It doesn't seem very godly at all."

"But you are right that it is necessary, I suppose," Charlotte said, still rather irritated by her allusion to Mr. Nicholls. "Then where?"

"The post office." Anne nodded in the direction of the building that was just across the street.

"This will surely not work," Emily said as they began to cross amongst the throng of carts and townspeople. "They won't give a private address to three strangers. We could be anyone—murderers or thieves, even."

"We shall see," Anne said, and indeed within a few minutes of her mentioning Miss Lucas's name and telling the postmaster about how she had lost contact with her childhood friend, he had proudly told anyone who cared to listen that he remembered the addresses of every single citizen of the town, and even wrote it down and provided full directions.

"That should not have worked," Emily said, smiling at how pleased Anne was with herself. "It was your sweet face that won that information, Anne. You simply do not look like a murderer or a thief, but then again I suppose that such an innocent countenance would perfectly position a person to be either."

The house that the postmaster had sent them to was fairly sizeable. A little smaller than the parsonage, it was a three-storeyed terrace nestled against the rearing cliffside that loomed impressively over the row of houses. All the houses were well kept, but this was the prettiest, for a window box full of huge daisies garlanded every one of the six front windows.

It was such a delightful little house, Anne decided enviously, for although it was made of the same steel-grey stone as every other building in the district, someone had painted its windowsills white, and the front door a very deep blue that reminded her of the swell of the ocean at Scarborough.

The door was answered by a young girl of around thirteen with a constellation of freckles across the bridge of her nose and a gap in her teeth. Although she was dressed in a maid's dress, her long, tangled ginger hair was worn loose down her back, and the look in her pale eyes was decidedly wary.

"What?" she said bluntly, eyeing the sisters.

"Good afternoon," Charlotte said. "We are calling on Miss Isabelle Lucas."

"Are you?" the girl replied, her unfamiliar accent, which was both flat and sharp to Anne's ears, sounding as if she might have been discovered in the hovels of the East End of London.

Anne tried not to show that she was amused to see that Charlotte, who considered herself prepared for every social nicety, was unprepared for that response.

"Please will you tell your mistress that the Misses Brontë of Haworth have come to call on her," Charlotte said, attempting to peer around the girl in the hopes of finding someone more civilised inside.

"No," the girl replied before remembering herself and affecting something of a refined accent. "I mean, no, sorry, madam, I cannot—my mistress is not at home at present. So clear off."

"Look." Charlotte took a step closer, and although she was a good head shorter than the strange creature at the door, she seemed to inflate with the well-practised authority of a school mistress. "We are here on important business, and your impudence will not be welcomed by Miss Lucas once she hears of it."

"Oh, won't she?" The girl seemed highly sceptical. "You ain't met her, then. Anyways, my mistress told me to let no one in the house, and the only person I take orders from is my mistress." The girl lifted her chin, as if daring Charlotte to challenge her further.

"Well, when will she return?" Charlotte asked, rather deflated by such a spirited defence.

"Dunno." The girl shrugged and made to shut the door. This time it was Anne who stepped forward and blocked the closure of the door with the force of her hand.

"Oi, get off," the girl demanded, and behind her bravado Anne saw a glimpse of childish vulnerability.

"Be calm," Anne told her gently. "You've no need to be afraid of us. We aren't policemen or . . . other officials."

"Are you teachers?" the girl asked her, narrowing her eyes. "You look like teachers."

"We are not," Anne said, and in that moment at least it was the truth. "We are detectors. Do you know what a detector is . . . ? What's your name?"

"Kitty," the girl said. "I don't know, nor do I care, what a detector is."

"We find things out," Anne said softly, "to help the good and the innocent, and to stop the wicked and the bad, and to bring them to justice. What do you think of that?"

Kitty tipped her head to one side as she appraised the women. Anne smiled at her encouragingly.

"How can three old ladies do that?" she questioned. "You ain't Robin Hood or Dick Turpin."

"No, we are not. We are just three teacher-looking *young* ladies, and do you know what, Kitty?" Anne winked. "That turns out to be the perfect disguise."

Kitty almost smiled, and behind the brittle expression of a girl who had already been hardened by the reality of life, there was the faintest trace of a curious child still present.

"If you truly know my mistress, you'll know where she is anyways. Those that she is closest to know all, like I do. But I will never tell. She gave me her instructions, and I will follow them to the death. You understand?"

"You are very loyal and very brave," Anne said softly. "Has Miss Lucas been very kind to you? Perhaps she rescued you from a place where you were very afraid, and given you a home. I think she would be very proud of how you seek to protect her."

"And that's why I ain't telling you nothing," Kitty replied sharply. "No matter how much you try and talk me round."

"Very well," Anne said, waving a hand to silence Charlotte before she could interrupt her. "However, I must tell you we are trying very hard to help someone else that your mistress cares about. We don't know Miss Lucas, that much is true, but we think that she would like us to find her; we think she wouldn't want to miss a chance to save someone whom she cares about a great deal in the same way that she saved you."

"Who is the someone?" She leaned in to Anne, her voice a whisper.

"Her name is Elizabeth," Anne said. The girl's eyes widened just for a moment, before her habitual scowl returned, and Anne realised that the poor child was afraid.

"Are you friend or foe?" she asked eventually, looking each of the sisters in the eye in turn.

"We are friends," Anne said. Removing her glove, she offered the girl her hand. "We only want to help Elizabeth and her children."

Something Anne said clicked with the girl, who held on to her fingers for a moment longer, before pulling her down until her ear was next to the girl's lips.

Anne listened as the girl whispered.

"Thank you," she said, with a nod. "I promise you, your mistress will not be angry with you."

"She better not, else I'll come and find you in the night and slit your throat," the girl said, slamming the blue door shut in their faces.

"I like her." Emily nodded.

Charlotte looked at Anne enquiringly. "Well, where are we headed next?"

"You will soon find out," Anne replied.

My soul is awakened, my spirit soaring
And carried aloft on the wings of the breeze;
For above and around me the wild wind is roaring,
Arousing to rapture the earth and the seas.
—"Lines Composed in a Wood on a Windy Day"
by Anne Brontë

37

❧ ❧

Charlotte

The carriage pulled over at the side of the Lancashire Moor Road, and the sisters emerged into what appeared to be the middle of nowhere.

"Where are we going, did you say?" Charlotte asked Anne. "For this doesn't seem to be anywhere."

"Wycoller," Anne said, looking around at the wild and beautiful country that seemed entirely unpopulated by anything human. "I asked the driver to bring us to Wycoller, just as Kitty told me to. She said I wasn't to tell you where we were going until we arrived. It seemed important, but come to think of it, I can't think why. Oh Lord, has she taken us for fools and sent us here as a kind of warning, telling us to stay away?"

"Well, at least we are only about two hours' walk from Haworth," Emily said. "And don't worry, Anne—Kitty sent us to exactly the right place, although maybe on a fool's errand. This is Wycoller, or about as close as you can get to it by road."

"Well, what is Wycoller then?" Charlotte asked. "Is it this tree or that sheep?"

"If you'd listened to Tabby's stories as closely as I did when we were children, you would know the answer to that question," Emily told her. "Wycoller is a village—an ancient settlement that's been here long since pagan times. Right up until twenty years ago, it thrived. There was a big house, Wycoller Hall, and a number of humble dwellings that made up the village—most of the village folk were weavers. Then the hall passed into the hands of some fool who couldn't pay his debts, and he gradually started to sell parts of the house off until it became a ruin. Then the mills came, and the factories full of weaving machines, and family by family the people of Wycoller left to find work in the towns. They had to, to survive." Emily took Charlotte's hand, leading her to the edge of the road. "Don't you remember, Charlotte, how Tabby told us that when she was a girl she'd go down to Wycoller and creep along the stream, hoping to catch sight of the fairies? And how Tabby said that all the new factories and the noise that came with them had chased all the fairies away into hiding everywhere except here, the place where people never come?"

"I do," Charlotte said, remembering a dark afternoon, and Tabby's tall tales, told to distract the unhappy children. "I do remember Tabby telling us that story, and that afternoon, though it rained and rained, you and I hunted for fairies in the garden. Anne was a baby, and Mama . . . was ill. I do remember."

Emily held her hand a little tighter.

"Nowadays," Emily said, "there isn't a living soul residing in Wycoller, though some say a lady in black haunts the ruin of the hall on the night of a full moon."

"But if this is Wycoller, then . . ." Anne scanned the hills, dotted with trees and a few sheep. "Then where is it?"

"There"—Emily pointed to the densely wooded floor of the valley—"hidden in amongst the trees. And the only way there is on foot across the fields and down through the forest. Unless you were one of the old folk, like Tabby, you'd never think to visit there—you'd never know it was there at all. When you think about it, it really is the perfect place to hide."

A deep, dreamy sense of peace settled over Charlotte, the last of their small party, as she followed her sisters through the long, golden grass of the meadow. Her fingers outstretched, she brushed her palms across the tips of the ears of seeds, plucking a sprig of first harebells and then fireweed from the meadow, tucking the small wildflower bouquet into the buttons of her blouse. What had that old gypsy woman meant about a flame within her, that if ignited might burn forever? It seemed impossible to Charlotte that such a prediction could be true of her, and yet something about it chimed within. It was a sense of possibility.

As they descended into the heart of the valley, they followed the barely detectable path into a deep, tree-covered tunnel, where midday sun dappled in flashes like a school of minnows and the exposed roots of the trees seemed to reach out in a bid to catch all passing intruders. It seemed to Charlotte that the deeper they travelled, the slower time passed around them—that perhaps, as they walked on, it might even begin to turn backwards.

After a short while they emerged from the wood into more meadow, and they saw that standing in amongst the grass, boneset and bridewort were jagged, tooth-like standing stones, none of them taller than Charlotte herself. Some were arranged in clumps, like a crowd of curious spectators, but mostly they stood in lines that led down into the valley, at least three or four rows that Charlotte could see, radiating out across where the meadow emerged from the trees.

"How strange—this is nothing like the drystone walls around Haworth," she said.

"That's because no one knows who put them there," Emily told her, placing her hand on top of one of the stones, blotched with bright yellow lichen. "Tabby used to say that all the ancient peoples from all over the moors would travel here once a year to meet and make human sacrifices."

"I don't remember Tabby saying that," Charlotte said.

"Well, she did, but I shouldn't worry about it—the pagans are all long dead now."

For some reason that didn't particularly make Charlotte feel any less unsettled by the strange, spectral spectators that lined the last of their route into the village. Finally they descended down a foliage-strewn stone staircase, the air cooling around them as the canopy of trees above thickened. All was silent except for the sound of birdsong and the gentlest murmur of the wind in the trees. It felt like being in a dream, Charlotte thought: a beautiful and strange dream where nothing quite made the sense that it should.

All of a sudden they were confronted with the ruin of Wycoller Hall, appearing out of the trees like an abandoned ship emerging from the mist.

"How extraordinary." Anne gasped, running at once into the empty archway where a door had once stood.

"Isn't it?" Emily followed her at once, but Charlotte was rooted to the spot, as her eyes roamed over every empty window frame, every broken-down chimney stack. Though she knew the prosaic truth behind the hall's ruin, it seemed impossible not to imagine it as a kind of Sleeping Beauty's castle, sent to sleep by wicked magic for more than a thousand years.

"Charlotte, come inside," Anne called, and after a moment Charlotte walked into the dark interior. Half of the boards on the upper floor were missing, and quite some portion of the roof, though not all. Many of the stone flags that were laid on the floor were absent, and rich, dark grasses had sprung up in their place. As Charlotte stood in front of what would once have been an impressive fireplace, she wondered what on earth the strange little key-shaped cavern to the right of it could possibly have been for. A movement from within startled her so that she had to stifle a shriek with her gloved fist as a small bird flew out of the strange enclosure and through the glassless window.

"Shall we brave the staircase?" Emily called from what would once have been the entrance hall. "Perhaps Miss Lucas is hiding upstairs."

"Well, that would frankly be ridiculous," a voice said from behind Emily. "It's terribly dangerous up there, you know—you'd certainly break your neck."

As Emily turned to the sound of the voice, Charlotte found herself staring at a young, barefooted woman in a loose, purple silk dress, with her dark hair curling down to her waist and the greenest eyes that Charlotte had ever seen—eyes that were alive with curiosity.

"Hello," the woman said. "I am Isabelle Lucas, and please do forgive my attire. We don't get many visitors here in Wycoller, so I tend not to dress for company."

38

Emily

"Are you lost, perhaps?" Isabelle smiled at them. "Can I put you on the right path back to the road?"

"We are not lost," Emily said, taking a step towards the strange creature as if she were a curiosity at the fair. "We have come here to talk to you, Miss Lucas."

"To me?" Isabelle Lucas's smile was just as bright, her eyes just as sparkling, but Emily noticed a tightening in the tone of her voice, which of course could be nothing more than the horror of unexpected visitors, something Emily knew all too well. "What on earth could you have to say to me? And how did you know I would be here? No one knows that I come here—that's why I am so very fond of it."

Emily liked Isabelle Lucas at once.

"We persuaded your maid to tell us," Emily explained apologetically. "And I can see why you like it here—it's rather like stepping into another world, a world rid of other people."

"Kitty told you I was here?" Isabelle seemed surprised, and rather impressed. "You must have had something interesting to say, then, to prise that information out of her. I rescued her from a very dark and dangerous place, and she is fiercely loyal. And sometimes just fierce."

"It wasn't Kitty's fault," Anne interjected hurriedly, worried that Kitty might be in trouble. "She could see that we had an urgent need to find you."

"Urgent?" Isabelle laughed and began walking away from the ruined manor house, the sisters following in her wake. "Ladies, I cannot imagine why a hermit artist such as myself should ever be of use to anyone who is not determined to buy one of my paintings. Are you determined to buy one of my paintings? For if you are, I'm afraid you will have to wait a little. I am having a very productive summer, hidden away here, but nothing is ready for sale yet."

"You're an artist?" Anne asked her. "By trade I mean, not just as a tutor?"

"Indeed I am." Isabelle smiled at her. "Rather a good one too. I told Kitty not to tell anyone where I was because there is always someone wanting to interfere—usually a gentleman, telling me how things should be done, what I may or may not paint, how I may or may not live. It's as if the male of the species cannot bear that I have agency over my own life, and insists on meddling where no meddling is required or invited. If you only knew how many of them kept trying to marry me. It's quite tragic, really it is.

"Come," she beckoned them on. "Come to my humble abode. I've taken up residence in Chapel Cottage. I shall make you tea and you can tell me all about what it is you think I can help you with, though I am bound to say I can't imagine a single thing."

Emily and her sisters followed the woman with no shoes or stockings through the long grass to the sweet little cottage, where wild roses grew around the door, and she suspected that her sisters were thinking and feeling exactly as she was: a kind of heady wonder that such an independent existence could ever be possible for a woman. And yet it was. Here was the proof that, under the right circumstances, anyone could be free to live the life they chose.

Isabelle poured tea into a mismatched set of cups as Anne walked from one unfinished painting to the next.

"These are really quite wonderful," Anne said with delight, speaking over her shoulder. "I'm no critic, of course, but each one fills me with such a sense of joy and freedom!"

"Then you are the best critic that there has ever been." Isabelle smiled, handing Emily a cup with no saucer.

"And so different," Anne enthused, "in style and subject, one from the other. Almost as if more than one artist made them."

"Yes, if you studied art you will know that copying another's style is a good way to learn, and even now I'm keen to learn, so I've been emulating an artist called Landseer—you may have heard of him?"

But Anne was lost in another painting.

"So, tell me, Emily, why have three such ladies—sisters no less—come all this way to find Isabelle Lucas?"

"It's about your friend, Elizabeth Chester," Emily said. "You taught her painting and drawing when she was still unmarried—Elizabeth Honeychurch."

"Elizabeth?" Isabelle stiffened in her seat, her smile becoming immobile. "Yes, my dear Elizabeth. Such a sweet girl, and so full of life—a little too much, her father would say. I haven't seen her for some time. Nor has she written me for months, although I kept writing to her. I have been worried, but I assumed that her marriage, her baby were taking up all her time. I expect her to come back to us eventually, as she always does. Please don't tell me that she's unwell?"

"Not that we know of," Emily said, looking at her sisters as they joined them, each choosing a mismatched chair to sit in. "But we have a tale to tell you that you may find very distressing, so please forgive me."

"Oh no." Isabelle's smile faded completely, her complexion turning to ashes. "What's happened to my Elizabeth now?"

Emily saw no point in holding back the details of the matter, for it seemed Isabelle Lucas was a woman of strong constitution, so she told her the whole story from the very first moment they had visited Chester Grange until they'd stood on the doorstep urging Kitty to reveal her whereabouts. And though Isabelle was a rapt audience, it was most dissatisfying.

Emily had been so sure that Isabelle Lucas would provide the key to this mystery, certain that perhaps Elizabeth might even be here in this most perfect of hiding places. And yet there was nothing in the way Isabelle reacted, nothing in her horror-struck expression, that led Emily to believe she was hiding something from them. There was only increasing distress and fear for her friend.

"And so," Emily told her, "we followed Mattie's suggestion to come to Hebden Bridge to look for you, and then we followed Kitty's advice to come here. Do you know how these letters would have been sent in Elizabeth's hand the day after she was taken?"

Emily handed the letter and the parcel wrapping to Isabelle, whose hand covered her mouth at the sight of her friend's handwriting.

"I'm sorry, it's been so long since I have seen her hand." She composed herself for a moment, winding a rope of her dark hair around her wrist and securing it to the back of her head with a pencil.

"I . . . I don't know for sure what the answer is . . ." Emily watched her chew at her lip, her concern for Elizabeth written in the knitting of her brows and the tremble of her hand. "But . . . but when I tutored Elizabeth her father was very strict about what he considered to be good manners, and he made her write letters to her grandmother on her mother's side and a selection of rich aunts every week. He hoped they would favour Elizabeth in their wills. But she hated it—she said every letter was the same, that nothing ever happened in her life to write about. So she'd write them in batches, a month's worth at a time, each one barely varying from the next. And she'd date each one on the date that it should be sent and entrust me to post them in turn. Her father never uncovered her scheme, and she found it so pleasing that she managed to dupe him *and* secure a hidden hour every week to do with just as she pleased—though what she got up to in those hours was quite another matter . . . anyway. She may have still taken this approach with letters home. I do recall her telling me in the last letter I received that every day was the same, only enlivened by the children."

"But would she have duplicated such a letter to her own mama, even if she was afraid and upset?" Emily asked. "Or sent letters to herself from Hebden Bridge?"

"Perhaps." Isabelle shook her head, at a loss. "Elizabeth is a complex person, as strong as she is weak, as determined as she is relenting. I do know that she always hated the idea that her father should ever see he'd made her cry when he chastised her, which he did very often. She hated to show any weakness at all. Instead she carried out small acts of rebellion that only she knew of." Isabelle's mouth curved into a smile. "In fact, we'd often call each other 'Rebel' as a sort of fond nickname, more like sisters than pupil and tutor. Often she'd tell me of the little jokes and secrets she'd write into the letters that no one would know were there except for her, and sometimes me of course."

"Or her mama," Charlotte said. "Remember, Anne, how Mrs. Honeychurch told us that she felt Elizabeth's mention of lavender was a secret message to her to please come and rescue her?"

"I do," Anne said. "Poor Elizabeth—but wouldn't she tell you, her friend and confidante, the truth of her marriage? Frederick Walters said you and she were very close."

"You spoke to Freddie?" Isabelle seemed surprised. "You really are very, very good detectors. And I suppose he told you the strange situation that Mr. Honeychurch pressed him into?"

"He did, and we find it hard to fathom"—Emily nodded—"that the rumour of one affair might be preferable to another."

"Oh dear." Isabelle turned her face away from the sisters for a moment, and they waited until her shoulders stilled and her breathing became even once more. "I'm afraid that I may well be the last person that Lizzie would confide in about her marriage. You see, I tried very hard to persuade her not to marry Robert Chester. I'd heard such things about him, and I knew Elizabeth would be happier unmarried."

"Really?" Anne asked, leaning forward. "Do you believe that because you are unmarried?"

"In part," Isabelle said. "I am the agent of my own destiny, and I would rather that than marriage to any man. But also because Lizzie is someone who was meant to do *something*, something *beyond* what life as a wife would allow. I saw so much potential in her. Elizabeth felt differently, though." Isabelle stood up, walking over to a plan chest that leaned up against the wall, looking thoughtful as she rested her palms against it, weighing her words carefully. "You see, Elizabeth had known great love once before in her life— she knew what it felt like, that passionate need for another, and she longed for it again. Her courtship with Chester gave her hope that it might be possible to love that way again, that their marriage would be an eternal, grand, passionate affair. Try as I might, I couldn't dissuade her from her path—she was determined. Elizabeth would have hated to admit to me, of all people, that she was unhappy; she would have hated to have conceded that I was right."

For a moment there was nothing but almost perfect silence, interrupted only by the chime of china, and the birdsong outside the open window. The more they knew of Elizabeth Chester, Emily thought, the less she understood her, or indeed the human heart at all. What could drive a person wilfully to choose a path to destruction, other than something like wild optimism—or perhaps something else, some kind of need to suffer, to atone for a secret sin?

"Mama." A girl child's voice startled Emily as she appeared behind Isabelle's chair. "Who are these people?"

"These are the Misses Brontë, Celeste, dear," Isabelle whispered to the child, who seemed to be about five. "Friends of Mama's. Misses Brontë, this is Celeste, my daughter."

"Good day, Miss Celeste." Anne smiled sweetly. "My sisters and I are charmed to meet you."

"Say hello like I've taught you, dear," Isabelle prompted the little girl, who performed a wobbly curtsey that Emily had to admit was rather charming. "Did you wake from your nap already? I expect you would like some milk with bread and jam, wouldn't you?"

"Yes, Mama," the little girl said, eyeing Emily with one velvet-brown eye through her cascade of wild, dark hair. Emily noticed her high cheekbones and thought what a beautiful child she was. It must have taken a very rare and beautiful man to make her, for she looked nothing like her mama.

"Then come and sit on my lap for a moment while I cuddle you, you dear, sweet little thing." Isabelle laughed, covering her daughter's face in kisses, her joy fading as she held the child pressed tightly to her bosom, holding her close as if she was afraid to let her go.

"Celeste is such a pretty name," Anne said, smiling at the shy child. "Oh, and you are such a beautiful little girl."

"Celeste"—Isabelle kissed her daughter on each cheek—"why don't you go to the pantry to fetch the jam and some fresh bread, and I will be with you in a moment."

"Very well, Mama," Celeste said, casting one last, long look at the three strangers before disappearing into the back of the house.

"What a delightful child," Anne said. "I'm so terribly sorry that you lost your husband."

"Oh, don't be sorry." Isabelle smiled. "For I have never been married."

39

Emily

"I . . . Oh." Anne coloured bright red, suddenly finding the stitching of her cuffs fascinating.

"Celeste's father." It was Emily who broke the silence, her sense of curiosity overcoming her. She did her best to frame her next words as delicately as she knew how. "He must have been a remarkable-looking young man."

"Indeed," Isabelle said, adding dryly, "how astute. He was born overseas, parentage unknown. As a young boy he went to work on a ship, but still his life was hard and cruel. And yet his intellect, his diligence saw him rise to ship's mate, and that was how he came to find himself in Liverpool and then Leeds, conducting business in his master's stead." Isabelle smiled faintly and at last opened the top drawer of the plan chest, drawing out a sketched portrait.

"This is George," she said, taking one long look at the work before turning it towards the sisters to view. George was indeed uncommonly handsome, with a light that the artist had captured in his eyes that seemed to Emily to speak of a very deep and gentle soul.

"How did you meet such a man?" Charlotte asked breathlessly.

"He came to make a trade with Honeychurch at the mill while Elizabeth and I were visiting one afternoon. You could feel it like a thunderclap when they met. They looked at one another, and the air was electric with it."

"They?" Emily asked.

"You seem like fine women, Misses Brontë," she said, as she turned back to them. "So I am about to trust you with a very deep secret, one which you must never disclose to anyone, for it is not mine to reveal."

"We swear it," Emily said at once, glancing at each of her sisters, who nodded too.

"The scandal that poor Frederick agreed to cover up for Honeychurch was because Lizzie's father could not bear the idea that his daughter had taken a bastard ship's mate as her lover, a man of no lineage who looked as if he might come from a very far corner of the world. No more than that. That she had loved him with all of her heart and soul, and he her, meant nothing to him. For me, though, well, it was a wondrous thing to see—it made me believe for a little while in the possibility of love overcoming all." She sighed deeply, turning the portrait back towards her, cradling it gently against her breast. "They planned to escape together, to find a place far away where they might be happy. They were both so young, so naïve, they thought that such a dream might be possible, and I hoped with all my heart that it could be too. But before they could make their escape good, the affair was discovered, and more than that. It soon became apparent to me that Lizzie was with child. I helped her hide the signs from her mother. And I aided her father in his plans to spirit her away out of sight."

"Oh my," Charlotte whispered. "Oh dear."

"Dear George—dear, sweet, brave George—should have run. Lizzie begged him to, but he refused. Instead he came to Honeychurch to ask for Elizabeth's hand. I don't know what was said, or what happened next, only that he was found dead in the canal two days later. The cause of his drowning was never determined."

"Oh, dear Lord," Anne whispered. "Poor George. Poor Lizzie."

"Elizabeth was broken." Isabelle shook her head, tears rolling down her pale cheeks. "I truly thought she might die, and perhaps she would have if it hadn't have been for Celeste. She was determined to bring George's child into the world. Her parents publicly announced that they had sent her away to school, and let rumours of a dalliance with Frederick act as a smokescreen for the truth. In reality Lizzie and I travelled here, to Wycoller, to this very house, where we spent the rest of her confinement, just us two. She gave birth to her daughter, a child that she loved very much, that she begged to be allowed to raise as her own, but her father would have none of it, threatened her with the asylum if she would not agree to give the child up. And I knew he would make good on his threat, for he is the worst of men, the kind that see themselves as righteous, just and true, even as they execute the cruellest deeds. Elizabeth was so very distressed, so desperate not to be parted from her child, and begged me to take her, to raise her as my daughter, but to allow her to visit whenever she wanted. I promised her that one day Celeste would know the truth about her real mama, that she would always have two mothers. It wasn't perfect, but Elizabeth visited and wrote until just after she was married. That's why I never understood why Elizabeth would stop writing to me, because right up until that last visit she would always be enquiring of Celeste. Indeed, the last time I saw her she told me how it would be her dearest wish to have all three children gathered under one roof, and me as well. But she stopped writing, and never replied to my letters . . . I waited for her to come back to us. I never thought for a moment that she might not."

"If she was so unhappy, so afraid at Chester Grange, perhaps she just wanted to protect you and Celeste," Emily offered. "Keep you safe from that cruel place. It is certain that Chester would have been enraged to find out that she'd borne a child."

"Perhaps," Isabelle said sadly. "One thing I can tell you that is certain and true about Elizabeth: her children are her life, both her own and her stepson. And I can promise you that she would never, not ever, leave them willingly, not while there is breath in her body. She would fight until the death for her children, kill for them. I know that much about my friend. Her children mean the world to her. Whatever she did, it was for them."

Emily surprised herself by reaching out to Isabelle, her hand covering the artist's, mourning alongside her this woman who had lived so little in such a short space of time, and then vanished into thin air. Perhaps that was the price of really existing in the world? Perhaps the price was always death.

"I had so hoped we would have found her here," she said, feeling the weight of Elizabeth's absence heavily in the air. "I had convinced myself that you would be hiding her, and she'd be safe and we'd be able to help her. But now I cannot see a way forward."

"We still have the other paper," Charlotte said. "The one sent from Hebden Bridge. That paper led us here to you, Isabelle, and I feel it must have some greater significance."

"Perhaps she came to Hebden Bridge to see me, and Kitty did not tell her where I was, though she would know I'd be here, and I can't imagine why she'd post a letter back to her own home," Isabelle said unhappily. "Dear God, if I thought that there was a chance I could have helped her, and I failed her . . ."

"Mama." Celeste reappeared, her cheeks smeared in jam, carrying a plate of bread, thickly spread. "Don't be sad, Mama—you can have my supper, if you like."

"I don't think that could be the case," Emily said kindly. "However this envelope was sent, it couldn't have been by her—she was ill in bed all day on the day before she vanished. We have a witness who told us so."

"A witness." Isabelle nodded. "My life has not been a conventional one, and perhaps I am a little more world-weary and worldly than ladies such as you. Human beings are fallible, they are weak. And if it is the testimony of a witness that makes this puzzle impossible to solve, may I suggest that your witness must be lying?"

Emily turned to Charlotte; their eyes met.

The answer was no, of course: no, because the witness had been someone they thought they knew, the very person for whom they'd embarked on this mission of discovery.

Had Matilda French been leading them a deadly dance all this while?

40

Anne

"Any news?" Mattie was waiting for them at the top of the steps just inside the open front door of the parsonage with Branwell standing behind her when the three sisters returned, a little before three in the afternoon.

Anne was glad to see her brother up after his adventure last night, respectably dressed and apparently sober, but her mind was whirling at all they had seen and discovered in their encounter with Isabelle, and her pleasure at seeing Branwell looking well was soured by the questions they were going to have to ask Mattie.

"Papa's concerns over Miss French's arrival and your absence again have led him to ask me to watch over you all," Branwell told them as the sisters bustled in, removing their bonnets and shaking the dust of the roads from their long skirts. "He has asked me to accompany you everywhere you go until this flitting about is all done with." Branwell smiled. "Sisters, I am the leader now."

"Of course you are," Charlotte said. "Then you had better keep up your good work of the last two days and remain respectable, Leader Branwell, if you are to be any use to us."

"I do believe the good ship *Respectable* has already sailed," Emily said, pausing to kiss Branwell on the cheek. "Let's hope her sister vessel the *Sober* makes it safely into harbour, brother mine."

"I shall lead you to victory." Branwell clicked his heels together and bowed, making Matilda blush and smile all at once. "The moment after you have told me where to go." He was such a darling idiot, Anne thought, repressing a smile.

It had been a long, hot walk home, because they were all tired and not a little discouraged. Emily had been so certain that they were going to find Elizabeth at Wycoller with Isabelle, and that she was not there had shaken her confidence in her detecting abilities quite considerably. *What if not every mystery could be solved?* Emily had asked as they trudged home, heads bowed. *What if sometimes the universe did just swallow up a person and never returned them?* Each of them found the whole idea rather terrifying and, for Anne at least, a little beguiling. For there was something unexpected that Anne had discovered today—something all the more exhilarating because she had never considered it until she met Isabelle: the notion that her life might be a better one, a richer and more free one, without a husband in it. Before she had only ever considered two possibilities: marriage or unfulfilled spinsterhood. The idea that a life alone could be a life well lived. No, even the best version of her life had never really presented itself as possible before, and somehow she found the notion both comforting and exciting all at once, her horizons suddenly stretching outward to destinations she had never previously allowed herself to imagine.

"Martha, where is dear Tabby?" Charlotte asked.

"She is nodding by the stove, miss," Martha said. "She seemed awful tired today, so I told her to put her leg up and I'd see to all. Should I wake her?"

"No, let her rest, Martha," Charlotte said. "Would you be so kind as to bring us tea, please?" Martha nodded at once.

Emily followed Matilda into the dining room, and with Branwell behind her, the tiny room was hot and cramped. Anne and Matilda took a chair each, and Branwell stood in the corner by the door like one of his toy soldiers of old, Charlotte at the window, and Emily occupied the space in between.

"What did you discover from Miss Lucas?" Mattie asked them. "Does she know anything of what happened?

"She told us a good deal that was helpful about the person that Elizabeth was . . . is—but nothing at all to indicate where she might be now."

"Oh dear." Mattie's face fell in concern. "So then we must return to Chester Grange at once, and send for a constable and get the children away from there somehow. I haven't slept a wink with worrying about them."

"I agree," Anne said, her eyes meeting Charlotte's. Her sister nodded, a movement that was echoed by Emily.

"Mattie"—Anne leaned in a little closer to Mattie, keeping her voice soft and gentle—"you said that Elizabeth Chester remained in bed the day before her disappearance?"

"Yes, indeed." Mattie nodded. "Yes, she never once emerged from her room."

"And yet we have this." Anne took the parcel wrapper out of her case and handed it to Matilda. "In Elizabeth's hand, addressed to herself. And according to the postmark, posted in Hebden Bridge one day before she disappeared—the day that she was in bed, posted back to her own home. How can that make sense, Mattie?"

"I . . . I don't know." Mattie looked at the package. "Do you think it is important?"

"It is important if you've been lying to us, Mattie," Emily said. "If you've been hiding the truth, then it is *very* important. We have evidence, a parcel wrapping that indicates that Elizabeth Chester may have been in Hebden Bridge on the day you said she was in bed, on the day that you took her tea and soup. Did you lie about that, Mattie, to confuse matters? Did you lie about where Elizabeth Chester truly was on that day?"

"I most certainly did not!" Mattie protested hotly. "I did not lie, because I didn't tell you that I had taken her tea and soup. I told you I *made* her tea and soup, and that is the truth! But I didn't take them to her. Mrs. Crawley took every meal up to her that day—she insisted on it. She said Mrs. Chester wasn't fit for visitors outside of herself."

"Mattie, if you are hiding something from us . . ." Anne pressed.

"Anne, please," Branwell said, reminding them all of his presence, "remember that Matilda isn't the suspect here, but a young lady and a friend. Gentle yourself, I beg you. It's unbecoming to see you harangue her so."

Anne pressed her lips together at being schooled in seemly manners by her brother, but in this instance she thought he was probably right.

"I mean," Mattie said hesitantly, reaching out for the scrap of paper, "Mrs. Chester always wrote a return address on her correspondence. It could just be that she sent this to Hebden Bridge and it was returned on this date by coincidence?"

"Coincidence," Anne said, looking at her sisters. "You mean this may not be a clue at all?"

"It may be," Matilda offered, eager to please her friends. "Or . . . or it may just be a letter. But even then, even if it was returned to Mrs. Chester, it found its way into her husband's study—perhaps it was even intercepted. And if it contained secrets . . ."

"If," Emily said, slamming her palms down on the table so that the pens they had left there rattled and rolled across the surface. "If! Not one of us thought of a simple explanation for that letter. Because we discovered it we thought it must mean something. We're very poor detectors if we are unable to discern what matters and what does not, wasting our time chasing a phantom."

"No, we haven't wasted anything," Anne said. "The letter led us to Isabelle Lucas. It led us so much closer to discovering the truth of Elizabeth, and I'm sure that by and by it will lead us to what that means to the mystery. Not everything we discover can be a chess piece, certain to move us one step nearer to a conclusion. To reach understanding we must gather all that we can, whether it makes sense at first or not, like your stone, Emily."

Emily slumped into a chair, reaching up for Charlotte's hand as her sister came to stand behind her.

"But while we learn from our mistakes," Emily said, "a woman's life hangs in the balance."

"There is something, though—a theory that has just come to mind that wouldn't have if we hadn't questioned Mattie about this," Anne said. "We've always assumed that Elizabeth was taken in the night, but if she was confined to her room the day before, and the only person to see her was Mrs. Crawley, then it's possible that whatever happened to her happened on that day, in broad daylight. And that might explain why no one heard the dogs barking in the night, why there were no signs of exit or entry from her room. Because her abduction had already taken place, and everything else, as Emily said, was theatre." Anne hesitated, making a determined effort to stand firm behind her thoughts. "I don't have evidence that that is the case, but it is a theory."

"That Mrs. Crawley would abet Chester in hurting his wife?" Emily said. "But we no longer believe that it *was* Chester."

"Emily's right, I'm afraid, Anne," Charlotte said. "I can't think of a single reason for Mrs. Crawley to lie about Elizabeth's location the night before she disappeared, if Chester is not guilty of this crime."

"Unless . . ." Emily said thoughtfully, making Anne smile. It was always something to behold when Emily was about to have an idea. Emily turned on Matilda, startling her rather. "Mattie, tell me, is there anything about the children that is unusual, out of the ordinary?"

Mattie looked perplexed.

"They are a perfect delight in every way," she said.

"I don't mean to insult them," Emily said. "I mean only to try to shed light on what is happening at Chester Grange. Anything *physically* unusual at all?"

Mattie frowned, twisting one of Branwell's handkerchiefs in her hands.

"It makes no difference to how much I love him, but Mr. Chester told me that I was never to let anyone see Archie's feet," Mattie said, unhappily. "And he has such dear little feet too. But Chester is ashamed of them, because there is webbing between his toes, which is really quite pronounced, though it will not hinder his life in any way, the doctors say. So I don't really see what on earth that can matter at all."

"Oh, it matters," Emily said, rising in her chair, triumphant. "And so, sisters, brother, Matilda, we come a step closer. We know something more than we did before."

"What can we possibly know?" Anne pressed her, intrigued by the look of realisation on Emily's face.

"The night I visited the Grange I saw Mrs. Crawley in her nightgown prowling about the house to keep an eye on Mr. Chester. For once she wasn't wearing those strange, indoor gloves, and as she opened the library door, I saw her bare hands: there was webbing between her fingers."

"Like Archie's feet?" Anne queried. "Does that mean it is a contagious condition?"

"Not at all," Emily told the room. "After seeing Mrs. Crawley's hands, I wondered about the same thing, and looked up the condition in Papa's medical dictionary. It is, in fact, *hereditary.*"

"Which means . . ." Charlotte's eyes widened as she looked to Anne and then back to Emily. "It means that either this is a huge coincidence, or that Mrs. Crawley is somehow a blood relative of Archie's."

"Their grandmother, I'd wager." Emily nodded. "And though I cannot determine how, I'd also suggest that she is almost certainly Chester's true mother. And what did Isabelle tell us that a mother would do for her child?"

"Die for them," Charlotte said, nodding gravely. "And perhaps even kill."

41

Charlotte

As the coach dropped them a mile from Chester Grange, Charlotte paid the driver to wait where he was and wondered for the first time about the wisdom of approaching the house incognito with what amounted to a small army of five people. Unlike Emily's first covert visit, though it was late, it was light still, the dusk taking its time settling into night.

And so, Charlotte concluded, it seemed unlikely that a group as large as theirs could remain undetected for very long. Swiftly, she made an assessment of the party, and decided whom to take with her.

"Mattie." She pulled her friend away from Branwell, who was whispering something into her ear, while his hands seemed to be on some covert missions of their own. "You must come with me, and you, Emily. You managed to fend off the dogs before, and should they search us out again, I'm sure they will do your bidding. Anne and Branwell, you must stay here and keep watch."

"Keep watch?" Branwell spluttered. "What use is my manly strength keeping watch?"

"Well"—Charlotte thought for a moment—"if we are discovered and need assistance, then you may sweep in and rescue us."

"And how, precisely, am I to know the exact moment when you will require rescuing?" Branwell asked.

"There will be a sign," Emily said confidently.

"What sign?" Branwell demanded.

"I don't know, but you will know it when you see it," Emily told him. "Besides, it's better that you are out here, dear leader. Think of yourself as the general on the high ridge, overseeing operations. We may be leading the charge, but you are heading the intellectual campaign."

"I wish I'd gone to the pub," Branwell said, collapsing down to lean against a tree.

"And why me?" Anne asked. "Why must I stay behind and look after Branwell?"

"How insulting!" Branwell protested as he produced a hip flask from inside his coat.

"Because, Anne . . ." Charlotte realised that she did not actually have a legitimate reason other than to keep an eye on Branwell. "Well, because you are the youngest, and besides, we are attempting to go unnoticed, a feat that will be made all the harder if we travel en masse."

"But . . . but . . ." For a moment, rage made Anne quite speechless. When she found her words, however, they were furious. "How my age matters a whit, I do not know. It is I who have been in the house before with Branwell, I who have seen the entirety of Chester Grange and I who discovered clues—lots of clues. If anyone should stay behind, it is you, Charlotte. All you've done is boss people around and annoy them."

"She does have a point," Emily said with a shrug.

"I'm not staying behind," Charlotte protested. "Because, well, I'm . . . well I'm *not*, and there's an end to it."

"Oh, dear Lord, will you all go and let a man drink in peace, please?" Branwell pleaded. "Charlotte, you are so small you only count as half a person anyway, and Emily is so unsociable that she is practically invisible. And let us pray that if you are all together, then at least I won't be able to hear you talking."

"Very well," Charlotte conceded with some exasperation. "Come along, then. We haven't got all night. And, Branwell, do try to stay sober."

"Too late for that." Branwell lifted his flask to toast them as they marched into the night.

Of course the door to the pantry creaked as Mattie let them in, the groan of the grinding hinges seeming as loud as a ghostly moan in the silent kitchen. The fire was almost dead in the grate, just a few embers still faintly glowing in the dark, and at first all seemed peaceful.

Then they heard it: the shouts and cries of a man's voice echoing throughout the house. Privately, Charlotte had thought it extremely likely that Emily had been exaggerating as she had described, with ghoulish delight, Robert Chester's nocturnal activities at Chester Grange. Rather, though, it seemed she had been underplaying it, for with each howling cry, the hairs on the back of Charlotte's neck stood up, and the primal impulse to run in the opposite direction was very strong indeed.

"Chester," Emily whispered. "Drunk again, and tormenting his poor dead wife."

"Take us to the children first," Charlotte whispered, not at all keen to see that spectacle in person. "Once they are safely away we will find Mrs. Crawley and tell her all that we have discovered."

"What *I* have discovered," Emily reminded her.

"Heavens, Emily, we are in the middle of conducting a highly illegal activity," Charlotte spluttered. "It's hardly the time for quibbling."

"I don't know what that is," Emily said. "But I do know I discovered the webbed-feet thing, so."

"This way," Mattie said. "And perhaps be a little more silent?"

It was easy enough to avoid Chester: the library door was wide open this time, firelight spilling out into the hall, dancing brightly on the wood-panelled walls. Fortunately, the central position of the grand staircase meant that the intruders didn't have to attempt to scurry past Chester unnoticed, and they were able to make their way upstairs without bearing witness to whatever unnatural acts in which he might be engaged.

Each one holding her breath, they crept up the stairs, taking each step as delicately as they were able, gathering their skirts close and high so that they should not make any sound at all, not even the swish of wool brushing against a wall. On the first landing the hallway was still and full of shadows, utterly dark except for the thinnest sliver of light that came from under the doorway that Anne recognised as the nursery.

Mattie's feet picked up speed as she rushed towards the door, the sisters hurrying after her.

At least all seemed well in the nursery.

The fire burned brightly behind the guard, and it was as warm and safe a little room as it had always been.

Mattie rushed over to Francis's bed, stroking the hair back from his face for a moment before turning to the cot.

"The baby," she whispered to Anne. "Little Archie—he isn't in his crib."

"Do you know where he might be if not here?" Anne asked.

"No," Mattie half sobbed. "I have no idea where he might be if not here."

It was then that they heard a movement in the adjoining bedroom that had been Matilda's. Racing to the door, Anne flung it open.

There in near dark was Mrs. Crawley with the baby in one arm, folding children's clothes into a small trunk.

"What's this?" Mrs. Crawley cried out, taking in the sight of four female faces staring back at her. "What business have you here?"

"Please let me have the baby," Mattie said, advancing into the room, her arms outstretched. Upon seeing her, Archie cried out, reaching his arms out towards her in return. Outside, the wind suddenly picked up, rattling the latches at the window and extinguishing the fire in the grate in a single gust.

"I shall not," Mrs. Crawley said, although Charlotte noticed a quiver of uncertainty and, yes, fear, in her voice. "What are you talking about, harlot? You should not be in this house. I saw the way you mooned after my master. Mr. Chester will shoot you if he finds you in his home, and no court would convict him."

"He is very good at escaping justice, that's true enough," Emily said.

The wind howled down the chimney, and Mrs. Crawley clasped the baby even tighter.

"Are you planning a trip, Mrs. Crawley?" Charlotte asked pleasantly, her impeccable manners going some small way to defusing the tension. Still Mrs. Crawley backed away towards the window, as the only remaining candle wavered and almost blinked out. "Are you leaving? Because you know now that no one is safe from him, and you want to protect them? Is that why you are leaving with the children?"

"I am doing no such thing." Mrs. Crawley was struggling to keep Archie in her arms as he whimpered, fighting to be free and with his Mattie. "It is just that we have no help with the children since madam here decided to run off, after Mr. Chester refused her advances, and so I'm up late sorting laundry."

"That is a despicable lie!" Mattie gasped. "And I know you, Mrs. Crawley. I know you wouldn't spend your time folding dirty linen. Please let me take Archie—you are upsetting him, please." But Mrs. Crawley only held him tighter, turning him away from Mattie as she edged nearer to the window.

"Oh, I know your game." Mrs. Crawley spat the words over her shoulder. "I've seen it a hundred times before. You think you'll get him to fall in love with you, marry you and you'll have a tailor-made family and a fortune to boot. But you don't know the half of it, Miss French. A governess would never have been good enough for Mr. Chester. He'd used you, and planned to throw you away like all the others."

Matilda held her composure as she took another two steps closer to Mrs. Crawley and Archie.

"That might have been a foolish notion of mine once," she said quietly, tears standing in her eyes, "but for a very long time now I have only cared for the welfare of the children. Please let me take Archie—he is afraid, and no baby should ever be afraid, Mrs. Crawley."

"I'll look after him," Mrs. Crawley insisted. "He'll be all right with me once he's used to me. Babies just want to love and be loved, hey, little one?"

Turning away from the night that peered in at the window, Mrs. Crawley looked around the room. While Charlotte and Mattie had been talking to her, Emily had softly closed the door between this room and the nursery.

Mrs. Crawley was quite surrounded, and yet she did not seem to be the kind of woman to be easily intimidated by anything.

"You are leaving, though, aren't you?" Anne asked her. "You are taking them away from this place?"

"Though it is none of your business, if it will send you on your way, then yes, I am taking the children on a trip." Mrs. Crawley was defiant. "Where they will be safe and happy."

"So that's where you draw the line," Emily said, scathingly. "You will stand by him, obscure his crimes, perhaps even commit them for him. But then, I suppose that is the nature of motherhood, you'd do anything to protect your son . . . We know that you are Chester's mother, Mrs. Crawley."

"How dare you say such a thing," Mrs. Crawley sobbed. "I am his house-keeper, though once I was his nurse. That is all. And I am taking the children away from all this chaos for a little while. Please step aside, or I will call my master."

"No you won't," Emily said. "For as much as you love him, you are afraid of him. You don't want him to discover that you are taking the children away. You want to protect them. I suppose it is better that you have at least some moral compass than none at all."

"Emily, dear, don't presume," Charlotte said lightly. "We don't know for sure what Mrs. Crawley has done for her son. Perhaps you would like to tell us, Mrs. Crawley? Perhaps we will be able to help you find safe haven for the children?"

"I do not know what you speak of." Mrs. Crawley made a start towards the door and, seeing her way blocked by Emily, backed against the bite of the stone sill. "You will all be gone from this house at once." She did her best to assert her authority one final time. "Or I will call Mr. Chester no matter what the consequence and I will let him see to you."

"I don't believe that you will." Charlotte spoke with a gentle smile on her lips and very quietly, so that Mrs. Crawley had to lean forward to hear her. "Because you love these children, and you don't want them to witness one minute more of violence, or come to any harm. If you did not, then you wouldn't be trying to remove them from his grasp now, would you? Let us take them."

"You don't understand—you know nothing of what I've seen!" Mrs. Crawley cried out, turning away from them, the baby in her arms, just as the window was torn open, and for one terrible moment it looked as if she might cast Archie out of the window and follow him soon after.

"No!" Mattie shrieked, rushing forward. But Mrs. Crawley only sank to the floor, the baby crying in her arms, and after a moment, as Mattie knelt down beside her, it became clear that Mrs. Crawley was quietly weeping. Taking Archie from the old woman's arms, she carried him away to the other side of the room, cradling him close to her.

"Tell us, Mrs. Crawley," Anne said gently, closing the window. "Unburden yourself to us and let us help you. What don't we understand?"

"That I am taking the children to their mother. I am taking them to Elizabeth at last. Don't you see it is I that helped her get free of my son? I that got her safe passage out of the house, and did all I could to show that it were him that were a killer, though no one would really look? For though I love him with all my heart, I could not stand by and see him kill another wife."

42

Anne

"Elizabeth is alive?" Anne gasped. "She's safe, unharmed?"

"She is," Mrs. Crawley said. "We had to wait to move the children. I thought they'd arrest him at once and they would be reunited at once, but you three girls are the only ones to truly see all that I laid out to be discovered. The constable went in the wrong direction and my son continued free, and the more frightened and angrier he became, the more I feared for my little darlings. For though they have lived through such darkness, they might yet be saved, and I will not rest until it is done."

"Elizabeth is safe." Anne turned to Charlotte, ready to laugh in relief. "She is alive."

"I knew it!" Emily said, and although that was almost entirely untrue, they were all just so relieved that not even Charlotte protested the claim.

"But you are telling us that Robert Chester killed his first wife?" Anne sat down on the bed, thinking of the torn and bloodied glove, the plea for help. "Poor Imogen Chester didn't take her own life after all?"

The room was still and tense. It seemed that every floorboard was straining to listen, and though she didn't show it, Anne was sure she could feel the weight of another sitting beside her on the bed, a chill in the air that brushed down her right side only.

"I am," Mrs. Crawley said with a long and heavy sigh that seemed to release a great burden from her shoulders. "Robert *is* my son, may God forgive me. All my life I have done my best to look after him. I have always done my best to care for him, when no one else would. And I've loved him with all my heart, every day of my life, stood by him, no matter what he's done. The man he is, it's all because of me, you see. It's *all* because of me. But when he came close to killing another wife again, then I knew there was no saving him, no turning him back from ruin. I've seen Robert Chester do terrible things in the past, and I've looked away because I loved him. But I couldn't look away anymore. I thought if I could find a way, a way to stop him, I could save Elizabeth and my poppets at the same time. So I made this plan, this half murder. I knew the constables wouldn't look very hard for Elizabeth, not if my master told them not to, or sent them on a false trail. And I knew that Robert Chester would believe whatever I told him. I'm the only person who he can trust, you see? He trusts me enough to let me lead him into a trap."

"This whole scheme, the blood, the tooth—it was all you?" Anne shook her head in disbelief. "You meant to have him hanged for a murder he didn't commit so that Elizabeth and the children would be free of him?"

Mrs. Crawley nodded.

"I came to accept that was the only way to free us all, him included, from the pain he caused. And he never paid for Imogen—I made sure he never paid for Imogen—and that is my burden." Mrs. Crawley covered her face with her hands, the webbing masking her face. "And he needs to pay. He will never be saved if he doesn't pay. Perhaps he will hang. But I'm still his ma, and I must try and save his soul, because it's all my fault, you see, all my fault. I must save his soul even if it costs me my own."

The sisters shook their heads in disbelief, trying to follow backwards through the maze of rights and wrongs that Mrs. Crawley seemed to think would correct any evil that her son had committed.

"And Elizabeth went with you willingly?" Anne needed to know for certain.

"Yes, we made the plan together, the three of us." Mrs. Crawley nodded.

"Three?" Anne asked.

"Me and Elizabeth and this strange young woman called Rebel, who'd visit in the night dressed head to foot like a man."

"Isabelle Lucas is the man in the woods, the mysterious man the gypsies sold pigs blood to," Anne said, turning to Emily, aghast. "Isabelle Lucas is Rebel!"

"And Elizabeth *is* at Wycoller," Emily said. "That's why the paintings on the wall looked like they were painted by two people—because they were. Elizabeth loves to paint and draw too. I bet that portrait of George was by her. Elizabeth was hidden at Wycoller while we were there, and Isabelle fooled us all. I knew I liked her."

"I'm to take them to their mama tonight," Mrs. Crawley said. "I was going to say that Mattie here had run off with them."

"But . . . I haven't!" Mattie said unhappily. "And that would soon have been discovered."

"But it would have given Elizabeth and her friend Rebel time to find a boat," Mrs. Crawley said. "They wish to travel to New Zealand and begin a new life far away. But now I am discovered, and I must face my fate. So you will have to take the children to her, will you? And send the law here. I shall confess all, everything about Imogen, and more, and I shall say I killed Elizabeth and the children and they may hang me, and I shan't mind if I know that those sweet souls are safe, and perhaps, perhaps then the Lord will forgive me."

"Mrs. Crawley, the Lord doesn't want you to hang for something you haven't done," Anne said.

"No, but I should have hanged for that which I did do," she said. "He kept Imogen locked in the attic for days before he finally killed her, tormenting her day by day and I *knew* what he was doing, just as she did. She knew she would never leave the attic alive, never see little Francis again." Her voice cracked as she wept. "When Robert came to me and told me she was dead, I didn't scream or cry out, I didn't think of her or her boy. I helped Robert carry her poor damaged body to the ramparts and throw her down. That poor, broken girl. He loved her as much as he hated her, and he hated me for helping him dispose of her. It was me that felt his anger that night—he gave me this scar as a thank-you." She touched the matrix of thickened skin on her cheek. "But this isn't punishment enough—I should hang for what we did to Imogen, and so should he."

Anne didn't know what to say, so strange was it to feel sympathy for one who had committed such evil acts .... How could that be possible? It seemed to her that the whole world had changed since they had begun detecting, that she had seen into the shadows that she had always known were there, and she had not flinched or looked away. Somehow she found courage in knowing that, and something deeper: a quiet determination to show the whole world the cruelty and injustice it concentrated so hard on pretending didn't exist.

"I believe we should take the children to their mother now," she said solemnly to Emily and Charlotte, who both nodded in agreement.

"Mattie, will you help me?" Anne asked.

At once Mattie and Anne went into the children's room, and a few moments later returned, now with a still sleeping Francis in Anne's arms.

"Take the servants' stairs, and go out the back. He's too deep in his drink to notice you leaving." Mrs. Crawley wept. "And look after them, I beg you."

"Please don't fear, Mrs. Crawley," Charlotte said kindly. "We will make sure your grandchildren are soon with their mother, and safe."

43

❧ ⚬ ❧

Emily

Emily stood on the threshold as Mattie and Anne spirited the children away down the hall, vanishing through a door hidden in the panelling, safe from discovery by Chester. A part of Emily wished she could follow them and explore all the hidden passages of Chester Grange, imagining what other secrets she might find hidden away there, but somebody had to stay and protect her sister.

She could hear Charlotte and Mrs. Crawley talking in low voices in the bedroom, as if they were old acquaintances exchanging quiet reminiscences. How Charlotte could sit so comfortably with a woman who had borne witness to such destruction and remain silent, Emily did not know. It was a curious characteristic of her sister that she could see the humanity in every person she met, from the lowest to the highest. Charlotte would understand the path that had brought Mrs. Crawley to this moment, where Emily never could.

.Perhaps Robert Chester was Mrs. Crawley's son, but was that bond enough to justify complicity? Emily thought of Branwell, no doubt dozing off the gin that he had brought with him under the tree where she had left him, made impervious to the cold and wind by alcohol.

There had been a time when they were children that Branwell had truly been the leading light of their little band, the beginning and the end of everything they did. Branwell had intelligence and wit—he had a deal of talent—and yet none of it was enough to bring him any happiness or contentment within himself. It was as if all of his life he'd been waiting for his genius to be discovered, for his talents to be lauded, without him actually having to do anything. Branwell thought of himself as destined for great things but did no great things to earn that distinction. He failed them all again and again, and himself in every second. And the truth was, it did mean that Emily loved him less; she loved him just a little less for not being the man he could have been, and even less still for not even trying.

Daring to venture a little further from safety, she crept along the landing to the window at the end, taking the sounds of Chester shouting and crashing about below as a signal of her relative safety. As long as he was down there, they would not be discovered here.

There was a break in the dense cloud cover, and now night had truly fallen, allowing enough moonlight to seep through for Emily to catch sight of the small party of Anne and Mattie, carrying two children. Strange, shadowy beasts they made as they headed towards the treeline, and she smiled, for there she saw hope—the promise of a future restored to two little boys.

If only there was a way to do the same for her brother, to restore him to that bright-haired boy who had once shown them all the way.

Turning back, Emily was stopped in her tracks by something quite extraordinary. At the other end of the landing there was a light, silvery and white, as if a moonbeam had found its way inside and curled in and around on itself, transforming into an orb. It looked a little like the fool's fire that you'd see sometimes up on the moor: fairylike flames that, legend had it, led the dim-witted and impure of thought to their doom. But this sphere of light didn't flicker or blink like fool's fire did—it just hovered there, casting a metallic glow around it.

There had been times in her life when the men and women of her imagination had seeped out into the world around, walked from room to room with her at home, or accompanied her and Keeper up onto the moor, but this was not like that. Like the cold hand in the study, this came from without and not within, and that made it all the more fascinating. With the smile of a curious child, she reached out towards it, drawn to it as a moth would be to a flame.

And yet, before she could touch it, it dissipated in the same instant that she felt a rush of cold air that seemed to pass right through her. Emily turned to look behind her, half expecting to see the light there now, but whatever it was, it had vanished without leaving the faintest trace. Yet in her mind's eye Emily could see two words, as clearly as if they had been etched into glass: *Thank you.*

When she returned to the bedroom, Charlotte was sitting next to Mrs. Crawley on the bed, her hands folded into her lap and her head tilted to one side as she listened to Mrs. Crawley talk, the words tumbling out of her as if they had been building behind a dam of silence.

Emily was glad that the children, at least, were on their way to safety, but the danger was still very present, for if Chester discovered that she and Charlotte were hoping that Mrs. Crawley would confess everything she knew and help bring him to the gallows, then his destructive fury would be unleashed upon them all.

"I was just a girl, you see—hardly more than a child," Mrs. Crawley was telling Charlotte. "They took me from the workhouse at barely more than fifteen, and I couldn't believe my luck: a roof, a bed, food and even wages. It seemed that the Lord had finally shone his light on me, for my early life had been very hard and full of sorrow. It was a much busier house then: full staff, cooks, maids—a butler." Her eyes shone as she thought of it. "I was hardly ever spoken to by the mistress of the house then. I remember thinking how elegant she was, and how beautiful, but she always seemed cold, like she was made of marble. And though they had been married a long time, there were no children. I had been there less than a year when Mr. Chester, the late Mr. Chester . . ." Mrs. Crawley sighed. "He would always stop and ask me how I was, bring me a sweet treat he'd saved just for me. He was kind to me, the only person who ever had been. Then one day, as I was walking back from an errand through the gardens, he came to me and swept me up in his arms. He told me that he had tried so hard not to love me, but love me he did. He spoke to me, looked at me, touched me like no other ever had. I was young and I fell in love." Mrs. Crawley rubbed her hands over her ruddy face. "It was only a few months before I discovered that I was with child. I had no inkling myself—it was the cook that told me, and she gave me a right hiding for it too. I went to him and all gentleness was gone. He told me that I would be dismissed at once, unless I agreed to give up the baby to him and his wife, to be brought up as their own son. If I agreed to that, he told me, then I could stay on as wet nurse and nanny. Even then I didn't realise that this had been their scheme all along, that on that day that they came to the workhouse they were looking for a likely candidate. Well, I had no choice—I couldn't go back to the workhouse with a babe. It would be death for us both. So I gave them my baby, and they kept me on as nursemaid. At first it scarcely mattered that I was not allowed to call him son, for we were together every day. My mistress was very little interested in him. But as he grew, he wanted less of me. And as he grew he understood he had a father that was cruel and incapable of love. And as for his mother, she couldn't bear to look at him and would not be in a room with him for longer than she had to be. And slowly, very slowly, what good there was in him rotted away, infected by opium and drink. I watched my dear, sweet boy become cruel and vicious. I watched him turn into a monster. When he was twenty years old his father died, and soon after his mother. But I remained always at his side, in the hope that I might find a way to bring him out of the dark and back to the Lord. And then I saw him one day treating a young maid as his father had treated me. I took him aside and told him the truth—all of it—and how I loved him and watched over him every day, and that he was loved and always had been, no matter what he did."

"And you had no effect on his conscience at all?" Charlotte asked, although to Emily the answer to that seemed blindingly obvious.

"None. He said that if I was his mother, then I must do his bidding and keep his secrets, and that it was I that had made him, and I alone that must bear witness to what I had done. He used to go to sleep sucking his thumb, sitting on my lap," she said almost dreamily. "Those were the happiest moments of my life: the weight of his body against mine, my heartbeat echoing his. I swore I'd always protect him. I swore it to that dear little boy who never harmed no one."

Emily started, hearing a sudden movement from outside the room. Going to the door, she pressed her ear against it and listened. Now there was only silence, and yet a few moments ago she'd heard the creak of a floorboard and, out of the corner of her eye, seen a shadow pass below the door, she was sure of it.

"Mrs. . . . What is your first name?" Charlotte asked, with such patience that Emily thought she might join the wind in screaming.

"Alice," Mrs. Crawley said, tasting the unfamiliar word as she spoke it. "Though she who bore that name no longer lives, she walks the halls of this place as much a ghost as Imogen."

"You've seen her ghost?" Emily asked at once.

"Seen her?" Mrs. Crawley shook her head. "No, I don't have to see an apparition to know that her soul is trapped here. After she died he was sick with sorrow and longing for the very woman he'd destroyed. So he went back to the graveyard and dug up her bones. He keeps her here with him, just as he used to imprison her in the attic when she displeased him. She is his slave, unable to rest."

"There is a path to redemption for you, I'm sure of it," Charlotte told her. "Come with us, Mrs. Crawley. Come with us and tell the authorities what you know about Chester's first wife. It is in your power alone to stop him now. Let his children and his wife be free of him without having to run to the other side of the world. Come with us and confess all. We will be with you, I swear it."

The next thing Emily felt was a tinder-flash of pain and, unsure of how she got there, found herself sprawled on the floor, tasting her own blood.

And suddenly, the room was filled with Robert Chester, bellowing with such rage that he might have been the very devil himself.

44

⤳⤙⤛⤵

Emily

The room lurched and tipped as Emily scrambled to her feet, attempting to steady herself as she took in the situation. Her heart was hammering in her chest, and all at once she felt alive with superhuman strength born out of true terror.

Chester flung himself at Mrs. Crawley, who screamed as he struck her with the skull he held, knocking the candle into the curtains that surrounded the bed, which at once became alive with flame.

Emily may have sworn under her breath as she pulled her startled and frozen sister off the bed, attempting to send her towards the door, but Charlotte didn't move—she just stared at Chester attacking Mrs. Crawley, and the flames that grew more vigorous by the second.

"Get off her, you brute!" Emily said, grabbing at Chester's arm and pulling at him, but her strength was no match for his.

"Charlotte." Emily turned back to her sister. "Move! You must get out at once!"

Still, Charlotte was transfixed following the path of the fire as it leapt onto the ceiling with arachnid grace. Emily realised that she had to choose what to do next: drag her sister free of the fire, or try once again to stop Chester from killing Mrs. Crawley. It was a choice she refused to make.

"Unhand her, you devil!" she shrieked like a banshee, throwing her whole weight into Chester, unbalancing him just enough for Mrs. Crawley to be able to roll from under him. Instinctively, Mrs. Crawley grabbed the fallen brass candlestick, and Emily saw her strike Chester with what looked like every ounce of force she could muster, stunning him as the flames engulfed almost the whole of the room.

Mrs. Crawley folded herself over the prone body of her son, weeping and stroking his face, and Emily realised there was no longer a choice to be made: neither mother nor son was leaving now.

But she and her sister were, she was quite determined. Although fire blocked every exit, this could not be their end. Apart from anything else, Papa would be quite destroyed.

"Charlotte." She took her sister by the wrist, shaking her out of her stupor. "We must get out now! Try the window!" But the bed was now fully ablaze, making it impossible to cross the room that way.

Desperately, Emily kept hold of Charlotte as she tried the door to the nursery, the heat in the handle burning her palm at once. Black smoke thickened in the air, and the heat alone seemed to singe her lashes and hair.

"Emily!" Charlotte cried out. "I believe we may be undone."

"We are not undone," Emily told her firmly. "This is not how I want to be undone. I don't want to die, Charlotte. I want to live. And by God, I will."

In a few swift movements, Emily ripped strips from her petticoats, thrusting them into a pitcher of water that stood on the dresser, soaking them through. Handing one to Charlotte, she showed her what to do as she wrapped the other around her nose and mouth. Then she used the last of the water to soak a small strip, which she wrapped around her hand.

The air was now almost impossible to breathe. Not only was it full of smoke, but it felt so hot that Emily was sure her very lungs were alight, and the flames were just a few inches from the hems of their skirts. One moment more and they would be lost.

"Now," Emily said, opening the door with her bound hand, dragging Charlotte behind her.

As the sisters ran into the hallway, the flames followed them, dancing onto the paintings and curtains, chasing down the rugs that lined the landing.

"Emily, your skirts!" Charlotte shouted, and when Emily looked down she saw the fabric of her dress was alight. Together the sisters beat her dress with their hands, Emily rolling on the floor until the flames were out. And scrambling to her feet, without looking back, she took Charlotte's hand, and they ran.

No matter how fast they travelled, the fire pursued them, unrelenting. Though she felt her legs might crumble to ash below her at any moment, Emily refused to stop, pulling Charlotte through the house towards the faint hope of safety.

They were almost out when she heard the frantic bark of Chester's dogs, and heard their bodies thud against the closed door of his study.

"Emily, no!" Charlotte cried as Emily ran in the wrong direction towards the shut room, and released the hounds that raced alongside her back to Charlotte, women and dogs spilling out into the blessed, cold night air, where they ran and kept running, even when the last of the danger was far behind them.

It was only when they were a safe distance from the house that the two collapsed into the long grass and looked back at the inferno that was raging where they had been only minutes before.

"Dear God," Charlotte half wheezed, half sobbed in relief as the flames caught hold of the building, lighting up every room. "This is more than a quiet woman such as I can stand, Emily. We might have died! I am done with detecting for good."

"Nonsense." Emily's cough shook her shoulders before she filled her lungs with the fresh Yorkshire air and coughed once more. "We live, Charlotte." She gasped. "And what's more, don't you see how *very much* we live? We live as brightly and as brilliantly as every one of those flames, and just as fiercely. Remarkable. How remarkable, that the proximity of death can make one truly know what it is to be alive."

"There will be men here from the village soon," Charlotte said. "And a great many questions will be asked. I think you and I and the Chester children should be far away from here before then. Whatever happens next, at least a kind of justice has been done."

"And Imogen Chester is free at last." Emily smiled. For it might have been her eyes playing tricks on her, but for one moment Emily thought she saw a silvery moonlit figure in a window, looking down on her, before vanishing into the fire.

"I'm here to rescue you!" Branwell toasted his sisters as he arrived, flopping down on the grass beside them.

"And only a *tiny* bit too late to be useful," Emily said, glad to find as she took in his bemused expression, a swell of fondness in her heart for her useless brother. "But do tell me what alerted you to our need?"

"You said there would be a signal," Branwell said, nodding at the burning house before them. "A little extreme to set fire to the biggest house for fifty miles, but still, my darling Emily, I wouldn't put it past you."

45

Charlotte

The first bright edge of autumn was in the air as August drew to a close, and the four Brontë siblings were happy to find themselves walking down the now coppery path that led to the haven of Wycoller.

"Greetings!" Isabelle called out to them, and as she opened the front door to her cottage, little Archie tottered out barefoot, as she was.

"The baby is walking." Emily smiled. "How nice."

"Yes, it was the same with Celeste—let her once get her toes in the grass and the cold waters of the stream, and she was off before you knew it."

"How wonderful." Anne laughed, falling to her knees and stretching out her arms, lifting Archie high into the air as he half walked and half stumbled into her arms.

"What a perfect little angel," Charlotte cooed, rubbing the back of her finger against the baby's smiling cheek. "Such a joy."

"Come inside, do," Isabelle said, offering her hand to Branwell, who was surprised that when he attempted to kiss it, Isabelle shook it firmly.

"My sisters tell me you are a painter, Miss Lucas," he said as they followed her into the house. "I am a painter, you know. I am to study at the . . ."

Branwell was silenced as he walked into Isabelle's conservatory, flooded with September light, and looked around at the works she had upon the easels, which surpassed his own efforts by quite some considerable way. "But it's just a passing interest of mine: my real skill lies in the writing of novels, one of which I have just begun to embark upon."

"Novels? How wonderful." Isabelle laughed at Elizabeth, who rose from a small table, where she had been sitting with Francis and Celeste, teaching them their letters. Charlotte smiled to see how they had been reposing, Elizabeth's arms around each child, Celeste's head resting on her shoulder. All three children under one roof after all. She wore the mourning dress of a widow, which was fitting, because after Chester's death Elizabeth returned to the world, telling all of how she had wandered off in a fevered state of ague, but that a kind, unnamed reverend and his sisters had found her and nursed her back to health, and how lucky it was that their governess had taken the children to see their godmother on the night of the fire. And when her father had demanded she and the children live under his roof, it had been Mrs. Honeychurch that had refused his demand, telling him their daughter was her own woman now. And indeed her radiant smile and the bloom on her cheek spoke of one who had found a life, rather than lost one. "Your sisters should be writing the novels—I imagine the past few weeks have brought them much inspiration."

"Indeed," Emily said, fixing her gaze on Isabelle. "She was hidden in the ruined house when we came, but how did you know we were coming?"

"I have a telescope on the top floor," she said. "Fortunately, Celeste was playing with it when she saw you coming down the hill."

"A telescope," breathed Anne. "I would very much like to see it."

"Kitty, dear?" Elizabeth called, and the girl came out of the kitchen, greeting the sisters with a smile that showed that a great deal of the care and wariness she had displayed when they first met was slowly ebbing away in favour of security and happiness.

"Will you take Anne up?" Elizabeth asked. "And, Celeste, will you show this nice lady how to look through your telescope?"

"Yes, Mama." Celeste clapped with delight at the thought. "Come, Miss Anne."

"You are a very fine actress," Charlotte said to Isabelle, as Anne and Celeste left, hand in hand. "Not one of us guessed that she was here."

"Let's just say that for most of my life I have had to hide my true feelings," Isabelle said. "The more I hide, the more freedom I have to live life the best I can. You should try having a few secrets, Charlotte—it's good for you."

For a moment Charlotte thought of one evening in Brussels with Monsieur Héger, and let her heart close around it, holding it deep within.

"Please, will you tell us?" Emily said. "The letters? The envelope that Elizabeth sent to herself? Was that a clue or not?"

"Francis?" Isabelle smiled. "Will you take Archie into the garden to find some flowers for me?" Francis leapt up with joy to be free of his learning, taking Archie's hand and guiding him slowly out into a cottage garden alive with the last blaze of summer flowers.

"Chester must have found Elizabeth's predated letters and sent the one dated that Tuesday in the hopes it would keep her family at bay," Isabelle said. "As for the other?" She glanced over at Elizabeth.

"My mama started a small fund in an account for me, held at the bank in Hebden Bridge. She didn't tell Papa, but one of my aunts left me a small income and she wanted me to have it rather than have it go to my husband. I couldn't go to the bank myself, so I sent a bulk package of self-addressed envelopes requesting they send me information on the balances once a month. The fund was very near being enough for a passage to New Zealand, but Robert must have found that statement. He withdrew all the money at once, as was his right. Not that it matters now."

"What a very dull resolution to a mystery that kept us so perplexed," Emily said. "I note that Elizabeth seems to have all her teeth? We worried so much over that tooth. Where did it come from?"

"Oh, I was ever so pleased with the tooth," Isabelle said happily. "The tooth had formerly belonged to Kitty, but she had lost it after a brawl with a local lad, a brawl she won, I might add. I paid her handsomely for it, on the understanding she would refrain from brawling."

"And finally," Emily asked her. "What about the pebble?"

"Oh, Emily, please accept that it is just a pebble!" Charlotte laughed at her sister.

"Oh my." Elizabeth snatched up the pebble, holding it to her chest. "I thought I'd lost all of these for ever. Oh, Emily, thank you. You don't know what they mean to me."

Emily smiled at Charlotte. "Do tell us."

"I was allowed a few days with Celeste after she was born. I wanted to be the first to show her the sea, so we travelled to Whitby, Rebel and I. It was a long journey, and I was not really fit to travel, but I was determined and young and foolish. Rebel and I agreed that when the time came, she would remain in Whitby with the baby, and I would return to Leeds with a nurse Papa had sent. I begged him to send Mama but he said if she knew about Celeste it would kill her."

Elizabeth bowed her head for a moment.

"At the moment that Elizabeth gave me Celeste, I gave her a handful of pebbles in return," Isabelle said. "I told her, these pebbles are my promise to you to that one day you will be free to be with your daughter. I'm not taking her from you, I'm exchanging her for this promise."

"What a beautiful sentiment," Charlotte said. "What a really wonderful friendship you two ladies have. You are as close as sisters, perhaps closer."

"Indeed." Isabelle smiled at Elizabeth. "Perhaps closer."

"And now." Charlotte reached for Elizabeth's hand. "All is well."

Just as they were leaving, Charlotte stopped in the doorway with Isabelle. "I realise now that of course the note we found in Mattie's room wasn't from Chester to her, was it?" She smiled. "She might have found it when she was in Elizabeth's room and taken it, wishing it was for her, but actually it was to Elizabeth from you, wasn't it, Rebel?"

Isabelle Lucas smiled at Charlotte, hugging her close for a moment.

"I do believe you are rather good at keeping secrets after all, Miss Brontë," she said. "And now that Elizabeth, the children and I are all together at last, no man will ever put us asunder."

46

Anne

They circled the table, the three of them, as Charlotte read aloud her latest letter from Mattie.

Dear Charlotte, Emily and Anne,

I am writing to thank you and Mr. Brontë once again for helping me secure this new position. The family are very good and kind, and treat me very well. The children are well behaved and very merry to be around, and on my half days I can walk into town, where there are all manner of interesting things to keep my attention. I will write more soon, but for now please know how deep my gratitude runs. For without your friendship and courage I feel certain that I would never have found such a sense of ease in my heart and mind ever again.

Sincerely yours,
Matilda French

"And now"—Charlotte stopped by the sofa and produced something from underneath one of the cushions—"there is something else I wish to put to you, Emily. You will not like it, but I beg of you to hear me out."

She held out one of Emily's notebooks filled to the brim with her poetry.

"That is mine!" Emily reached out to grab the notebook, which Charlotte let her take. "How dare you, Charlotte. How dare you take something so private and paw over it with your grubby little hands. It is *mine!*"

Emily held the book tightly to her breast, surprising her sisters with the force of her fury.

"Please, Emily, let me explain: these last few weeks have shown us a great deal, and one of the thoughts that has occurred to me since we met with such women as Isabelle Lucas and Mrs. Prescott, is that there are other ways for us to find our independence than in teaching. I came across your book lying quite out in the open . . ."

"Pah!" Emily narrowed her eyes.

"And, I knew how much poetry you had written," Charlotte continued carefully. "But not how very wonderful it is, Emily—truly. As great as any I have ever read. And it is worthy of an audience, I truly believe it. And you know that I would not compliment you unless I really had to."

"It is mine, and for me alone," Emily told her furiously. "No one else will be interested in these words—they are just my thoughts put down on paper."

"I believe that you are wrong." Charlotte held out her hands to Emily and Anne. Anne took one, but Emily went to the window, where she continued to clutch her notebook to her chest, eyeing Charlotte with a look that if the barometer could have read it would have signalled forthcoming thunderstorms. "My dear sisters, we need to make our living, we know that. And we have all of us thought of teaching or working as governesses, but in the last days I have come to realise that if we have just a little courage, there are more possibilities for each of us. We live with a mighty passion, and why might our words not have just as much meaning and force upon the world of literature as those of any man? For we are just as brave, just as bold, just as determined as any one of them. So I propose that we compile a collection of our poetry and seek a publisher."

Anne gasped a little as she turned towards Emily. "Think of it, Emily— our own income; our freedom. Just like Rebel!"

"Over my dead body." Emily scowled at her sisters and slammed the door loudly behind her as she stomped out of the house.

"Well," Anne said thoughtfully, "how do you think that Emily took to that idea, Charlotte dear?"

"I think she's coming round to it," Charlotte said.

Both the sisters were surprised when, a few seconds later, Emily came back into the dining room, closing the door behind her.

"Have you changed your mind already?" Charlotte asked her.

"I found the boy from the Bull lingering out back like the idiot he is," Emily said. She produced a letter from the sleeve of her dress.

"It seems that the Bell brothers have been presented with another case."

At once, all the sisters gathered round the letter, their curiosity already taking flight as a new adventure beckoned.

Dear Reader,

When my mum first took me to the former home of the Brontë sisters, the Parsonage in Haworth, when I was about ten years old, I couldn't think of anything worse than walking into a dreary old house that some dead writers used to live in, and complained the whole way.

But from the moment I stepped over the threshold of what had once been the Brontë family home I was hooked, and embarked on a lifelong love affair with Charlotte, Emily and Anne, their lives, their literature and the remarkable legacy they have left behind.

As I came to read their books and discover more about them I began to see them not as remote authors of dusty and impenetrable fiction, but women who fought for their right to have lives as rich and as notable as their male counterparts, refusing to believe that their gender consigned them or their talent to a polite and quiet existence that would eventually fade to nothing.

The idea for *The Vanished Bride* comes from the conviction that the sisters' short lives were just as compelling and exciting as their novels. And although we know a great deal about them, there is also so much more that we don't know.

It's that imaginative space that has allowed *The Brontë Mysteries* to be born. Of course there is absolutely no evidence to suggest that the Brontë sisters were ever part-time amateur sleuths. Also there is no evidence to suggest that they were *not*.

Not everything in *The Vanished Bride* is pure fiction; a large percentage is based on known biographical facts or inspired by them.

August 1845 is the first time they had all been under one roof for several months.

Branwell had just left employment at Thorp Grange under a cloud of scandal involving his employer's wife, obliging Anne to leave her own position there too.

Charlotte, suffering deeply and painfully with unrequited love for her Brussels tutor Monsieur Héger also returned home. And it was in the following September that Charlotte persuaded her sisters to begin to consider writing as a professional endeavour.

In *The Vanished Bride* Patrick Brontë writes a letter to an unmarried mother, recommending that she doesn't rush into marriage until she and her intended have financial security. This may seem unlikely and far too modern an attitude for a Victorian Parson, but it is based on a genuine letter that Patrick wrote in 1855 to Eliza Brown (sister to his servant Martha Brown) who found herself unmarried and with child.

> *In regard to your proceedings, and those of your friend James, you both have acted very properly. You have done all things openly and wisely—which is the best way. As the times are hard, and likely to be so, during the winter you should be in no haste about marriage. You should not marry till you have a fair prospect of being able to live without debt and poverty.*

We also see Emily buying material for a dress made up of a thundercloud and lightning pattern, which might seem too good to be true. But we know, thanks to the recollections of Charlotte Brontë's good friend Ellen Nussey, that Emily did indeed buy material with this wonderful design. According the Ellen:

> *Emily chose a white stuff patterned with lilac thunder and lightening, to the scarcely concealed horror of her more sober*

companions, and she looked well in it; a tall lithe creature
with a grace half-queenly, half-untamed.

Most of all *The Vanished Bride* is a novel written with fondness, warmth and appreciation for three legendary and revolu-
tionary authors that have had a lasting impact on my life and so
many others. And, I hope, it's a pretty good yarn too.

With love,
Bella Ellis